Sunlight, Moonlight

Sunlight, Moonlight

Hwang Sun-won

translated by
Sol Sun-bong

///Si-sa-yong-o-sa, Inc.

Sunlight, Moonlight

ISBN : 0-87296-037-4

First printing 1990
Si-sa-yong-o-sa, Inc.
55-1 Chongno 2-ga, Chongno-gu
Seoul 110-122, Korea

Jacket Design by Kim Jin-pyong

This book is a co-publication by Si-sa-yong-o-sa, Inc.
and The International Communication Foundation.

Printed in KOREA

Preface

Sunlight, Moonlight, published in 1964, is the fifth novel of Hwang Sun-won, one of the leading Korean novelists in the post-Liberation era. It is a story of people who come from that special social group, *paekchong*, that formed the lowest bottom of society or rather an outcast class in traditional Korea, socially stigmatized and proscribed to the hereditary occupation of animal slaughter, as they struggle with the mystery of their stigma that limits their fate and freedom, and conditions their essential being. But it is not basically a novel dealing with social problems—the problems of a society that traps people in the toils of oppression and discrimination. It has more to do with what the writer perceives to be a basic given of human existence: the loneliness of the individual, an intolerable cause of suffering but also a condition one must pass through if one were to attain true self-knowledge.

Hwang Sun-won, born in 1915, near Pyongyang, north Korea, began publishing poetry from the early 1930's but later turned to short stories and novels, collected in the mid-1980's in eleven volumes, es:ablishing himself over the years as one of the representative writers of modern Korea. One of the distinctions Hwang Sun-won has achieved lies in the sheer perseverance with which he has dedicated himself to the job of being a writer, which is a difficult feat in view of the fact that there has been so much to deflect a writer from his craft in the political and social upheavals of modern Korea as it went through Japanese colonialism, the Liberation, ideological struggle between the Left and the Right, the Civil War, military dictatorships, industrialization. It took great dedication and asceticism for a writer to remain dedicated exclusively to his craft, while political passions swept through the country in continuous waves or while political and material ambition or just the necessity of earning a living in the extreme condition of poverty exerted its seductive or coercive influence. Hwang remains a symbol of a writer totally dedicated to literature in the dark times of the human soul. It does not mean that he was insensitive to political and social events around him; he sees his characters in the midst of these events but his main concern is to depict how they live more permanent themes of human existence in the midst of or in spite of these events. In *Sunlight, Moonlight,* too, the writer takes a group of people in a very peculiar social situation and puts them through the existential journey of loneliness, suffering and self-discovery.

Translation of *Sunlight, Moonlight* was commissioned by the Culture and Arts Foundation of Korea and the Si-sa-yong-o-sa, Inc. I would like to take this occasion to thank them for enabling me to translate it. I owe a deep gratitude to Mr. Hwang Sun-won for the permission to translate, though the permission was obtained through the good offices of the Si-sa-yong-o-sa, Inc., whose editorial staff have been most kind in other sundry businesses of publishing as well, for which my sincere thanks.

August 8, 1990

Sol Sun-bong

CONTENTS

PART THREE

PART ONE

CHAPTER ONE

The Closed Eyes

After Kwangnaru and Chonho-dong, the bus arrived at Ichon. The whole trip had taken no more than twenty minutes. Professor Chi got off the bus following a woman with a child on her back and a middle-aged man. There was no one waiting to get aboard the bus at this juncture and the bus took off immediately. Professor Chi walked back a little way along the road which he had just passed on the bus and then turned into a narrow country road running southwest.

About three miles ahead, one could see Namhansan standing like a gigantic *pyongpung* (folding screen of paintings or calligraphy). To one side of this mountain range soared the pointed peak of Kaeksan touching the floating white clouds.

Professor Chi, attired in a casual shirt, mountaineer's hat and a pair of sneakers, walked in a sprightly gait, almost like a young man. He thought, for a second, that maybe he would like to wear his sunglasses, but decided not to. The left side of his rather bony shoulders was tilted slightly upwards to keep the leather strap of his camera from slipping off. He held the camera in his left hand so that it wouldn't bump against his side too much.

It was in the afternoon of the day before that Professor Chi had received a call from a farmer living in Pundinamut-kol. The message of the call was that a pounding-stone from the Paekche Period had been found in his land. He wanted the professor to come down for confirmation at his earliest convenience. This was indeed a glad news for the professor.

Last autumn, Professor Chi had visited an old temple site at the foot of Kaeksan in the company of some of his students. The group's chief purpose for going there that day was to enjoy the scenery and fresh air. But it was the second visit for Professor Chi who had visited the area some time before. He had gone there to take a look at a rock-cut Buddha which was supposed to be from the Paekche Period. On the occasion of his outing with his students, he wanted to take another look at the Buddha along with his students.

The Buddha was cut on a granite wall standing at the back of what used to be the premises of the old temple. Next to the granite wall with the image was a waterfall of about twelve feet.

The Buddha on the granite wall was holding the medicine bottle in one hand while his other hand was raised to call mankind to his side. The approximate measurements of the image were three feet in length and one and half feet in width.

When he had first heard about the rock-cut Buddha supposedly of Paekche origin, Professor Chi had felt quite excited. Although his major field was literature, he had more than average concern for old relics, especially those from the Paekche Period. The following were the words engraved along one side of the Buddha: The repair work on this stone Buddha was finished on the Twenty-Seventh Day of the Second Year of Taepyong and Chongchuk. Long live His Highness the Emperor.

It was these engraved words that had drawn especial attention of the historians to the image of the Buddha itself. Since there was no year-name throughout Korean history that was called Taepyong, it was clear that the name came from China. Some among the historians seemed inclined to think that the date pointed to the second year of the rule of Emperor Ching of Chinese Yang which corresponded to a date sometime before the fourth year of the rule of King Widok of Paekche.

Although Professor Chi was no professional archaeologist, he held his own view on this matter. Instead of interpreting the 'taepyong' as referring to the year-name of Yang Dynasty, Professor Chi opted to fit it into the second year of the rule of Taejong of Chinese Song whose year-name Taepyong-Hung-guk also had the words 'taepyong' in it and fell in the Year of Chongchuk by the sexagenary calendar. The further evidence in favor of Professor Chi's interpretation is that neither Koguryo nor Paekche Dynasties used the year-names borrowed from Yang whereas the Koryo Dynasty used that of Song from the time of King Kyongjong. What was more, the instances of abbreviation of the Chinese year-name 'taepyong-hung-guk' into the shorter appellation 'taepyong' were quite numerous. For instance, there were books from Song Dynasty that carry titles such as Taepyong-Oram or Taepyong-Kwang-gi. The fact that there was a coin minted during the Koryo Period with the name of Taepyong-Tongbo was, from Professor Chi's point of speculation, another very solid factor in support of his conjecture over the rock-cut Buddha.

The decisive reason why Professor Chi considered this work as dating not from the Paekche Period but from the Koryo Dynasty, however, was the shape of the Buddha itself. There were, in short, no esthetic simplicity and dynamism common to other Paekche remains in this rock-cut image of Buddha. What characterized the delineation of this Buddha, instead, was a sense of sweet gentleness cradled in soft curved lines just as in other Buddhas of the Koryo Period. One more factor that was significant in Professor Chi's estimation was the fact that the Buddha was cut against the surface of the coarse granite. According to the content of the engraved words at its side; the Buddha had been cut earlier than the epitaph. And yet, the lines of the Buddha remained quite clear and unbroken while the engraved words of the epitaph were rubbed off in places. But how could an image cut into the surface of coarse-grained granite have weathered nearly one and a half millenia without losing shape? Would it not be far more sensible to consider it as having been made during the Koryo Period, nearly half a century after the Paekche era?

While applying wet drawing paper on the stone engraving which had been wiped clean for the operation and tapping it carefully with a brush to teach his students how to take a rubbing that day, Professor Chi had said to himself once again that his conjecture was more correct than that of the historians. What had made his visit to the temple site especially rewarding, however, was something else. An old man who lived in a hut built on the site of the old temple had told Professor Chi that a relative of his who lived in a village called Pundinamutkol about two kilometers from the temple site had found an earthenware while digging a hole in the earth to store the manure. Professor Chi had gone to this place on his way back from the temple site without much expectation. To his surprise, however, the vessel which had a handle was an unmistakable specimen of Paekche earthenware with its characteristic beauty of simplicity and crudity. Professor Chi had bought the vessel from the farmer giving him a sum far above what the farmer might have expected. And he had also left his Seoul address with the man so that he could let him know if he should come upon any other such buried objects. And the farmer had reported to him that in the same manure pit where he had found the earthenware, he discovered what looked like a pounding-stone used by women for smoothening the cloth.

In 1925, there was a big flood that had swept off the tall dirt bank on the far side of the river in Kwangnaru. It was known that in the wreckage after the dirt bank had been pulled down by the flood, a Japanese by the name of Fujida Ryosakura had excavated so many items of Paekche earthenware that it took many a number of apple crates to carry them away. This had both excited and chagrined Korean historians. Even after this event, however, earthenwares and old tiles had been excavated in the Kwangju area now and then, but never before had a big item such as a pounding-stone been reported to have been discovered. There was a good reason why Professor Chi found the farmer's report about the hidden pounding-stone significant. Up to the date, the historical conjectures had traced the first use of the pounding-stone to the time of King Kongmin of Koryo Dynasty when Mun Ik-jom smuggled the cotton seeds from China. It had not been thought plausible that such an implement would have been needed in periods earlier than when the chief materials used for Korean garments were hemp and silk. Yet, the historians had been unable to establish this theory on an incontestable basis. If, therefore, on the evidence of this pounding-stone from the Paekche Period, the date of its first use could be fixed anywhere in that era, the historians would be faced with a very challenging situation to deal with.

White wild flowers were in bloom along the road when he came with his students last fall and the harvesting had been long over. Today, however, the fields were packed with water-fattened rice plants, all ready to burst into ears.

About two kilometers ahead along the road which was barely wide enough to let an oxcart pass, there was a *hyanggyo* (traditional school unit) standing in the middle of the flat land. Professor Chi saw that the big ginkgo tree standing in front of the *hyanggyo* was heavy with green pointed leaves today. To the right of the *hyanggyo*, there was a fairly large village shrouded by a mountain at the back. All this was in the opposite direction from Kaeksan and the temple site. Past the village and around the mountain bend was a reservoir on the left-hand side and if one looked beyond the reservoir, one saw two towers against the background of a hill on the other side of the water. These were the towers which Professor Chi had taken his students to see on their way to Pundinamutkol last fall. Standing about twelve feet apart from each other, the two towers were moss-covered and were unmistakably from the Paekche Period. One had five stories while the other had only three. Both the towers had their foundation stone broken off in one corner. Professor Chi had noted with a mild interest that the three-storied tower, that is, the shorter of the two towers, was leaning slightly to one side. He turned several bends up the moderately slanting road throwing his glances at the towers across the water. Pundinamutkol was on the other side of a stream that lay at the end of this hilly road.

Although it was still fairly early in the morning and there were patches of white clouds in the sky screening off the sun now and then, Professor Chi could feel the heat of an August day against his skin. By the time he reached Pundinamutkol which made three to four kilometers of steady walking, he was drenched in sweat.

The farmer who had called Professor Chi was luckily home. So that the visitor could sit down, the man spread a straw mat on the ground in his yard. Asking for a bowl of water, Professor Chi drank from it and, with the water left in the bowl, he wetted his handkerchief to wipe his face and neck with it. While the professor occupied himself in this way, the man went into the house and came out with the object which he had judged to be an old pounding-stone. Seeing that the man was bringing it out of the Inner-Room, Professor Chi could tell how precious the man considered his finding to be.

"I was digging to make the manure-pit a little bigger and then I felt this at the tip of my shovel," said the man.

Having been buried a long period underground, the stone had a yellowish tint which the farmer's careful wiping had not been able to remove. Professor Chi saw that it was a block of granite. Measuring six to seven inches in the width, two feet in length, and about two inches in height, it had the shape of a pounding-stone although it looked a little too thin. In the course of his careful examination of the object, however, Professor Chi began having doubts and then felt downright disappointed by the results of his probing. The two surfaces, the top and the bottom, as well as the longer two of the side surfaces were ground smooth so that only the small surfaces on both ends of the stone were coarse. Actually, these two parts were completely natural granite surface without even chisel marks. A close scrutinization revealed, also, that one of these surfaces was slightly smaller in dimension than the other.

"This is a broken part of a tomb stone. It's broken in a way that makes it look like a pounding-stone, though."

"A tomb stone? Then, why are there no words cut into it?" asked the tall, strong-boned farmer incredulously.

"I guess it got broken off before it could be used as a tomb stone. Maybe it got a crack while being ground and split up or something."

Hearing Professor Chi's explanation, the farmer looked somewhat shamefaced and began to fill his long pipe with tobacco in silence.

It was apparent that Professor Chi's precipitated trip in this hot weather had been for nothing, after all. Even so, he could not just turn back and go away without showing some token of gratitude for the pain the farmer had taken to let him know about the discovery. He, therefore, offered to treat the farmer to a drink. The latter modestly declined the offer verbally, yet followed Professor Chi out of his house for the drink

A boy of six or seven was eating juicy-looking steamed corn holding the cob with both hands and letting his navel show between his shirt and trousers.

"Are there about thirty houses in the village?" asked Professor Chi.

"We have twenty-six houses here."

"Is it called Pundinamutkol because there are a lot of *pundi* trees?"

"Not really. We just have a couple of them standing in

front of the village over there."

The farmer led Professor Chi to a drinking place at the back of the village at the very foot of the mountain. It was an ordinary house turned into a tavern.

They entered a room and sat down leaving both the front and the back door wide open. Wind from the mountain ridge drifted in pleasantly. There were several chestnut trees in the back yard across which one could see tombs which covered the mountain slope in a great number. It must be the village cemetry, thought Professor Chi.

Sounds of cicadas which Professor Chi had heard continuously since he had entered this village now sounded as if they were being poured into his ears from directly overhead. Looking out at the mountain, Professor Chi noticed that a few graves had the mark of a cross on their tomb stone.

"Is there a church in this village?" he asked.

"No," answered the farmer. "But there's one in the village on the other side of that mountain."

In a little while, a woman who looked a few years past fourty brought in the *makkolli* on a tray from which the paint had been peeled off. There were also two drinking bowls and a dish of turnip pickles.

"This is good homemade *makkolli*," said the farmer drawing closer to the tray.

Professor Chi could not drink or smoke. Sometimes, he would be obliged to drink a little wine at some gathering and then he would instantly have a headache. Now, too, he tried not to drink the *makkolli* himself but kept on pouring for the farmer who kept on saying that he had had enough but kept on emptying the bowl. In other words he seemed to be one of those *ani paekchan* (drinking one hundred cups while repeatedly saying: no more)' drinkers.

The farmer said he would from now on dig other spots to see if he could find anything interesting for the professor. Then, just as he was nearly done with the cup of *makkolli*, he said, looking out through the back door,

"Hm, that old man's here again."

Looking in the direction he was looking, Professor Chi spoted an old man bending down over what looked like a new grave. Seeing that there was no tuft on the mound yet, Professor Chi thought that maybe the old man was mourning for someone who had just died and been buried.

"He didn't even sod the grave. And now he is pulling off even the grass that comes out from the ground by itself."

Professor Chi couldn't understand how anyone could wilfully not sod his relative's grave. Just then, the farmer said again in a lowered voice,

"It's a knife-man that's buried in there."

"A knife-man?" asked Professor Chi bewildered. "You know, a *paekchong* (butcher). It seems people weren't supposed to sod a butcher's grave in the old days."

It was something new to Professor Chi.

"Is that true?"

"Yes. That's why that old man there's pulling off the grass so the grave will be bare. If the grave is sodded or if grass should grow on it, the ghost of the dead person cannot go to heaven, they say. There are three butchers in this village and that one is the oldest of them. He lets other things be handled in the world's way but keeps to the old way about the graves of his dead ones. Very stubborn old man he is, I assure you."

"I heard somewhere that there's an old butchers' village hereabout. Is this the village they are talking about, then?"

"I think so. There were about ten *paekchong* houses in this village when I was young. Then some organization or some such thing took them away one after another until finally only three houses were left."

Professor Chi, too, remembered something.

"Is this organization something called Hyongpyongsa?"

"That's right. That's the name of that organization."

After the March the First Movement in 1919, Japan had changed their militaristic policy toward Korea to one meant to appease Koreans somewhat. One result of this change of policy was materialization of many a social organizations in Korea. Hyongpyongsa, an association of Korean butchers was one of them. The first letter *hyong* came from the Chinese character meaning 'scale'. The Chinese character for *pyong* meant 'equality'. And with the last letter *sa* coming from the Chinese character meaning 'organization,' the name of this organization of butchers could have meant no other than that men are born equal or at least ought to be treated as if they were equal. That this dishonored race who had suffered the contempt and mistreatment by the society at large finally came to organize themselves as a social force was a significant and, on their part, much belated manifestation of their human rights. Aside from the headquarters in Seoul, Hyongpyongsa established branch offices all over the country.

Surprised that the professor had any knowledge of such a thing as a butcher's association and pleased to have found a common topic, the farmer went on,

"This Hyongpyongsa had a lot of power at one time. Once, one butcher in this village was insulted by a man living on the other side of that mountain. It wasn't really much of an insult. All the man did to this butcher was to talk to him without honorifics although he was younger than the butcher. Anyway, all the butchers in this village ganged up against this man. The only butcher who didn't go with the gang was that old man there. He said what they were doing was no business of a butcher."

Professor Chi, too, remembered some such acts of retaliation on the part of the butchers written up frequently in the newspapers for a period.

"Is Hyongpyongsa still active?" asked Professor Chi.

"No, it has disappeared completely. And it's no wonder either because who would like other people to know that he is a butcher at a time like this? I mean which butcher would let the whole world know that he is a butcher when he can live like other people if only he can hide his origin. But, to tell the truth, there's something this Hyongpyongsa did for the butchers, too, because after there was such an organization people came to treat the butchers better and the butchers themselves came to feel freer to mix with other people. In this case, of course, the butchers don't let others know about their past. All other butcher families except three from our village, also, are living elsewhere making their living some other way than butchering. And come to speak of it, all the members of the three remaining butcher families, too, except that old man there, live in a way that isn't much different from other people. One house even sent a daughter to college. Even the younger brother of that old man is head of a company called Taeryuksangsa in Seoul. It's really the case of a dragon coming out of a stream, as the old saying. . . ."

"Did you say Taeryuksangsa?" interrupted Professor Chi in a surprised tone and suspecting for a second that he had misheard the farmer because of all the noise the cicadas were making. The farmer on his own part seemed suddenly afraid that maybe he had said something that he shouldn't have said, seeing the professor's unexpected reaction to his causerie. With a somewhat hardened face, therefore, he said hurriedly,

"I am not really all that sure what it is called. . . ."

Professor Chi in the meantime thought to himself, what a strange revelation it would be if the name he had heard was really what he had been led to think. He urged the man to drink more. Again saying no with his mouth, the farmer picked up his *makkolli* bowl.

"How old is that old man, do you know?" he asked the farmer.

"I think he is one or two years past seventy."

"I would like to offer my greetings to him, if you can arrange it for me," said Professor Chi reading the farmer's expression.

"Well, I don't know. People have come to talk to the old man with the pretext of making researches about how butchers live and so on, you know. At first the old man seemed to oblige them kindly enough. But lately, he seems to avoid them altogether," said the farmer still with an uneasy face, but he added, "but since you wish it, I will go and ask him."

Before he went out of the room to speak to the old man, however, the farmer warned Professor Chi,

"Even if he agrees to talk with you, don't ever bring out the topic of his trade."

After a few minutes, the farmer came back from the back of the house accompanied by the old man from which Professor Chi could tell that the negotiation went well. Professor Chi noted quickly that the mistress of the tavern was showing much respect toward the old man. Professor Chi also registered in his mind that, from close up, this old butcher gave one a strange impression. The coarse cotton jacket he was wearing seemed to accentuate his short stature. Hair had just begun to grow back out of his clean-shaven head but clearly the color of the hair was black as was that of his eyebrows. But his beard which also was newly growing out of his shaven chin was snow white. His eyes were gray and he had unusually red lips. The mistress of the tavern came in with a *makkolli* bowl for the old man and placed it deferentially in front of the old man.

As soon as the introductory greetings were over, Professor Chi ordered a fresh jug of *makkolli* and filled the bowl for the old man who took it with an impassive face, his sitting posture stiff and erect. Yet, he did not seem reluctant to accept the invitation to the *makkolli*.

As he kept on emptying the *makkolli* bowl, the old man's face became somewhat flushed and his lips became redder. The flush on his face seemed to grow luminescent between the blackness of the short hair and the whiteness of his beard.

"I admire you for keeping yourself in such a good health,

sir," said Professor Chi trying inwardly to find a resemblance between the old man's face and the face he was thinking of.

"You mean how come my hair hasn't turned gray yet?" said the old man with a wry smile which gave some sort of an expression to his otherwise completely apathetic face.

"One should have gray hair in old age. But what can you do? It's not as if one can make one's hair turn gray at will."

Professor Chi started turning his eyes away from the old man not knowing how to react to the latter's apparently defiant manner of speaking. But just then the old man spoke again,

"Perhaps, you, too, heard the story of a man whose hair turned gray during one night which he spent atop a tree chased by a tiger. But mine has stayed black although I had both my son and grandson die before my very eyes during the Korean War. I don't suppose this means I have different kind of blood stream in my body."

Mildly purturbed by the old man's angry voice, Professor Chi said placatingly,

"I didn't mean to offend you in any way."

The old man closed his eyes without saying any more words. Just then, there came a thumping noise from the back. Looking out, Professor Chi saw the mistress of the tavern hitting a chestnut tree on its lower bark. Wondering what the woman could be doing, Professor Chi watched on. All the cicadas had suddenly become very quiet. Only then did he realize that it was to quiet the insects that the woman had made that incomprehensible gesture and it was for no one but the old butcher that she had taken the trouble.

The old man reopened his misty gray eyes and said,

"The blood my son and grandson shed was the same red color like everyone else's."

"I see that you have a very painful memory of the war," said Professor Chi not knowing what else to say and poured more *makkolli* into the old man's bowl.

The old man drank the *makkolli* quietly, and then as if suddenly discarding his bitter anger of a moment ago sighed deeply and closed his eyes again. The flush around his eyes and between the wrinkles on his forehead was darker pink now.

Picking up his camera, Professor Chi snapped a quick picture of the old man not bothering to focus the lens properly. The old man sat on with closed eyes. It was difficult to tell whether or not he heard the clicking of the camera.

"You seem very tired. Maybe we'd better not keep you any longer," said the farmer in a polite voice. But the old man sat on a few more minutes in immobility, his eyes still closed. But finally he opened his eyes and said,

"The picture should take care of my share of the expenses."

He stood up. There was such a finality in his tone that Professor Chi could not think of detaining him even for formality. Both he and the farmer stood up after the old man to bow goodbye to him. The mistress of the tavern ran in from the backyard and saw the old man off to the outside of her gate. The old man walked off at a steady rapid gait in his straw sandals which looked a little too big for his bare feet.

Professor Chi who was not used to drinking, especially in the daytime, felt his headache coming on even though it was little enough that he had drunken. Still, he picked up the *makkolli* bowl in front of him and emptied it. The cicadas made noises with abandon now that the woman of the house no longer tried to quiet them.

"It seems I offended the old man," said Professor Chi.

"No, it's not that," said the farmer, and then, after a brief silence, he went on, leaning toward Professor Chi,

"It's just that he has much pain weighing on his mind. It's not just that he lost his son and grandson. He also killed a man."

According to the farmer's account, the old man's eldest grandson escaped from the camp of the so-called Voluntary Army draftees of the Red Army during the Korean War and took hiding at home. But somebody in the village reported this to the North Korean Security headquarters. It was a son of a fellow butcher who had joined the North Korean Youth Corps and got himself elected the chairman of the Youth Corps branch of this village. Both the grandson and his father, that is, the old man's son were shot dead, the father for hiding the son who was 'the subversive element' as everyone who did not go along with the communists was called in those days.

"It was really terrible," said the farmer. "And then, some time later, the Allied Army landed on Inchon. And two nights after the National Army recaptured the capital, the villagers heard a horrible scream in the dead of the night. We all ran out. It was that old man. He was holding a knife in one hand and shouting at the top of his voice: 'I've killed a man!' He was standing in front of the house of this young man who had been the Youth Corps chairman and was the cause of the deaths of his son and grandson. The old man had killed the father of this young man. The young culprit himself had fled away following the retreating People's Army. The old man explained later that he had killed the man with his butchering knife wishing his victim to go to heaven after death."

"How can killing a man with a butchering knife send the victim to heaven?" asked Professor Chi incredulously. It seemed that he had become tense without being aware of it.

"Well, there's an explanation to it. The butchers treasure their butchering knives a great deal. They clean and polish their knives very diligently so that not a speck of rust could settle on them. The knife which the old man used in killing the man that night was an especially valuable one to the old man because it had come down to him through generations of his butchering ancestors as a family treasure, so to speak. What it all means is that since the old man had killed his enemy with the knife which had killed a countless number of cows and oxen, the dead man was sure to go to heaven."

Professor Chi felt his curiosity mounting about this race called the *paekchong*. He decided to satisfy his curiosity by asking a few questions to the farmer. What he could find out as a result of his questioning was as follows. Nothing of any importance in the butchers' lives was unrelated with the cows and oxen. Even the straw rope a family hangs across the gate for announcing the birth of a child has, in addition to the customary red peppers, charcoals, and pine leaves, pieces of ox tails strung onto it. This was to chase away the evil spirits. At weddings, the main ceremony is held in front of a painted image of a cow. At funerals, the mourners keen imitating the cow's cry. This was to let the Heavenly King in the Upper World know of the coming of the deceased. Hair of the ox tail is stuffed into the ears and nostrils of the dead person and underneath the coffin, too, hide of a cow or an oxen is spread. Also, cow or ox hooves are placed on top of the corpse in which case the more worn-out the hooves are the more quickly can the deceased make his travel to the Upper World.

As to the clothes, just as the *chonmin* class of old Korea did, the butchers were forbidden to wear the long outer garment or to wear the *kat* on their head. They had to wear coarse hemp or unrefined cotton and their customary headgear was *paeraeng-i* (a semblance of a *kat* made with bamboo). One really distinguishing characteristic in the butcher's outfit was the lack of a collar-strip around the neckline of their jacket and the replacement of thread-botton for the cloth ties on their jacket front. The omission of the ties was to prevent the evil spirits from catching up to a person by hanging onto the handy long ties. On their foot, the butchers were advised to wear no socks or, if hey have to, wear only black socks. Also, they had to wear just the straw sandals. The purpose of wearing black socks, too, was to chase the evil spirits. The butchers were to shave their heads and not grow beards.

"Nowadays, nobody minds these things. It's just that old man who's still keeping to these rules."

Professor Chi drew to his mind's eye the tie-less coarse cotton jacket the old man was wearing, his shaven head, and beardless chin.... And... his crude straw sandals that were too big for his bare feet....

Asking about their marriage custom, Professor Chi got from the farmer an answer which he had half guessed all along.

"In the old time, they married only their own kind. But now, most of them are scattered all about to live among other kinds of people. In short, there aren't enough families who have kept up with their tradition for them to make marriages only among themselves. What makes it harder is that ordinary people won't go through with the marriage once the origin of a butcher family is known to the other party. I told you about this girl who's going to a college, didn't I? Anyway, this girl once got engaged with a boy who lives in Seoul. But when the boy's family found out about the girl's father being a *paekchong*, the marriage blew off. She took it very hard and dropped out of the school, too. Now she is back in the village."

"Are those butchers left in the village able to make living by just butchering the cows?"

"Not at all. During the summer time, they can't kill the cows because the meat rots too quickly. And what they can make by killing a few cows during the cold period brings them hardly enough to live by. Their main source of living is farming just like the rest of us."

"Are there any rites they offer when butchering the cows?"

"Well... in the old days, the butchers did things like sprinkling clean water all over the slaughterhouse. But not any more. Only the old man who was here offers some sort of a rite on the August Full Moon Day and that seems to be about all."

When the topic shifted to the food the butchers ate, the farmer said,

"They don't eat meat, no matter what kind. They neither

drink nor smoke, nor eat the garlic. I mean they didn't used to. Now it's different. It's only the shortage of these things that's keeping the butchers from them now. But again, the old man alone still keeps away from these things."

Professor Chi could not help reminding the farmer that the old man had consumed some amount of *makkolli* only a short while ago in their own company.

"Ah, that. There's explanation to it, though," said the farmer unperturbed. "He began to drink in small amounts after what happened during the war. But even so, he never drinks as much as to get himself drunk."

The farmer did not speak for a while, and then went on,

"One thing that's clear is that the butchers have a very high respect for their trade. The cows and the oxen, too, they don't think of just as ordinary animal. There's a story that explains their attitude toward them. It goes like this. In ancient time, the Heavenly King of the Upper World had a prince who took interest in nothing but women. The Heavenly King was so angered by this that he turned his son and one of the court ladies into an ox and a cow and sent them down to our world. When sending them off, however, the Heavenly King promised them that when the two should die at the end of a hard-working life on earth, their souls would be called back to heaven. And the Heavenly King also promised to allow the souls of men that put oxen and cows to death, too, to come up to the Upper World. So, the butchers think of their butchering as a penance they do to go to heaven. The old man still believes in these things. He thinks he sent his victim to heaven because he killed the man with a butchering knife."

Professor Chi seemed to see some more logic in the butchers' way of thinking.

"Is it possible for me to take a look at the old man's butchering knife?" he asked the farmer.

"What for?" said the farmer.

"I would like to buy it if that makes it easier."

"You'd like to buy his butchering knife?"

"Yes, I would."

The farmer's eyes opened wide when he was fully assured of Professor Chi's intention and he shook his head earnestly, saying,

"That's impossible. How could you think of buying something in which generations of butchers' souls are living?"

"Let me take a look at it, at least," said Professor Chi wishing honestly to find out what it looked like. "I don't think he would show it to outsiders because it's believed to invite the evil spirits. A long time after his killing of the man, it seems that he'd shown it to someone who came from Seoul. The person who wanted to look at it went so far as feeling the knife with his fingers, it seems. That night, the old man dreamt that a troop of cows stampeded down from the heaven and began to circle around the knife. One after another, the cows began to lick the knife while circling it. And then, the cows that licked the knife turned white instantly. Soon, all the cows became white and still they were circling the knife. Then the old man saw that all the white cows were shedding tears profusely. Suddenly, the old man understood the message. He went to the knife and kneeling down licked at it the way the cows did. Immediately, all the cows that had turned white recovered their original color and ascended the heaven."

Finishing the story, the farmer looked at Professor Chi as if in expectation of the latter's admiration of the profound mystery the story conveyed. And then, he went on,

"The knife was never again shown to the outsiders after that. But there are some who were helped by that strange butchering knife, too. One person had a nightmare every night. He slept with that knife in his arms for one night and he was freed from the nightmares. A child had the malaria. But when the child's forehead was touched with the knife, his fever was gone. And then.... Oh, yes, it was the son of the widow woman of this very tavern who was cured by the knife. The child could not utter a sound even when he was past two years of age. The old man had the boy brought to him and made him put his lips to the knife. As soon as his lips were lifted from the knife, the child called, 'Mother!' I was there. I watched it all. The boy has yet a year to go to the elementary school. But he already writes his name and is quite smart."

The farmer then called for the woman turning his head toward the kitchen.

The mistress of the tavern appeared brushing back streaks of stray hair with one hand.

"Is Pong-pal-i gone somewhere?" asked the farmer.

"He's gone to the stream. He said he would catch a fish for me. But why do you ask? Did you want him to run an errand for you?"

"No, I just asked because I couldn't see him around at home. But I see that he's all grown now if he says he will catch a fish for his mother."

The woman seemed pleased with this remark. Smiling in a way that made her look younger than her age, she went back toward the kitchen.

"Does the old man still do butchering?"

"No, not any more. Now his second son has a job at some slaughterhouse in Seoul."

Professor Chi offered to fill the farmer's *makkolli* bowl again.

"Oh, no, I really shouldn't drink any more. And you've had so little," said the farmer earnestly, but let Professor Chi fill up the bowl.

"What is the name of the old man? I ought to have caught it when we were introduced a while back but I think I missed some of the sounds. I only caught his surname Kim and the end sound which sounded like 'dol'."

The farmer threw a suspicious glance at Professor Chi although he now showed clear signs of inebriety. But finally he answered,

"It's Kim Pon-dol."

"Is Pon-dol his original name?"

"I don't know. That's the only name I know."

Taking out his note pad, Professor Chi wrote the name down in it. Then he picked up the bowl of *makkolli* in front of him and drank it down although it was obviously going beyond his usual limit to do so.

For several days on end after his visit to Pundinamutkol, Professor Chi engaged himself with reading and studying the chapter on the butchers in the Japanese author Ayugai's The Miscellaneous Manuscripts and other writings on the same topic. He wanted to find out more about this strange race than he already knew. His wish was that Chon Kyong-hun would come by to pay him a visit soon. Chon was a graduate assistant who studied from Professor Chi. He had a habit of coming to see the professor at his house on a more or less regular basis. Lately, he seemed busy looking for a new boardinghouse.

On the third day after Professor Chi received his last telephone call from his one-time student, however, Chon Kyong-hun walked in, wiping sweat from his face that looked flushed from the afternoon sun. He was wearing a white cotton shirt which had been neatly starched and ironed.

Even before Chon Kyong-hun had had time to finish his cold *misu* tea, Professor Chi asked,

"Have you heard of butchers' villages extant somewhere in the Kyonggi-do area? Excluding Kwangju and it's vicinities, I mean...."

"Are there still such villages?" asked Chon Kyong-hun adjusting his thick-lensed glasses on his nose. He seemed to have been listening to the sound of piano Ta-hye's pupil was making in the adjacent room.

"They aren't large-unit villages like in the old days but there still are some places where the butchers are gathered in small groups."

Hearing this, Chon Kyong-hun blinked his eyes across the thick lenses but said nothing. Professor Chi knew that it was only about a year ago that Chon Kyong-hun had started wearing these glasses. He also knew that the young man's eyes became bad from his reading books late into the night because he had had to work his way through high school and college after coming south during the Korean War from his native province Hwanghae-do.

Professor Chi told Chon Kyong-hun about what he had found in Pundinamutkol and, at the end of his recount, said,

"It's rather remote from my major field, but I feel like studying about this interesting race."

"If you wish me to, I will find out what I can on my part," said Chon Kyong-hun, throwing a rather puzzled look at his favorite professor who might have appeared to him as having too many unnecessary curiosities. Professor Chi, however, appeared impervious to whatever inner puzzlement his one-time pupil might be experiencing in secret. With a gleam of quiet excitement in his eyes, the older man sat on without saying anything for a while, his hand with the fan arrested in the mid air. When he finally resumed his fanning, Chon Kyong-hun said,

"It looks like In-chol hasn't come back from Taechon, yet."

"Yes, it seems he hasn't because I should suppose he would have paid me a visit if he has."

"I tried calling him yesterday again but was only told that nobody knew when he'd be back. It's been over a fortnight since he went, isn't it?" asked Chon Kyong-hun.

"I think so," replied Professor Chi still wrapped up in his thought.

"Must be that he finds it a lot of fun staying by the sea," said Chon Kyong-hun. Then, after a brief second of hesitation, he went on, "Actually I have something to talk over with In-chol. And his taking so long to come back is making me somewhat restless. It's about what I think is a very good opportunity for In-chol. A family whose daughter I once tutored is having a new house built and they say they wish to find an architect who has a sense for the modern architecture. I told them about In-chol explaining that although he is still a graduate student he is sure to come out with some interesting new ideas. They took my suggestion favorably and asked to see In-chol for a tête-à-tête. This appears to me as a rare chance for In-chol. And I want the appointment to take place before the other party change their mind."

"Well, it seems to me that they are no ordinary people, either, if they are willing to give such a big task to one who is still a student. But you are right. I, too, think, he would be able to think up something new. He will be here pretty soon. Don't worry. And since I expect him to come to see me immediately after his return, I will tell him to get in touch with you. To tell you the truth, I am in a bit of a hurry to see him, too," said Professor Chi and continued fanning himself slowly and mechanically staring at a point in the air absentmindedly. Then he spoke again,

"And I would like you to do what you promised a while ago."

"I will, sir," said Chon Kyong-hun and looked out at the yard through the window.

Under the hot August sun, the leaves of the summer flowers in the garden were drooping down languidly. The piano pupil in the other room seemed to be making mistakes often. Chon Kyong-hun could tell that the child was being made to repeat certain parts of the music many times over.

Ta-hye! called Chon Kyong-hun once, inwardly. His emotion responded to this silent act with some pleasurable sense of expectation. But in order for him to have any expectation in respect of that name, there ought to have been some word from the mouth of his old professor. In all their conversations up to now, however, Professor Chi had never mouthed a word that could be taken as that kind of a symbolic utterance. Then, it occurred to Chon Kyong-hun that for some time now, he had been unconsciously waiting for this utterance to be made by the professor every time he came here to visit with him. This realization made him blush so that he could not take his eyes away from the flowers in the yard to look at the professor.

CHAPTER TWO

Back in the Street

Stepping down the last step of the staircase leading to the basement teahouse: Montparnasse, In-chol entered it. His eyes did not adjust instantly to the semi-darkness of the hall inside the teahouse. Only the jazz music from a radio struck him with a strangely naked sense of immediacy. Soon his eyes saw better and he took a general inspection of the inside of the teahouse. Now he knew that it was the wallpaper which was drab grey that had made this hall even darker than many other similar interiors of underground teahouses. There were overhead electric fans but the air was still sultry.

Most of the seats were occupied. Even in a crowd of so many people, however, In-chol had little trouble finding Na-mi. She was sitting at a corner table facing this way. But there were two other people, both men, sitting at the same table. Seeing this, In-chol decided to take a seat at an empty table near the entrance instead of walking up to her. Sitting down, he thought briefly that Na-mi had seen him. She did not come up to him, however. Maybe she got angry because he was about twenty minutes late in coming? Wondering, he ordered a soda drink to the waitress who came to his table with the usual wet towel. He wiped his forehead with the wet towel using it to push the stray sweat-soaked frontal hair back. Then he picked up the fan lying on the table and started fanning himself.

Slowly the memory of the picture he had seen at Professor Chi's house a while ago came back to him. It was the picture of the old butcher with his closed eyes. He was surprised that an image he had looked at briefly just once should come back to his mind's eye in such clarity.

In-chol was excitedly talking about his trip to the seaside sitting on the sofa in Professor Chi's study this afternoon.

"I read in the newspaper that the beaches were unprecedentedly crowded this year, is that right?" Professor Chi had asked.

"Oh, yes, there were people everywhere. But what about you, Professor? Hadn't you gone even to the riverside throughout the summer?"

"That's right," said Professor Chi and then as if to excuse himself he added, "I've had things to do."

"But what about Ta-hye? Why doesn't she ever go anywhere? Why doesn't she go swimming in the sea or at least a river, a high school swimming champion like her?"

"That's what I am wondering, too, you know. I even urged her to go along with you and your friends to Taechon this time. But she said she won't go unless I went, too. You see? And she's no child any longer. She can't expect her old father to tag along everywhere she goes. I suppose, though, that it's her piano lessons that kept her from going. She is very particular about her responsibilities, as you may know."

In-chol could hear the sound of the piano lesson even while this conversation went on.

"I don't think the piano lessons are really all the reason she isn't going to places. Certainly, even she can take a week off from her work? I think the real reason is she feels she needs to look after you in place of *samonim* (honorific for teacher's wife, usually). And, of course, that's what she has been doing for quite some time now, isn't it?"

It was true, too. Ever since his wife died in Pusan where they lived as refugees during the Korean War, he had left everything related with housekeeping to his daughter Ta-hye. And the latter had been able to carry out this task so well that he had never felt inconvenienced because of an ill housekeeping.

The maid came in with slices of watermelon on a tray.

"I shouldn't have listened to the storekeeper. He said the watermelon was ripe. That's why I didn't insist on his cutting out a wedge for test. But look at this! I will go and give him a hard word or two later. I surely will," said the maid loquaciously, putting down the watermelon on the table between In-chol and the professor.

In-chol smiled listening to the maid's harangue. He was by now quite used to this woman's talkativeness. And the watermelon was actually just right for eating as the storekeeper seemed to have assured the woman.

Professor Chi urged In-chol to help himself to the watermelon and picked up a slice himself.

"This is good after sweating, and, of course, this will make more sweat to flow.... But it won't be long before we will all complain of cold weather," said the professor looking at In-chol picking up a second slice of watermelon and biting into it.

Professor Chi felt at a loss as to how he could bring up the topic he had in his mind. Although he had been waiting for In-chol to show up quickly, he did not quite know how to broach the matter he had been intending to talk over with In-chol now that the latter was sitting right in front of him. To make his talk more natural, he decided to start it from his inspection of the pounding-stone, going through the whole account of how he had been notified by the farmer and how he had been disappointed that the stone was not a Paekche relic as he had been led to believe. Only after this rather lengthy digression did he carefully touch upon the butcher theme, detailing his student on the various pieces of information he could gather during his visit to Pundinamutkol.

Although In-chol seemed to be listening more or less nonchalantly, Professor Chi found himself scrutnizing his pupil's face to see how he was taking it all. But he had to get to the heart of the matter any way. So he continued,

"But most of the butchers have given up their inherited trade and live like the rest of the world hiding their *paek-chong* origin. But there's at least one exceptional butcher. He is an old man past his seventy. This person alone is still keeping all the old rules and customs of his race. You might call him The Last of the Butchers if you like. It seems, though, that he now leaves the job of butchering to his second son who's having a job at some slaughterhouse in Seoul...." said Professor Chi still trying to sound as casual as the circumstances allowed.

In the end, Professor Chi had told In-chol all about the old man, even the incident of his manslaughter. Only he kept the fact of the old man's younger brother running a business by the name of Taeryuksangsa a secret.

When he was through with his recounting, Professor Chi walked over to his desk and brought back a note pad and a paper bag from one of its drawers.

"This is the old man's name," he said pointing at a spot on a page of the small note pad.

"Kim, Pon, Tol," read In-chol pausing after every letter.

Professor Chi was keeping his eyes on the young man's face, but he could read no sign there. But then, since In-chol's father's name was Kim Sang-jin, it was apparent that the old man's name did not even belong in the same class of kin relationship degrees to be that of a brother of one with In-chol's father's name. Even so, he took out two photographs from the paper bag and handed one to his pupil, saying,

"This is how he looks."

In-chol took the picture in his hand and glanced at it. As soon as his eyes took in the image on the photograph, however, he was struck by some powerful feeling. Surprised by his own emotional reaction, In-chol kept on studying the picture of the old man sitting with his eyes closed. It was not a face he knew or could recall having seen anywhere at any time. But then why had he experienced that strange pang of feeling when he first glimpsed at this picture? Perplexed, he put down the picture on the table before him.

Professor Chi saw that In-chol's facial expression changed when he looked at the picture, but what he read in the young man's face was not close to an emotion a person might show upon seeing the face of a blood relation under unlikely circumstances.

"What do you think of the face you saw there? You don't think he looks atrocious enough to slay a man, do you?"

What In-chol felt inside him listening to these words of the professor was an urge to refute the latter's implication altogether. To In-chol, an act of manslaughter of that type committed right after the Korean War could not properly called a crime of atrocity. Shouldn't such a word be used to describe things of a different nature? He did not speak his thoughts out, however. Instead, he finished the slice of watermelon in his hand and put the rind down on one side of the tray.

"And this is a picture of the graveyard of the butchers," said Professor Chi handing him the other picture.

"You see that there's no sod on these graves? It's because they think the dead person's soul cannot go to heaven if his grave is sodded. But in the present day, no butcher believes in that story any longer. Only, there's this stubborn old man who's trying to keep other butchers, too, from sodding their dead relatives' graves. In that sense, this fanatically stubborn old man may lawfully be designated the last of the trueborn butchers."

"What did you say the name of the village you visited was?" asked In-chol.

"It's Pundinamutkol," answered Professor Chi, still without having found the response he had been expecting, but at the same time relieved that In-chol most possibly was not related to the old man. "You can go there taking a suburban bus at the Ulchiro 6-ga. You get off at a place called Shinjang, walk about four kilometers, and you are there. I am going to go back there again at the Full Moon time. It seems that there's a rite offered for the dead cows and oxen then. Of course it's officiated all by the old man by himself. I want to be there to look at it, and if I get the chance to do so, I want to take a look at this butchering knife he has. I am not at all sure that the old man will let me do that, though.... Anyway, I intend to study up on this theme of *packchong* since I am this far in it already. I asked Chon to make a research and find out about other existing *paekchong* communities for me."

"How is Chon-*sonsaeng* (appellation for one usually in teaching position)?" asked In-chol referring to Chon Kyong-hun in that honorific term to be correct in his interpersonal etiquette. Chon was only a few years older than In-chol but what did it matter....

"Oh, I almost forgot. He wants you to get in touch with him immediately. Or, have you received a message from him already?"

"No, I haven't."

"It seems that the family who used to have him tutor one of their children want a new house built. And Chon recommended you as master architect, it seems."

"Really? But how could I? I am hardly in a position to take such a big commission. I have no experience to speak of."

"They seem to have a particular wish that the house plan be drawn up in a new style by a rising young talent, like yourself, I should say. Why don't you give it a try?"

Even so, In-chol could not feel enthusiastic about the prospect. He looked at his wristwatch. It was a quarter to six o'clock. He stood up from the seat.

"Going already? Why not stay on for supper and some more chat?"

"I have a date with someone," said In-chol.

At seven o'clock, he had promised to meet Na-mi at Mont-parnasse. The two had become rather close at the sea this time.

"Oh, is that right? But Ta-hye must be about through with her lessons, now.... You know she talks about you now and then. Actually she was complaining that you never sent another word after a picture postcard," said the professor.

The reason why In-chol decided to leave the professor's room now actually was to see Ta-hye for a minute before leaving this house.

Na-mi walked over to In-chol's table when he had finished his soda drink. She was wearing a sleeveless blue blouse and a shortish pleated skirt, also of a blue dye but darker than the blouse. A black belt was giving an attractive accent to the slimness of her waistline. There was a nearly intangible smile on her face as she came up to him.

"Let's go over there," she said still standing.

Together they walked over to the table where the two men were still sitting. One of the two stopped his speech in the middle and looked up. Leaning a little forward (but still without sitting down) Na-mi introduced In-chol and this man to each other.

"On this side we have the star of our New Theater, Pak Hae-yon-*sonsaengnim*. And on this other side we have the architect of our future, Kim In-chol-*ssi*," the girl intoned in a slightly sarcastic tone.

The man was in his late thirties apparently. He protruded his hand for a handshake, without standing up In-chol felt that his hand was wet and cold.

"And this is Producer Nam Chun-gol-*sonsaengnim*," said Na-mi again completing her job of introducing.

Taking his pipe out from between his lips with a slow motion, the producer held out one hand in In-chol's direction, but it was clear that he didn't expect the handshake to actually occur.

Only then did In-chol remember about Na-mi's telling him by the sea that she was training to become a stage actress. Taking the seat next to Na-mi, he took another round of the hall with his eyes. Plaster masks of Beethoven and Goethe were hanging on the wall at the back of the counter. On the walls on the left and right ends of the hall could been seen framed pictures of famous foreign movie stars.

".... So what I was driving at was that our New Theater has decayed to the point of irremediability. We no longer have actors or actresses who are willing to live or die on the stage. No, we don't see that kind of passion and professional pride any longer. Nowadays, it's a common story for a player to go off to take a part in a movie even in the middle of a rehearsal. All it takes is a bigger pay. What can you do with a situation like this? I grant that for some people, it is an act of necessity, I mean, a necessary act of earning bread. Yes, sometimes, one is obliged to act in a certain undesired way. But there's one point beyond which I cannot concede. It is that some acting people have the dumb and unforgivable idea that they can make a success of their acting career while trying to get the better of both professions, that of a stage actor and that of a movie star. Those people are self-conceited fools. They are victims of a tragic fallacy, if you ask me. And because of this fallacy, they end up by ruining themselves and the theatre as well. Do you understand what I am saying? And do you think only the actors and the actresses are to blame for this? Not at all. Producers, managers, and many others with different responsibilities in the theatre ought to share the responsibility. At least this is what I think," concluded Pak Hae-yon apparently continuing a talk he was engaged in when In-chol and Na-mi appeared on the scene.

"But why should there be such rigid clear-cut lines between the stage and the film-making? Why can't a person act on the stage and also be in a movie? What would your definition make an old-time actor like Louis Jouvet? And in our time, too, we have such good actors as Lawrence Olivier, Jean-Louis Barrault, and many others who are good stage actors as well as being very good movie stars, don't we?" said Na-mi seriously.

"What Miss Cho has just said has a point, of course," said Pak. "But one must not confuse these people's scope of artistic calibre with what our theatrical crowd that call themselves actors and actresses have, or... I should say, rather... lack. Let me put it in a different way, though. Those westerners you mentioned are like grown-ups who can very well walk on their own two feet. But if they like to, they may very well ride whatever transportation means comes handy their way. Not our performing artists who are like toddlers who can barely tag along after their mothers.... Even before they have learned to walk, however, our actors and actresses try to ride the automobiles and in that process forget what they had learned about walking on their own two feet. I wouldn't worry much if these kids will learn to even handle the automobile riding, you know. In short, there's no comparison between the two cases."

"What do you think could revive our New Theater, then, Pak-*sonsaengnim*?" asked Na-mi.

"Revive our New Theater? You know, Miss Cho, that riviving means rebuilding something that had been there but could not continue. It can't apply, therefore, to our New Theater because, in my opinion, our New Theater has never lived. It annihilated itself as soon as it was born, in other words.... I don't mean to say that we cannot rescue it from a total collapse. But in order for it to be rescued, certain requirements must be met. The most imperative of these, in my thinking, is the harmony between three principles. This, of course, means, the harmony between a good playwright, a good actor, and a good producer. Another requisite which is as important is that all the theatrical people who believe themselves to belong to any of these categories accept their fate as theatre artists with courage and determination."

"But didn't you say a while ago that those who are in charge of managing theatrical affairs, too, ought to take the blame of the failure of our theatre? If so, shouldn't you rather say that harmony between not three but four factors should be striven for?" said Nam Chun-gol who had been pretending to be intent on sucking his pipe up to this point.

"What you seem to be thinking is a wrong thought. We can't define a manager as an artist. At most, we should acknowledge his part as an active sympathizer and cooperator. So, it is still the question of how we can realize an ideal harmonization of the three elements, competent playwright, good performer, and an able producer. But is this easy?"

Just at this point, however, Nam Chun-gol stood up, saying,

"I have to excuse myself. I am sorry I can't stay on and enjoy your talk. I have another appointment to keep, unfortunately." Then, turning to Na-mi, he said, "I will see you later, right?"

Na-mi nodded in agreement. After paying his courtesy to In-chol with a silent goodbye which involved only a slight movement of his head, Nam Chun-gol left the teahouse.

Pak Hae-yon picked up the cup placed in front of him. His face looked tired. Then he opened his mouth again,

"But the problem is... no, let's not talk about this any longer...." Pak Hae-yon said and then turning in the direction of a waitress hollered, "Say, can't you turn off the radio and put a record on. Let's have Greco's Fallen Leaves, shall we?"

Even before the music he ordered started, however, Pak stood up and without a word walked toward the entrance. "He's going to have a drink. He can't stand it if he hasn't some alcohol left in his blood stream. He's always loud and talkative like that. Maybe that's his way of letting his professional frustration out of his system," said Na-mi.

"Let's go somewhere else," In-chol said. Then, seeing

Na-mi throw a glance at her watch, he added immediately, "Oh, I forgot. You have a date with that other man, don't you?"

"There has been a workshop for would-be actors and actresses this summer. And today is its last day. So, they are planning an open discussion session for this last day. And I am invited to participate in the capacity of an observer."

There was neither heistation nor any sign of apology in Na-mi's tone of voice and attitude. In-chol said, "I see."

In-chol felt piqued, however, because today's date had been suggested by Na-mi herself in the train coming up from Taechon. This teahouse, too, had been Na-mi's choice. Now that In-chol has seen that this was a place frequented by Na-mi's other acquaintances, he could not help suspecting her motive in making him come here. But Na-mi did not look as if she were in any way aware of his chagrin or doubt. In-chol could not read any regret or remorse in her lightly eye-shadowed eyes which were unusually large in her smooth-skinned darkish face with lips that had been merely touched with rouge. What would have been her expression when he had kissed her by the sea that night? She was aloof and even cold to him today. But his was not what she was that night. There was nothing about her today that could make a man embrace her at an impulse. The discrepancy between the girl of the night sea and the girl who was sitting opposite him today, however, had the beneficial effect of calming down In-chol's somewhat aroused feelings of a while ago.

"I will sit here a little longer. But you'd better go if it's time."

"I will see you tomorrow, then," said Na-mi and springing lightly up from the seat, went to the counter and paid the bill. She turned briefly and nodded her head by way of a goodbye and then walked straight to the door.

Turning his eyes away from Na-mi, In-chol experienced a bitter disappointment as when he has just torn off a building plan he has given a lot of thought and time to. He lit a cigarette, wondering if he should call Ta-hye and ask if she would like to take an outing. Just at this moment, however, he saw Pak Hae-yon coming toward him.

"Oh, Mr. Kim... that is your name, isn't it? But why didn't you go with Miss Cho? Ah, that's right, they are having this discussion thing.... Say, somebody, will you turn on the record, please. Greco's Fallen Leaves!"

Na-mi took the last step of the staircase leading from the basement teahouse to the street outside. She felt free. And she felt pleased with herself for having so cleverly handled today's appointment with In-chol. She had been so cool and indifferent with him! And why not? Is giving one kiss to a boy such a big deal? I am a free woman, as always!

Before she could reach the restaurant where the discussion was to be held, however, Na-mi was stopped by someone in front of the Municipal Hall. It was Chon Kyong-hun.

"Oh, is that you, Chon-*sonsaengnim*, I didn't recognize you because of your new glasses."

"I heard you'd gone to Taechon. When did you return?"

"Just yesterday. But how have you been? Not so busy as when school's open, perhaps?" asked Na-mi throwing a glance at the books Chon Kyong-hun was holding against his side. Oh, once a bookworm always a bookworm! But he does look somewhat academic with those glasses on, said Na-mi inwardly.

"Shall we go and have some tea somewhere?"

"Actually I am the one who would have liked to invite you to tea, but not now. I have an engagement, and there's no time. I will give you a rain check, though, all right?"

Na-mi was not lying. She would really have found it rather agreeable to sit with this dull bookish man for a spell.

"Goodbye, then," said Na-mi and started to walk. Then as

if remembering something, she stopped again and said,

"I just remembered. My father seems to be waiting to see you for some reason. He made some such remark only this morning."

"Well, I've been busy changing the boarding houses and so on. I ought to have called on your father. But my going by myself wouldn't have meant much, anyway. I was supposed to take someone to see your father, you see. And this person has been away. I called his place today and found out that he has just come back from his trip. Would you please tell your father that I will go and see him before noon tomorrow?"

Parting from Chon Kyong-hun, Na-mi went to the restaurant. Instead of going straight up to the second floor where the discussion meeting was to be held, however, Na-mi went to the restroom and touched up her face with a little more rouge and eyeshadow which she applied a little more generously than before. She smiled to herself in the mirror and then leaving the restroom climbed the steps lightly to go to the discussion meeting.

Just as Na-mi had predicted, Pak Hae-yon had had his drink and In-chol saw that his face looked much less fatigued now. He sang along with the voice of the record by patches:

Toi qui m'aimais,
Et je t'aimais....

"Not me!" Pak suddenly ejaculated. "I have never loved anyone and no one has ever loved me. The reason I like to listen to that song is just to get the feel of the thing called love. For me, love is just a word that I find in such things as the Bible, literature, or pop songs.... But what about you, Mr. Kim? Have you loved someone or be loved by any one?" asked Pak Hae-yon staring at In-chol with watery eyes. Then he continued, "Do you know what I think? I think that only strong people are able to love. I mean those who are strong enough to hate. Because hate and love are two surfaces of a mirror. Without one, the mirror does not exist. But who among us have that kind of strength? Who can love and hate in equal intensity? Maybe, you wouldn't like to be included in the category of the human specimen I am speaking of. I will just include myself in it."

Then, he sang again in a low voice:

Et la mer efface sur le sable,
Les pas des amants désunis.

"That's right. No one who has not loved can experience separation. A weak character like me cannot know what it means. All I know is dependency. Mr. Kim.... I have a plot for a play. It's about a village where only weak characters are gathered to live together," said Pak Hae-yon and, then sat silent for a minute making a grimace as if he were concentrating on a thought. Then, he spoke again,

"The scene is an opening in front of a small village with about half a dozen grass-roofed huts standing against the backdrop of a bare dirt hill which is the same dull red color as the dirt walls around the huts. There's no vegetation of whatsoever kinds as far as eye can see across the dirt fields that surround the village that are also the dull red color as are the walls and the hill at the back of the village. In the midst of all this, there's an electric pole constituting the only noticeable man-made construction in this world of red dirt. Since countless people have leant against this electric pole, it is worn smooth around where human backs might have touched.... When the curtain rises, it is midday, ablaze and scorching-hot with the sun. A man walks in onto the stage. It's better that he be an old man. He is wearing work clothes, also of the same dye as the dirt hill and the dirt fields. His head is bare. This old man walks over to the electric pole and sits down putting his back against it. After a while, another person walks in. This time, it doesn't matter if he is a young

man or middle-aged. He, too, goes to the electric pole and
sits down leaning against it like the old man. More people
come in one by one and all of them go to the electric pole
to sit down against it. This continues until not one more
person can sit down against the electric pole even if everybody squeezes himself to the utmost. Yet, people keep on
arriving there so that now there forms a long line of men
and women of all ages, even infants sucking at their mothers'
breasts. They are waiting for somebody to get up and leave
an empty space in the tightly-knit human chain around the
electric pole. The red burning sun is pouring heat and blind-
ing light upon them all.... What do you think of this, Mr.
Kim?"

Pak Hae-yon paused in his recitation and looked at In-chol
who was a little surprised to find this man acting as if they
had known each other for a long time.

"It's interesting," said In-chol.

For a few seconds, Pak Hae-yon sat silent staring at the top
of the tea table. Then, he said, again,

"There are one act and three scenes. The setting and the
characters are identical throughout the entire scenes. Only,
there will be some changes in the order of appearances by
different characters. In other words, I would have the old
man appear first in the first scene but let a young man or a
middle-aged person be the first to come on the stage in the
second scene. And the denture made on the electric pole by
repeated contacts with the human backs deepens as the play
progresses. By the time the play reaches the last scene, there's
such a deep denture around the pole that it is likely to break
in two any minute. Also the sun becomes larger and larger
with the play's progression and heat and light, too, grow in
intensity. There will be just a single stage light which is red.
And this red also will grow into a more and more angry red
with the change of scenes. One other stage effect that is required is the screeching calls of the crows which will become
more noisy as if the number of crows were getting bigger and

bigger.... I wonder if this is all.... Oh, there's just one more detail which is that the characters' figures will change gradually, from thin to fat or the other way round. Which way it will be depends upon the producer's judgement.... So, what do you think? Do you think this will make a play?"

"Aren't the characters going to say anything? I mean, is this going to be a pantomime?" said In-chol looking at Pak Hae-yon as if to study his face anew.

"Well, to tell you the truth, I haven't decided it yet. I would like to have them speak their lines but the trouble is I can't think up the words. That's why I have not been able to complete the play. But I am convinced that the words will come out of their womb one day, I am sure of it," said Pak Hae-yon, suddenly looking very tired.

"I think I'll go now," said In-chol not to tire the older man any more. But the latter seemed not ready to be parted from In-chol yet. He said,

"If you are not in too big a hurry, I would like to take you to a show. This is a Comédie Humaine performed by real people in a real setting. It's far more entertaining than a stage performance."

Dusk had descended on the alley outside the teahouse when the two men walked out of the building. The house of real entertainment where Pak Hae-yon led In-chol was no other than a tavern a few buildings further into the same alley. When the two arrived there, Pak Hae-yon hurriedly entered the tavern pulling In-chol by the sleeve.

Drinking was not one of the things In-chol was much fond of. He drank a little in the company of his friends, but never did he make an occasion to drink on his own initiative. But he decided to drink somewhat freely this evening. For the past hour or two, he had felt depressed. The viewing of the old man's picture. Na-mi's behavior, these things seemed to have brought about this spell of low-spiritedness. Drinks, he felt, would be the right thing for him in his present mood.

It was a fairly big tavern with six to seven stools along the counter and about half a dozen tables sprawled about in the hall. Although there were several empty stools facing the counter, Pak Hae-yon chose a table in one corner of the hall. Before he reached the table and took a seat, however, he exchanged greetings by nodding his head with a number of different people.

After ordering the girl who waited on the tables to bring half a *toe* of rice wine, Pak Hae-yon asked In-chol what kind of *anju* (food eaten along with drinks) he would like to have. His finger was pointing at a miniature blackboard on the wall at the back of the counter on which were written a list of names of foods. In-chol read under the heading Today's Menu five to six different names of *anju*. He told Pak Hae-yon that anything would be all right with him, and the latter ordered dried pollack.

With a mild interest, In-chol observed that Pak Hae-yon had a strange sort of a way with his drinks. First, he poured a cup as soon as the order of rice wine arrived on the table and drank it down in one gulp. He let about ten minutes pass and then poured a second cup which he again drank down at one stroke. It seemed that he enjoyed the sensation the drink gave him while it spread out in his body. Another characteristic In-chol noticed was that Pak never touched the *anju*. In any case, a new vitality came back to him erasing the look of fatigue from his face, and he began to talk without stopping: In-chol got the impression that consecutive talking helped him relish the sensation of intoxication the better.

"I promised to let you watch a performance, didn't I?" said Pak. "The setting is as you can see. As for the dramatis personae, there are so many of them that I could not possibly introduce all of them to you. I will therefore select only the more conspicuous of the characters and give you their profiles. Most of these chosen ones have the illustrious record of having played on this stage for more than one year. Anyway...you see the tall one sitting on the third stool from right facing the counter? That man ran for the National Assembly in the last election and lost. He sold away his house to pay to debt he ran into during his campaign but still got stuck with several million *hwan* in debt. There's nothing strikingly new in these things, of course. But his election speeches were something quite novel and characteristic, I should say. One of the promises he made was that he would cut down the liquor tax in case of his election. His reason was that he wanted drinkers to have their fill of wine and liquor. Of course, there was an understandable cause for this. That man himself is a drink-lover. He even won a prize once in drinking. It was at a drinking competition held at the Kumchon Hall. He won the second highest prize in it. That man doesn't get drunk easily. I believe he is the strongest in drinking among all the drinkers here. But he is very entertaining once you can get him drunk.... Now I want you to look at that fatso sitting last to the left. He is a literary critic. He is at the height of his popularity these days. Only a short time ago, he was a mere extra who barely showed his face on the stage. But now he is one of the leading actors of this theater. He is full of lectures on existentialism and Camus, Sartre, Kierkegaard, Jaspers, and all the others, you know. But I have a funny thing to tell about that learned man. Once I chanced to leaf through a book of literary criticism he wrote in the course of which action I found out that he was explicating Naturalism in literature as meaning a return to nature. Isn't that something?"

There seemed to be no bottom to his reservoir of causerie. But In-chol had, for some time now, been listening to his words with as much attention as he had for the general noise-making in the hall.

"What are you thinking of so deeply, Mr. Kim?" Pak asked suddenly.

In-chol raised his head and saw Pak Hae-yon staring at him with drink-bemused eyes. What he had been doing was to examine the face of that old man which he had called up in his memory. He could not explain why, but that face gnawed into his nerves as he got deeper and deeper into drinks.

"I see that many of our chief actors are absent today," said Pak. "But at least there will be Mr. Nam and Miss Cho by and by...." Then turning his eyes toward the entrance, he suddenly exclaimed,

"Ah, there's one actor who is worthy of introduction. Look carefully. Do you see a paper sack he's clutching against his side? Do you know what's in it? There are notebooks in which he prepares his lectures. He is a philosophy instructor at a university. Why does he go around with his lecture notebooks during vacation time? There's a very good reason for that! He carries his spending money inserted between the pages of his notebooks. The money he thus hides away in his notebooks comes mostly from writing articles for newspapers or magazines. And he keeps this fund for his own use without his wife's knowing it. As to his pay envelope from the university, he can't do a thing about it because it is confiscated totally by his wife every time. She gives him money for his pack of cigarettes and bus rides. That's all. And if you ask me, I have a strong feeling that she will lose not much time in sniffing out his secret fund tucked away in those notebooks...."

In-chol wasn't listening to him any more, however. Na-mi's coming here? Okay, then, I will sit on and see her once more, he said to himself. He picked up his drink. Then it occurred to him, despite his considerably drunken state, that falling in with Na-mi once more in this kind of a place would make him play a very awkward role. This thought made him smile to himself bitterly. But suddenly, he began to wonder what action Ta-hye would advise him to take in a situation like this.

Although the door was left open, only the child practicing at the piano came into his vision. As always, Ta-hye was invisible to him from the angle where he was looking in. Softly, he entered the room trying not to disturb the lesson.

Ta-hye saw him and smiling a warm welcome gave him an eye signal telling him to wait till the lesson would be over. The room was not very large. But it had windows on all its walls except the one with the door which made it very pleasant. Right now, however, the air in the room was humid although all the windows and the door were open.

In-chol unbottoned his cotton casual shirt and fanned himself, watching the child play the piano without attention. Ta-hye, too, was moving the fan up and down, trying to give some wind to both herself and the child whose untrained performance seemed to be making the air more sultry and unbearable. How could Ta-hye be listening to that kind of noise day after day, wondered In-chol with sympathy. He glanced at Ta-hye's profile noting the white-striped russet color dress which wrapped her body loosely in its generous folds. Her hair was tied up in a pony tail. In-chol thought she looked more pale than he had last seen her. Ta-hye was twenty-six this year. Was she going to live just like this, in her father's house, year after year until she becomes an old woman? Wondering, In-chol looked at his watch. It was twenty minutes to seven. It won't take more than fifteen minutes from here to Myong-dong, calculated In-chol inwardly.

Just then, the girl stood up from the piano picking up her practice book.

"I see that you have a date with someone. Isn't that why you looked at the watch?" said Ta-hye sitting down on the sofa facing In-chol.

"Why do you look so pale in the middle of a summer?" asked back In-chol without answering Ta-hye's question.

The two of them who had grown up together from childhood experienced a short period of social awkwardness in their relationship, especially in the way they spoke to each other, while they both grew out of childhood and then adolescence. But now, after they had become adults unquestionably, they were back to their earlier speech habit that was devoid of all honorific stylizations.

Ta-hye looked at him wordlessly as was her and his habit
when they have not seen each other for some period of time.
Her clear and thoughtful eyes always made him feel relieved
and disturbed at the same time. Although they were of the
same age, somehow Ta-hye's way of looking at him as she was
doing now was more like that of an older sister looking at a
brother younger than herself. This was a feeling In-chol had
had ever since their common childhood....

"You are tanned even to the white of your eye."

"I wouldn't be surprised. I spent all my waking hours on
the beach.... And you... you have become thinner."

"Spinsterish, you mean."

"I think, though, you look even prettier as you are."

"I see you have had your practice in teasing old maids,"
she said in a mock ironical tone and then asked in her natural
voice,

"Did you get to learn swimming?"

"Ah, yes, it wasn't difficult."

"How far can you go, five meters? Or, ten?"

"I can swim two hundred meters like nothing."

"Liar!"

"Will you come to the Han-gang with me and put me to
test?"

"The Han-gang?"

Ta-hye had had her fantasy while In-chol was away in
Taechon. It was about two young people, man and woman,
going to the sea. It was not to enjoy swimming or any other
seaside activities that these two came there but for health
reasons because the man was in a weak physical condition.
He had never had a strong physique and then lately he was
having some breathing difficulty. The fresh sea air might alleviate his pain, they had thought, and they came to the seaside. As for the woman, she was healthy and was a good
swimmer. But she did not go into the water like others. She
only went in with the man and stayed there so long as he

could take it and then came out with him. They were contented with this life. In the morning they went out to the sea
and gathered shells left on the wet sand after the ebbing.
They laughed and shouted with joy doing this. During the day,
they liked to rent a boat and row out to the sea. The sea gulls
followed them emitting funny squeaky sounds. The woman
often imitated the birds' call and the man laughed happily.
At times, too, a motor-engined boat would swish past them
causing their boat tip to one side from the impact of the
water squirted by the machine-operated boat. At these times,
the woman folded her arms over the man's shoulder protecting him. With her eyes, she told him, don't worry because I
am here with you. In the evening, too, they went out to the
beach together. They could hear the sound of the music
floating out of somebody's country house built on a low hill a
little way off. The windows of this house were dyed red with
the setting sun. Turning their heads back toward the sea,
they saw that the sun had dyed the sea water into red, too.
They took a walk along the beach looking steadily at the
crimson sea water, silently. One very windy day when the
angry waves rose tall and wild in the sea making it impossible for anyone even to think of going into the water, the
man suddenly ran in. At first the woman thought he was
going in for only a very short while but would come back out
right away. She thought this because he was not good at
swimming at all and it was such a very foul weather. Yet he
did not turn back but started swimming a little. Next instant,
the fierce, overwhelming tide swept him away. Only then
did the woman take in the full meaning of what was happening and ran into the sea after the man.

The night before they were scheduled to take the train
back to Seoul, In-chol took a walk with Na-mi along the
night sea. They reached the point where a large rock stood
blocking the way. Although the sea looked calm enough to
the eye, the sound of the waves hitting against the sand was

loud and sharp. They had to turn back. But just then Na-mi made a suggestion. She said why not go in for a dip. Throwing off the beach gowns all at once, they ran in. And they went out quite a distance, swimming side by side. In-chol suggested, let's turn back now. But the girl pretended not to hear and went on ahead. Although the sea was calm, Na-mi was going much too far for her to make the return trip safely. There was nothing else for In-chol to do but follow after her hoping that she would turn back of her own accord. This she did in fact. But even in darkness, In-chol could see that her swimming form was getting out of order. In the next moment, she said to In-chol in a panting voice that she could not swim any more. In-chol was by no means a skilled swimmer, yet he did not lose his head when Na-mi declared that she could no longer swim. In a calm voice he told her to try swimming on her back. And then pushing her on, he managed to help her make it to the shore.

Ta-hye's fantasy continued. I must rescue him even if I drown myself doing it. I must save him. By the time she reached where he was, struggling through waves as big and tall as houses, the man was about to sink in the water, completely beaten and exhausted. She swam out dragging him with great difficulty. When his body was brought out of the water, she sucked at his nostrils again and again. Finally, he recovered his breath. But after this day, he became so ill that he had to be hospitalized. The woman asked the man, why did you take such a big risk? I wanted to throw myself against the waves, said the man in a weak voice.

Reviving this fantasy in her memory, Ta-hye looked at In-chol with a quiet smile. Lately, she fell into daydreaming often. Maybe it came from her living too inactive a life despite her ability to take charge of things in a composed, persevering, but competent way.

"Why are you smiling like that?" asked In-chol.

"I am just happy that you didn't try anything foolish but

came back safely?"

"Didn't try anything foolish? What do you mean by that?"

"I mean I am glad you didn't run into an accident at sea."

Oh, she and her worries, said In-chol inwardly with a good humour. What Na-mi did that night certainly was something foolish, he thought. But I...I kissed her for the first time that night....

After she pulled herself out of the water, Na-mi had staggered a few paces on the sand in utter exhaustion and then threw herself down flat on the beach. And In-chol lay down beside her. It was a moonless night. Only, some stars were twinkling in the dark sky. But even the stars were sparse that night. Why are there not more stars, he had wondered, on a clear night like this. Suddenly he felt extremely languid and he closed his eyes. Na-mi was still panting by his side, which made him recall the thoughtless prank she had played a while ago and made him feel a mild anger toward her. He felt the cool sensation of the wet sand on his back. It was not an unpleasant feeling. The sound of the tide scratching at the sand just below his feet and the clashing noise of big waves hitting against a rock a distance away kept their regularity taking turns in noise-making. All of a sudden, In-chol felt the desertedness of the beach at night. And in this deserted emptiness of the night, he was conscious of himself gradually tightening into a tiny hardened knot. Next moment, however, this tiny knot reverted to expanding until it became one with the vast night. He felt a need to become his normal self. But just at this moment, he became aware of something smooth and soft flesh rubbing him on his shin. At the same time, he felt the tingling of the sand grains against his skin. He pulled himself to a sitting position. Na-mi was still lying flat on her back, completely immobile. Her panting was gone and she was breathing in normal even tempo, now. In-chol covered her lips with his. He felt the soft coldness of the girl's lips. Still lying flat on her back, she did not show any reaction to his move. He took his lips away. There was a taste of salt on his tongue. Suddenly, Na-mi threw her arms around In-chol's neck. Then, in a posture of a child hanging onto an adult's neck, she sought his lips and rubbed her lips against them. Letting himself go in the direction of the weight pulling him, he bent his upper body down, his lips still folded on hers. He felt hot and resilient flesh darting into his mouth for a fraction of a second, but almost at the same instant Na-mi pushed his chest backward jerking her head away.

Without realizing, In-chol was looking at Ta-hye's feet. They were well-shaped nice slender feet. On all the tidily lined-up toes, he could see pretty dimples marking every little joint in them. The slightly-upturned thumbs of her feet had cute pink bellies.

As if sensing In-chol's eyes on them, Ta-hye pulled in her feet gathering them close together.

"You have pretty feet," said In-chol.

"Are you feeling all right? You are acting funny today," said Ta-hye pulling her feet up on the sofa and covering them with the hem of her skirt. In-chol noted that there appeared just a tinge of light pink flush on her cheeks.

What do the feet of Na-mi who had tickled him on the shin on the night beach look like? Come to think of it, he had never looked at her feet during all the hours they had spent in close contact at the sea.

"Are you looking at the watch again?"

"I have to go some place, that's why."

"Are you meeting a girl?"

"Yes."

"What kind of a girl is she?"

"She is somebody I got to know at the sea."

"So that's why you didn't write again after just one post-card. But this is a wonderful news. What is she like? No, tell me these things another time. And now, go. You have to be punctual when you are seeing a lady. Otherwise, you are lost. And...if she is a nice good person, grip onto her this time. You mustn't lose a good girl through lukewarm attitude in your usual way. All right? Now, go!"

Ta-hye knew about all In-chol's relationships with girls, even the boring details. Today, too, In-chol might have told Ta-hye everything if only he had not been pressed for time. Even what happened on the night before his return to Seoul....

"Oh, I see that the actor over there is about to begin a performance. He is the one least strong for liquor."

The instructor of philosophy was coming toward the table where In-chol and Pak Hae-yon were sitting. He carried his sack with lecture notebooks tucked under one arm and held the drinking cup in his other hand. He took the seat next to Pak Hae-yon and, putting down his cup in which there was only a little drink left, said,

"Do you know, Pak-*sonsaengnim*, what kind of a woman is the greatest in this world?"

"Well....I would say a Nepalese woman who lives with about half a dozen husbands may well deserve that name. Is my answer correct?"

"Nope!"

"Well, then, is she a negress who weight thirty-four *kwan* (one *kwan*, 3.75 kg.)?"

"No, again!"

"Then, is it that western woman who gave birth to quintuplets?

"I must say you lack imagination. So, I will tell you the answer. The greatest woman in the world is one who doesn't suffer from hysteria after she is forty."

Relieved that there was someone now who would take charge of Pak Hae-yon and his bottomless talk, In-chol got up. Neither Pak Hae-yon nor the philosopher seemed even to notice what he was doing. In-chol went to the cashier and after paying the bill walked out of the drinking house.

A Comédie Humaine? And what is Pak Hae-yon? Isn't he

also only one character in this thing of which he thinks himself to be an objective spectator or producer? It was when he was almost at the end of the gayest section of Myong-dong abright with neon signs that he nearly bumped into a group of people who were coming from the opposite direction. Hurriedly In-chol stepped aside making room for the group to pass. But just then, he remarked that two of the three in the party were Na-mi and Nam Chun-gol. The other was a young man he did not know.

"Oh, you've been in that teahouse all this time?" said Na-mi whose arm was in that of Nam Chun-gol.

In order to avoid a long talk, In-chol nodded his head once.

"By the way, In-chol-*ssi*, you have a sister by the name of In-ju, right? She attended this workshop that just closed today. But why didn't you tell me about her?," asked Na-mi, and then giving a backward glance once, she continued, "We just said, goodbye to her back there.... She is such a talented girl. Don't you think so, Nam-*sonsaengnim*?"

Nam Chun-gol took his pipe from between his lips and managed to say,

"She is a promising student."

What an odd thing to hear, said In-chol to himself. How could she think of attending an actors' workshop? Must have made the decision during my absence. She has talent? Yes, she can do whatever she chooses to, at least on the average level. In-chol continued to think about this matter while he walked on after saying goodbye to Na-mi and her party. As he came near the bus stop in front of the Midopa Department Store, however, he suddenly heard a voice behind his back,

"Excuse me, I hear you are an older brother of In-ju-*ssi*."

It was the young man who was walking with Na-mi and Nam Chun-gol. He was breathing hard from having run after In-chol. He said again,

"I attended the workshop with In-ju-*ssi* this summer.... I think she is wonderful.... And my name is Shin Myong-su."

The young man bowed to In-chol hurriedly, and then

turning back began to run again.

In-chol stood on in immobility for a while, sunken in thought.

CHAPTER THREE

The Arabesque

In-chol woke up at the sound of the paraquets and the *kumhwajo* coming from his sister's room nextdoor. It seemed he had slept off last night's drinks. He felt rested. Even the birds' songs which sounded somewhat out of tune gave him only a pleasant and refreshing sense of joy.

Last night, he had gone to bed weïghed down with fatigue because of what happened between Na-mi and himself, the picture of the ōld butcher Professor Chi had shown him, and all the talks and drinks he had had thanks to Pak Hae-yon. And maybe this fatigue had enabled him to have such a good sleep.

On his way to the bathroom downstairs, he ran into In-ju in the corridor.

"Oh, good morning to you, our illustrious star!" he exclaimed in mock admiration.

In-ju looked at him her eyes wide open behind the long eyelashes that reminded one of the bamboo shafts of an elegant fan. Her face looked surprised and guilty as when a small child who has done something without the parents' knowledge has been caught.

"You might have told me, though. I always thought you considered me worthy of that much trust. But maybe I was wrong?"

"I wanted to let it known after I have spent more time

with it. I am sorry, *obba* (older brother).

"If you have an intention to stand on the stage, give your-self to it. Maybe, I will have the honor of decorating the stage for your debut performance?"

In-chol ate breakfast and came back up to his room up-stairs. Then, he heard the bell on the wall ring once. This bell served as a signal between the lower and upper quarters of this house. If it rang once, it meant there was a telephone call. Two rings were the signal for the meal. Three meant there was a visitor.

In-chol picked up the receiver at head the of his bed. The call was from Chon Kyong-hun. He said that he had been waiting for In-chol's return everyday and said he needed to see him right away. In-chol guessed that it would be about the matter he had already heard from Professor Chi. True, it was a rare opportunity for In-chol. But In-chol's mind was still no more drawn to the proposal than when he had first heard of it from the professor.

He had an unpleasant memory from a commission he had fulfilled on a house for the first time as an architect. It was a house of a man in an executive post in his father's company. He had given his time and energy to this project eagerly and unstintingly. Yet as he watched the construction go up in front of his eyes on his repeated visits to the site, he could not help experiencing deep painful disappointments because of the great gap between what he had drawn up and the thing that was being materialized as an actual house. It was not as if he had not known the obvious fact that the drafts on the paper cannot be directly transformed into a full-scale construction without some adjustments. But there was absolutely no com-parison between the thing that was being built and the original plan he had drawn with so much passion and devotion. A greater part of the change was caused by the construction director but not a few changes had been made because of what different members of the family felt about different things. In-chol ended up suffering a serious mental damage. He did not yet know what kind of people Chon Kyong-hun wanted to introduce him to, but he did not wish to involve himself with anything like that again, not until he should have finished his graduate work, anyway. What he wanted to do now was to concentrate on his thesis.

But he did not wish to act unappreciatively toward Chon who, after all, meant to help him. So, he promised to meet him at a teahouse and packing his swimming trunk in a carryall bag left the house. He had meant to go out and swim in the Han-gang anyway.

Meeting Chon Kyong-hun at the teahouse and hearing from him various things about the project and the people who wanted the house built, however, changed everything. Once more, In-chol felt a temptation to try it. Especially since the would-be owner of the house who was a banker specifically wanted a young architect to draw up the plan....

When In-chol was finally persuaded to meet the party, Chon Kyong-hun went to the counter and made a call to the banker's house. But it was an unexpected response that Chon Kyong-hun could get through the phone. He was told that after waiting a period of time, they had found another architect with the belief that maybe the one Chon Kyong-hun had mentioned did not wish the job, after all. If so, was that why Na-mi had said her father wanted to see him?

Coming back to his seat, Chon Kyong-hun apologized so shamefacedly that In-chol felt uncomfortable. Repeatedly, he blamed himself for not having called that house before and he explained that the banker wanted to begin the work before the cold weather begins. In the end, In-chol could no longer bear to hear Chon Kyong-hun's apologies and watch him fidget with the bridge of his eyeglasses. So he said,

"It turned out that way all for the best because I hadn't wanted to take the job in the first place. And in any case, it would have been difficult for them to have a house completed before winter although I don't know what type of a house they have in mind exactly." Then, changing the subject, he said,

"By the way, did you know that Professor Chi is doing some research on the butchers?"

"Yes, he is very much involved with the subject. But then, he always goes in deep into a subject, doesn't he, once his curiosity is aroused?" said Chon Kyong-hun who seemed relieved that In-chol changed the subject of their conversation.

"I never knew that such a thing existed as a separate community. I always thought people became butchers when they were poor and had no other means of livelihood."

"Well, I myself have been doing some study on them at the request of the professor and according to what I have found out...."

"Oh, then, is it something that can be studied seriously from some historical perspective?" asked In-chol interrupting Chon Kyong-hun.

"There aren't really much of what you could call historical data on the subject, but in the Choi Chung-hon section of the History of Koryo Dynasty, for instance, we find a reference to a social group called the Yangsuchok. This was a sort of a vagrant group who did not have a fixed place of residence but made their living by hunting and sale of *kori* (bamboo chests) which they made. And the general scholarly view seems to consider this group the predecessor of the later-day butchers."

"You might call them Korean gypsies, then, might you not?"

"That's right. Like gypsies, they are roamers," said Chon Kyong-hun, and then, readjusting his glasses once more, continued, "Yangsuchok comes from the Chinese characters, *yang* meaning the willows, *su* meaning water, and *chok* meaning measure. Often, the name is shortened to just Su-chok. There is a scholarly opinion of viewing Suchok as really standing for *suja* which is to say that for the second letter *ja*, *chok*, the Chinese character meaning 'measure' had been used. Then, what does *suja* mean? It means the present-day *kwangdae* (performers at the folk level). So then, the race of

Yangsuchok hunted, made bamboo chests, and also sang and danced to make living as they moved about from place to place."

"It's interesting." said In-chol intrigued by Chon Kyong-hun's explication. "Roamers who hunted and performed.... Just like gypsies.... When did this race occur on the Korean scene first?"

"We don't know exactly, but in the Choi Chung-hon material I mentioned a while ago, it is conjectured that they are the survivers of the Paekche resistence forces against the troops led by the Koryo founding king Taejo."

"Then, when did Yangsuchok become butchers?"

Chon Kyong-hun explained to In-chol the origin of the word "butcher', or, *paekchong,* in its traditional appellation. *Paekchong* meant different things in different ages. During the Koryo period, for instance, it meant the people who did not partake of the land distribution administered by the state. The latter-day meaning of the word *paekchong* came to be attached to it only in the Choson Dynasty. It referred to those of the Yangsuchok race who made a living out of butchering. Those whose main source of livelihood was making bamboo chests were called *kori-paekchong.*

After this additional information, Chon Kyong-hun said,

"Professor Chi wanted me to make inquiries about the butcher villages that are still remaining in our society. And I have found out that there's at least one in Yangju-gun. As soon as I have the name of this village, I and the professor will go there for a look."

In-chol felt in good mood today. Even while he was swimming in the Han-gang, this uplifted mood continued. The water of the river was a bit heavier on his body than the sea water. But he was resolved to cross the river today. While crossing the river trying out different techniques he had come to acquire, he thought continuously about this interesting people who roamed throughout the land earning their daily bread by hunting, handicraft, or performing as singers and

dancers just as their luck would allow them. He succeeded in
crossing the river. It was not as difficult as he had thought.

A little distance in the direction of the Hwashin Department Store from the Anguk-dong crossroad was a rather
decrepit barber shop on the right-hand side of the street. It
was past ten o'clock in the morning. The barbers were
dozing in the customers' chairs because there was no one at
the moment who wanted to have his hair cut. A narrow
crooked alley ran from where this barber shop stood, flanked
by low-lying ancient houses.

Whenever he stepped into this alley, In-chol felt as if he
were back in his eternal home site. He had lived in this alley
for twenty years before his house moved to Chae-dong about
five years ago. Although the passage was crooked and hemmed
in by houses, In-chol felt he would be able to walk through
this alley with his eyes closed.

From about twenty meters inside the alley, he began to
hear the sound of the piano. It came from Ta-hye's house. In
the summer when houses kept their windows open, one could
hear this sound of piano from quite afar. Since the piano had
belonged to Ta-hye's mother who had brought it along when
she married the professor, In-chol must have been listening
to its sound ever since his birth. But he was surprised to hear
the sound of the piano on this particular day because he had
Ta-hye's promise to go to the Han-gang to swim.

In-chol hurried to Ta-hye's house passing four to five houses
on both sides and pushed the ring. There was a sound of rubber shoes being dragged against the ground and then the
sound of the latch on the gate being pulled off.

"Ah, it's you, the dark-skinned young lord!" exclaimed the
maid of this house with exaggeration. This woman who was
in the middle of her forties had found a younger woman for
her husband about five years ago to atone for her infertility
and had ever since been living at Professor Chi's house as a
maid. She was a spirited lively woman, but at times, she was

a little burdensome because of her excessive talkativeness. Even now, she seemed reluctant to let In-chol go without some more of her bantering. At the back of the retreating young man, therefore, she shouted,

"It's a pity you don't have a kinky hair. You'd have passed for a negro, otherwise!"

In-chol did not talk back but kept on walking with a good-natured smile on his face. He threw a glance at the 'piano room' that stood separate from the main building. This time, it was Ta-hye who was at the piano. She was playing with her head a little tilted upward. In-chol thought she looked a little lonesome.

Professor Chi was not in sight when In-chol went into the house.

"The professor went to the country with Chon-*sonsaeng-nim*. They left early in the morning," answered the maid when In-chol inquired her about the whereabouts of the professor.

They must have gone to this village of the butchers that's supposed to be somewhere in Yangju, thought In-chol to himself. He strolled over to the 'piano room' passing flower beds with the sun flowers that were in bloom exhibiting sundry bright colors.

"Why don't you give yourself a break sometimes," said In-chol standing at the doorsill.

"Come on in," said Ta-hye pausing and smiling to him quietly, as usual.

"No, I won't go in. Let's go. Right away!"

"Come in for a minute, anyway."

"Why is it so difficult to go anywhere with a woman? You wouldn't need to make up your face when you're going to the river for swimming. So, let's go."

In-chol entered the room, however, and sat on the sofa. Ta-hye came over and sat opposite him.

"I can't go," she said.

"What are you talking about? You mean you've changed your mind overnight?"

"It's not that. I even packed my old swimming suit which I wore in my high school days, but....I suddenly found out that I couldn't go."

"Why? Is it because your father's away and you have to watch the house?"

"No, it's not that either. There's *ajumma* (general, unceremonious, appellation for women. In this case, the maid) to do that."

"Then what?"

"You wouldn't know."

"Why not?"

"Believe me, you wouldn't know," said Ta-hye with a slight blush on her pale face.

Suddenly In-chol understood. He smiled, nodding his head as if to say 'oh, that!'

"Why are you smiling? Why are you nodding your head, you wicked boy!" said Ta-hye blushing deeper. Then she said in a more sober voice,

"Anyway, I am sorry. I really wanted to look at you swim with my own eyes."

"Didn't I say I can cross the Han-gang like nothing?"

"Don't try to show off. You can get into trouble doing that," admonished Ta-hye seriously. "And you must give your body a plenty of warm-up before you go into the water."

In-chol laughed, amused and pleased by Ta-hye's worry over his well-being.

"It's no laughing matter. You must remember what I said."

When he was going to the elementary school, he had fainted a number of times in the middle of the Morning Ceremony or some other such ceremonial events. He would be standing with his eyes on the face of the principal or some other person on the platform delivering a speech. Then, suddenly, a bluish fog would begin to spread over the three-story school building at the back of the speaker and the blue sky above it. He would close his eyes tight for a second and re-open them hoping this would chase away the foggish illusion. The fog seems to be gone for a fraction of a second, but soon it is back this time dyed in grey hue. Again he closes his eyes a second and reopens them. Every time he repeats this rou-tine, the atmosphere before his eyes turns more and more ominously greyish. Finally, this grey fog which gets darker all the time covers up everything, the speaker on the plat-form, the school building, the blue sky and even the words spoken by the person standing on the platform. And soon, he can't even see the head of the boy in front of him because a darkness as black as the color of the boy's hair is screening the head from his vision. Then, this time, it is In-chol himself that is dissolved into this ever-thickening darkness.

When he regained consciousness after each of these spells, he would invariably be lying on the bed of the school in-firmary. The strange thing was that throughout all the stages of his first seeing the bluish fog to the point of his fainting, he never felt any kind of a fear. After fainting several times, he even had the composure to measure the length of time he could hold out against the black assailant that would finally gulp him down. In time, he came to savor the sweetish sensation that spread throughout his body just before his losing consciousness. The only thing he disliked about this routine was the smell of the antiseptic solution that pene-trated his nostrils as he lay in the infirmary. Whenever he woke up, however, he saw Ta-hye looking down at him with solicitous eyes. In-chol closed his eyes again relieved that Ta-hye was there by his side.

Then there was this other recollection.

It was a little before the winter vacation started at the end of the fifth year in the elementary school. The teacher was making the kids who got right answers for the arithmetic question they were given by the teacher go home ahead of others, it being the last class of that afternoon. Although In-chol hardly ever failed in giving the correct answers as far as arithmetics were concerned, somehow he gave the wrong answer that time. The teacher who was a sort of an eccentric was a believer in democracy in education. Instead of subjecting the kids to any corporal punishment, therefore, he was making them retrieve their notebooks which the teacher kept throwing out of the window to the school ground two stories below. Those who repeatedly gave wrong answers had to make several trips up and down the stairs to have their notebook back. In-chol, of course, found the right answer on the second try. But a mischievous impulse possessed him before he could hand in the correct answer to the teacher. It was to write down a wrong answer on purpose. The number of the kids remaining to work over the question decreased in time so that in the end there was only In-chol left in the classroom with the teacher. The teacher asked In-chol what was the matter with him that he who was always so good in arithmetics was making repeated mistakes today. The short winter sun was already going down and the teacher was uncomfortably standing around by the cold stove with his coat collar pulled up. But once more, In-chol handed in the wrong answer. This time, however, the teacher did not look at the notebook but with a strange smile on his face blurted, 'Go home, rascal.' In-chol left the classroom without saying goodbye to the teacher. He walked across the wind-swept empty school yard. Just when he reached the gate, however, he saw Ta-hye standing on one side of the gate shaking with cold. She seemed to have been watching his doings all this while. She said, 'I thought you would faint.' In-chol said, 'Why would I. I enjoyed it thoroughly.' And he tried not to pant in front of Ta-hye.

"Then, we have to put off our swimming match indefinitely, right?"

"Let's set the date again one week from now. But maybe the water will be too cold by then."

In-chol was standing up from the sofa but Ta-hye halted

him saying,

"Wait a second. Aren't you filing your report on that girl you went to meet the other day? I could have called you to call off the swimming match but I didn't. It was because I wanted to hear the story from you. Did you meet her all right that evening?"

"I did."

"What is she like?"

"A senior in the drama department of some college. Name, Cho Na-mi."

"Oh, she is a little star? Do you see her often?"

"No, I haven't seen her after that day."

"Why not? Have you arranged to meet no more than once or twice a week?"

"That's not it. We have stopped seeing each other."

"Why?"

"Why not? We don't see each other because we don't want to."

"Has there been a problem?"

"No, I just decided to quit because she didn't seem to like me much."

"That's the trouble with you. What matters is how much you like her. You can't expect a woman to be forward from the beginning, can you?"

"Let's say, then, that it's me who don't like her too much."

"That being passive. Even if I had been that girl, I wouldn't have liked you much if you acted in that lukewarm way. You must show more enthusiasm as long as you like a woman to some extent."

"It's really you who have made me that way."

"What are you saying? I have always advised you to be positive and aggressive, haven't I?"

"That's an influence you've given me wordlessly from way back, from when we were little kids."

Ta-hye blushed faintly. Feigning a resentment, however, she said,

"You've become very wicked, you know."

"Well, then, the wicked boy will now say goodbye to her ladyship."

Ta-hye walked him to the gate. But In-chol halted just outside the door, exclaiming softly,

"Look, the Chunhyang and Lee-*toryong* are taking a walk again!"

Ta-hye followed him out of the gate and looked in the direction he was pointing with his chin.

A tall stout old man was walking one step behind a shriveled little old woman who was moving so slowly and painstakingly that to the onlookers' eyes she seemed to be taking a full minute to make one step forward.

Waving a second goodbye to Ta-hye with one hand, In-chol walked on toward the outer end of the alley passing the old couple on the way. But Ta-hye stood a while longer outside her gate watching the two old sojourners.

The old man was carrying a wooden chair in one hand. In this chair he was going to sit the old woman once they reach the pavement by the street at the end of this laborious journey through the winding alley. He will, as usual, stand a whole hour or even for two or three hours behind this chair where his old wife would be sitting watching the passing vehicles and pedestrians, thought Ta-hye to herself. Finally, the old woman would tire of watching the people and the running vehicles and wish to go home. Again, the old man would follow one step behind her carrying the chair as the couple make their toilsome return trip through the alley to their home....

After this old couple moved into this alley last year, they became the hot topic for gossip among the neighbors. One rumor had it that the old woman had been a *kisaeng* (geisha) and had a daughter from a man who was other than the tall old man with whom she was living now. The daughter married a man who became a high government official last year and bought the present house for the old couple as a gift. But nobody in the neighborhood had ever seen the daughter or the politician son-in-law.

Of the four rooms of their house, the old couple used just the Inner-Room and took renters for the remaining three rooms. It seemed they made their living with the rent money they collected from these rooms. All sorts of stories circulated on the basis of the reports these renters provided the curious neighbors with: The old man helped the kitchen work, making fire and bringing water from the well. He also went to the market with his wife carrying the shopping basket on his arm. In time, the rowdy prank-loving barbers nicknamed the couple: Chunhyang and Lee-*toryong* (characters in a famous old love story). Another rumor had it that the old woman was in the habit of whacking the old man on the head with a whip she carried around in the house. This happened when the old man didn't respond to her commands promptly enough, having failed to comprehend them as soon as they were given. The old man obediently put out his head to take the whack, according to the same rumor. All this was known to In-chol, as well, through the chat-loving maid at Ta-hye's house. Professor Chi who was there with In-chol and Ta-hye when the maid made this report on the old couple had commented, 'There's nothing odd there. It's no instance of sadism or masochism but a rather understandable attestation to the fact that there are many ways of manifesting love. Except that if it were the old man instead of the old woman who did the whipping, we could not call it love but persecution. In-chol, nonetheless, had joked that Professor Chi himself would not have liked it much if his wife had been in any way like the old woman in question. In-chol had made that joke because he knew how Professor Chi was unadept for practical matters of quotidian life, certainly more so than the average scholar type whose impracticality was a platitude to Korean thinking. For instance, Professor Chi left everything, from maintaining some order in his book-laden study to choosing a new suit, to his wife who looked after him uncomplainingly although she was herself a working woman having many piano pupils to teach at home. After his wife died from heart disease during the Korean War, Ta-hye had been performing all these duties for her father.

Yesterday, it was clear, with the sky high and blue. One had the feeling that autumn was already there. But today, it was raining all day and there was a fairly strong wind, to boot. It was a shifty whimsical wind which blew in one direction a moment and then came back the next moment to rattle the screen door on the other side. The little holes on the iron net covering the screen door were full of water so that no air could pass through them. The water drops that had gotten through the net crawled down the window panes looking as if they were live worms making their wiggly way down the precipitous glass cliff. Suddenly, the screen door and the window clattered noisily.

In-chol was sitting in front of his desk looking out at the yard through the glass panes. He could see that the trees in the yard were rocking in any direction and some leaves were fighting not to be torn away from the branches. A length from the top part of the stalk of the morning glory that had crept up a tree was fluttering about in the air, having, apparently, been broken without being cut off from the main stalk by the whipping wind. Two blossoms of morning glory were attached to the broken stalk dancing fanatically in the wind.

In-chol picked up the copy of the journal Art And Architecture that had just arrived and turned the page. There was an article on space and housing by an author whose name hadn't appeared in this magazine for some time now. In-chol who liked this author's writing, began to read the article right away.

Only toward noon did the wind calm down. Now there was only the rain which kept falling in varying degrees of thickness. The two blossoms were long gone from the broken stalk of the morning glory which was now drooping down with its wide-bosomed leaves folded up in two.

When the rainfall became lighter, In-chol began to hear the squeaking of the parakeets from his brother's room next-door. What would these sour-tempered birds have been doing during the hours of storm this morning, wondered In-chol. Just then, he heard the bell ring once in a long stretch of noise. He walked over to the phone and picked up the receiver.

"Are you busy?" said a voice at the other end of the line. It was a woman's voice and he could not offhand tell whose it was.

"Who is this, please?"

"It's me.... Don't you recognize my voice?"

Still, In-chol could not guess.

"How unpardonable! You've already forgotten my voice!" said the voice defiantly. And then there was a high-pitched laughter.

"Oh...."

"So, you know, now?"

It was Na-mi. In-chol was himself surprised that it had taken him so long to recognize her voice. Part of the confusion, of course, was caused by the distortion caused by the machine, but the more direct reason for In-chol's failure to know her voice sooner was that she was speaking as if she were in a highly excited mood which altered her voice somewhat.

"Are you busy, now?"

"Not really."

"Then, spend a short while with me."

"But it's raining...."

"What's a little rain? I have a business to talk over with you. I must. You know Grill Chonwon that's in Chongno? Meet me there. Right now. I'll be waiting there," said Na-mi and then, without waiting for In-chol's answer, hung up.

After giving it a brief thought, In-chol took out his rain-coat from the closet and put it on.

He caught a taxi in the street. Through the window of

the vehicle, he could see the fallen wet leaves of the platanus pasted flat on the asphalt. Highlighted by the glossy black of the rain-soaked asphalt, the leaves looked more alive than when they were hanging onto the bare branches. Rain streaks kept coming down on them. The vitality of the fallen leaves remained in In-chol's vision for a long while....

Na-mi had come out with her father. Even before they were introduced, In-chol could tell that the middle-aged man with graying hair was Na-mi's father. It was not exactly because there was such a strong resemblance between the two of them, however....

"I hear your father is Mr. Kim Sang-jin," said Na-mi's father when the waiter retreated with their orders.

"Yes."

"We are acquainted through some business your father has with our bank."

"Is that so? I didn't know."

"Is he well?"

"Yes, he is."

"This is an interesting coincidence, anyhow. I am sorry we made you come out in this rain but...." Here the older man threw a glance at his daughter and then said, "Why don't you tell him?"

Mr. Cho, that is, Na-mi's father, sprinkled some pepper over the soup just brought in by the waiter. In-chol was bewildered. Why had Na-mi wanted to see him so suddenly? And why was her father sitting here with them? Unable to find the answer, he glanced at Na-mi questioningly.

"You know Chon Kyong-hun-*ssi*, right? He stayed with us for a time a few years back. He tutored my sister. He came to the house yesterday and the conversation fell on you. I knew then that it was you that had been recommended to draw our house plan by him. A small world, isn't it?"

It was indeed a small world. That it had been Na-mi's house where Chon Kyong-hun had tutored was a rather surprising news to In-chol, too.

"To make it brief, I asked my father to give the job back to you. Since my father wanted from the first to commission a young architect to do the work, it was no problem. My father is very fond of young talents....But...you will take the job, won't you?"

Wiping himself on the mouth, In-chol turned his eyes on Na-mi's father and said,

"I thought you had given the job to another person."

"You don't need to concern yourself with that," said Na-mi before her father could open his mouth.

"Well, my daughter nagged me so much I had little choice. I went and paid him off this morning," said Mr. Cho with a pleasant smile, halting in the middle of spreading jam on a piece of bread.

"I have little experience," said In-chol.

"That's all right," said Na-mi hardly waiting for In-chol to finish his sentence. "All you need to do is consult me about the general shape of the house. That's all. Will you take it?"

"What kind of a house do you have in mind?"

"The lot is about a hundred and eighty *pyong*. We want a garden of some sort. The house itself which we want to have two stories doesn't need to be more than sixty to seventy *pyong*. It will have to be steam-heated. We would like the outside of the house to be finished with tiles or stone. As to the general structure and style, you may consider my daughter's opinions to some extent, but for the most part you decide for the best yourself. Just one thing, we want to have it finished before winter which means that you will have to hurry up."

"But that's impossible," said In-chol. "How could I draw a plan for that size of a house to be finished before winter? I should think, though, that the architect to whom you'd given this job might be able to meet your order since he had the head start, so to speak...."

"What if," interrupted Mr. Cho, "you drew just a ground plan for a start so the work can be started. You can finish the rest of the drafting job while the foundation is being laid, couldn't you? I will do what I can to get the construction licence with what you can give me offhand."

"I think that settles the matter very well," said Na-mi. "But first we will have to take you to the site for a look."

Na-mi was acting as if there was no question, any longer, of In-chol refusing to take the commission. And, in fact, In-chol, too, was feeling more or less resigned to taking the job since he did not have the nerve to go against the aggressiveness of the father-daughter campaigning.

Na-mi was the first to finish the dessert which was brought to the table when the meal was over.

"One should think a girl would be daintier in her table manner," commented Mr. Cho judiciously.

"What are you saying, father? You said yourself that we must hurry since the house has to be finished before winter, didn't you? So, let's go and look at the site. Aren't you going to a two o'clock meeting, besides?"

When they were walking toward the exit, Na-mi whispered to In-chol,

"Papa is a charming person, isn't he? He never refuses me anything. . . ."

A creamy-yellow car was waiting outside the restaurant building wet and shiny from the rain. In-chol took the seat next to the chauffeur and Na-mi got into the back seat with her father.

"I wish the rain would stop," said Na-mi as if to herself looking out at the rain that was falling at a steady pace.

The house site was at a foot of a hill at a midpoint between Mukchong-dong and Changchungdan. Getting off from the car, In-chol opened his umbrella and followed Na-mi and her father for his first look at the house site. On the southern side was the flowing low range of Namsan and to the east, one could look out at the residential area of Changchungdan. A wide vista of downtown Seoul was spread out at its northwestern angle. In short, it was a fairly attractive site for a house.

Mr. Cho told In-chol that he had bought up three houses to make a lot of this size by pulling down all three of them. In-chol could see that Mr. Cho had had the lot nicely leveled out forming a smooth oblong ground lying lengthwise between south and north. In-chol decided that the house would best be sat at its northern end facing south. Using his legs, he measured out the part of the lot that would be covered by the house.

On their way back from the house site, Na-mi said she would go with In-chol to his house right that afternoon and talk things over with him concerning the house plan. As the car passed Tonhwamun and turned into the by-street leading to Chae-dong Elementary School, Na-mi stopped the car saying,

"We will walk the rest of the way, father."

"But I have the time to drive you there," said Mr. Cho glimpsing into his wrist watch.

"It's not necessary. Besides, I feel like walking in the rain for a bit."

"Weren't you complaining about it raining just a while ago?" asked Mr. Cho relieving In-chol's unuttered urge to ask the same question.

"That was a while ago and now is now."

After the car slid away, the two young people started walking, their umbrellas spread out overhead. The rain was pouring in fairly thick streaks now. Feeling that Na-mi was lagging behind, In-chol turned back to find her trying to pull up the hood attached to her coat. In-chol began to resume his walking, when suddenly Na-mi came up to his side thrusting herself under the shade of his umbrella, having folded her own in a quick motion.

"Shouldn't the gentleman have asked the lady to come in first, in a case like this?"

"I would have done so if you hadn't had an umbrella."

"I knew that's how you felt!" said Na-mi with discontent in

her voice. She walked in silence for a few minutes and then opened her mouth again,

"Why haven't you come out to our teahouse since that day?"

"It didn't suit my taste."

"You know, In-chol-*ssi*, you are different from other men," said Na-mi in a somewhat contemplative tone, and then asked,

"Do you think your sister would be home now?"

"I don't know. But with rain pouring like this, she probably hasn't gone out."

"I like In-ju-*ssi* so very much. She is beautiful, bright.... And she is very close with me. She told me you are very devoted to her... and... she to you...."

In-chol was surprised that In-ju had told someone whom she had come to know so recently such an intimate matter.

"Aren't we there yet?" said Na-mi. "Maybe I shouldn't have asked to be let off from the car."

Na-mi seemed by nature a vivacious girl, but today she acted as if she were excited to the point of impetuous restlessness over something. Secretly, In-chol was uneasy about the fact that he was taking a job offered by the father of this girl. He felt that he would be interfered with incessantly by Na-mi in the course of carrying out his duty toward his temporary employer. I should have followed my first instinct, said In-chol to himself without voice.

Stepping into the *hyon-gwan* (roofed-in porch) after In-chol, Na-mi said to the maid who took the umbrellas from the two of them, 'Tell In-ju-*ssi* somebody is here.' The maid, however, responded that In-ju was not home.

"Did she go out alone?" asked In-chol remembering that Shin Myong-su had been to the house for a visit the day before.

"Yes."

"About what time?"

"She left about an hour ago."

"Let me know when she comes in," said In-chol to the maid.

"Where is In-ju-*ssi*'s room?" asked Na-mi after pulling up her stockings which seemed to have slipped down a little when she was taking off the rain-shoes.

In-chol walked to the room next to the one facing the *ung-jopshil* (reception room) and pushed the door open. A small-size mirror-chest, a desk, and an elegant traditional-style wardrobe came into Na-mi's view. It was a tidy nice room with shiny *ondol* floor.

"What a neat attractive room this is!" said Na-mi in a somewhat sobered voice, entering the room without asking.

When the two climbed the stairs to In-chol's room, however, Na-mi exclaimed, sniffing disgustedly,

"This room stinks!"

Na-mi made a gesture of covering her nose in order not to smell the foul air of In-chol's room while she ejaculated once more,

"This room stinks of a male-odor!"

"Should it stink of a female-odor, then?" said In-chol laughing inspite of himself.

"I wonder what makes a room occupied by men smell in this way. I once went with a friend of mine to her house in Inchon and we were given her brother's room to sleep in. I couldn't sleep because the room smelled so badly. Finally, driven to my wit's end, I fetched a bar of soap from their washroom and put it by my pillow and only then could I get to sleep."

In-chol took out a cigarette.

Taking off her coat, Na-mi threw it over the back of a chair and sat on its seat. She took an inspecting look around the room which was fairly large as far as the size went. A blue thick rug covered the entire space of the floor at the inner end of which a bed covered with a white sheet was seen. At the right angle from the foot-end of the bed stood a clothes cabinet. Drafting tools of different shapes were lying atop a square work table drawn close to the window. Next to this was a smaller table on which was an architectural model made with plaster. Against the wall partitioning this room from the one adjacent to it stood a moderate-size bookshelf. A black-and- white unframed photograph of a snow scene of a mountain valley packed with stalks of snow-heavy winter trees was pinned down at four corners on the same wall next to the bookshelf.

"Is this house your own experiment?"

"No, we bought this one. It's a sturdily built house but doesn't have much of a look."

"Why didn't you draw a plan for your own house?"

"This house belongs to the boss."

"Well, then, you will build your home-sweet-home yourself?"

Just at this moment, the maid came in with a dish of pared apples on a tray.

"In-ju-*ssi* has many friends, doesn't she? Men friends, too?" asked Na-mi picking up a piece of apple on the pointed tip of the fruit-fork.

"I can't say she does. She isn't much of an outgoing character. So it was a bit of a surprise for me to know she is thinking of a performing career."

"You mean she's an introvert? You don't know your own sister! She is very outgoing and outspoken."

How could she be different persons inside and outside the house, In-chol asked himself. His sister who had graduated from a girls' high school last year had taken up home economics as her major, obedient to her father's wish and was known to her family as a quiet and shy person.

Walking up to the bookshelf, In-chol picked out a thick-volumed book of architecture and came back to his seat with it. Going through the book, In-chol began to show pictures of different style houses to Na-mi, who examined each picture with interest and then concluded that she would like to have all those houses built for her and live one month each in every house by turn. 'Greedy, am I not?' she said looking up at

In-chol with a smile.

Finally, however, Na-mi seemed stuck on one picture of a house. She gave it a long look.

"That's a spanish-style house," said In-chol.

"It has roof-tiles similar to our traditional tiles," said Na-mi. "I like the way this roof stretches down smoothly. This is a hothouse on the second floor, isn't it?"

"Tell me about your family," said In-chol.

"We are a fairly small family. My father, my mother, and my brother who's going to college next year is all there is, except me, of course. But we will need at least five rooms, one for my parents, one for my brother, one for myself, one for the guests, and one for the maid. And, then, I want a big hall-room upstairs.... What if we turned the whole upper area into a hall-room? So people can rehearse for plays or do some such activities, you know."

"I see you have your mind set on the theater."

"That is my sole demand on the house, really. The rest is yours to do what you like with it.... It seems your sister's taking long to come home."

Na-mi threw a glance out of the window making this last remark and then suddenly she sprang up from her seat uttering: 'Oh, no!' Her two hands were brought up to cover her mouth in a gesture of a great shock.

Looking in the direction her eyes were staring at, In-chol saw that the pouring rain had turned into a fine fog-rain although the sky was still heavy with slate-colored clouds. Then, In-chol saw it, too! It was a fat fist-size toad that was restlessly perched on the narrow ledge along the windowsill nearly rubbing himself against the rain-bestrewn screen door.

"What shall we do?" said Na-mi in a childlike helpless voice.

Without answering, In-chol walked to the connecting door to the adjacent room and hollered,

"Hey, In-mun, the toad is out!"

The connecting door must have been locked. One second

later, a boy in his shorts and T-shirt hurried in through the
front door of this room, and without so much as looking at
the two in the room went to the window, opened the screen
door, and picked up the toad without hesitation. The toad
who had his backside gripped in the boy's fist, wiggled his
thick limbs clumsily while his rain-waxed whitish beige
throat bulged angrily. The boy went out with the toad,
again without giving one look at the people in the room. All
this while, Na-mi was standing in one corner of the room
with her eyes tightly closed.

"You don't need to be afraid. It's just one of the pet-toads
my brother's keeping. He also keeps birds, tropical fish, and
white mice. He was upset a few days ago because one of his
toads got away and that one must have been it...."

"You mean he keeps toads in his room?"

"Oh, yes. I think he lets them loose to go about in the
room regularly, too."

"And he sleeps in that room?"

"Of course, he does."

"How sickening!" Na-mi said with disgust, twisting her
lips in a grimace.

In-chol walked over to her, and without knowing why he
took her cheeks between his two palms and pushing her head
gently back, kissed her. Since she had her mouth half open
from the grimacing, their teeth met with a tiny tingle. Then,
closing her lips down on his, she passed her arms around his
waist. When In-chol lowered his hands from her cheeks to
her back and tightened his embrace, however, she pushed
him back hard on the chest.

"I must go now," she said.

In-ju who did not come home until late in the afternoon
came up to In-chol's room and asked,

"Who's been here, *obba*?"

"Oh, it was Na-mi," said In-chol raising his head merely
but without trying to pull himself out of his deep thinking.
He was pondering about his new job. However, he did not

forget to ask Na-mi, "And what's been keeping you out for so long in this rain, sister?"

"Why did she come?" asked Na-mi back without answering In-chol's question.

"I've taken the job of drawing a plan for her family for their new house. And that's why she came."

"You are going to draft a plan for her new house?"

"That's right. It all happened accidentally."

"I hear she came into my room, too."

"Yes."

"I don't like you, *obba*. Why did you show my room to a stranger when I'm not there?" said In-ju fluttering her rain-moist long eyelashes in quiet anger.

"It's nothing to make a big fuss about, is it?"

In-ju left In-chol's room and went downstairs. Since she had been out in the rain for hours, the skin of her body felt sticky. She walked to the washroom and began to give herself a thorough washing. She usually took a long time to wash herself. She in fact spent twice as much time in the washroom as any other person in this house.

While scrubbing her skin again and again so that it began to turn pink, In-ju muttered to herself. What kind of a woman is she, that she should come into a person's room in her absence! I wonder if she knows about my meeting Nam-*sonsaengnim*. I wonder if that's why she came. But I'm seeing Nam-*sonsaengnim* only for the sake of learning how to act. So, let her do what she likes, I won't care....

She poured more water on herself and began to rub her body all over with a lathered wash cloth. Nam-*sonsaengnim* knows so much about acting, she said to herself. I will finish the book he lent me today in a hurry and borrow more books from him.

After lunch today, In-ju had gone out to teahouse: Spring. It was a small quiet place located in Chungmuro where they had dropped in by chance the day before yesterday. They liked the place and that's how they came to meet there everyday since then.

Nam Chun-gol was there when she arrived. As usual, he showed his welcome by pulling his pipe from between his lips. In-ju went to the table and sat opposite him.

"I am sorry I am a little late," she said.

After they ordered tea, Nam Chun-gol handed In-ju the translated collection of Ibsen's plays which he had promised to lend her yesterday.

"Read through this. And if you find any of the plays better than the rest, read it over," he advised.

They left the teahouse after a while and began to walk in the rain. When they reached the end of Chungmuro, Nam Chun-gol halted a taxi without consulting In-ju and got into it ahead of her. Thinking that maybe he wanted to take her to some performance, In-ju followed him into the taxi. But the destination Nam Chun-gol gave the driver was Uijongbu.

"Let's take an outing to the suburbs," said Nam Chun-gol seeing In-ju's questioning eyes fixed on his face.

In-ju felt offended that he was taking actions without asking how she felt about them. And so she sat rigidly on the seat trying to leave room between herself and Nam Chun-gol.

"The rice is ready for harvesting," said Nam Chun-gol when the taxi was passing Miari.

"That's the sign that we are in autumn, now," said In-ju mechanically and thought to herself that what she said was just like a clumsy repartee of an ill-written drama.

They got off at Uijongbu and began to walk in the opposite direction from the thoroughfare. A misty rain was falling softly. Soon they reached a point where the houses ended and a muddy stream was flowing beneath a bridge making an unexpectedly loud noise. A little way from the bridge was an orchard hedged in by a row of acacia trees. A narrow path came into view that went round the acacia hedge. They walked into this path. On one side of it stretched a bean field. In-ju felt almost instinctively that it was not the first time that Nam Chun-gol was taking this road. She wondered if he had come here with Na-mi.

Something like a barrage of thick raindrops hit against the canopy of the umbrella In-ju was holding up. But the sound it made was too dry to be that from raindrops. In-ju peeped out of the umbrella and saw that hail was pouring down on the bean field. It was a rather fine-grained and gentle pour for a hail which melted away as soon as it touched the green leaves of the bean plants with its whitish-soft grains. Then, the hail stopped as if a sudden wind had whisked it away. Again, the misty fine rain took over. The short spell of noisy commotion made by nature had been instantly swallowed up by a deep silence.

Nam Chun-gol handed his umbrella to In-ju in order to refill his pipe and put light on it. The aroma of tobacco drifted through the wet air giving a strange sensation to In-ju's nostrils which had never smelled it outside a teahouse or some such enclosed space. Nam Chun-gol took his umbrella back and resumed walking.

"Na-mi-*onni* (older sister, but used broadly among females of differing ages) is nice, isn't she?" said In-ju feeling that she was acting too tense.

"Yes, she is nice."

"How long have you known her? Have you known her for long?"

"Certainly longer than I have known you, In-ju."

"Of course, you have. But that's not what I've asked."

"Let's see, then. I met her at this College Acting Competition thing. So it must have been the early spring of this year."

"I liked her right away. She seemed so frank and honest. But as time went on, I came to feel as if she were not as straightforward as she was making out to be. But it is quite possible that I am judging her wrong. Do you think I am?"

"I think there's a point in what you just said," said Nam Chun-gol and pictured in his mind the way Na-mi kissed and passed her arms around a man and then, as if it had been a scene ordered by a script, slipped back to where she had been before the kissing and embracing.

"You don't like it that Na-mi is friendly with your brother?"

"That's nothing I have a right to like or dislike."

"Well, I said that because I heard that you are so very close to your brother.... You have just one brother who's older than you?"

"No, I have one more who's older than this one."

"What does he do?"

"He's the magistrate of Kwangju-gun. He was a man before I got out of my childhood and he stayed away from home a lot. So I am more deferential to him than close and sisterly."

"Yes, that happens in such a case."

Suddenly In-ju felt like telling this man everything about her family background so that he could be of help to her as she plans her career in future.

"We have different mothers. My eldest brother's mother died early. Our present mother gave birth to my other older brother and a younger one. As for me, I have been brought into the family from outside," recounted In-ju in one breath, and remained silent for a few seconds. Then, she continued,

"My mother died when I was seven years old. I have no other memory about her except her lying in bed with some sickness. But at times, she sat in front of the mirror and made up her face taking a long time. Later, when I was grown up, I came to think that maybe these were the times when my father was coming to our house. One night I opened my eyes to see my mother shedding tears looking at her image in the mirror. That is the face of my mother I most vividly remember. Maybe, it was a night my father broke his promise and didn't come to the house...."

Then, changing her tone, In-ju said to Nam Chun-gol speaking as one who was determined to find out something,

"I am not going to marry. I will do anything rather than depending myself on a man. Do you think I have talent for acting, I mean enough to devote myself to it for the rest of my life? What do you think?"

In-ju looked into Nam Chun-gol's eyes.

"How can I answer that kind of a question in an instant?" said Nam Chun-gol and looked back at the girl who was, to him, like a child who was totally innocent of what difficulties might lie on one's way to a successful, or even an unsuccessful, professional life. But what he saw behind the long eyelashes were eyes that were shining not with tears but with some inviolable clarity of an honest and determined mind.

Last spring, Nam Chun-gol had come to this place with a young woman. Although the acacia trees around the orchard were trimmed down every year so that they would not prosper out of control, still, there were occasional blossoms remaining on some unmutilated branch to spread their strangely seductive fragrance throughout this secluded area. While walking, the young woman who was actually a girl started talking about some novel she had read. Mainly her story was about the heroine whose purity was trampled on because of an over-developed ambition in one male character. The girl who was Nam Chun-gol's companion for the day was full of sympathy for the victimized female character. It was when the two were passing a point which must have been somewhere hereabout that the girl had finished her story and raised her head to look at Nam Chun-gol. As if she were the heroine of her sad story, the girl had a sorrowful expression on her face. When Nam Chun-gol put his arm around her shoulder, the girl buried her face as if she had been waiting for him to make that gesture. Nam Chun-gol remembered feeling rather turned off by this attitude of the girl.

But today Nam Chun-gol walked on without a word, turning his eyes away from those of In-ju. When the entrance to the orchard came into view, the two turned back. Returning to the thoroughfare, they entered a teahouse. In-ju ordered orange juice and Nam Chun-gol ordered a highball. When the drink was brought to him, Nam Chun-gol scooped out a couple of ice chunks from the glass and told the waitress to bring a double order of whisky. When it came, he poured it onto his drink.

In the taxi taking them back from Uijongbu, Nam Chun-gol sat with his eyes closed. On the occasion of the spring outing with the girl, he had taken her to a hotel room upon reaching Seoul. The girl had hesitated very much to undress. Later he found out that it was not just bashfulness that had made her so hesitant. She had a number of bean-size moles on her body. While Nam Chun-gol kissed these black moles one after another, the girl had got so hot that the black protrusions themselves felt like little burning coals against his lips. Opening his eyes, Nam Chun-gol glanced at In-ju's lips. He noticed that on the left corner of her upper lip was a tiny black dot. Somehow, this little dot gave her face an infinitely cold atmosphere. The girl of that day had no blemish on her face. He closed his eyes again. Remembering that inviolable gleam in In-ju's eyes, Nam Chun-gol thought about what transformations this young woman's piteously brave determination might go through in the years to come. How will she adjust to these shocks and frustrations.... Then, for no clear reason, he began to have the presentiment that maybe he, Nam Chungol, would be playing some part in the vicissitudinous course of life this girl would be following. I would treasure and care for this girl, he said to himself. But this was a feeling he had never had for any of his female companions or acquaintances up to now.

I will be seeing Nam-*sonsaengnim* again tomorrow and listen to his talk about the theater and acting, thought In-ju, still pouring more water onto her flustered body.

CHAPTER FOUR

A Short History

In-chol's drafting work progressed smoothly. His fear that Na-mi might interfere too much proved wrong. She only called him once for the entire week after her visit. In-chol could, therefore, give himself to the work without unnecessary tension or trivial worries. At times, In-chol sat for hours in front of his desk with a vacant mind waiting for an idea to come up. But mostly, his work progressed steadily so that by the end of the second week he was almost through with the floor plans. He needed only to polish them up a little. Looking down at what he had drawn up, In-chol felt that he would like to go out to town for a change. He shaved himself and left home as dusk was falling.

He went to Myong-dong and decided to drop in at Montparnasse. Na-mi was there with a young man In-chol didn't recognize. This did not need to bother him because he had not come there to see her specifically although he had not excluded the possibility of meeting up with her at this teahouse.

He walked up to their table noting that Na-mi's face showed a mild surprise at his appearance. The young man who was sitting with Na-mi stood up seeing In-chol come up to their table. He bowed to In-chol. Only then did In-chol see that it was no other than the young man who had run after him to introduce himself to In-chol in front of Midopa the other night. Instead of sitting down again, Shin Myong-su stepped out further from his seat. Then he said, 'Please excuse me,' and walked out after bowing to In-chol once more. In-chol thought that Shin Myong-su looked a little dismayed.

"I would have liked to have a chat with him. He was at our house the other day. But we never had chance to talk to each other," said In-chol sitting opposite Na-mi.

"He is so naive you can't even make a decent conversation with that boy."

"This place looks pretty grim today."

"What are you talking about? It's filled with people, isn't it?"

"Maybe I get that impression because those acquaintances of yours I met here the other night are absent today."

"I guess Mr. Pak is in his usual drinking house and as for Mr. Nam, he seems busy these days."

"Oh, I see. And that's why you were sitting by your lonesome self with just that boy to keep you company."

"No, no, don't call me lonesome, not yet!" protested Na-mi wide-eyed.'

In-chol thought her eyes looked beautiful that way. As if sensing his inner feeling, Na-mi blinked her eyes once and then looking up into his eyes asked,

"But what brought you here this evening?"

"I came out to see you."

"Liar! Don't forget that your greatest charm is in your candor, In-chol-*ssi*. But you look somewhat pale... and thin, I should say. Is the work going well?"

"I think the floor plans will be complete in a few days. But I can't say for sure because I may get stuck even at this stage."

"Let us know as soon as they are ready. My father says he has arranged to get the work started without the license for construction for now. Oh, I wish the house will be finished quickly...."

"But the house hasn't started to go up yet. What's the hurry? Are you dissatisfied with your present house?"

"No, I'm not. It's a nice enough house even if it's a bit old. Since it's in Naesu-dong, the transportation situation is quite good, too. Only, I am impatient to see our new house done now that we've decided to have one."

"As I said before, it will be very difficult to see the house finished within the end of this year."

"Pessimist! Don't you see that we are in such a hurry that we have arranged to start the work even before we can get the license for construction? Where there is will, there's a way! Actually, I am so impatient to look at your house plan, too! Really!"

"I am afraid I will disappoint you...."

"Well, I would rather be disappointed than be deprived of expectation."

"Well, let's drop the subject, shall we? After all, I came out to town so I can forget about the work for a bit...."

"Oh, is that so? Then, come with me. I will help you get relaxed."

When the two stepped outside from the teahouse, Na-mi started walking in the direction of the tavern where In-chol had been taken by Pak Hae-yon the other night. Na-mi turned back before entering the drinking house and said, 'I hear you'd come here the other night?' She walked in without waiting for In-chol to answer.

Stepping into the hall, Na-mi exchanged greetings with a number of clients sitting in the hall by nodding her head silently. Pak Hae-yon was sitting on the other side from the entrance with a man neither of them knew. Pak waved to them by way of signaling them to come to his table. Yet Na-mi chose a table leaving quite a bit of a space between them and Pak Hae-yon and sat down.

"You order whatever you like for us both," said In-chol sitting opposite her.

"Let's have *yakchu*."

"What about *anju*?"

"Raw squid is the best you can get in this place."

Na-mi wrinkled her face tasting the drink that was presently brought to their table.

"I see you are not very well qualified to be anybody's drinking companion."

"Don't rush me. Just wait and see."

Just at this moment, they heard a voice speak right beside them,

"Is it all right for one to come sit with you uninvited?"

It was Pak Hae-yon who was standing with a drinking cup and a wine jug. Then, sitting himself down with a thud beside Na-mi, he hollered to the man he had been sitting with to come over to this table.

"That's a chap who went to the middle school with me," he said, and then added, "He is in mining business."

Na-mi was not hiding her displeasure at Pak Hae-yon's bringing in a stranger amongst them. But Pak Hae-yon seemed only overjoyed to see In-chol again.

"Long time no see, Mr. Kim! Take this cup from me," he said and poured wine into In-chol's cup. He then said, turning to Na-mi,

"What's with Mr. Nam these days? He only peeps in here, and that only for a minute, late in the evening."

"Why do you ask me?" said Na-mi retortingly.

Pak Hae-yon looked at Na-mi with blood-shot eyes for a second and then turned to In-chol, saying,

"It's really you, Mr. Kim, that I came to have a talk with. I will just have that talk out and go. Won't be in your way.... You see, this friend of mine...." said Pak Hae-yon showing with his hand that he meant the man who was now sitting beside In-chol. "This miner friend of mine who now has a position at some university is saying that he would like to quit his teaching job starting this fall. He says he feels like switching to another occupation. It seems that he had had an offer each from a mining company and a company of some industrial specialty or other. The trouble is he can't decide which is better, the mining company or the industrial one...

If he went to the mining company, he says, he may be exposed to too much coarseness and crudity. If, on the other hand, he went to the industrial company, he says he may be bored to death poring into piles after piles of paperworks. He can't decide.... And if I should suggest one thing, he jumps to the other. We have been going through this several dozens of times this evening. Yet, he says I have to decide for him. Can you believe it?"

In-chol had no other way but mouthing some noncommittal words of sympathy and smile. Na-mi, too, was smiling when In-chol turned his eyes to her to see her reaction.

Pak Hae-yon turned his head toward his friend who was sitting wordlessly with a good-natured smile on his face, and said,

"Ah, I just remembered something! You listen, carefully, now.... 'Choose this, and you will regret. Choose that, and you will regret. Whether you choose this or that, you will regret just the same'.... How is this?"

"You are not the same man that you were. I asked you repeatedly because you didn't show the kind of sincerity in your attitude that used to be there. That's all," said the man who had not said a word until then but sat on with his good-natured smile on his mildly drink-flushed face.

"What? I am not the same man I used to be? You mean my friendship toward you has cooled off? No, no, no. That's not true. Don't you remember? It was the same when you were taking the job at the university. You were agonizing you and me both for days whether to take the university position or the job offered by a mining company. But when it came down to making the final decision, you had to do it by yourself. That is what's going to happen this time, also. Wait and see."

Just then, the front door to the hall opened and a man came in. He had a longish sun-tanned face and a rather small stature. He looked a few years past forty. After nodding this way and that as he proceeded into the hall, this man remarked to Pak Hae-yon,

"Defending the castle, as usual?"

"I hear you'd been to Soraksan," said Pak Hae-yon. "Did you have a good time there?"

"Not bad.... It's cold up there. But here it's still only autumn...."

"But it's almost hunting season, now, isn't it?" said Pak Hae-yon to the man who was proceeding toward the counter to take one of the stools.

As if it was his duty to do so, Pak Hae-yon offered an introduction. According to him, the man who just talked to Pak Hae-yon was a dentist by profession whose hobby was to go camping in the mountains during the summer season and go hunting during the winter. At times, he brought here a pheasant or a hare he had killed to have it cooked and shared with the habitués of this tavern.

"In short, he is one of the core members of this place," concluded Pak Hae-yon. Then, after gulping down his drink in his characteristic style, he said to his middle school alumnus sitting opposite him,

"Drink! Bottoms up! You will know what's best for you when you've had the right amount of drink in your system.... You, too, Mr. Kim, hand me your cup.... And you, Miss Cho, you are acting strange, today. Why aren't you drinking at all?"

Na-mi picked up her cup which was still nearly full. Just then, the front door opened and Shin Myong-su who had left the teahouse a while ago showed himself in the doorway. Without coming any further into the hall, however, he signaled to Na-mi to step out for a minute. Na-mi walked to the door and went out closing the door after her.

"I hear that young man, too, is one of the theatrical illusionists. None of them knows what harsh world it is out there...." mumbled Pak Hae-yon addressing no one in particular.

Na-mi came back in a short while.

"Say, Miss Cho, why don't you advise the young man to

give up the stage, eh?"

"Are you offering that advice for my benefit, also, by any chance?" said Na-mi. "You can't tell a person to stop doing what he or she likes doing."

"You mean another person can't tell him or her to do this or not to do that? You have a point there, Miss Kim, I must admit...."

Na-mi stood up and excusing herself briefly to Pak Hae-yon and his companion said to In-chol, "Let's go!"

When the two came out to the crossroad where the Municipal Hall stood, they took the alley that ran in the opposite direction from the Hall. The neon signs on the shops flanking the alleyway were not as bright as they would become when the night would ripen.

"What does that Mr. Pak do for living?" asked In-chol walking at Na-mi's side.

"Nothing. It seems his wife's making some money some way.... A friend of his who's working at the radio station tried to help him offering him a script-writing job for the radio. But he declared he would rather starve than demean himself in that way. My honest feeling is that maybe he is not able to do the job."

Na-mi pushed open the door of a bar and stepped in. Some customers who were drinking beer on one side of the hall and a bargirl who had been sitting across from them turned their heads to look at the newcomers. The two walked to the counter and took a stool each.

"What would you like to drink?" asked the bartender with a mechanical smile on his lips.

They ordered scotch whiskey.

"Hard liquor is easier to drink. Maybe I have a bigger capacity for drink than you are, In-chol-*ssi*," said Na-mi finishing the drink before In-chol did. Then she asked him for a cigarette, saying,

"One has to learn to do all sorts of things in order to become a stage performer. Do you see my point?"

The pinkish color that had appeared around her eyes when she had emptied her first glass of whiskey gave way to a palor by the time she was having her third round of whiskey.

"You'd better let go, now. I don't get the impression that your capacity for liquor is as great as you claim," said In-chol.

"Why do you say that? Is that because I'm turning pale? That's no problem. And please don't worry about me. I won't make you carry me home on your back.... And now tell me. Do you think there's such a thing as true love between man and woman?"

"Just as I thought, you aren't strong for liquor at all. Otherwise, you wouldn't be asking such strange questions."

"You don't wish to answer? If you ask me, though, everything is a show. The act of living, the act of love, grief, joy, everything's just a show.... Merely a show...."

"How about cutting out banal generalizations? In any case, I don't find your act of acting very convincing," said In-chol feeling the inebriety brought on by the mixture of wine and liquor on his temples.

"But even unconvincing acting is an acting of a sort.... Why don't you finish your drink? We are cutting it short here so we can move onto another scene. You can drink more there."

In-chol poured the remaining whiskey down his throat.

Outside, the neon signs were ablaze in the blackness of the night town. Na-mi put her arm into that of In-chol who registered in his consciousness that her gait was perfectly steady and balanced.

"You've walked this way during the daytime, haven't you? The glass tubes of the dead neon signs are then as ghastly as intestines of a cadaver, and...the shops, too, look like houses of mourning. One must, therefore, walk in this kind of an area only at night."

In-chol felt her breath tickling the side of his neck as she elocuted these words. Na-mi stopped in front of another bar.

"Let's not go in. You don't need to show off," said In-chol.

"From this moment on, I want you, In-chol-*ssi*, to divert my mood."

"Let's go somewhere and drink tea," said In-chol starting to walk in the direction of a teahouse off the main alleyway. But Na-mi was keeping her position looking as if she were pondering about something, and then she said,

"I will take you somewhere else, then, somewhere nice and decent. Maybe, you will meet people you know there...."

She started to walk toward Chungmuro. In-chol, who bought a newspaper along the way, followed after her.

Na-mi led In-chol into a teahouse that was near the Chungmuro 2-ga. Walking into the hall after Na-mi, however, In-chol experienced a considerable surprise because facing the front door from one side of the small hall of the teahouse was Nam Chun-gol sitting with his pipe between his lips as usual, and his female companion who was showing only her back toward In-chol was almost unmistakably his sister In-ju although he could not confirm it by the face. For a split second, In-chol felt like turning back but he summoned up his composure and walked further inside the teahouse.

"Oh, Kim In-ju-*ssi*, how are you?" said Na-mi boisterously walking up to their table and taking the seat next to In-ju.

When she turned to look at the friendly intruder, something glinted in In-ju's eyes. Then she seemed to attempt a smile but failing in this she let her face become ossified.

Supressing a sudden disgust and anger he felt for Na-mi, In-chol sat down beside Nam Chun-gol. Na-mi, however, seemed impervious to whatever turbulance she might have caused in In-chol's mind at this moment.

"It's so quiet and nice here, isn't it?" she said in an innocent voice. Then, after looking all around inside the small teahouse, she called the waitress with a wave of her hand. She said, "Bring me a soda drink, and... what will you have, In-chol-*ssi*?... Well, bring two soda drinks, please." Noting that the paler on Na-mi's face had once more given way to a pinkish flush, In-chol took out a cigarette and lit it.

"I love your necklace, In-ju-*ssi*," said Na-mi cocking her head a little forward as if to look at In-ju's jade-colored porcelain necklace closely. "It's very becoming on you." Then, she added, "But then, everything looks so good on you...."

In the next second, however, her eyes spotted a collection of Chekhov's plays on the table in front of In-ju. She exclaimed,

"Oh, what do we have here? Chekhov! He's divine, isn't he? Did you read all the plays in this book? Oh, you've just borrowed it to read? Well.... I remember there were lots of very fine dialogues in this book...."

She began to leaf through the book and then seemed to have found a page that interested her. She gave it a brief reading with her eyes and then said abruptly,

"Listen to this....[Chebutykin—(moved) My beautiful lovable Irena...my precious..., you've gone away from me. You have gone so far away that I could never hope to see you again.... So, I am left alone, like an old migratory bird that can no longer fly.... But fly, my beloved Irena, fly!].... No, this isn't what I was looking for...."

Na-mi drank from the glass of soda drink that had been brought to the table and went on searching through the volume of Chekhov. And then, she halted and read aloud,

"[Koolyghin—Do you know, we're thirteen at table? Rodé —(loudly) You don't really believe in these old superstitions, do you? (Laughter) Koolyghin—When thirteen people sit down to a table it means that some of them are in love. Is it you, by any chance, Ivan Romanych?].... But we...we need nine more people to make us thirteen...."

"You have been drinking, Na-mi," said Nam Chun-gol.

"A little.... Oh, I just thought of something fantastic," said Na-mi. "Let's go somewhere all together and have a drinking party." Na-mi looked at In-ju, still smiling.

"I think I'll go home," said In-ju, standing up. "I can't drink like you, Na-mi-*onni*." Then she picked up the volume of Chekhov plays from Na-mi's hand.

"You make me feel quilty! I'd have to take the blame for ruin mood of this gathering if you go off like that," said Na-mi with apology in her voice. "C'me on, let's give it a try. It's not as'f we can meet up all together like this every night!"

"I am sorry. I really must go. I was about to leave, any way. Excuse me," said In-ju pulling herself out through the narrow space between the tea table and Na-mi's knees. She gave In-chol one brief look, saying, "I will see you later, *obba*."

But In-chol, too, stood up. He wanted to get away from the awkward scene.

"Oh, you're going, too, In-chol-*ssi*?" Na-mi said in a surprised tone but didn't try to stop him.

As they walked toward the main thoroughfare outside Chungmuro, the brother and sister did not exchange any word. When they had reached the Central Post Office building, however, In-ju said as if to herself, "Never saw such a worthless character!"

In-chol wondered whom In-ju could have meant because from her tone and diction, he sensed that she could not have meant Na-mi. Then, who? But In-ju told him herself in a second,

"I mean that good-for-nothing boy Shin Myong-su. I just saw him standing by an electric pole across the alleyway from the teahouse we were in."

In-chol remembered how the young man had looked off-the-balance at Mont Parnasse and how he had asked to see Na-mi at the tavern a while back.

"You didn't come to that teahouse by chance, did you, *obba*? Na-mi took you there, right? ... I'm so disgusted. How can a man make an occupation of spying on a woman?"

"You get that way when you're in love."

"He's only a boy."

"What about you?"

"You must believe this of me, *obba*. I'm seeing Mr. Nam only to learn about acting from him. Do you believe me?"

"You wouldn't try to make excuses like that if you were as grown-up as you seem to think...."

They got on the microbus in front of the Midopa Department Store. Until they reached home, neither of them said another word. While they were away in town, a serious happening had taken place at their house.

The maid told In-chol and In-ju that their older brother had come during their absence. When the two entered the *ung-jopshil,* their father and his eldest son were facing each other across the tea table with uncommonly solemn expressions on their faces. Something uncanny was felt in the air. When In-chol was leaving the room with In-ju after they offered their greetings to their brother briefly, his father called from his back,

"In-chol, you had better stay here."

In-chol went back in and sat on a chair.

"That's right. In-chol, too, should know...," the voice of his older brother said. In-chol knew from the voice that his brother, In-ho, was upset and excited.

It seemed that In-ho had come while their father was still out and had been waiting for his return alone. In-chol could see only one fork on the edge of the fruit dish on the table. He also noted that his father was still in his office clothes.

In-ho's face which was not even wrinkled at an age nearing fifty was bleached white with tension and some excessive emotion he seemed to be experiencing inwardly. He said, again,

"Really, I don't know what I should do in a situation like this. I feel as if I were plunged in a bottomless pit. I don't think I will ever be able to crawl out of it."

He paused for a while and then continued,

"I am sorry, father, but I cannot help resenting you. With that kind of a deplorable past to hide, why did you not stop me when I wrote to you about taking a post in Kwangju-gun? Why did you let me straggle into a tiger's cave on my own two feet?"

"You mean, now everybody knows about it?" said the older man whose severe-looking face with its high cheek bones betrayed his inner turmoil.

"Whether or not anybody has sensed anything so far is of no consequence. It is bound to be known and spread within a short time. There's no question about it. You know how quickly rumors of this sort can go around...."

"How did it happen? How did you chance to meet your big-father (older brother of father)?"

When he heard the word 'big-father' fall out from his father's mouth, In-chol was startled. It was as if he had just heard a very fearful word. Next instant, however he understood. Everything seemed to fit into place, the strange uneasy feeling he had been experiencing lately albeit without quite knowing it himself on the conscious level, the things said between his father and brother....

"I did not go to Kwangju accidentally. I had had my plans. This is something that I had not intended to tell anyone yet, but my motive in getting myself appointed to the Kwangju post was to prepare myself for the event of running for the National Assembly in the next election. I knew from looking into a copy of the census register that our family was originally from Kwangju area although later we had our register transferred to Seoul. I figured that it would be wiser for me to run in a district where I have some connections to rely on. So I did what I could to get my appointment settled on Kwangju-gun instead of anywhere else. After I was posted there, I began my private operation right away, giving free access to everyone with request or opinions to my office and so on because I thought that this sort of a thing would show me up in the eyes of my prospective electorates. But how could I have known that this would draw me to a ruin by bringing to my office this afternoon that old man who was...."

"I acted unwisely. The reason why I did not stop you from

going there was that I wanted to see with my own eyes that
my children will not be touched by my past...even if they
should go back to the land from which I fled."

The older man paused for a second and then continued,

"It was about fifty years ago that I left there. Since I was
only a second son of my parents, I separated my name from
the family register and had mine established independently
in a Seoul register office. My brother was opposed to my
doing it at the time. He accused me of betraying my an-
cestry. After moving out of the province, I cut all my ties
with that place, even contact with my brother. I changed my
name which was originally Cha-dol. I named my children
with 'in' as the basic character which would have been 'ki' if
I had followed the rule of kin relationship. Traditionally,
none of our people were allowed to use the characters 'in,'
as meaning 'virtue' or 'ui', as meaning 'justice' in our naming.
But I dared go against this taboo, also. But what was the
use? Every effort I put in to insure security and honor for
my children has gone to a complete waste, has it not? Why
had he come to see you, anyway?"

"He had a request, he said.... And you should have seen
him...such an incredible mixture of everything unthinkable
and grotesque.... He was wearing coarse cotton work jacket
and no outer garment which everybody who is anybody
wears to go to places even in a provincial area.... And then,
on his feet he was wearing crude straw sandals without socks!
Believe me, I never met his likes! His beard was white but
hair was pitch black.... His request, too, was of a most
bizarre nature. He said that there was a cemetry in his village which was being partly used by Christian converts. He
wanted these Christian tombs moved to some other place. He
says it's because the roots from the sods on these tombs stretch
over to his side of the graveyard. I guess you, father, know
what this means. I mean the idea that a butcher's soul can't
get to heaven unless his grave remains unsodded.... What
nonsense is all this? Yet I couldn't treat this old man just like

a lunatic. So I talked to him in a genial fashion and made
him leave."

In-ho paused for a second as if he were recollecting the
bitter incident in his mind all over. Then, he opened his
mouth again,

"After this old man left my office, one of my staff came into
my office and told me that the old man had appealed in the
same manner to my predecessor as well. He then added that
the younger brother of that old man was said to run a big
business in Seoul. This one remark my subordinate made hit
me on the head for the first time. I became impatient because
of the doubt that began to torment me. So I sent the office
boy to fetch the old man who came immediately maybe thinking that I was going to grant him his request. I ordered off
everybody else so the old man and I could have a complete
privacy and began by scrutinizing his face feature by feature.
Luckily, I could find no resemblance with you, father. Somewhat relieved, I asked the old man, 'Have you heard of the
name Taeryuksangsa?' He did not answer, nor did he change
his facial expression. Instead, he began to stare at my face intently. No, it's more correct to say that he was glaring at me
as if in anger. And I read everything in his eyes. That was
the moment when I fell into a bottomless despair from which
I could never come out whole again. There was a long heavy
silence between the two of us and then the old man got up
and left the room. But his eyes... his eyes never left me. Even
now, I feel as if those two strange eyes were glaring at me.
Whenever I have this feeling, I feel my heart thump with
fear. Oh, to think that the race who aren't even allowed to
have their tombs sodded are our ancestors!"

Suddenly, In-ho clutched his head with his hands on both
sides and shook it a few times violently.

In-chol, on his part, recalled the incomprehensible emotion
he had felt upon laying his eyes on the old man's picture at
the house of Professor Chi. Maybe, that's what they mean by
'the call of the blood'? Wondering, In-chol contemplated the

fact that the old butcher whose picture he had seen was his own uncle. He found himself accepting this condition in equanimity and it was this fact, rather, that surprised him a little. His eyes caught the cut up peeled apple in the dish on the tea table which had taken on a dirty russet color having been left uneaten for hours, and idly he thought to himself that probably his brother had not eaten even one piece out of the dish.

Seeing that his younger brother did not look surprised, in the least, In-ho said,

"You don't seem to realize the gravity of the situation our family is facing. In any case, though, it's maybe better that things turned out this way because it leaves you time to prepare yourself before you go into the society on your own. But for me, this is the end. My end started from the moment that old man's eyes glared at me...."

In-chol tried to understand his older brother's reaction to these eyes of the old man which seemed to bear such a tremendous effect on him, but he did not succeed in this. He knew, however, that the real issue was not the eyes but the immovable verdict that they were all descendents of the butchers. Until he had heard about them, In-chol had not even suspected that there was such a separate race on earth. That was why he had listened to the professor's talk nonchalantly. When Chon Kyong-hun had mentioned the Yangsuchok, In-chol had felt rather thrilled that even in Korea there had been a lineage of a gypsy tribe, but that was all. Now that it had become clear that these things were not unrelated but indeed very closely related with him personally, he could no longer feel as if the Yangsuchok were an interesting object of a more or less idle curiosity and the butchers' world were separate from his. Slowly, he became aware of the black cloud enveloping the persecuted race of butchers come down on him to snatch him into its ominous shadow. In other part of his consciousness, he kept wondering why this revelation had so upset his normally self-possessed unemotional brother but was not dealing a similar effect on him at all. Could it be because I am still not in the society as my brother implies, he kept on wondering inwardly.

"I think, also, that there's already someone in my office who knows about our family background. It's that same man that told me about the old man having a brother who owns a big business in Seoul. I think he deliberately didn't say the name Taeryuksangsa although he knew it well enough. I guess he wanted to see how I would react to his remark. If so, how could he not know the relationship between me and the old man? He knew it all, and he wanted to see how I would treat the old man after hearing the information he offered me. So, how am I going to face that man in my office from tomorrow morning? What do you suggest? It wouldn't be just that one man, either, to be sure. The news must be out among all the staff members by now."

In-chol saw that his brother's lips were parched and his hands that were laid on his knees were trembling faintly. But his brother was speaking again,

"I am a finished man, now. All finished! But why did that old man show up before me? If only he hadn't...."

"Look, son," interjected their father in a shaky voice abruptly. "I hear you calling him 'that old man' repeatedly. I hope you would stop calling him that if you can help it."

In-ho's well-shaped face turned color when he heard his father say this, but the older man spoke on,

"He is the one who tied the butt of an ox-tail around your ankle on your Hundredth Day."

"Butt of an ox-tail?"

"Yes...so that you would have a long life...."

"So that I would have a long life? What...what good would a long life do me...now...now that I can't even live among de...decent people?" exclaimed In-ho stammering and in a hysterically self-deriding tone, his pale distorted face struggling to sneer.

Just then, however, the telephone on the side table beside

the sofa rang in a startling loudness. Although the phone was closest to In-ho, he did not make a move. In-chol went to the phone and picked up the receiver.

"It's me. You haven't forgotten my voice, again, have you?"

"Oh, hello," responded In-chol vaguely, feeling relieved that he had answered the call himself. The caller was Na-mi. "What is this? Aren't you glad to hear my voice? Anyway, can you guess who I am with, now?"

"You'd better go on home, now."

"Wow, you sound like an old uncle! Or like my father when he's lecturing me.... But, anyway, guess who I am with. Come on, guess!"

In-ho turned to In-chol with a grimace and said sharply, "Can you cut it short?"

Na-mi seemed to have heard this. She asked,

"Who's with you? Your father?"

"I am somewhat busy right now. I'll have to hang up," said In-chol putting the receiver down.

Even before he could sit down in his former seat, however, the telephone started ringing again. He knew it would be Na-mi almost certainly. He went back and picked up the receiver.

"How could you hang up even before the talk was over? I must give you a grade zero on etiquette toward a lady. Anyway, though, please spare me a brief while. Can you really not guess who I am with now? If you really have no idea, I will throw you a hint. I said goodbye to Mr. Nam at that teahouse. If so, who could it be? You still don't know? Oh, well, you must be less bright than you look, In-chol-*ssi*...."

Na-mi's slightly nasal voice indicated that she had drunk some more after they were parted.

"I must hang up," said In-chol feeling his brother's displeased stare on him.

"Oh, my, aren't you even allowed to receive telephone calls in your own house? What a pity! Is your father that strict? So different from my papa, isn't he? Going back to the main theme, however, the person who is with me is...no other person than me, do you get it? I am with me in my own room. That's why I am not in the least lonely. You said something about my being lonesome or some such nonsense to me today, didn't you? It was a total misconception. I can never be lonesome as long as I can be with myself. Can you believe this?"

In-chol did not answer.

"Well, looks like I've been reciting a soliloquy, haven't I? So then, I will make my exit."

There was a sound of laughter and then she hung up. Feeling oppressively apologetic toward his brother and father, In-chol walked back to his seat and sat down.

"I know everything, now. Why our aunt had killed herself, and why except her we have had no other relatives...." said In-ho after waiting a while with his eyes fixed on one corner of the tea table as if to allow the atmosphere to readjust itself after the disturbance of Na-mi's call. "Wasn't it because the family secret was exposed that she killed herself?" pursued In-ho looking at his father who was slowly rousing up from some deep thinking he had sunken into during the quiet interval. The older man gave one look at his son's miserable angry face and then turned away.

In-ho had two mutually conflicting memories of their aunt who had married when In-ho was nine years old. She was so beautiful stepping onto the bridal chariot attired in her wedding garments that even now he could recall the image vividly. Several years from that day, his aunt had come home accompanied by her mother-in-law, this time looking so ghastly, her face emaciated and tanned black, eyes sunken, and even the bones on her hands standing out painfully. This was another ineffaceable picture of his aunt he had kept all these years. After the mother-in-law left, his father had come into the inner quarter of the house from the *sarangchae* (outer quarter of a house mainly used by the master and his guests). His aunt had thrown herself at his father's feet when he stepped into the Inner-Room. In-ho had seen her bony figure heave spasmodically under the encasement of loose-fitting clothes. His father had stood silently looking down at his sister. Then his mother had taken him by the wrist and together they had walked out of the room to go to the kitchen. After she had taken refuge in the kitchen with In-ho, his mother had crumbled down on the kitchen floor pulling In-ho down with her. She had clasped him against her bosom wordlessly while In-ho felt her arms around him trembling without a pause. Although there was no light, In-ho knew that his mother was crying. Since that day, his aunt lived with them at their house working alongside his mother in all the household chores. She spoke to his mother now and then but In-ho rarely saw her smile. As a girl, she laughed easily. Sometimes, her face turned red from her trying to suppress laughter so that In-ho ended up nicknaming her 'Aunt Carrot.' In any case, however, he was happy that his aunt was back with them. A few months passed without much event. Then, one day, his aunt went to her husband's house. The next day at dawn, In-ho's family heard the news that his aunt had killed herself.

Breaking his long silence, the older man uttered,

"It is as you say, son."

"Did you hide it from the groom and his family, then, when marrying aunt to their house?"

"Yes."

"How did it come to the open in aunt's case?"

"It seems your aunt herself had made the confession."

"She did? Why do you suppose she did it?"

"I don't know.... We'd heard that she and her husband were exceptionally happy with each other. Maybe, this was the cause of the whole trouble. It could be that your aunt began to feel guilty about the fact that she was hiding something from a husband who was being so good to her. But when she actually told him the secret, everything went into pieces and their marriage was finished over the night. I am pretty certain your aunt had no idea that it would bring just that kind of a disastrous result...."

He paused a few seconds as if he found it difficult to go on, then he opened his mouth again,

"In the end, her husband went so far as declaring that your aunt had cow's hair on her abdomen.... After she was brought home, I determined never to let her go back to her husband's house even if they changed their minds. Then, one day we were notified that they wanted to go through a divorce formally. I offered to go for the last confrontation without your aunt but she insisted that she would go on her own because it was her business. So we let her go. She hung herself in their storage shack the night of her arrival there.... I had taken your aunt along with me when I was moving out of our country home. I and she were always very close. Yet, I could not even bury my sister's body with my own hands. I dared not to for fear of ill-willed rumor. It later dawned on me that maybe that was the very reason why your aunt had gone to her husband's house by herself saying she would take care of the divorce matter and then hung herself immediately after her arrival. What I mean is she chose to die while her name was still on the family register of that house because then they would not spread the news of your aunt's disfame for their own protection. We sold our house in Pugahyon-dong right away and moved to Kyonji-dong because I was still afraid of being exposed and disfamed...."

In-ho thought of his mother who had died after a Caesarean delivery of a dead baby the winter the family had moved into their Kyonji-dong house.

"Then, does my mother, too, come from a...?"

"Yes, son. In those days, our people could not even think of marrying outside the tribe...."

"What about nowadays, father? Would a girl marry one of us after they find out who we are?"

The older man exhaled slowly before he opened his mouth

to answer this question,

"That is the reason why we must keep our identity in secret. That is the only way. It is a painful and severely burdensome task to live with a secret...but...I am sorry I could not put an end to this family burden while it was on me...."

"I wish we have been brought up as butcher's children to continue the family lineage. We would have suffered less that way."

"You speak like that because you don't know what great suffering there really is in that kind of a life," said his father, his face turning more gloomy and pained upon hearing his son's last remark. "No matter how painful the present situation is, we must keep on trying all we can to guard our secret as long as it is possible. Even at this moment, I do not regret my having persevered in my effort to hide our identity. You boys can never imagine how contemptuous and slanderous people are toward our people. I will not go into describing it to you at this stage, but...."

The older man seemed to have decided not to speak any more, but after a while he spoke once more,

"Even now, I can't forget the anger and shame I felt when I used to go to gather fuel wood with your big-father and had to carry some of the burden of other boys of the village every time. We never dared to protest. It was a natural thing we had to do as sons of a butcher. Once, a boy whose burden I was carrying down the mountain slope tripped on a stone and fell on his knees. This made other boys laugh. Then the disgraced boy suddenly got up and tripped me down with the stick he was carrying for his A-frame. And he reviled me for having kicked the stone loose deliberately to make him fall on it. With the heavy burden of fuel wood on my back, I fell on my face. Hot tears welled up in my eyes and I grabbed a stone that was lying within my hand's reach to throw at the rascal. But just at that moment, your big-father stepped in between me and the boy. We, two brothers from a cursed house, stared into each other's eyes for a long while. In the end, I let go of the stone. But I did not get up. I put my face back on the ground and stayed still...."

A silence fell on the room. Even In-ho had become quiet with his head bent low. But the older man resumed his reminiscence in a low voice,

"This is also from my early boyhood. There was a wrestling contest sponsored by the County Office one Tano Day (a festival in May). My father, that is, your grandfather was chosen as champion of our village. He fought well and pushed onto the final. In the hot midst of this decisive match, though, somebody in the crowd suddenly shouted, 'Let a butcher fight a cow!' As soon as he heard this, my father released his adversary from his clutch and crumbled down on the ground.... That evening, back at home, I saw my father looking up at the sky squatting down on the dirt floor of his work shack. He stayed like that for a long time and I merely watched him in silence. Just then, I heard a noise outside our brushwood gate and in the next second saw three stout-looking men walk into our yard. One of them I recognized to be the one who had fought with my father at the wrestling final that afternoon. And do you know why they came? They came to ask my father to butcher an ox for them. They even showed a Permit For Butchering they had got before coming to my father. And outside the gate was the ox, with bells, bright-colored neck-cloth, and all, that the man had received for winning the championship at the final contest. Without a word, my father picked up his ax and butchering knife and followed the man out. Your big-father and I tried to go with him as we customarily did on such occasions. But this one time, our father did not allow us to come along. It was when the dusk had completely covered our little house that I saw my father walking into our yard with a pair of ox horns and a butt of an ox-tail in his blood-stained hands. He hung the horns and the butt of the tail on one wall and stood gazing at them for a long long while.

From that time on, an uncontrollable anger filled me every time I looked at these horns and the butt of the ox-tail. And this anger grew even stronger as I became older. I resolved to get out of that hell. And I planned for it. It was just after your Hundredth Day that I took the fated action...."

When he judged it to be the right time to make the re- solved move, Kim Sang-jin had left without even so much as consulting his brother once, taking only a younger sister aside from his immediate family. His destination was Seoul. In the capital, he could get an admission to a government-funded academy for training apprentice land-surveyors because the Japanese Government-General had a grand plan of making a survey of all thirteen provinces of the Korean peninsula by the new scientific methods and thus was in need of a large number of trained surveyors. His first appointment after fin- ishing the required course at the academy was going to the Kwangju area and make an overall survey of all the lands within the county. To his own surprise, this job proved to be exceedingly rewarding. Since most of the landowners were afraid of being over-taxed by the Japanese colonialist govern- ment, they tended to disclaim portions of their land espe- cially if the soil was in poor condition. What Kim Sang-jin did was to adroitly register these publicly disclaimed lands under his own name. No need to say that this was a tremen- dous risk to take on the part of the young apprentice surveyor, but Kim Sang-jin was in those days so driven by a sense of desperation that it did not seem to matter whatever might happen as a consequence of his misdeed. In any case, the total property he could amass by this devious strategy a- mounted to ten acres of farmland and twenty acres of forest land. By the time he was through with his surveying work in Kwangju, Kim Sang-jin had formally become a licensed sur- veyor. Before the second birthday of his first son In-ho, Kim Sang-jin had removed his name from the family register in his home province and reregistered it as head of an independent family in a Seoul register office. Several years later, land prices went up dramatically whereupon Kim Sang-jin sold off all the land he had appropriated and started a construction business, thus putting an end to his career of a surveyor. He had at this point asked his brother to come up to Seoul and become partner in his new business but had been flatly refused.

"The construction business was a success and my capital grew. After the Liberation, moreover, I tried my hand at some other businesses, as well. Finally, I started the company I own now. All this time, however, I concealed my identity. And I never resumed contact with my brother in the provincial home. I scolded you a while back about calling your big-father 'that old man,' but actually I have no such right, I who have been as ungrateful to my own brother as anyone I know. But what could I do! My aim was in raising you children just as other children of normal families."

"But how do you think the provincial people found out about your running Taeryuksangsa?" asked In-ho in a voice that had grown much calmer by now.

"I don't know, son. But right after the Liberation, country people came up to Seoul frequently and maybe somebody from our village found out about me and my company while staying in the city."

"Which means that we cannot be sure when, where, and how we may be discovered. When I think of it, I cannot but tremble in my heart. And I am almost convinced that words have already gone around in my work place," said In-ho, his voice getting excited once more.

In-chol, who had been conscious of the gap between his brother's reaction to the newly-developed situation and his own apathy toward it, felt his heart begin to ache with pity and affection for his father after hearing his father reminisce about his childhood and about his own father's sorrowful defeat at the wrestling match.

In-chol's eyes caught In-ho's face which looked as if he were listening to something intently. Then In-chol noticed that the crickets had been chirping at full throat for some while. Wishing to forget the oppressive feeling in his heart, In-chol, too, listened to the sound with concentration. But now his brother was standing up from his seat and with almost a tip-toe walked to the door. Reaching the door, In-ho jerked it open. Only then did In-chol realize that it had not been the chirping of crickets that his brother had been so intent on.

His mother who seemed to have been standing outside the door for some time took one hurried step or two backwards startled by the sudden opening of the door. She was many years past fifty, yet her face still retained the freshness of a younger woman. Her immediate response at being thus caught was to look not a little dismayed. But she covered it up with a smile quickly and said,

"I came to tell you dinner is ready."

The voice with which she said this was weak and strained, however.

"All right. We'll come right away," said Kim Sang-jin in a deliberately casual voice, and then turning to In-ho, he asked,

"You haven't eaten, have you?"

"I am not hungry," said In-ho, and then, closing the door after In-chol's mother moved away from the doorway, he muttered,

"What an utterly...." But his eyes glanced at In-chol and he shut up.

Although his father urged him to stay the night at the house since it was already too late, In-ho insisted on returning to his home outside Seoul. He said that he had not told his wife about his coming to Seoul and so had to go back. His not telling his wife about this visit had been out of precaution. His not having ridden his office car, too, derived from the same motive.

There was no other option but to go by his father's car. Yet he did not want to be driven by his father's chauffeur. He did not think it wise. So in the end, In-chol was obliged to offer to drive him home with his father's car.

In-chol drove slowly and carefully. Soon his brother got impatient and told him to go faster. Sensing that his brother was still upset from what had come to pass that day, In-chol said in an amiable voice,

"I have to be careful on an unfamiliar road."

"The worst will be getting killed, is that such a big deal?"

"Is there any need for death? Anyway, one's instinct makes one be careful once he sits on the driver's seat."

In-ho fell silent, his eyes looking straight ahead into the darkness outside. After they had ridden some more way, In-chol asked,

"Do you know if there's a place called Shinjang near here, brother?"

Instead of answering, In-ho moved his head sideways once. The movement, however, was so slight that In-chol could not be quite sure whether it had not been a mechanical reaction to the bumping the car incessantly ran into on the uneven dirt road.

"Do you know if the old man, I mean, big-father who came to see you in your office lives in a village called Pundi-namutkol?"

"No, I don't, but why do you ask?"

"I just wondered because I seem to have heard of a number of those people living in such a village."

Conversation dropped again between the two brothers. After a long silence, In-chol spoke again,

"I don't think I can blame father for the choice he made. What remains to be done at this point seems our choosing our own course of life."

"That's right. But is it easy? Tell me, what course would you take for yourself?"

"I am really not sure. I will have to think about it more. Maybe, this new revelation hasn't taken its proper effect on me personally yet."

The conversation dropped again. Some unknown insects

kept flying into the windshield and then scattered away. In-chol felt as if he were driving along a mountain road away from all human habitations.

Pulling out a pack of cigarettes from his pocket, In-ho put one between his lips. On the point of returning the pack into the pocket, however, he paused and protruded the pack toward In-chol. This was something that had never happened between the two brothers. Just as he had never thought of smoking in front of his father, In-chol had up to this day never smoked a cigarette before his older brother. He therefore shook his head even before he had time to think about the meaning of his brother's gesture. As yet, his attitude toward In-ho was dominated by deference than by affection and familiarity.

In-ho drew on his cigarette deeply a couple of times and then said,

"I saw In-ju for a brief moment this evening, but how about In-mun? Is he well?"

"Yes, he is."

With the burning cigarette between his fingers, In-ho seemed to be pondering about something, then he asked again,

"Tell me your honest opinion. Do you think I acted like a small-minded person tonight?"

In-chol noticed that his brother's voice was now calm and thoughtful. He wanted to reassure his brother quickly that everything was all right, so he said at random,

"No one who's not been in your position could know the hardship it involves."

Little by little, sparsely scattered electric lights of a provincial town came into view. It seemed that they were finally arriving at Kyongan, the town of his brother's temporary abode. When the car reached the outer edge of the town, In-ho stopped the car and said he would walk the rest of the way. Although he could not be sure, having never come out to his brother's place, In-chol guessed that there was quite a distance between this spot and his brother's house.

After getting off the car, In-ho walked away hurriedly and was soon engulfed by the darkness of the night. Looking in the direction his brother disappeared, In-chol ruminated on the words his brother had spoken just before their parting. His brother had asked him if he thought he had acted like a small-minded person tonight. Even now, however, his brother was intent on hiding himself in the folds of the darkness as if he were mortally afraid of being seen by someone, like a frightened boy.... Slowly, a feeling of a spontaneous fond affection which he had never felt toward In-ho formed in In-chol's heart. He turned the car and drove away almost in a light mood.

It was just before the curfew hour when he reached home. He washed up and ate the supper the maid brought in. Then he went up to his room. Although the entire event took no more than five hours, he felt as if he had come through many more hours of a very stressful ordeal. He started to undress to sleep. Just then, however, he saw the door of his room open softly and his mother coming into the room.

It was very rarely that his mother came up to this part of the house at night. And even during the daytime, it was almost as difficult for one to meet her within the house as it was to see his father home who went to work in the morning to come home at varying hours in the evening. Mostly she was kept busy with church works such as visiting the faithful at their homes because she was one of the stewardesses at her church. Then, too, she went to the mountain retreat for prayers now and then which kept her away from home for a stretch of a week or even ten days. On those rare days when she did not go out, she kept to the Inner-Room praying or reading the Bible so that she was not seen by the family members much.

His mother walked up softly to In-chol and then after glancing toward In-mun's room quickly, asked in a low voice,

"Something has happened, hasn't it?"

"What has happened, mother?"

"You all are trying to deceive me," said his mother looking into In-chol's eyes.

"Why should we try to deceive you? Really, nothing has happened."

The reason In-chol decided not to disclose tonight's event to his mother was that he felt there was no call for worrying his mother. It was not because he saw the need to hide the matter from his own mother out of precaution.

There was a saying his mother was in the habit of repeating in regards to his brother In-mun. She said that the cause behind his brother's excessive fondness for such living things as toads or mice lay in his having inherited the seed of sin from his parents. What she meant by 'parents' sin' actually was the sin her husband committed by going to another woman, that is, In-ju's mother, whom he visited frequently when In-mun was being conceived. She seemed to feel that her husband's sin of adultery somehow rubbed off on her newborn baby. It was after giving birth to In-mun that his mother had become Christian. If he were to tell his mother what really had taken place tonight, it was almost sure to aggravate his mother's already over-developed guilt consciousness further.

But his mother was persistent. She asked again still keeping her voice down,

"You know that your older brother never comes here except once a year on your father's birthday, don't you? So, then, why was it that he came today?"

"Nothing you should concern yourself with, anyway, mother. We only talked about business matters."

"You are lying. I can see through you with my spiritual eye. Do you know how great is the sin of lying?"

Suddenly, the white mice squeaked noisily in the next room which startled Madam Hong. She threw a glance in the direction of the noise, then she started mumbling something in her mouth with her head bent forward. In-chol thought that maybe his mother was praying. After a while, Madam

Hong raised her head and tiptoed out of the room.

Only after making sure that his mother had reached the foot of the stairs did In-chol undress and get into his bed.

CHAPTER FIVE

Three O'clock
in the Morning

There were two houses of butchers living in Suam-dong, Pyollae-myon, Yangju-gun at present. Before the Liberation (August, 1945), there were eight such houses but some of them moved out of the village during the period of excitement and social change after the Liberation. The Korean War caused more butcher families to disappear from this village because some of them had collaborated with the North Koreans during the latters' occupation of this district and then with the end of the war fled away from fear of retaliation. That was how there now remained only two butcher families here. Even these two houses, however, did not rely solely on butchering for their livelihood. They did some farming, wove baskets and mats, or made small things like pot brushes during the warmer season and only in the winter resorted to their inherited profession of butchering.

This was the second time that Professor Chi and Chon Kyong-hun were visiting this village. On their first visit, they had not been able to talk with anyone who could give them the information they wanted.

The two butchers both of whom looked to be past fifty seemed reluctant to see the visitors at first. When they were assured that Professor Chi and Chon Kyong-hun were not likely to insult or in any way harm them, however, the two men agreed to talk with them.

What they told the visitors were not too different from what Professor Chi had heard at Pundinamutkol The legend about the origin of the ox and the cow on earth was in the main the same with the Pundinamutkol version aside from some variations here and there. Especially, in that the ox and the cow were sanctified, the story told by the two butchers was no different from what the professor had heard in the other village that time. Only, whereas in the Pundinamutkol. legend, the Prince is turned to an ox in punishment for his lechery, the story told by the two butchers had the Prince steal the forbidden fruit which only the Heavenly King had access to and upon eating which the Prince is turned into an ox. The Heavenly King who thus discovers his son's misbehavior is angered into chasing his son down to the Lower World. Yet, like in the Pundinamutkol story, the Prince's soul is allowed to return to the Upper World when he dies at the end of a toilsome life in service of men. The two butchers, however, did not give the impression of believing in the sanctity of these animals the way the old man of Pundinamutkol seemed to.

Some new things the visitors could hear in this place all concerned customs of either the birth or the death in the village. When a woman is having a difficult delivery, the husband goes up on the roof and makes the gesture of pulling a heavy burden in the manner of an ox yoked to the cart. Then, the woman's suffering ceases and she delivers her baby safely. When a woman is barren or keeps miscarrying, burnt cow dung is applied on her abdomen and then she gets cured of her infertility or inability to have a safe delivery. Ground hoofs of a cow or an ox, is believed to cure all sorts of ailments when swallowed with water. When a person is dying, the ribs of a cow or an ox are laid underneath his head to prevent the body from decaying. If the urine of a cow or an ox is sprinkled above the head of a dead person, his soul which is lightened in weight by this procedure flies upward to the heaven the more swiftly. It was surprising how many of these folk beliefs were connected with the cow and the ox.

Most of these customs, the butchers informed, were now forgotten and nowadays the butchers even sodded their dead ones' graves like other people. Asked by the professor if there was a rite for the dead cows and oxen on the August Full Moon Day, the two butchers responded that they knew nothing about it. Then they added that the only custom they still kept faithfully concerned the rules against killing the animal on certain days. On the Buddha's Birthday in April, for instance, butchering of the oxen or the cows was strictly forbidden, and on the lunar New Year's Day and the Day of Cold Food, too, butchering was as good as forbidden.

Upon hearing that in the old days butchers used to recite songs in the form of incantation, Professor Chi had Chon Kyong-hun write down the words which varied slightly according to the season. They were as follows:

(spring)

When spring melts the snow and covers ten thousand mountains with flowers, ascend the Ox Prince to heaven leaving his grassland behind. In heaven, he will be praised by the Heavenly King for suffering in service of men. Take pity on him, O Buddha, *namu-amitabul.*

(summer)

The grass by the stream is green and rich. The grass in heaven belongs to the Prince. The Heavenly King will welcome thee with a golden cloak and a large banquet. Take pity on him, O Buddha, *namu-amitabul.*

(autumn)

There will be a large crop in autumn in heaven. The Prince will rest peacefully after a toilsome life in man's world. Since the storage house of heaven will belong to the Prince, he will live a long happy life in heaven. Take pity on him, O Buddha, *namu-amitabul.*

(winter)

Snow flowers that fly and pile in heaven will make our Prince happy and joyful. Resting in his Father's arms, he will point to man's world. The evil spirits of men will then bow down before him. Take pity on him, O Buddha, *namu-amitabul*.

These songs were memorized by the two butchers jointly who filled up for each other whenever their memory failed them. One of them who called himself Lee was a fourth generation butcher in this village while the other whose name was Chong said his family had lived there for three generations including him.

The two visitors left the village after buying a couple of pot brushes from the butchers in token of appreciation for their hospitality and started back home. On the way, the professor and his pupil exchanged conversation on what they had heard that day from the butchers.

"It seems their reverence for the animal is close to a religion, don't you think so, professor?"

"Yes. But my feeling is that the original motive had little to do with religion in their case. I once heard that an Indian congressman declared that rather than killing the oxen or the cows it was better for their country to go to ruin. This I call a truly religious attitude in regards to the animal. But our butchers' reverence for the same animal originates more from a sense of their profession than any religious feeling. In other words, the butchers felt a need to rationalize or justify their act of killing living animals in some euphemistic way."

"There seems to be a definite affinity with Buddhism in their way of thinking, though. It comes out both in the cow legend and also in the wording of those songs. And their taboo against butchering on Buddha's birthday especially seems to be a positive indication of their leaning toward Buddhism, I think."

"I agree. Their food habit, too, resembles that of the Buddhist monks, in fact. Such a habit as avoiding strong spices, I mean. But this, too, I consider to have grown out of their sense of their lowly social status rather than from a religious motivation. In order to understand this aspect of their structure of consciousness, we ought to remember how persecuted these people were socially in the bygone days. Persevering through life in the face of extreme social discrimination against their race, these people developed an existential need to find some other social class to affiliate themselves with, and this need made them define their image as something that was not far from that of the Buddhist monks doing penance. This self-identification with the monks must have consoled and gratified the butchers not a little. Especially after the monks began to be persecuted in the Choson Dynasty, there might have developed between these two discriminated classes a spontaneous mutual feeling of affiliation. To change the topic, the two butchers said most of their old customs are now forgotten, but I am pretty certain that still enough of the old ways are kept alive. Especially those curatives they use at child birth or deathbed."

"I suppose so. But one thing I cannot help admitting after everything is said and told is the fact that they had such high reverence for the cows and oxen."

"That's what shows on the surface. In my opinion, all these attitudes and customs clearly indicate is only the fact that they were so wretchedly impoverished and oppressed people. And I wish I could find out how this race actually originated in our society."

"Until I read Kim Sang-gi's theory of their being descendants of the immigrants and prisoners-of-war of the Chinese tribes of Kitan and Jurchen I had believed just as it is claimed in Choi Chung-hon-*jon* that they descended from the last survivors of Late Paekche."

"Yes, there are those two mutually diverging theories of their origin. And I want to make this occasion a constructive opportunity to find out for myself which of those two theories is more valid."

"You work too hard, *obba*," said In-ju peeping into In-chol's room without coming in. "Why don't you go out and take some air. I just talked with Ta-hye *onni* on the phone. I said I would call you to the phone but she said I had better not because you are busy. All she wanted to know was that you are well and healthy, she said." Then she went down.

In-chol looked out of the window at the tree which he had lately developed a habit of contemplating in order to divert his mind from the stress of a continuous work. The sprig from the morning glory was still hanging there, dried up and ungainly. Watching the dried-up dead end of the morning glory, In-chol's mind often flew back to the sight of the wet platanus leaves green and vital against the glossy-black asphalt. At the same time, he felt that even if he should witness similar spectacles at some points in the future, he would not be able to experience the same kind of refreshing and joyful sensation as he had felt that day looking at those fallen leaves.

At night, In-chol took a brief rest now and then, smoking a cigarette or listening to the songs of the crickets coming from the night garden. Whenever his consciousness registered this sound, however, In-chol could not help remembering the night of his brother's sudden visit. Then the things he had heard from his father that night, his father's bitter childhood, his grandfather's mortification, and his aunt's tragic death came to his mind in increased vividness and intensity of emotional appeal. Then, too, he remembered how angry, shaken and miserable his brother had been that fated night. And he recalled how he had for the first time in his life felt close and intimate toward his brother, In-ho. When his thought reached this point, he would shake his head as if to clear it of these sundry impressions and emotions, and concentrate again on his drafting work.

He worked day and night not leaving his room except to

wash up and eat downstairs. Maybe he wanted to be freed from the complex impact of the event of that night that oppressed his mind. Maybe that was why he was driving himself like a work-crazed person.

On the day the drafting was all finished and blue prints were taken, In-chol contacted Na-mi's father to arrange a meeting between him and the person who would be directing the construction work on the site. At this tête-à-tête which took place in the presence of Na-mi's father, In-chol requested the man who was in his middle age to consult him when he felt a need to make a change in the plans he drew. Mr. Cho, Na-mi's father, on his part asked In-chol to drop by the site whenever he found time to do so. In-chol parted from the man and Na-mi's father hurriedly, feeling mildly disturbed that he did not like being with these men for longer than was absolutely necessary.

He went on to Professor Chi's house from there. Past the decrepit building of the barbershop and winding around many bends of the crooked alleyway flanked by low-roofed old houses, In-chol walked on with his head bent down until his feet reached the gate of Ta-hye's house. Then he paused and raised his head. To his mild surprise, the bell which ought to be on the gate-post a little above the eye-level was not there. He looked again from left to right, and then realized that he was standing in front of the house next to Ta-hye's, further inside the alley. This was a house, too, in which he and his family used to live. He seemed to have passed by Ta-hye's house in his thought-filled obliviousness. But the profundity of contemplation which had made him even forget where he was going was of a nature which was impossible to explain even to himself in any clear terms. He walked back to Ta-hye's gate front and pushed the bell. The maid who opened the gate to him looked as if she were going to say something to him and then she seemed to change her mind about it. Professor Chi who was sitting in front of a low desk out in the *taechong* (wooden-floored hall-like area connecting two most important rooms in the inner quarters of a traditional Korean house) looked pleased to see In-chol. The bookcase that stood against the inner wall of Professor Chi's study area which was made by joining the *taechong* and the Opposite-Room was heavily laden with books. In one corner of the wooden-floored section of the study, one could see porcelain vessels, earthenwares and pieces of old roof tiles, and next to these was standing a roll of rice paper sheets which had been already used to make rubbings of old relics. All these were maintaining the order they used to present to the onlookers' eyes. Only, In-chol was not the same as he had been up to only a short time ago....

Sitting down opposite In-chol, Professor Chi asked him about his family in his usual courteous way. And then he said,

"Is your work proceeding smoothly? You look fatigued. But one forgets physical discomfort when one's doing something one likes doing."

"There's something I wanted to ask you, Professor. I remember your saying that you plan to visit Pundinamutkol coming Full Moon time. I wondered if you would be keeping to this plan."

"Yes, I am. I am going there on the Full Moon Day."

"Another thing I wanted to bring up was about that picture you'd shown me some time ago. You said that a son of that old person in the picture was living in Seoul. Have you had chance to visit with him, Professor?"

"No, I haven't had the chance. But why are you asking this?"

Professor Chi was puzzled by this sudden keen interest in these matters shown by In-chol who had been so indifferent to the old man's picture upon his first viewing of it.

"Not that there's a lot of good you would get out of meeting this person, come to think of it, because he would be a young person and so would have little information to offer about the traditional ways of his people. But do you know, Professor, which slaughterhouse in Seoul he is working in?"

"No, I didn't ask that."

"Would there be many slaughterhouses in Seoul?"

"I don't really know. I know of only one such place that's located just outside the Tongdaemun."

Professor Chi now looked at In-chol in earnest. In this stare, In-chol on his part seemed to read some deep meaning. At the same time, he realized that he had been asking too many questions that must have sounded, at best, odd to the professor. For what use did he want to know, anyway, wherever this butcher cousin of his might be working in this confused city?

"You do look very fatigued," said the professor repeating the remark he had made earlier.

The conversation dropped. Usually, In-chol was happy in this house whether he was taking part in a conversation or merely sitting around without exchanging any word with anybody. Today, however, he felt a stone-like weight oppressing his heart when the conversation stopped. After being conscious of this fact, he felt himself growing more rigid and unnatural by the minute.

Just then, the bell of the front gate rang and after a few seconds Chon Kyong-hun walked in bruskly. As if he had met a rescue in a desert, In-chol stood up to welcome him.

"It's been a long time. I hear you don't go out these days because of the drafting work," said Chon Kyong-hun stretching one hand for a handshake.

"It's just a fuss, not much of a good work done."

"But Na-mi seemed overjoyed that you took the job."

"She gets easily excited."

"By the way, have you heard of Na-mi's recent news?"

In-chol stared at Chon Kyong-hun wordlessly.

"It seems she nearly drowned in the Han-gang while riding a boat the day before yesterday. There was a man who was with her in the boat but he swam out by himself, it seems," explained Chon Kyong-hun without waiting for In-chol to say something.

"She swims pretty well herself, though."

"I don't know exactly what happened. Anyway, Na-mi swallowed a lot of water and started to sink when luckily the rescue arrived."

Somehow, In-chol could not take much interest in this report. Chon Kyong-hun now turned his eyes to the professor and said handing a book he had brought with him,

"I found this in a secondhand bookstore."

The title of the book was: The Traditional Village of Korea. It was a tattered-looking old book compiled by the Japanese Government-General with the covers warped and stained here and there.

"I bought this without a second thought because I found in it some reference to the old-time *paekchong* class. It says here, for instance, that a butcher was allowed to wear a *manggon* on his head but never a *tanggon*. A *paekchong* woman was never allowed under any circumstances to use a *pinyo* as a hair fastener."

"Yes, I heard of those customs."

"The *paekchong* class was not allowed to be buried in a coffin and at wedding the bride and bridegroom were forbidden to ride the bridal chariot and a horse respectively. Instead, the bride rode only the floor board of a *kama* (bridal chariot) and the bridegroom an ox. Whereas an ordinary person wore a *sangtu* (man's traditional hair style with the hair gathered in one knot on top of the head) after he is bespoken for marriage, a *paekchong* could wear it only after he is married and is father of a child."

Here Chon Kyong-hun stopped for a second and adjusted his glasses on his nose. Then he continued,

"Another thing I found out from reading this book is that the *paekchong* class engaged themselves in not only butchering and weaving of baskets but also hired themselves out to execute the criminals sentenced to death by beheading. Since they were not treated as proper and rightful citizens of the society, too, the *paekchong* class were exempted from military duties and also from paying taxes. And it seems that some of them accumulated wealth on the very strength of this discrimination by the society. One amusing circumstance the book records is how some from the *yangban* class who were reduced to borrowing money from the well-to-do butchers used the honorific form of speech with the latter on the occasion of their requesting the credit but lost no time in switching back to their customary tu-toyer fashion when paying the debt."

"Didn't you read in the newspaper some time back about the son of an old butcher killing a young man who spoke to the old man without honorifics?"

"One thing clear is that the butchers were treated far more harshly than any other lower class people of our society. The servant class could in time become commoners, but not the *paekchong* class. They could never raise themselves to the level of common people. It is much advertised how the gaps between the upper and lower classes were narrowed thanks to the Kabo Reformation, but as far as the society's attitude toward the *paekchong* class is concerned, even the Reformation sparked no change whatsoever." Here Chon Kyong-hun paused a second and then in a slightly changed tone, said, "As to the origin of this singularly oppressed race, however, this book, too, offers no information. It only vaguely conjectures that these people are likely to descend from some foreign immigrants. And if I remember right, this is the opinion Professor Kim Sang-gi seems to hold, too. Is that right, Professor?"

"That's what's said in Ayugai's Miscellanious Manuscripts. That is, it is speculated in this document that maybe the race who are known as *paekchong* in our traditional society descends from the Yangsuchok who were originally a tribe residing in the northeastern district of China but later emigrated to Uiju, a territory belonging to Koguryo during our Three Kingdom Period. But this, too, is no more than a rather forced guesswork, if you ask me."

Concluding his remark on the subject in this way, Professor Chi turned his eyes on In-chol who had been sitting in silence while the dialog continued between the professor and Chon Kyong-hun.

"You look tired and pale. Have you been sick lately?" asked Professor Chi, his eyes still scrutinizing In-chol's face.

"I haven't had much sleep, sir, but otherwise I am quite all right," replied In-chol who had been feeling more and more oppressed listening to the conversation the professor and Chon Kyong-hun had been carrying on.

Now that he had said the words, however, In-chol was convinced that he really lacked sleep. He now remembered that ever since he started working on this house plan, he had never had his fill of a night's sleep. Yet, he knew well enough that the paleness of his complexion which Professor Chi was noticing at this moment was not altogether caused by the amount of sleep he had been missing these last several weeks. He stood up feeling as if he were carrying a sackful of pebbles inside his body.

The sound of some child taking a lesson came from the 'piano room' as usual. In-chol turned his eyes toward the room to see if he could catch a sight of Ta-hye through the window across the blossoming heads of cosmos and chrysanthemum, but the open window offered no view of Ta-hye. He walked past the window and proceeded toward the front gate. Never before today had he gone away from a visit to this house without saying hello to Ta-hye. He had moreover promised to go to the Han-gang with her in another week when he had last been at this house. And then he had been kept so busy and could not keep his promise with Ta-hye. Even so, he felt at the moment reluctant to be seen by Ta-hye. Then, suddenly, he remembered the maid's strange attitude when she was admitting In-chol into the house a while back. She had started to say something and then stopped. What was it that had prevented this garrulous woman from accosting In-chol with her usual chatty familiarity?

Walking through the winding narrow alleyway in the direction of the street, In-chol recalled how only a couple of nights ago he had declared to his brother whom he was driving home in their father's car that the newly revealed secret of his family had failed to take its full effect on him personally. And how little time had been needed for this little personal event to so powerfully overshadow his life....

In his dream that night, In-chol was standing in the midst of a vast crimson sunset. Everything visible, the sky, the earth, the mountains, trees, and the houses were one uniform crimson color. Then, he noticed that the crimson sunset was actually on fire, making big flames and myriad fire sparks. And In-chol knew (he had known it from the first, in truth) that the crimson sunset, the flames and the sparks really originated from the breath he himself was exhaling. He knew, too, that he was inflicted with some terrible disease that was making him spit out such unthinkable things from his insides. As a boy, In-chol once betted with a schoolmate of his over eating red water color. He had licked it up clean from its little dish in the case containing a set of different watercolor pigments and had won the bet. At first, no reaction seemed to occur in his body, but in a little while, he felt an acute nausea which eventually made him throw up. The drawing paper on his desk was dyed with the red liquid that spouted out of his mouth. He was sent home right away and was made to stay in bed for several days. Ever since that time, he was visited by a fantasy of a sunset ablaze with flames and sparkles whenever he felt weak and was likely to get sick. He usually dreamt in black and white, but his particular dream always came in technicolor. Waking up in the middle of his dream that night, In-chol felt a heaviness and dull pain oppressing his body.

Next night, also, he woke up from a dream he could not remember. And from this time on, he woke up at about the same hour unfailingly whether or not he had been having a dream. He would light a cigarette and read the time by the match light and it would be invariably three o'clock in the morning or closely thereabouts. No matter how late he went to bed, he woke up at this hour every night. And after waking up like this, he could never get back to sleep right away. He would toss and turn in his bed going from one thing to another in his thought for a good couple of hours and then only at dawn he fell back into a second sleep to wake up only past ten o'clock in the morning. He usually woke up from some confusing dream in this second sleep. And after spending his night in this way, he felt heavy in the head all day long.

He had not had many dreams before, but ever since he fell into the habit of waking up in the middle of the night, In-chol began to dream far more frequently. The dreams he had, however, were so disoriented and confusing that they did not make much sense except that there was one constant theme which came up again and again albeit in moderately varying contexts:

In-chol was descending a staircase. He could not tell whether it was a twilight or a dawn. All he could tell was that the surrounding atmosphere was filled with an indeterminate dusk streaked with a misty whiteness. Also, it was cold and wet. Putting his foot down on the steps one after another, In-chol thought to himself, 'This is a house I've planned. But why is it that there is not one window on this house? And why is it that there is not a single electric light here? I must ask the construction director. Feeling the wall next to the staircase, In-chol found out that the surface was very uneven and was so damp that the palm of his hand with which he felt it became wet. 'Why is this wall still unfinished?' Wondering, In-chol kept stepping down the stairs. He had a vague feeling that he was going down these stairs because he had to pick up a sheet of paper on which were printed the questions he had to answer. Or, maybe he had an appointment to meet someone down there.... In any case, he had to hurry. He moved his legs faster. But the stairs continued down further and further. There seemed to be no end to it. Then, finally, In-chol realized that this was no staircase inside a house but a road made completely with steps. He went on and on down this road of descending steps but woke up before he could ever reach the end of the road. Once, descending these steps in the gloomy shadow of a dusk or a dawn, he felt very strongly that there was someone he really had to meet. But there were still so many steps down ahead. Then suddenly he became aware of the startlingly sharp resounding sound his feet were making on the steps. The footsteps were producing terrible echoes in the space through which the incredibly long staircase ran. He took his steps more cautiously looking down on the steps. To his surprise, his eyes saw, for the first time, that each of these steps was covered with the leaves of the platanus! The leaves were shining in their refreshing wet greenness. More carefully, he picked his way down the steps putting his feet softly upon the shining green leaves. Even so, his feet were causing a tremendous resounding in the empty void surrounding the staircase. He examined his feet with attention. Since he was wearing rubber shoes on bare feet, he saw no reason why he was being the cause of such a terrible resounding. Then, he saw! He saw the marks of ox hooves left on the leaves covering the surface on the staircase.

Another dream In-chol often had was one in which he contracted smaller and smaller indefinitely. Sometimes, people whom he passed looked as tall as an electric pole to his eyes, and the sparrows flying above his head were the size of an eagle. Once, he was walking along a dried-up dirt road. As far as his eyes could reach, there was no grass growing nor a tree standing on the dirt hills he could see at some distance. Each step In-chol took raised a cloud of dry dust that buried his feet invisible. In-chol knew that, in this empty field of dry dirt surrounded by bare hills, there was someone who was waiting to meet him. He trudged on making more dust-cloud. The sun was pouring down a fearful amount of heat through the still atmosphere which not a whiff of wind stirred. In-chol felt an acute thirst but there was not a drop of water nor a spot of shade where he could take a short rest. There was no other option but to trudge on. But all of a sudden, his eyes caught something a short way ahead of him on the dirt road he was following. It was the sight of a tall object around which many people were gathered. Invigorated by this scene, he hastened his steps and went up close to the tall object. It was a giant-size letter T around which a group of people were sitting, leaning their backs against it. A long line of people were waiting to spot an empty space around the T. In-chol examined those standing in line only to find out that there were Pak Hae-yon, Na-mi, Nam Chun-gol, his older brother, his mother, Ta-hye, Professor Chi and Chon Kyong-hun in the line. To his surprise, however, none of them seemed to recognize him although clearly their eyes saw him. He started walking toward the end of the line to stand like other people. Just as he was passing by Ta-hye, however, she stretched an arm and pulled him into the line right behind her. At the same instant, however, Ta-hye's backside grew so large that In-chol could not help feeling unbearably small and insignificant in the face of this gigantic back image of Ta-hye. Then, suddenly, he felt something landing on his shoulder with a staggering weight which pinned him down on the ground so that he could not move. He turned his head and saw that the thing that had fallen on him was no other than the letter T. He scrambled up with the letter T which was continuously trying to press him down on the ground. Then he saw that all the people that had been standing in line were nowhere to be seen, nor those who had sat around it. Now, there was nobody except himself. He started to drag his feet along the dirt road again, staggering under the great burden of the gigantic letter T....

Then there was another dream in which he walked into a dark cave. The darkness grew thicker as he went further inside it and it looked as if the labyrinthine passage through the cave would never end. Yet in one corner of his mind he felt relieved that the darkness and the obscure passage were likely to continue forever and something even intimated to him that it was this darkness and obscurity that he had been traveling so far to seek. 'If I could only melt out into this darkness!' In-chol thought and kept on going deeper into the black labyrinth. His mind was quite peaceful now. And this gladdened him. Just then, he heard a voice from behind: In-chol! In-chol! Pretending not to hear the call, he kept on moving forward. Then, the voice said: In-chol, can't you hear me calling you? Only then did In-chol halt and turn back. But there was no one there. So he asked: Who are you? The voice said: It is I, the one you have been looking for. But I have not been looking for anyone, said In-chol. Don't lie, the voice said. I know everything. You should not take fright at this point. You were destined to meet me. So come out! All right, then, said In-chol, I will come to you! And In-chol started walking back out of the cave. He walked to a point where the mouth of the cave could be discerned in its whitish luminosity. Then, In-chol was out of the cave, standing in the full sunlight. He shouted at the top of his voice: All right, I am here! Where are you? The voice said: Right beside you! In-chol looked all around, but there was no one in sight. Where are you, he asked again. Right beside you, I said, the voice answered. You cannot see me because your eyes are still blinded by fear. Shake off fear from your eyes and look at me, the voice went on. In-chol tried to look again opening his eyes wider but just at this moment he woke up from his dream.

In-chol got on the streetcar headed for the Tongdaemun in front of the Hwashin Department Store. Why had he chosen the streetcar instead of a bus or a microbus? He did not know why, himself. Maybe, he felt an instinctive aversion to the prospect of listening to the savage calls the driver's attendants would be sure to emit at every stop to collect even one more passenger aboard the vehicle before it would start again. Getting off at the Tongdaemun, In-chol walked past the Steam-Locomotive-Car station and stopped at a cigarette booth to ask directions. The booth-keeper mumbled something handing out the cigarette through the hole in the front screen of the booth, but In-chol could not catch what he said. Only, from the movement of the man's head, he guessed that maybe he had to walk on ahead for some more distance.

After walking for a while in the same direction, In-chol thought that maybe he had gone too far. He stopped in front of a woman peddler who was sitting with some shriveled pieces of fruit in a basket by the sidewalk and asked her. With a tired look on her face, the woman pointed toward an alleyway that started from the house next to the one against the outer wall of which she was sitting.

The alleyway was barely wide enough to let a truck pass. In-chol went about twenty meters inside this narrow road when he came in sight of an empty pen marked off with stakes. Across from this empty pen was an opening and on the far side of this opening was a large one-story building which In-chol could, without much difficulty, recognize to be a slaughterhouse. Across the alleyway from the empty pen was a building with a signboard that said: Association of Cattle Merchants. In-chol went up to the front of this building and walked in through the entrance. Four or five men were sitting at desks that were laid in two rows in the hall inside the building out of which In-chol chose the one that was closest to the entrance and walked up to it. He said, "Excuse me." The man who had been holding the evening paper up in front of his face (although it was only a little past one o'clock in the afternoon) reluctantly looked up.

"I would like to know if a person from Kwangju of Kyong-gi-do is working here. His name starts with 'ki' and his family name is Kim."

"There's no one that fits your description in this office,"

the man answered with finality. Then turning his eyes away from In-chol, he talked to his colleague at the next desk holding the newspaper out to him,

"Look, didn't I say so? You insisted that it was a suicide but I said no, didn't I? It says here clearly that it's a manslaughter. And the killer is no other person than the man's own son."

The man who sat at the next desk snatched the paper from the first man's hands and began to scrutinize it.

"He doesn't do the office work. He is a butcher," said In-chol.

"Why don't you go in there and ask," said the first man who seemed to realize only at that instant that In-chol was still standing by his desk. He was pointing in the direction of the slaughterhouse with his upturned chin as he said this. Then, as an after thought, he added, "I guess they are all gone home, now. You can come back in the morning, no later than eight o'clock."

Walking out of the office building, In-chol looked across at the slaughterhouse. Just as the man had said, the place looked completely deserted.

When In-chol visited this same spot the next morning, however, he was surprised to find several dozens of cows and oxen tied to the stakes of the pen. And the opening next to the slaughterhouse was fairly crowded with men who were going about briskly seemingly tending various businesses of their respective responsibilities.

Crossing the opening straightway, In-chol entered the open door in the middle of the slaughterhouse building. Something made him halt involuntarily in the middle of the doorway, however. It was the stench of blood and fat mixed in a peculiarly unpleasant way.

The interior of the slaughterhouse was not dark. Large-size doors and windows surrounded it and through these openings the morning sunlight was pouring in abundantly. Yet, strangely enough, In-chol could not discern the things that

were going on inside the slaughterhouse at one glance. He
only saw that men in blood-stained rubber boots and greasy
work clothes were moving swiftly about between the bodies
of the cows and oxen thrown about here and there. There
was one cow that fell right in front of In-chol's eyes while blood
gushed out of its neck. Then there was a huge bulk of meat
which was a cow or an oxen without head or skin hanging on
an iron hook. The groove dug in the cement floor was full
with blood. A man was pulling a wheeled trough laden with
the intestines of the animal out of the back door. These sights
were reflected on In-chol's retinae scatteredly without any
vestige of order. Only the vague feeling that the inside of the
well-lit slaughterhouse was paradoxically dark made any
cohesive impression on In-chol's consciousness. To whom
should I ask about him? In-chol wondered. Nobody was
paying attention to him. Each man was only intent on the
work he was engaged in. It then came to his notice that
compared with the section of the slaughterhouse where he
was now standing, the other side looked less crowded and
confusing. Picking his way through the cement floor sticky
from blood and grease, therefore, In-chol went over to the
far section of the slaughterhouse.

Just as In-chol reached the less crowded part of the slaughterhouse, a man came in through a door on the left pulling in
an ox after him. He had his coarse hemp trousers rolled up to
his knees. The ox in the meantime was trying to back out
rolling his eyes as if in fright. Once he was dragged into the
slaughterhouse, however, the animal let himself obediently be led to a spot not far ahead from In-chol to the left.
In-chol could see the mouth of the animal spewing out white
foam.

A stocky short-necked man in a regular work suit came up
close. He looked some years past thirty, and except that his
eyes were slightly blood-shot, his face was completely expressionless. In one hand, this man was grabbing a mallet fixed
with a sharp-edged steel pipe for a head. The man who had

pulled in the ox bent down so that his head was almost equal in height to the underside of the animal's chin and blind-folded the ox with his palms. At the same time, the club fell on the animal's forehead with a frightful force. With a dull thud, the ox fell on the cement floor looking as if he were trying to kneel on his four limbs. In-chol could not tell whether the ox had emitted a moaning sound or no sound at all. The man who had hit the ox with the mallet turned on his heels. In-chol felt that he might be the one whom he should consult about the purpose of his coming to this place. Before he could take any action, however, the man with the fearful mallet had walked over to the other side of the slaugh-terhouse. In-chol wished that this man would not be the cou-sin he had come out here to look up.

The man who had dragged in the ox now stuck a long bamboo stick into the hole the second man's mallet had made on the ox's forehead. The body of the ox went into a violent convulsion and became gradually still. A middle-aged man also wearing a work suit came and along with the first man turned the animal's dead body on its side. Then he cut its throat. A boy who was in an identical work suit as the middle-aged man rushed over with an empty can and filled it with the blood gushing out from the animal's throat. He then took it to a larger can and emptied the blood into it. The head of the ox was severed from the rest of its body. The boy carried the head with its frightened rolled-up eyes out through the back door. In-chol saw that the severed edge of the muscle was still twitching spasmodically. With the help of the man in the coarse hemp trousers, the middle-aged man now laid the animal's body over the groove so that its back fitted against it. He began to skin it. As the knife kept on moving rapidly, the dimension of the red meat covered with whitish grease became larger. In-chol could see this huge lump of grease-surfaced meat twitching here and there. The man with the knife wiped his bloody hands on the skin. Then he cut the feet off the animal's skinned body.

In-chol watched, thinking that he would ask his necessary question to this man as soon as he looked as if he could spare a few moments.

The fore legs were cut off next and then the chest was halved with a saw. Lastly, the hind legs were slung on a huge iron hook so that the cadaver could be pulled up with a spinning wheel. From between the hung-up legs, the intestines tumbled out. Someone came with the wheeled trough into which he dumped the fallen-out intestines and pushed the trough out of the slaughterhouse. Lastly, the skin on the back was separated, whereupon the entire ox hide dropped onto the cement floor looking like a crumpled leather bag. A new stench of blood-grease mixture stung In-chol's nostrils. But now, no twitching could be noticed in any part of the cadaver which was now no more than a big lump of meat hanging by an iron hook. The man with the knife began to cut the lump into different parts which were then carried out to a vehicle waiting outside. In this way, a living ox turned into lumps of meat within a short time while a complete silence and order dominated the inside of the slaughterhouse. Still, In-chol could feel only as if all these sights and movements were no more than some disjointed scraps of happening made unintelligible by the strangely deep darkness of the slaughterhouse.

Seeing that the man was nearly finished with cutting up the meat, In-chol walked up to him and asked him if he knew the one with such and such name coming from such and such a place. He shook his head, however, on which only his blood-streaked eyes were noticeable in the otherwise totally expressionless face. Somehow, this man's wordless gesture with his head seemed to tell In-chol the more definitely than any other possible means of communication the fact of his ignorance as to the object of In-chol's query. To his surprise, this unambiguous denial of the knowledge of his unaquainted cousin on the part of this man relieved In-chol's mind considerably. It was not without an information about the existence of another slaughterhouse located in Miari, however, that In-chol finally walked out of this one through its back door. He felt dizzy. In fact, he now realized that he had gone through a number of dizzy spells back in the slaughter-house itself. He seemed still to hear the sound the steel mallet had made against the forehead of the ox, the dull thud made by the falling of the ox on the cement floor, moaning sound the ox might or might not have emitted. He still seemed to see the convulsions and the twitchings of the lifeless body, the blood that had gushed out of the animal's throat making a whitish foam, the grease-covered meat lump, the cascade of intestines that had glistened in wetness.... All these memories came back to him cluttered in confusion. But why had he watched the whole process of butchering, standing there? Why? Why had he kept his position even while he felt dizzy every now and then in the course of the men's operations. He lit a cigarette. There was a bitter taste on his tongue and he felt nauseated. He dropped the cigarette on the ground and squashed it out with a foot.

He noticed that there was another fairly large building across the backyard of this slaughterhouse. It seemed that that was where the intestines of the slaughtered animals were dealt with. In-chol saw a trough laden with steaming intestines being wheeled into this second building.

He started to turn around the building, and then suddenly his feet halted as his eyes caught a sight taking place near the wall of the building. What drew his attention was the sight of the old Chunhyang and Lee-*toryong* whom he often saw on his way to and from Ta-hye's house. They were hold-ing bowls filled with the blood of the slaughtered animal. It seemed that the old man was urging the old woman to drink the content of her bowl. He took a sip from his own bowl and then smacking his tongue as if to say that it was very delicious nodded to the old woman by way of saying, 'You try it, too. It's very good!' The old woman slowly raised the bowl to her lips in the manner of a child reluctantly taking bitter herb medicine.

Crossing the opening, In-chol walked out of the slaughter-house compound. Passing the pen where the cows and oxen were tied in, In-chol saw an ox trying to put his fore legs onto the back of a cow over the partition wall between them. White foam was oozing out of the animal's mouth. In-chol thought about the foam that the dying ox had spewed out back in the slaughterhouse which was no different from what he now saw on the mouth of the excited animal in the presence of a female.

Should I visit the slaughterhouse in Miari tomorrow morning? In-chol asked himself walking along the staked pen. But what is it that I want to accomplish through meeting this cousin? Would it not be wiser, after all, to turn his eyes away from the world this un-met cousin belonged to and lead his life the way his father had tried so hard to enable him to? In-chol let himself be drawn into this self-debate which he had been incessantly conducting internally these several days and nights.

PART TWO

CHAPTER ONE

On the Way

For the first time lately, In-chol felt relaxed and peaceful. For one thing, he had finished his drafting work altogether. The blue prints were now in the hands of the construction director. It was not as if he had not had moments of frustration doing this work. Yet, on the whole he felt that he had earned much valuable experience thanks to this commission. More than anything, he had come to learn how difficult, but how necessary, too, it was to maintain a harmony among various elements that make up a house (not to speak of the importance of an overall structural harmony) while, at the same time, achieving individuality and uniqueness whenever possible. Even such a small point as how to design the ceiling of the *hyon-gwan*, or the decision to make the staircase form a spiral cloister took several days out of his work time.

Registering the feel of the paper money that amounted to three-hundred-thousand *hwan* which Na-mi's father had sent over by way of 'showing appreciation' as the latter put it, In-chol thought to himself that the reason why he could finish the drafting work so promptly was thanks to the visit he had made to the Miari slaughterhouse to meet his cousin.

On the third day after his visit to the slaughterhouse near the Tongdaemun, In-chol resolved, after a great deal of hesitation, to go to the one which was supposed to be in Miari.

He felt that he would not be able to concentrate on his work
nor do any kind of a consecutive reading unless he went to
this place and find out what he could. He set out very early
in the morning.

Getting off the bus at Miari, he walked in the southeastern
direction for some distance. Gradually, houses became scarce
and farmland began to come in sight. Then, in a little while,
In-chol's eyes caught the sight of a slaughterhouse compound
that was very similar to the one he had seen near the Tongdaemun. At the back of the low-lying one-story buildings was
a small mountain with a fairly dense growth of pine trees.
One side of this mountain was connected with a quarry
where large chunks of rock were lying about exposing their
whitish bare skins. Maybe no quarry work was in progress.
There was no one to be seen there. Or, maybe, it's because
it's too early in the morning now, thought In-chol, walking on
in the direction of the slaughterhouse.

When he entered the entrance gate of the compound, he
saw a group of people who were standing or moving about,
and approximately a dozen cows and oxen tied to the pen in
front of a building in the opposite. He went straight to this
building and walked in. There was no one inside the building which was the slaughterhouse proper. It was smaller
in size than its counterpart in the Tongdaemun area. Just
as in the latter case, however, the inside of the slaughterhouse gave the impression of an ominous darkness despite
the fact that this one, too, had large open doors. And the
mixed stench of blood and grease was rampant in this one,
also.

As he was walking out of the slaughterhouse, In-chol saw a
man in his mid-forties coming from the opposite direction.
He was wearing rubber boots and a work suit that had, by
now, become familiar to In-chol's eyes. In-chol asked him
about his cousin giving him only the family name and the
first letter of his given name as before.

"Kim Ki something, did you say? Maybe, it's Kim Ki-ryong, do you think?" said the man in work suit.

"He comes from Kwangju, Kyonggi-do," said In-chol.

"Then, that's Ki-ryong, all right. I saw him this morning...." The man took a sweeping look round the yard and then said, "He was here a while ago." Then, he shouted to a young man who was talking with someone across the yard, "Did you see Ki-ryong?"

"I just saw him walk out that way," shouted back the young man pointing to the gate.

"Must have gone out for a drink. But wait here a while. He'll be back soon."

Although in one corner of his mind, In-chol was glad that he could find his cousin so easily, yet he could not altogether help his heart sinking upon realizing that his search was now over. Instead of waiting for him there, he went toward the gate and walked out. He was nearly certain that this Kim Ki-ryong would be the cousin he had been looking for. He wanted to meet him where a lot of people would not see or hear them.

He could not spot any drinkinghouse, however, although he walked the whole way to the thoroughfare. The air of early autumn morning was clear and chilly against his cheek. On the yellowing ears of rice plants were clusters of dew drops sparkling in the first sunlight. Dazzled by their brilliance, In-chol closed his eyes.

"Are you looking for someone?" asked a thick male voice close by.

Not a little startled, In-chol turned in the direction of the voice. His eyes saw a shack house standing right by his side. The voice had come out of this shack house. In-chol tried to peer in through its open front door which was a coarse patchwork made with pinewood boards of uneven lengths. He could not offhand identify any human figure in the doorway which was in the shade. With his face still turned toward the open front door of the shack house, therefore, In-chol asked,

"Could you tell me where I might find a drinking place near here?"

"This place sells drinks, too," said the voice.

"Do you happen to know if somebody named Kim Ki-ryong is here, now?" asked In-chol going up to the shack house which did not bear any outward sign of a drinking house.

"Why do you ask?"

"I have some business with him."

"I am Kim Ki-ryong," said the voice.

Stopping short on the spot, In-chol waited for the man to come out. But nobody walked out of the shack house. Drawing up closer to the shack, therefore, he peered inside. Then he recognized a man in a black work suit standing in the middle of a dirt floor. Rather than the outline of his face, In-chol saw the shape and whitish hue of the drinking bowl held in the man's hand against the shadow that hung in the interior of the shack house. He did not even invite In-chol to step inside. His taciturnity notwithstanding, In-chol went in as if drawn by some invisible force. Only then, the man asked in a thick voice,

"Why did you want to see me?"

As In-chol's eyes got more used to the darkness of the interior of the shack house, they identified a man in his early thirties with a crew cut and a scanty beard. His face was eggshaped and he had a pointed nose. In-chol also noticed that his lower lip was considerably more meaty than his upper lip. In-chol told him about his own family and its relationship with the place name, Kwangju.

The Man listened intently, glaring at In-chol's face while the latter outlined the circumstance of his visit. In-chol saw that the man's two eyes shone but it was not certain that they were bloodshot like the eyes of those men In-chol had seen at the slaughterhouse near the Tongdaemun. Rather, he thought, my eyes might be more bloody than his....

In-chol had set the alarm at six a.m. before going to bed the previous night. As usual, he had woken up in the middle of the night and then had a dream. In this dream, he was looking into a mirror. The image of himself that he saw in the mirror

did not have a mouth but the ears were large as those of an
ox. Although he was shocked by the ugliness of this image, he
found himself consenting that this was how he should look.
And he said to himself: I must only listen to what other people say with these ears but never say anything myself. Then
he noticed that his eyes that he saw in the mirror were blood-
shot. He felt that he had seen these eyes somewhere. He
pressed his forehead with a finger whereupon a hole was dug
underneath the pressing finger, letting crimson blood gush out
of it. He felt no pain, however. The alarm went off just then
and he woke up. When he looked into the mirror while
washing his face, he saw that his eyes had bloody streaks in
them from not getting enough sleep.

"So, we are cousins to each other," concluded In-chol,
looking straight into the man's eyes.

Without answering, the man finished his drink in the bowl
and asked the old woman who was trimming vegetables in
one corner to fill up his bowl one more time. It seemed that
the old woman kept only one *toe* or two of rice wine for
merchandise at most. She poured whitish liquid of *makkolli*
into the man's protruded empty bowl.

"You came to the wrong person," said the man finally. "I
have no cousin." The tone of his voice was dry and indifferent. Seeing that In-chol was about to say something, he
interrupted, saying,

"I have no relatives of any kind."

Then, lifting the bowl to his mouth, he gulped down the
makkolli in one swill. Then, he said something which sounded
quite incongruous under the circumstances,

"I am sorry to say this to a stranger, but it seems to me
that you are too pale in the face. Maybe you should try the
ox-head for a cure. You will be surprised what difference it
will make to your health."

The man's voice as he was giving In-chol this advice sounded
as apathetic as when telling In-chol that he had come to the
wrong person.

He walked away in the direction of the slaughterhouse not hurrying, thumping his rubber-booted feet resolutely down on the unpaved ground.

To be honest, In-chol could not experience, in his confrontation with this butcher, the same 'call of the blood' which he had felt when looking at the old man's picture first at Professor Chi's house. All the same, he could not shake off the feeling that the man was unmistakably his cousin whom he had been seeking to meet these past couple of weeks. Yet the butcher was denying this fact. If so, wouldn't it be better, for all concerned, to leave it at that? The fact is, thought In-chol, maybe it's best if our two families remained separate from each other, just as father and big-father had done. When his thought reached this point, In-chol felt the tension which had been weighing him down in body and soul lately begin to dissolve, plunging him slowly into a sweet benumbing sense of bottomless fatigue.

A young man in the group standing at the bus stop seemed to recognize In-chol and made a move to greet him. Yet seeing that the latter's eyes did not register his presence there, he looked away.

One unusually clear and bright morning, In-chol visited the construction site. Not even the foundation work had been finished. Although the terrain had the advantage of being not rocky, it was found out, even before the earth was dug out six feet, that water seeped out of some subterranean channel making it difficult to lay the groundwork for the basement. As for the materials for construction, In-chol could see that all bigger items had been procured. The pile of 'natural stones' with which the walls would be finished drew In-chol's special attention. This was something he had discovered while having a picnic near Anyang several years ago. He and his friends had, that day, chanced to pass by a quarry in that area, when In-chol's eyes caught sight of slabs and chunks of natural stone freshly cut out from larger hulks.

Looking at these stone pieces that day, In-chol had a flash of inspiration about using these unpolished natural stone pieces to give a special architectural effects to a house or a building. What he found at the quarry on that day was a variety of gneiss which was, in color, a soft mixture of beige and light yellow, ingrained, partially, with whitish dust-like dots.

Examining each piece of the cut stone with appreciation, In-chol had pictured to his mind what the finished construction with these charming stones highlighting the outer walls would look like. He did not wish it to look like a conglomeration of inanimate objects but rather as a living thing that knew how to assert its raison d'être even if it would not be able to speak or move. When his thought reached this point, his heart filled with something akin to an extasy which, however, was inextricably linked with a sense of uncertainty and fear. The picture he drew up in his mind was more perfect and more beautiful than what he could ever put down in his drafts. Yet what would actually be materialized as a house would be sure to carry many defects and imperfections which he had not foreseen when drafting.

It was from this uncertainty and fear that he had resolved to take up Na-mi's random suggestion about making a model of the house to be built. At a teahouse where they had dropped in after a movie, Na-mi had complained that she could not visualize anything from studying what was put down on the drafting paper and went on to say that she wished he had built a house model instead of handing in just a lot of insensible drawings.

He knew that making a house model would take up a great deal of his time. Yet, he wished to do it not so much to oblige Na-mi but because he felt that by making a concrete tangible model of the house now, he might be able to detect what shortcomings the finished house might show. So he promised Na-mi that he would indeed make a model for her.

"But I want to take a short trip before starting this thing."

"You will go on a trip?"

"Well, maybe not really a trip, but I want to go somewhere and take a good rest especially now that I have a bundle of money in my pocket."

All he had to do for his graduation was to finish up the thesis and hand it in till the middle of December. He had gathered enough material for the thesis which was to be entitled: The Aesthetic Value and Structural Efficacy of the Eaves in the Korean Traditional House. He was going to write this up after a brief resting period. But now he thought he would finish up this house model first.

"Where will you go?"

"I don't know. Where do you suggest?"

"When are you planning to go?"

"Doesn't really matter."

"Who's going with you?"

"Nobody."

Na-mi looked up at him and asked,

"What if I went along?"

"I don't know...."

"You mean you don't want me to, right?" asked Na-mi with a faint smile.

She lifted the teacup to her lips. As soon as she took a sip from the cup, however, she began to cough. It seemed that the liquid went down the wrong way. Na-mi put the handkerchief to her mouth hastily. Suddenly, remembering something from looking at Na-mi make that gesture, In-chol asked,

"I hear you nearly drowned in the Han-gang lately."

"Who told you?" asked Na-mi opening her eyes wide.

"It's obvious your swimming lessons were useless."

"It's not that. It all happened because of that fool Shin Myong-su. Do you want me to tell you how it really happened? We rowed a boat to the middle of the river, and then, this idiot suddenly started accusing me for letting a relationship develop between Mr. Nam and your sister. He then said he would do what he can to retrieve In-ju-*ssi* and so will I please go after Mr. Nam and recapture him! I was so angry it took me a superhuman will power not to slap that insolent fool right across his face then and there. But I had to do something, I just had to, to give vent to my insufferable anger. So, I said, 'Okay, then, take this from me!' And I threw my weight to one side of the boat. My intention was to capsize the boat which was exactly what happened in the next instant. The misfortune was that I was the one who was caught on the underside of the capsized boat. Naturally, I swallowed some amount of water and passed out for a while."

"Which means that you took some more practical lessons in acting, eh?"

Na-mi seemed to find this comment quite amusing. She laughed merrily and then said,

"None of it would have happened, though, if Shin Myong-su was not so enamored by your very charming sister. Do you understand this point?"

"But In-ju seemed to think him a mere boy."

"I am not surprised, and yet, these chicks can get very hot once they take fancy to something."

"But he won't succeed in winning her heart no matter how hot he gets. And as to her relationship with Mr. Nam, it's only a relationship between a mentor and a pupil. There's no call for a lot of misunderstanding."

Yet, In-chol had lately sensed something more than that in In-ju's attitude toward Nam Chun-gol. He had met his sister in the hall downstairs as the latter was returning from school and asked her in passing, 'So, how's your apprenticeship in acting?' To his surprise, In-ju had blushed and after throwing a strangely intense look at him disappeared into her room without saying anything in response to his remark. In-chol had wondered if his sister had taken his question as asking: 'Are you still seeing Mr. Nam regularly?' Even so, why would that make her blush in that way in so far as her meeting Nam Chun-gol was no news to her brother?

"Mr. Nam has a wife, doesn't he?" In-chol asked Na-mi

abruptly.

"Why?" said Na-mi almost in an accusing tone. "What concern is that to me, anyway?"

"There's no need for you to get angry with me for asking it."

"Who got angry?" said Na-mi. "What I mean is, why should Mr. Nam's having a wife or no wife be the topic of our conversation. Why don't we rather talk about what you personally think of the idea of a marriage."

"What an abrupt change of topic!" said In-chol as if he were really surprised by the whimsicality of Na-mi's manner of carrying on a conversation.

Inside his mind, however, In-chol was thinking that maybe what Na-mi suggested was not such a far-fetched or uncalled-for topic. Had he ever thought of a marriage in relation to any of the relationships he had had with women in whatever degrees of intimacy they might have been? Would he develop any relationship with the thought of marriage even in the future? It did not seem likely. Ta-hye ought to get married first, thought In-chol, almost incongruously as he was ready to admit himself. He did not know why this thought came to his mind so naturally right at this moment. Now that the thought came to his conscious mind, however, he felt as if it had been in his mind for a long time, only more settled now than can be shaken off with any logical thinking.

"Did my question embarrass you?" said Na-mi, as if relishing this prospect.

"No, not really.... Let's see now.... A professor at my college once told us his own marriage plan. He said that when he was twenty five, he thought he would marry if he could possibly find a woman he could like within five years' time. When he was thirty, he thought he would marry within five years if only he could find a likable candidate. He made the same plan when he turned forty. He was forty-four at the time and he was still unmarried."

"Does that mean that you are like him?"

"I don't know. I guess that remains to be seen."

"I think men are all fools without an exception!" Na-mi said showing the white of her eyes to In-chol in real or fake exasperation.

Nam Chun-gol did not show up until it was past ten thirty. It had been with a special plan that In-chol had dropped in at the tavern Myong-dong, the gathering place of Na-mi's theatrical cohorts. In-chol had, earlier in the evening, had a drinking party after a penalty billiard game with some college alumni of his. Upon parting from them he had suddenly thought of dropping in at this drinking place where he might be able to run into Nam Chun-gol. It was not with any specific purpose that In-chol had taken this action, however.

When he returned to his room this morning after washing up, he found a notebook on top of his work desk with a short message that said: 'I wanted to show this only to you, *obba*. But don't ask me for any explanations.' It was from In-ju.

The contents of the notebook was written in the diary style. Yet there were no dates. As a whole, the entire writing was a random continuation of isolated short passages. It was easy to tell that all the entries were made since In-ju got herself interested in building an acting career. In one passage, he read the following:

(I can't tell whether or not I have talent for acting. Only, I cannot help feeling a great sense of joy just thinking about acting and theater. I wish I could live feeling this joy forever.)

In another place, he read:

(Mother, my pitiable foolish mother, why had she ruined her life by binding herself with her own miserable ineffectual affection for a man? Can't a woman live without depending on a man? What about an acting career?)

Then, there was this:

(Listening to N, I feel as if I could do things which I did not dare think of trying before. It is beneficial to me to meet N.)

There were more entries about her meeting N:

(We went for a drive in Uijongbu although it was raining. I was a little vexed by N's one-sided action but it was a pleasant excursion. N seemed in a melancholy mood later on speaking only in monosyllables. I wonder why.)

(I ate *naengmyon* with N. He made me eat an extra boled egg-half which had been atop his *naengmyon*. I had a feeling that he was treating me too much like a child. I did not like it. It's foolish to be treated like a young girl which I am not.)

(Once again, I want to make it clear to myself that N and I are associating only for the cause of the theater. Our relationship is unthinkable as well as meaningless without this bond.)

(N is so passionate when he talks about the theater and acting, but too often he looks depressed, especially lately. At these times, he only smokes his pipe without saying anything. I mustered up courage today and asked him the reason. 'Just to go on living is too complicated and depressing. You, In-ju, are too young to know this.' But I do, too. I am not too young to know it. I am so vexed that he insists on treating me as a child. I must grow up intellectually so that I could become fit as his conversation partner. Maybe, I should keep myself away from him for some time and think about this problem carefully.)

It was not difficult at all for In-chol to know who N was. Reading through In-ju's notebook, In-chol could not help smiling. He was pleased that In-ju showed the record of her recent life to him so candidly because this act reflected the healthy state of her mind. From his first meeting with Nam Chun-gol, he found himself feeling a mild dislike for the latter. Especially, he did not like the man's tone of derision when he spoke and the attitude of contempt which seemed to characterize his general carriage. From reading In-ju's notebook, however, In-chol came to realize that the derision and contempt only stemmed from the dilemma and agony he felt about life just as In-chol himself was experiencing. It was not because he had anything specific to say to this man that he wished to see him. He just felt like having a drink with Nam Chun-gol today. The man In-chol wished to see, however, did not show up.

The interior of the tavern was full of cigarette smoke and drink-thickened speeches among which In-chol could discern the voices of Pak Hae-yon and his drink-house colleague who was supposed to have run for the national assembly. Then, in the midst of the cigarette smoke, smell of liquor, and noise of the drunken conversations, In-chol caught a voice which was saying: 'Stop worrying. There's the Chusok bonus coming, right? So, what're you worrying about? Let's drink! C'm'on!'

The words gave In-chol a strangely acute sense of disgust. He stood up and walked out of the tavern. He looked up at the night sky. The moon was almost full. In-chol thought that the moon was unusually pale. Three nights from now would be the full moon, thought In-chol, and that would be the Chusok Day. From a public phone near the Municipal Hall, he called the Seoul Railway Station and checked the train schedule. Then he called Na-mi's house. It was a young maid of the house who answered the phone.

"What made you call so late?" said Na-mi in a genuinely

surprised voice.

"Didn't you say that it's okay to call you at any hour of day or night, unlike my house?"

"Are you drunk?"

"Will you go on a trip with me?"

"Go on a trip?"

"Meet me at the Seoul Railway Station before ten o'clock tomorrow morning."

Maybe I should have told her that the train leaves at ten o'clock sharp, thought In-chol checking with his wrist watch that there remained only six minutes to the departure hour of the train he wanted to catch. Already the passengers were going in through the gate which had been open since twenty some minutes ago. Stepping out of the waiting hall, In-chol looked toward the square in front of the station. The micro-buses came and stopped at the square at short regular intervals, letting off, each time, several passengers who started running toward the station as soon as they got off the vehicle.

Maybe I shouldn't have acted so one-sidedly without consulting her about her preference or convenience? But in one part of his mind, In-chol could not help feeling the certainty of her coming. A middle-aged man was lugging a huge trunk across the square. It seemed that he was trying all he could to hurry but the weight of his luggage was slowing him down. Then, In-chol saw a taxi stop a few yards short of the struggling middle-aged man. From it, Na-mi came out wearing a bright green sweater and tightly-fitting black slacks. She, too, was in a hurry. But already, even before she got off the taxi, she seemed to have caught sight of him waiting for her. She raised her hand looking in his direction. In her other hand she was holding a small traveling bag. Without waiting for her to come up, In-chol turned back and walked toward the gate.

"Your self-confidence is awe-striking," said Na-mi in a breathless but merry voice when she caught up with In-chol.

In-chol knew that she was referring to the fact that he had bought two tickets although she had not given him her verbal consent last night on the phone.

In-chol, on his part, was so irritated about her showing up only at the very last minute that he wanted to say something hurting to her. He pressed down this impulse, however, and merely walked on taking big strides on purpose.

The train started moving as soon as they got on the train and found their seats.

"We nearly missed this one!" said Na-mi, looking into her pocket mirror as soon as she was settled in the train seat. From the way her voice sounded, In-chol felt instinctively that Na-mi was glad about not missing the train and the chance to travel with him. This thought softened his mind toward Na-mi more effectively than any excuse she could have uttered.

"Where are we going, though?" said Na-mi again.

"To Pusan. For a start anyway."

Na-mi looked at him as if waiting for him to explain further.

"Then, we will go on to Haeundae, Pulguksa, Kyongju, and back to Seoul."

"It will take many days, then."

"Maybe, three days, maybe four, or... five.... I don't know. Maybe it will take a week."

"I told my family that I was visiting a friend in Inchon. I told you about this friend before, didn't I? I mean the one in whose brother's room I was put up but it smelled so bad I couldn't sleep until I put a piece of soap underneath the pillow, remember? Anyway, it's the same friend. I told my family that this friend of mine was sick and so I had to go to pay her a sick visit. I said it would take one or two days, though. Since it's the beginning of the semester and there aren't many classes open, I don't worry so much on that account, but what if this friend of mine comes up to Seoul even tomorrow and decides to pay me a visit at my house?"

Na-mi did not seem really worried, however. Rather, she

seemed to find the whole situation exciting.

The inside of the second-class car was not crowded. There were empty seats here and there. In the seat at the front of the one occupied by In-chol and Na-mi, an elderly gentleman was sitting alone with a magazine held up before his eyes.

The rice fields that stretched outside the window was already dyed in yellow with the ears of grains hanging down. Passing breeze was making soft yellow waves across the rice fields. Some farmers were already harvesting.

When the train passed by a village, In-chol was delighted to notice the pretty contrast the red of the drying red peppers made with the whiteness of the gourds that were ripening in their nests of straw mat atop the grass roofs. To In-chol's eyes, the beauty created by these natural colors and shapes under the bright sunshine seemed to be a thing that was separate from all other things surrounding them. Yet, as he kept looking at the same sights over and over again, he came to realize that these beautiful colors and shapes could not have been possible without the drabness of the thatch and the slanting line it drew against the background of the blue sky or the pine copse.

It was very cloudy when the two got off the train in Pusan. They took a taxi from the Pusan Railway Station straight to a hotel in Haeundae.

The hotel building looked lonely against the backdrop of the autumn sea. Maybe this impression came from a sense of desertedness which a summer resort place inevitably acquires after a season of a thronging crowd and booming business.

A boy led them to the second floor. The first room the bellboy opened for them was a tidy and pleasant-looking room with a good view of the sea. The bathroom was right inside the door to the left and there were chairs further in from the doorway. A double bed covered with a crisp white sheet was seen to the left, next to a wall. The boy went into the bathroom and turn on the water tap on the tub and came out. He inserted the key into the hole underneath the door-nob and then, telling them to call him if they should need anything, started to go out. At the same time as the boy slipped out of the room, however, Na-mi pushed In-chol out of the room and turned the key. The boy threw a commiserating glance at In-chol who, having had no thought of sharing one room with Na-mi himself, merely smiled indulgently at his sympathizer.

The boy opened the door to the next room which had the same structure as the first one. After the bellboy left, In-chol stepped out to the terrace with a lit cigarette between his lips. A black sea was scratching at the beach only a short distance from the hotel. The sky was overhung with heavy layers of clouds in varying shades of dark gray. In-chol stood there listening to the sound of the waves hitting the coast.

Leaning forward on his elbows against the railing of the terrace, In-chol went on watching the waves rush onto the sand scattering thousands of white horses. As he drew on his cigarette, sparks from it whiffed against his face giving it a tingling sensation. He threw away the half-finished cigarette.

A scrawny-looking dog with a brownish coat ran in from somewhere toward the spot where the cigarette butt In-chol threw away fell. After sniffing at it once or twice, the dog went away, losing interest. The hair on the dog's back stood up as it moved away against the wind. In-chol thought that probably the dog had been living on the scrap foods the vacationers threw away throughout the summer. That was why the dog was roaming about in the beach area although the warm, prosperous season was over. He kept on sniffing at different spots in the sand. Then, all of a sudden, he became immobile, staring in one direction with a fierce concentration. In the next moment, he started moving toward whatever it was that had caught his interest. Looking in the same direction, In-chol discovered another dog whose coat was black and white, or rather black spots against white. The

brown dog sniffed at the underside of the motley's face and
then he raised a paw putting it down on the neck of the
other one. After that, he turned back and started running
back toward where In-chol was looking out. The dog did not
run all the way up to In-chol's part of the beach, however.
Instead, he stopped at the midpoint and then ran back toward
the motley only to turn away again and run on in In-chol's
direction, jumping up and down as if with genuine delight.
In-chol could see how the dog's belly nearly scraped the sand
when he lowered his body to make another jump upwards in
his joyful gamboling. He stopped again at the same midpoint where he had stopped and turned and, running back
toward the motley, tried to get on its back. The other dog
did not yield without putting up a show of a fight. Raising
its prostrated body up from underneath the assailant, the
motley leapt over the brown dog. After the two dogs wrestled
and frolicked about in this way for some time, one of the
dogs began to run toward In-chol's side of the beach. The
other dog followed fast upon his companion. They had another wrestling bout before they could come as far as the
cigarette butt. Then, abruptly turning direction, they both
ran back away one dog following the other. The dogs repeated these movements several times over in the deserted
evening beach by the black sea dotted with whitecaps of the
waves. To In-chol's watching eyes, the play of the dogs appeared to delineate nothing less than the spontaneous and
vital movements of nature herself.

Suddenly, In-chol heard the sound of laughter right beside
him. It was Na-mi who, also, had come out to the terrace of
the room she had taken. The two terrace was separated only
by an empty space of about two feet. Na-mi was still laughing
when she asked him,

"Is it such a great fun to watch the dogs play?"

"You, too, had better watch carefully, Na-mi. Because it
will do you a lot of good if you can imitate their body movements on the stage later on."

Na-mi merely laughed without saying anything. They returned to their respective rooms a while later.

In-chol took a bath and then lay down on the white sheet in his undershirt. The boy knocked to let him know that it was suppertime. In-chol dressed and went over to Na-mi's room. It seemed that she, too, had taken a bath in the meantime. With a mild flush on her face, she was combing her hair in front of the mirror. In-chol saw that her feet which she was twining one against the other under the mirror-desk were still wet from the bathwater. In-chol remembered how he had wondered about Na-mi's feet while looking at Ta-hye's naked feet in the 'piano room' of Professor Chi's house. He remembered, too, that he had never looked at Na-mi's feet closely even once during the whole time they bathed and swam together in the sea last summer.

Compared with Ta-hye's, Na-mi's toes were slender and longish. The second toe was pushed up atop the thumb and the third toe which was the longest of all her five toes. In-chol thought to himself, 'These are the toes that scratched me on the shin at the seaside that night.' It was not an especially attractive foot, but it had the potentiality for diverse expressions.

The dining hall was nearly empty with only two foreigners sitting opposite two Korean women with a heavy make-up, drinking beer. After the dinner, In-chol and Na-mi walked to the beach slipping out of the side-entrance of the hotel that opened straight on the beach area.

Darkness was spreading fast and thick under low-hanging black clouds. The sea was even blacker than before which made the whiteness of the foams stand out more distinctly now. Together, they listened to the ponderous sounds the waves were making as they came and broke against the coastline. Sand grains, whisked up by the damp salty wind, blew against the nocturnal sojourners' faces.

In silence, they kept on walking side by side along the sandbank. When one of them stopped and turned back, the other followed the suit. If one of them should again change the direction after a while, the other, which of the two it might be, turned back without a demur. They repeated these actions as if they were the most natural thing they could be doing at the moment. It was giving In-chol a strange feeling that Na-mi was so quiet and acquiescent tonight.

It was pitch darkness all around, soon. Except for whitish lines made by the foams against the shoal, the sea was almost totally invisible now. Only, one still could feel the salty wetness of the air against the skin.

In-chol pictured to his mind's eye the sight of the dogs playing in the sand. He had not been able to tell, nor cared, which one was the male and which the female. Maybe they were both males or both females. Only the spontaneous beauty and rhythm of their movements came back alive in his memory.

Na-mi sat down on the sand folding her arms across her breasts. In-chol sat beside her.

"Do you know what I am thinking now?" asked Na-mi.

In-chol did not answer. Na-mi said again,

"I have been thinking about why it was that I came on this trip with you so unhesitatingly. But maybe our impulsive actions are more eloquent than our reasoning, don't you think?"

Passing one arm across her back, In-chol held Na-mi by one elbow with his hand. Then, stretching his other hand in the front, he held her chin up and kissed her. Both her lips and skin were cold against his.

They returned to the hotel. Saying good-night to her in front of her room, In-chol said to Na-mi,

"You'd better lock your door tight, all right?"

"You, too," said Na-mi as if she understood the meaning of his admonishment. There was a smile on her pale lips chilled by the sea wind.

Entering his room, In-chol turned on the radio that he found in one corner of the room. A radio drama had just ended and the weather report was on. It said that from late in the night, there would be rain across the country which would continue until next afternoon. Switching off the radio, In-chol left his room again and walked out to the sea. He went to the sandbank and stood facing the black sea. There was nothing but a profound and eternal darkness which had both the sea and the sky inside it. Only, one could still hear the repeated sound of the waves at regular intervals. In-chol felt the sea wind blowing against his face. As if to protest against some invisible force, In-chol went on standing there confronting the bottomless darkness. And he asked himself, why did I come here? And why did I take Na-mi along with me?

Then in the midst of the sound of the waves, In-chol seemed to hear a voice calling his name from afar. Hearing this voice, In-chol trembled once, almost involuntarily. He strained his ears to hear better. But the assertive sound of the waves seemed to be engulfing all other sounds so that he became conscious of nothing but the huge benumbing darkness of night by the sea.

After a long while, he turned back and started to walk toward the hotel. When he came close to the hotel building, however, he saw the silhouette of a human figure standing out on one terrace against the sheet of electric light flowing out of the room at the back through the glass panes. In-chol walked up to the underside of the terrace and identified the figure to be that of Na-mi. The two of them stared into each other's faces across the darkness between them.

"Where have you been? Why didn't you answer my calls?" said Na-mi.

Without answering, In-chol walked into the hotel through its side gate.

Na-mi was sitting in a chair with a pack of trumps in her hand when he entered her room. She seemed to be waiting for him to sit down in the chair facing her.

"You look pale," she said.

In-chol went behind Na-mi and holding her cheeks in his

two hands pulled it back gently and kissed her on the lips. Why would I look pale when my heart is burning like this, he wondered and rubbed his lips against hers with passion.

"Your lips are cold," mumbled Na-mi's mouth under his. In-chol did not let go of her lips, however. Slowly, Na-mi's arms came up around his neck and the cards fell from her hands while In-chol pressed his lips harder against hers. Suddenly, Na-mi bit In-chol's lips and snatched away her head.

The black tide of the night sea rushed into In-chol's head. Without a word, he pulled Na-mi's body up from the chair and, clutching it against his own chest, he pushed her toward the bed. It would be the Full Moon day after tomorrow, he thought. And Professor Chi would go to Pundi-namutkol on that day, he thought on, still pushing Na-mi toward the bed. Na-mi writhed her body from waist up, tottering backwards pushed by In-chol. 'Tell me your honest opinion. Do you think I acted like a small-minded person tonight?' 'No one who's not been in your position could know the hardship it involves.' In-chol pushed Na-mi down on the bed. Although Na-mi appeared shocked, she did not resist. Another and still another black tide rushed into In-chol's head to break in thousand fragments. Then In-chol saw a man's eyes shining from underneath all this commotion. He was saying, 'You came to the wrong person. I have no cousin. I have no relatives of any kind.'

In-chol raised himself from the bed and, leaving Na-mi where she was, walked toward the door. And while walking, he mumbled,

"Na-mi, we are going back to Seoul, tomorrow."

That night In-chol heard the rain drops hitting against the window panes mixing their sounds with that of the waves breaking against the sands. Yet he had a deep sleep uninterrupted by any dream.

CHAPTER TWO

The Knife

Old Man Pon-dol went out of the house while it was still as dark as in the middle of a night. He had the *turebak* (scooper used at the well) in one hand and a water jug in the other. The sky was very clear after yesterday's rain and there were many stars shining in eye-dazzling brightness.

Reaching the well which was a little way off from his house, he put down the jug on the ground and threw the *turebak* into the water. The sound of the *turebak* hitting against the stone wall of the well resounded in the clear quietness of early morning. The clear and refreshing sound was inexpressibly good to hear, and as in many many years in the past the sound made the old man feel as if his body and soul had been washed up clean in their totality.

Although he had rinsed out the water jug thoroughly last night, Old Man Pon-dol gave it another rinsing before he started filling it with the well water. When the jug was filled to the half, he stopped. Until two or three years ago, he could, without difficulty, carry a full jug of well water to his house. From last year, however, he reduced the quota to half because he found that his body was not as strong as his will.

Today, even the half-jugful of water seemed too heavy for him who panted from the strain the labor gave him. After carrying it home, he covered it carefully with a clean cloth and took it to the outer quarter of his house where he resided. Then he went to the kitchen and washed himself with heated water. Although he had a daughter-in-law who lived with her husband's parents after she became a widow during the Korean War, the old man did not let her heat the water for his ablution before the Chusok rite. Always, he heated the bathwater himself.

While he went through the ritual of bathing himself in the kitchen, he heard the church bell ring out from the village on the other side of the mountain. They were having early morning prayer meetings these days because this was one of their faith-reviving periods as they put it. The sound of the bell resounded in the quiet dark of early morning. Old Man Pon-dol coughed up some spittle deliberately and spat it out with force.

Returning to the outer quarters after the ablution, the old man changed into garments which had been washed, starched and ironed with care in preparation for today. Then, he sat quietly beside his son Ki-ryong who was still in deep sleep. There was still some time before daybreak.

From a few years ago, Old Man Pon-dol found it not easy to sleep soundly until daybreak. He would wake up during the small hours and then, too, restless to get back to sleep, sit with his knees drawn up against his chest until dawn. Since he did not smoke, it was a long wait in the dark by himself. Especially, today, the old man had woken up so early that he did not seem to have gotten any chunk of sleep to speak of. Ki-ryong had come down from Seoul only in the afternoon yesterday. After supper, he had gone out as if to visit a neighbor's house, returning only late in the night. As soon as he entered the room which he shared with his father during his home visits, he drew his pallet toward the wall on his side and started snoring away, his face to the wall. Smell of liquor drifted over to the old man who was mildly shocked by it. 'Living away from home in the big city made my son drink,' thought the old man listening to his son's snoring in the darkness. Worry and listlessness took his sleep completely away and he went from one thought to another turning in his bed.

Ki-ryong was sleeping peacefully now, no longer snoring. There was no smell of liquor either. Sitting by his son, the old man said to himself that as long as he would live, he would look after the affairs of home himself without bothering his son. It was only yesterday that Old Man Pon-dol had harbored the thought that maybe he would now hand everything over to Ki-ryong. This tempting thought had come to his mind while he was visiting the ancestral graves along with Ki-ryong and his second grandson Chae-uk. The specific purpose of their visit to the cemetery was to add earth over the tombs because the ancestral tombs of the butcher families needed adding new earth every now and then, earth crumbling down from their unsodded mounds almost constantly and regularly. Ki-ryong and Chae-uk brought earth in a straw carrier and threw it onto the mound which the old man spread out evenly over the mound with a shovel, carefully filling any dented spots he could find. When the work was almost finished, Old Man Pon-dol straightened his back, with the shovel stuck in the ground. Suddenly, the sun appeared between the clouds that had remained in the sky even after last night's rain had stopped in early afternoon. The sun was so bright that the old man felt dizzy. Letting go of the shovel, therefore, he squatted down on the ground. Although he did not like to get the direct sunlight on top of his head which had been freshly shaven for the big day, he did not have the strength to move his body away from it. Then, he felt a protective shadow falling on him from above. It was the shadow of his son Ki-ryong who had run to his father to see what was wrong. Recovering his strength in the shade provided by his son, the old man had had the momentary tempting thought of disburdening all his ancestral duties on this son and retire for good. In the next instant, however, he realized that it was a wrong thought that he had had in his moment of weakness. With a reawakened resolution that he would carry out his heaven-appointed duty for many many more days yet, he had come back home escorted by his son and grandson.

With Old Man Pon-dol walking at the head, Ki-ryong who carried the water jug in his arms and Chae-uk who carried the *chirung* (large carrier-container made with twigs of bush-clover) with various items needed for the rite walked behind him while Chong-*sobang*(informal appellation for men) who was a fellow butcher in the village took up the rear carrying a miniature-size manger carved specifically for this Chusok rite. It was a clear quiet morning.

The slaughterhouse was located in the valley at one end of the village in the opposite direction from where the cemetery was. In all, it was only an old building which was no bigger than an average storage house. The rusted tin roof had holes here and there and the cemented floor was cracked and chipped in several places so that reddish earth pushed out from beneath. Only the inner section of the slaughterhouse had its floor intact but the blood and the animal fat had turned it to a dirty blackish hue. Even so, the inside of the slaughterhouse was clean and tidy enough on this day of rite-offering.

From the top of a hill overlooking the slaughterhouse, Old Man Pon-dol could see some people standing around the entrance to the slaughterhouse. Who could they be? Wondering, the old man looked more carefully. One of them he could identify as Pun-i's father but the other two were unknown to him. When he went up to where these men were standing, however, one of the two strangers offered him a sort of a greeting making way for him to pass. Then, he knew. This man who was the older of the two strangers was no other than the man who was supposed to be a professor from some college in Seoul whom he had met through Pun-i's father. He ignored the other's gesture of greeting, however.

The manger was placed in the center of the slaughterhouse, lengthwise, beside which the jug of water and the *chirung* with things needed for the rite were lowered. Then, all except Old Man Pon-dol moved back to the doorway and stood in line facing inside.

Professor Chi took his position close to the doorway where he could take a good look at the proceedings of the rite inside the slaughterhouse. In-chol did likewise.

There were no food preparations for this rite. The sole major offering seemed to be the water which the old man had taken so much care to keep clean. And one other important item needed for the rite seemed to be a knife.

First, the old man stood in front of the manger, eyes closed. Then he took out a gourd dipper from out of the *chirung* and, scooping out the water from the jug, began sprinkling it all around the interior of the slaughterhouse. He scooped out another dipperful of water from the jug and poured it into the manger in twelve tippings during which ritual he counted the twelve months of the year: January, February, etc.... When this was over, he took out a black cloth-wrapper containing some beans which he threw in, again, in twelve castings into the manger. Some grains of beans spilled outside the manger although the old man bent down as if to make sure that all the beans fell correctly into the manger. The reason he spilled some of the beans was that his hands were shaky and Old Man Pon-dol himself was aware of this fact.

Next to be picked out from the *chirung* was a red cloth-wrapper which the old man spread out over the manger covering it. Then he sprinkled some more water over this before he took out a knife which had a considerable length to it. He placed it across the manger over the red cloth with hands that seemed to be shaking a little more now. Kneeling down in front of the manger, the old man bowed twice.

By the time Professor Chi had finished putting in a new roll of film in his camera, Old Man Pon-dol was mumbling some incantation with the knife pressed against his forehead with both hands. Then he stood up. The knife was now wrapped in the red cloth and, grabbing this in one hand, the old man started going around the entire space of the slaughterhouse making slashing movements with the wrapped knife in all four corners of the building. Returning to his original position, he put the knife down across the manger and bowed two more times, this time more slowly. This was the end of the rite. Anybody could see that the old man put his soul into every movement he made during the ceremony.

Coming out of the slaughterhouse, Old Man Pon-dol walked away without so much as glancing at the spectators standing near the doorway. One could see that there were drops of perspiration on his face.

Upon reaching his house, Old Man Pon-dol felt a great surge of fatigue. Going to his quarters, therefore, he lay down with a wood-pillow under his head. His duty was not over until he would have eaten, for breakfast, the rice cooked with the beans that had been used for the rite. Lying down, he randomly thought about this college professor he had met before and seen again at the rite today. He did not like the fact that this man was back here, probably to pry into something about him and his fellow butchers. There seemed no doubt about this man's motive for coming here today because this time he even came with one of his students to help him....I should never have allowed myself to be introduced to this kind of character from the first, thought Old Man Pon-dol with a degree of bitterness.

He turned his face toward the wall. A pair of ox-horns and a piece of ox tail were hung on that wall which was yellowing with age and wear. The horns, too, were discolored to a dirty brown-black and the ox tail had withered with passage of many years. Old Man Pon-dol, also, had changed in body and mind along with these age-old relics of an ancient butchering.

He remembered how these horns and ox tail had been hung on this wall on a Tano Day by his father's blood-stained hands. Ever since this day, he had watched his father staring at these remains of a dead ox now and then. As a boy, he had no way of truly knowing what thoughts and feelings passed through his father's mind as he stood in front of these horns and ox tail, yet, albeit blindly, the boy had tacitly believed that somehow these things were protecting him and his family from unforeseen misfortunes.

When his brother was persecuted by the other boys in the village like on that day when one of the boys had tripped him so that he fell on the ground with the burden of the fuel wood, he thought that as long as these horns and ox tail were hanging on their wall, it was all right for him and his brother to suffer molestations from other boys who were, after all, poor kids who lived in a world where there were no blessings from these sacred things. Seeing his brother pick up a stone to throw at his persecutor on that day, he had prevented it just by staring at his brother, willing his two eyes to tell his brother: Put the stone down. You must not hit him. We have our own way to follow. What they are doing to us is nothing compared with what good we are promised for following our way. It is a way we must follow no matter what happens.

In time the boy Pon-dol came to acquire an attitude or, rather, a philosophy which enabled him to overcome any contempt or harassment he might experience from others. He came to believe that those were only necessary trials a butcher was expected to win through if he were to deserve his calling. The horns and the ox tail he came to consider as some powerful amulets that would chase away all evils of this world for his family.

After he entered the trade of butchering himself, however, his faith in the horns and the tail transferred to the knife with which he killed the animals. The cows and oxen were sacred animals. It seemed in order that the knife which would send these animals' souls to heaven also should be invested with sanctity. His growing belief in the sacred nature of the butchering knife emboldened him to kill the man whose son had been the cause of the death of his son and grandson both and to think moreover that he had done the man a good service of sending his soul to heaven by killing him with the sacred knife.

At the same time, Pon-dol lived apart from the rest of the world so that his sacred world would not be easily invaded by the evil forces of the world that lay outside it. His ardent wish to have the graves of the Christians moved to another location, too, derived from this exclusivism of the old butcher. Even now, Old Man Pon-dol tried to recover his spiritual strength and equanimity by concentrating his thought on the knife which he had put away in the low-closet beneath the horns and the ox tail. I must look after this knife with more care and attention from now on, thought the old man. I don't think Ki-ryong has it in him, the old man said to himself and was about to finish the sentence when he hurriedly changed his thought and said, instead, 'He is still too young to know the value of a thing like that. It's up to me yet to take a good care of the knife because I am still able to move about quite well.' In the next instant, however, Old Man Pon-dol remembered how his hands had trembled while he was going through various movements for the rite. It's all because I didn't sleep enough last night, that's all, he reassured himself. But had they picked up the beans which I had spilled on the ground?

"Will somebody come here!" called out the old man in the direction of the inner quarters.

Seeing Chae-uk come into his view, he asked,

"Are all the beans brought home, every one of them?"

"Yes, grandfather, we brought the beans home without even shaking them out of the manger."

The old man guessed that the beans he had spilled on the ground had not been picked up. He scrambled up and started his trip back to the slaughterhouse. It was not because he grudged the few grains of beans he had involuntarily let fall

outside the manger. Only, he had firm belief that whatever
had been used for the rite should never be wasted or treated
carelessly.

"It's all very simple," said Professor Chi to Pun-i's father
when the rite was over, glancing at In-chol from the back as
he walked on ahead of himself and the farmer.

"I've heard that in some places, the monks are invited to
recite the incantation, but not in this village. It's been always
family of that old man who have done everything for the
rite-offering here in our village," said Pun-i's father showing
it visibly in this eager tone that he desired to make the professor's visit a worthwhile trouble in so far as they two had
become some sort of a team ever since his discovery of the
Paekche earthenware.

"Isn't there another rite they offer at the cemetery?" asked
Professor Chi, anyway, although he was nearly sure that it
would not be the case because why would the butchers fuss
with rites at their graves when they do not even sod them?

"Never. I hear that nowadays many butchers elsewhere
offer rites at their dead ones' graves but the family of that old
man have followed the butchers' rules to letter. And they do
not offer rites at home either on days like Hanshik or
Chusok. And this is, in a way, keeping the other butcher
families of this village, too, from rite-offerings at home or
cemetery."

"By the way, I don't think he recognized me. Otherwise,
he would have returned my bow."

"No, it's not that. He acted that way deliberately. It's forbidden to speak with anyone during the rite-offering. They
think it will invite evil spirits to talk with outsiders."

"Oh, is that so?" said Professor Chi, and then, changing
the topic, he said, "He is so fit and strong, isn't he? I was
very impressed by the way he swished that knife in powerful
strokes making his round of the room. I was as if the ghost
had really descended on that old man. Nobody seeing him
like that would have believed that he was in his seventies."

When they reached the village and were passing a house in the yard of which ears of rice were drying on a straw mat, they saw a woman come round the hedge of the house next to this one. Seeing Pun-i's father, she bowed to him. Her one hand was holding what looked like the Bible and the book of psalms. She was wearing her hair short and had on simple western-style clothes. Yet, she had a refinement which made her look somewhat incongruous with her surrounding. She looked to be about twenty two or three.

"Christians are increasing in number in a village like this, too," muttered Pun-i's father when the young woman was out of hearing distance. Then he continued, "Do you remember my telling you about a daughter of a butcher who had been betrothed to a man in Seoul but had the engagement called off because of her being a butcher's daughter?"

"Ah, you mean that girl who had gone to Seoul to study at a college?"

"That's right. The girl you just saw is the one. She started going to the church regularly like that. She seems actually to spend all her days there lately, it being a faith-reviving period or some such thing among the churchgoers."

"Does her family leave her alone?"

"What else can they do? Ever since the blowing off of the engagement, she locked herself in her room and for a long time didn't speak with her own family, even. In the end, her folks started getting afraid that she might do something terrible to herself and they lived on the edge of their nerves watching her. So, they were rather glad, it seems, when the girl began taking interest in the church at least and took her outings to go there."

"Is the man who helped with the rite this morning the girl's father, by any chance?"

"No, that's not the one," replied Pun-i's father taking his pipe out, "That girl's father isn't in the village at the moment."

According to what Pun-i's father related, the girl's father

had butchered a cow illegally several days ago. What was more, it was not a simple violation of the butchering law but he had killed a cow which somebody had stolen from some other party while knowing about the theft. The agreement was that he and the cow-thief share the spoil half and half. But they were discovered, somehow.

"The police got wind of it, and so the man had no choice but take a hiding somewhere for a while. None of us villagers suspected anything about his part in the stealing. Since people have the habit of killing their cows or oxen at Chusok time, we had thought that he was involved merely in some such usual dealings."

Professor Chi stopped at a point where he could see the jeep which In-chol had driven to come here. He could not see In-chol either inside or outside the vehicle, however. Seeing In-chol hasten away ahead of him and Pun-i's father, he had guessed that maybe his pupil was hurrying back to the jeep in order not to leave it for too long at the disposal of the village urchins. Yet, there were neither In-chol nor the children anywhere near the vehicle.

Where could he have gone, wondered Professor Chi. Then, he caught sight of the old man who was coming this way turning round the vegetable field. Instead of taking the path that ran toward where Professor Chi was standing, however, the old man was stepping onto the dirt bank stretching away from the vegetable field.

Marking the swiftness of the old man's movement once again in his consciousness, Professor Chi decided to bring up the subject which had really been his main purpose of coming out here today.

"Was the knife which he used at the rite today the one we talked about the other day?"

"Yes," said Pun-i's father turning his head quickly to look at his interlocutor.

"Couldn't you ask him to allow me to take just one picture of the knife?" said Professor Chi.

Professor Chi who had taken pictures of the entire precincts of the slaughterhouse far before the rite started had continued to photograph every scene involved with the rite-offering. Since the old man's attendants who had followed him were blocking the doorway, Professor Chi had to tiptoe frequently in order to take pictures of the proceedings inside the slaughterhouse. When the knife was pulled out of the *chirung,* he knew almost for certain that that was the very butchering knife with which the old man was known to have killed a man. Yet when he tried to focus his camera lens on the knife, either the view was hindered by the movements of the old man or the red cloth-wrapper shielded the essential knife from the eye of the camera. It was impossible to take a close-up photograph of the knife.

"I won't touch the knife. Just ask him to let me take a picture of it with my camera," said Professor Chi again, almost nagging, knowing inside his head that, if he failed to do it today, he would not have a second chance easily.

Pun-i's father seemed more cautious and timid than his well-built strong body led a person to think. He hesitated a long while before he managed to say,

"I could go and try, but I wouldn't count on much if I were you...."

Before he started going after Old Man Pon-dol, however, Pun-i's father first snuffed off the light of his pipe and only after putting away the extinguished pipe inside his pocket, did he begin moving in the direction the old man was taking. Watching him go through these gestures, Professor Chi could reascertain the fact that this farmer revered the old man a great deal. Could it be because of the special power this old butcher's knife was reputed to possess?

The shortish figure of Old Man Pon-dol in the meantime had disappeared over the low hill at the other foot of which was the slaughterhouse.

Stepping into the shade underneath the eaves of a house nearby, Professor Chi looked out across the field in the direc-

tion of the hill noting the clear bright sunshine that en-
veloped the entire hill area.

Finally, the tall stature of Pun-i's father came into view
atop the hill who seemed to be stopping there instead of following his way down the other slope. Maybe, he means to
waylay the old man there until the latter would take his road
back to go home, thought Professor Chi. Then, suddenly, he
saw Pun-i's father jump up as if startled by something and
dash down the hill.

Church bell was heard from the village on the other side of
the nearer mountain. It was a clear sonorous sound matching
the clear bright sunshine pouring down on the silent hill.

Try though he did, In-chol could not shake off depression.
Whatever bizarre display he might be witnessing in front of
his eyes, it was now his personal affair, in a manner of speaking. No longer could he idly savor the detached curiosity of
an interested spectator because what he was seeing were
gestures and customs his own ancestors had revered and
preserved generation after generation. And now it was his
own 'big-father' who was personally officiating the ancient
ceremony, enacting each ritual symbolism himself. This fact,
for In-chol, was so overwhelming in its striking singularity
that he felt dizzy and mildly nauseated.

Seeing Professor Chi shuffling from one spot to another
trying to photograph the scenes of the rite-offering, he had
felt obligated to offer his help to the professor. Yet, there was
something that prevented him from making that offer. What
was more, he even became conscious of a self inside him that
resented the professor for so detachedly taking picture after
picture of what was most serious and important affair for the
butchers.

As soon as the rite was over, therefore, In-chol had walked
away ahead of the professor and his companion. He wanted
to walk as far as the entrance to the village and wait for his
cousin there.

He had not waited for long when Ki-ryong appeared in the company of others involved with the rite. Recognizing In-chol, he handed the empty water jug to his nephew and came up to In-chol.

Just as if they had previously agreed to make that move, Ki-ryong and In-chol turned toward the mountain at the back of the village and started walking. They reached the upper slope of the mountain in no time. The village urchins who had gathered there throwing stones at the chestnuts to make them fall scattered away seeing Ki-ryong come up with a stranger. Catching, in-between the chestnut branches, the sight of a number of unsodded tombs side by side with ordinary sodded mounds with signs of cross stuck in front of them, In-chol thought to himself, that must be the ancestral cemetery I've heard so much about lately.

Ki-ryong who was about to sit down in the shade of a chestnut tree stepped onto a chestnut-bur that had fallen on the ground. Three shiny chestnuts rolled out of it which Ki-ryong handed over to In-chol. He crushed another chestnut-bur under his foot.

There was a bitter taste to the chestnut when In-chol ate it without peeling off the inner skin which was hard to remove without a knife.

"I knew you would come sooner or later," said Ki-ryong using the honorific form.

Despite the formal form of speech his cousin was using just as he had when In-chol had visited him at the Miari slaughterhouse, now there was a warmth in the way he spoke to In-chol as if he recognized the latter to be a cousin indeed.

"I wish you would not use the honorific form with me. I don't think there's a rule binding a person to speak to a younger cousin in honorifics," said In-chol.

Ki-ryong stared at In-chol intently. In-chol realized that his cousin's eyes shone in a striking way which he had not noticed in their last encounter at Miari.

"I told you before," said Ki-ryong finally, still using the

honorific form, "that aside from my family in this village, I have no other relatives. My father is an only son. How can I, then, have cousins?"

His tone was quiet and indifferent, just as it had been when he spoke to In-chol at Miari.

In-chol decided not to argue with him over this issue. As long as Ki-ryong meant to deny kinship between the two of them, how could he refute the other's assumption? Changing the topic, therefore, In-chol said,

"There's something I want to ask your opinion about. What do you think of the kind of rite that was offered this morning?"

"What do you mean?"

"Well, what I mean is, do you think that kind of a thing should be kept alive in the future. I mean, will you be doing the same thing if your father should pass away?"

"Why do you ask that?" said Ki-ryong as if on his guard, but he went on without waiting for In-chol's reply, "Think of the matter in this way. There's someone in this village who butchered a cow which another man had stolen from some other party. He took hiding when the police found it out and started looking for him. Yesterday, he came back to the village and proposed to his family that they move out of the village and make a new start somewhere. But do you know what? Their the oldest daughter objected to her father's idea. I guess you know what it means for people like us to move out of our village, don't you? However, this daughter's objection was very unexpected, and to tell you the truth, I myself was not a little surprised when I heard it from her father over the drink at the tavern last night because just about anyone in this village would surely have thought that this daughter would have been all for her father's proposition. She is one who suffered a great deal because of her origin although lately she seems to be getting some consolation from attending the church. Anyhow, this daughter kept on opposing her father about this matter of moving out of here and, what was more, she even urged him to give himself up to the police. The man was furious saying what kind of a daughter is she to tell her own father to give himself up to the police and so on. Now, tell me, what do you think of this girl's attitude?"

From his tone of voice, however, In-chol felt that he did not really want to know what In-chol thought about the matter. Only, there seemed to be some forcefulness in his voice although it did not betray emotion even now. In-chol noted the sharp ridge of his nose which was more prominent when looked at from the side. He turned his eyes away from his cousin. The sun was pouring down so much light and heat that In-chol could not keep his head straight. He looked down at the ground to avoid the sun.

"Maybe," spoke Ki-ryong again. "She is, even now, praying inside that church that her father give himself up to the police and become clean again. The commonsense would condemn her as a heartless child lacking in filial piety. But what is this commonsense? Isn't it something invented by weak people to live through life with some sort of a shield? To my thinking, the little we have achieved in this world owes nothing to these weakhearted people whose only law is commonsense. I mean all we have achieved in small or big ways...."

The church bell was still ringing.

"But going against the commonsense achieves nothing by itself, either, don't you think?" said In-chol.

"I would have thought to hear something different from one who made the decision to show up here like this today."

The church bell had stopped ringing.

From Ki-ryong's long speech about commonsense, etc., In-chol seemed to be able to guess that his cousin would be sure to follow the footsteps of his father offering rites to the cows and so on. But what good does he expect to get out of adhering to this kind of a primitive custom? All of a sudden, In-chol felt something like a burning suffocation in his heart. Irrelevantly enough, this sensation brought to his mind the

memory of a dueling scene in some French novel he had read
long ago.

Thump! A big ripe chestnut fell from an overhead branch
to the ground. Because of the surrounding quiet, the sound
of the chestnut hitting the ground sounded bigger and
heavier than it normally would have. With the transposition
of the shadow made by the chestnut branches under the
moving sun, In-chol's feet were now exposed to the sunlight
as he kept on sitting with his knees drawn up to his chest.

Suddenly, In-chol shook a hand in a jerky frightened movement. An insect had just crept up on the back of his hand. It
was a tiny green-colored bug which was common in any
grassland.

"Did it frighten you?" said Ki-ryong with something akin
to a faint smile for the first time in his conversation with
In-chol. He went on, "These things can unsettle you when
they come up on you when you are least expecting them. But
once you know what they are up to, they can't frighten
you.... By the way, hadn't you come with a company?"

In-chol told him about Professor Chi and then he went on
to the subject of the butchering knife. To be sure, he was no
longer taking this trouble to be of help to the professor.
Rather, he wanted to see what kind of a reaction Ki-ryong
would show to the proposition.

"What do you want with the knife?" asked Ki-ryong briefly.

"This professor who came with me wishes to look at it, it
seems."

Ki-ryong seemed to give it a thought for a moment and
then commented,

"He is a strange person to take interest in that," Ki-ryong
said, and then went on, "That knife is...."

Just at this moment, however, a child's voice called,

"*Samchun!* (paternal brother, especially a younger unmarried brother)" The call was coming from down the mountain
slope.

In-chol saw that it was the boy whom he had seen at the

rite this morning.

"Come home, quick, *samchun*! It's grandfather. He's just...."

Just as he had thought, quite a few grains of beans were left scattered on the cement flooring of the slaughterhouse. Bending down stiffly, Old Man Pon-dol began picking up the beans one by one thinking how each of these grains which had been used at the rite was precious. All of a sudden, however, his fingers stiffened and the grains of beans that had been in his hand fell through the spread-out fingers. At the same time, he felt a great dull pain at the back of his head. He fell forward as if to bow down on his knees.

When he regained his consciousness, he was lying down in his room at the outer quarters of his house. His son, daughter-in-law, and grandson came into his vision. He wanted to tell them not to worry, but he could not produce any sound with his tongue which had become like a stone. He became conscious of a streak of saliva trickling from a corner of his mouth down one side of his chin. He wanted to wipe it off, but he could not move his left hand or arm. Then, he said to himself, aha, I must be having the 'wind (stroke)', but it's nothing. This only happened because I did not get enough sleep last night. I will have a good long sleep and then I will be completely recovered.... He closed his eyes.

But why are they sitting around like this? Do they think I am going to die or something? Foolish kids! Then, Old Man Pon-dol remembered the scene of his own father's death. His father had suffered a great deal before death. His breath had stopped many times before it finally ceased for good. Every time his father regained consciousness, he had called the name of his older son Pon-dol and the name of the son who had deserted his family. His dying father's face had shown a mark of deeper suffering as minutes passed. He was suffering without being able to be freed from it no matter how many times he lost his breath, and it was because the gate of the

upperworld would not open for him to enter. The family
had to resort to the ultimate means of pounding the chopping
block three times with the butchering knife in order to announce his coming to the higher quarters so that they would
open their gate for his father to pass through. But...I am not
going to die yet, thought Old Man Pon-dol. No, I am not
going to die. He opened his eyes wide.

Ki-ryong could see that his father's eyes had more red in
them than a while ago. Answering his father's beckoning, he
drew up to him on his knees and brought his ear down to the
level of the other's mouth. His father made some guttural
sounds out of which Ki-ryong could not make any sense.
Mainly, the unintelligible sounds his father was making
seemed to be the noise of mucus boiling in his throat. His
father, however, kept trying to speak to Ki-ryong who failed
every time to catch what his father so wished to say to him.
Finally, the old man gave up and raising his right hand
pointed to the low-closet. Only then did Ki-ryong guess what
it was that his father had been struggling so hard to tell
him.

Going to the wall with the low-closet, Ki-ryong slid the
closet door open and took out the butchering knife wrapped
in the red cloth. He took it to his father's bedside and put it
down right beside the old man's right hand.

Lifting the flaps of the cloth wrapper with his good hand,
Old Man Pon-dol took out the knife and, bringing it to a
parallel level of his eyes, stared at it for a prolonged moment
looking as if he were exchanging some secret dialog with
the knife. One could see that the knife blade was trembling
minutely. Then Old Man Pon-dol brought the knife down
and drawing it inside the bed cover inserted it between his
left arm and the left flank of his body. Now, all I need to do
is to sleep a while, said the old man to himself, and closed his
eyes quietly. Soon, he was snoring.

Ki-ryong left the room. Lighting a cigarette, he drew on it
deeply a couple of times. Then he started walking toward a

group of people sitting in the shade outside the gate. Professor Chi and In-chol, too, were sitting there on a straw mat along with Pun-i's father and some other villagers who were gathered to hear the news of the old man.

Pun-i's father was the first to ask Ki-ryong about the condition of the patient. As if relieved by Ki-ryong's brief report, Pun-i's father said,

"I am so glad it's not any worse than that! You know, I thought at first that he was offering a bow or something because that's exactly how it looked to me. But he wouldn't get up. So I ran down to him. And just as I feared, he was lying on his face unconscious. It was some task carrying him on my back because he had no control of his body."

Ki-ryong thanked him for his trouble and then turning to In-chol he said,

"Could I ask for a ride in your car if you're not in too much of a hurry? I want to fetch a doctor from Kyong-an because there's none in this vicinity."

Only when the jeep had run some distance on the throughway after leaving the country road did Ki-ryong open his mouth,

"Maybe the matter is getting simplified."

In-chol could not guess what Ki-ryong meant by this.

"My father may die," said Ki-ryong again only confusing In-chol the more.

Slowing down the speed of the jeep, In-chol turned his head toward Ki-ryong who was looking straight ahead, his face completely expressionless as if he had not opened his mouth to say anything.

The jeep jolted over some obstacle on the road. When the normal balance was regained, In-chol felt that Ki-ryong was turning his head sideways to look at him. Then he heard his voice,

"You seemed full of hate back there."

All of a sudden, In-chol felt as if he could understand what it was Ki-ryong had been trying to say to him ever since they had started out on this trip. He tightened his grip on the steering wheel. Although he knew that Ki-ryong's face was at this moment turned toward him and he very much wished to read the expression on that face, In-chol did not give himself up to the temptation. He kept his eyes straight ahead. But, all the same, what Ki-ryong said was true. It was true that the minute he saw the old man walking toward the slaughter-house with his hair and beard clean shaven, wearing a coarse cotton jacket held together with thread-bottons and a pair of straw sandals on his bare feet, he began to hate him with all his heart. He hated him fiercely although he had never before seen this person except once in the picture Professor Chi had shown him. At the same time, however, he knew that the sense of aversion he felt for this old person was something which only one who was related by blood to him could experience. It was hate mixed with suffering.

"This is what I think. It is wrong to treat the *paekchong* class as something below the human level. But it is equally wrong to glorify their status. *Paekchong* should be considered only as a profession from the start to the end. Neither more nor less."

"Theories are always simple and clean. And I won't deter you from yours. One should be allowed to hate what he wants to. Even so, I knew that you would give us the service of your jeep," said Ki-ryong.

In-chol turned to look at Ki-ryong to see if his last remark was intended satirically. His expression, however, was as in-scrutable as ever. In the impassivity of his face and his mono-tonously level low voice, In-chol sensed, at least, a tinge of suppressed animosity. Strangely enough, however, he could not help feeling a strange closeness and warmth toward Ki-ryong.

"You told me that you wanted to look at the knife, didn't you?" said Ki-ryong in an unhurried tone. "But I don't think it's possible today. I will find a chance to show it to you an-other day. Maybe that day will come along quite soon. I might even be able to give the knife to you for keeps."

In-chol felt dumbfounded. How could Ki-ryong give away this knife which was like a symbol of faith for him and his whole family? Does Ki-ryong, too, have doubts about the world his father has built up, then? What is the connection between his attitude of a while ago and the pronouncement he just made? There seemed no way of guessing his inner thoughts.

Two trucks loaded with cargo was clattering away on the road ahead of them. Maybe because it had rained the day before, there was not much dust although the road was un-paved. Speeding up the jeep, however, In-chol passed over both the trucks.

"Where can I reach you in Seoul?" asked Ki-ryong.

In-chol told him the telephone number of his house.

Neither of them spoke again. The jeep went out onto the national highway. Just as he had guessed the other night when he had driven his brother In-ho, the road ran along a narrow gorge between two mountains where, now and then, one saw people offering rites at graves scattered across the mountain slopes. The valley area between these mountains were the rice and vegetable fields. Then suddenly, the vista seemed to widen and one saw houses in the middle of the fields. This was the town of Kyong-an. In-chol could see even at a remote glance that the place which was more like a large-size village than a town was too small and impover-ished to be qualified as the seat of a county office.

In-chol proceeded at a very low speed as soon as they crossed the borderline of the town. On their right side before the res-idential area began, In-chol could see the building of the county office. Looking at this building, In-chol thought to himself that maybe he had guessed wrong when he assumed that his brother was getting off from the jeep at a spot con-siderably distanced from his house. Maybe, it was possible that he was living somewhere near the county office, thought In-chol, because he would be living in the official residential quarters. Today, he must have gone to the grave of his mother with his family, thought In-chol, again. He felt a sudden impulse to tell Ki-ryong what had happened that fated day at his house starting from the incident of the petition about the ancestral cemetery Ki-ryong's father had brought to In-ho. Yet, he desisted from the temptation anticipating only more demonstration of impassivity on Ki-ryong's part.

They crossed a small bridge across a stream passing a cattle market on the left marked off with numerous stakes. Soon they saw a police station on the right. The clinic was right next to the police station.

Ki-ryong got off the jeep and went inside the clinic. He came back out in a short while following a fiftyish man with a semibald head carrying a 'doctor's visiting case.'

"You said the left side, right?" said the doctor as soon as he got on the jeep. "It's usual for that disease to disable a man on the left side and a woman on the right."

After a while of driving, the doctor spoke again,

"I don't like his falling into that deep sleep and snoring away, though....It's not a real sleep. It's a coma. And snoring is a bad symptom in that kind of illness."

The doctor took out a handkerchief from a pocket and wiped his smooth forehead over and over although there was no mark of perspiration on it.

Food was served at Pun-i's house upon In-chol's return from town. It was a tray layed out for two, Professor Chi and In-chol. Although In-chol had left home without eating break-fast, he did not have much appetite. He was only conscious of an empty stomach.

When he returned to the jeep, the doctor was already in it. He was sitting front beside the driver's seat. There were a number of village kids and also Ki-ryong standing among them.

In-chol started the engine. Then, the doctor who was again going through the exercise of wiping his unperspiring smooth forehead said to Ki-ryong,

"An absolute rest is the word. And use a very low pillow. I will see you then, day after tomorrow, when you will come to get the refill of the medicine."

Without moving from his place, Ki-ryong looked at In-chol. Silently, they said goodbye with their eyes. In-chol felt that a flicker of warmth passed across Ki-ryong's eyes. Yet his face remained impassive.

The jeep ran past the entrance of the village leaving the chasing band of children behind. For the first time since early morning, In-chol realized how tired he was. Leaning back against the back of his seat, therefore, he slowed the speed of the vehicle deciding to relax a bit.

"He will be all right, won't he, doctor?" asked Professor Chi from the back seat.

"I wouldn't say so," replied the doctor. "His blood pressure is above two hundred and twenty, you see. It's a wonder he survived the stroke at all."

"But he seemed so strong and healthy only such a short while ago. It's unbelievable that he could so suddenly...."

"You must never trust the strength of an old person. Rather it's the ones who ail often that don't fall so suddenly because they know how to look after themselves. Having too much confidence in one's own strength can be the cause of disaster quite often. Even if he comes out of this all right, it's likely that he won't be able to use the left side of his body. Since his speech nerves are affected, moreover, he will probably not be able to speak again. But this is a worry for later. Right now, the question is whether he will pull through alive. What amazes me, though, is that his mind is so sound in the midst of such a severe physical disorder. It's really striking."

Internally, In-chol was saying that it was only because his big-father had such a strong will to live. As if it were his incorrigible habit, the doctor again took out his handkerchief and went through the routine of wiping his forehead clean. And he said,

"Are you related to the family?"

"No. We came here on some business merely," said Professor Chi.

"Ah, is that so?" said the doctor. "And I thought maybe you were.... I happened to notice a pair of ox-horns on a wall of the patient's room and do you know what? There was a sharp-bladed knife stuck between his arm and the side. I don't know what kind of a ghost-chasing prescription it is but it was fearful to look at. Made my hair stand up, you know...."

Professor Chi remembered what he had heard from Pun-i's father, but he told the doctor neither the fact that it was a butcher's house that he had just visited nor that the knife was supposed to carry a special curative power.

In-chol on his part came to understand from the words of the doctor why it was that Ki-ryong had told him it was impossible to show him the knife today. At the same time as he became aware of this, a new surge of hate toward the old man welled up in his heart for some inexplicable reason.

"The old man in Pundinamutkol is my big-father," said In-chol driving the jeep back from the town where the doctor got off. "He does not know this himself."

In-chol's words were so easily spoken and so spontaneous. Professor Chi did not say anything. In-chol went on to tell him how Ki-ryong had promised to show him the knife on another occasion. He did not tell the professor, however, that his cousin had told him maybe he would give the knife to In-chol for good.

The jeep ran on along the road between the mountains, soundlessly.

CHAPTER THREE

Calculations

Having told Professor Chi the relationship between the old butcher of Pundinamutkol and himself, In-chol came to realize that it had not been an instantaneous urge to confess that had made him disclose it to the professor. Nor was it a result of a long-meditated plan either. Maybe it was a wish on In-chol's part to be freed from a suspicion that Professor Chi was in the knowledge of the secret of his family. Even if the professor did not know anything, it did not matter. What In-chol wanted was to get rid of the sense of oppression he felt because of his suspicion of what the professor might know.

His telling the professor in unequivocal terms how things stood might cause a serious change in In-chol's relationship with Professor Chi and Ta-hye, but at the moment, he was too beleaguered with his more imminently existential problems to worry about that aspect of his new position. He was only relieved and grateful that Professor Chi did not pretend to be surprised or try to console him. This equanimity of the older man effectively helped In-chol's own mind to calm down.

When the jeep was pulled to a stop at the mouth of the small alley leading to his house, Professor Chi said, getting off from the vehicle,

"Thank you for all your trouble, In-chol. Come to see us when you can spare the time."

Would I be able to visit him and Ta-hye at home just as I have done up to now, asked In-chol to himself. He did not know. What he did know at this moment was only that he was very tired and would be very glad if somebody else could do the driving for him.

Returning home, In-chol found a letter from Na-mi. When he read what was written in the letter, he chuckled despite his extreme fatigue. Na-mi's letter written briefly in a stationery sheet which looked larger because of the smallness of its content was as follows:

(Nero was an imbecile. From Nero's Old Friend Na-mi.)

What happened at the hotel in Haeundae could not be helped, not as far as In-chol himself was concerned. He could well understand, however, that his action must have appeared exceedingly bizarre to Na-mi. On the train coming back to Seoul, Na-mi had pretended to be dozing. Maybe I ended up inflicting an insufferable damage to her pride, of which she seemed so exceptionally particular, too. The only thing I can do at this point in her respect is to finish the house model as quickly as possible and hand it over to her.

He, therefore, spent every waking hour working on the model for days on end. He was glad that his head was clear in the morning after sleep. And it was a lucid and beautiful autumn weather everyday. In the morning, he went through a light warming-up movements in front of the window which he opened to change the air of the room. Along with the fresh outside atmosphere, the pleasant sounds of the birds from his brother's room next-door drifted in through the open window. On some mornings, he could see In-mun coming in through the outer gate carrying a large carton box against his side. Maybe he was on his way from the Samchong Park with his gathering of foodstuff for one or other animal-kind cohabiting with him. In-chol could see that the sneakers and the bottoms of his trouser legs were wet from the morning dew. The morning-glory that crept up the bark of the tree in the garden still bore blossoms although of a smaller-size than in the summer. The leaves, however, were turned to withered yellow-green now.

It was when he was almost finishing his work on the model that he received a call from Ta-hye. It was an invitation for dinner next day. About a week had passed since In-chol had been to the village of Pundinamutkol.

Something told In-chol to look up in the calendar. Just as he suspected, the next day was Ta-hye's lunar-calendar birthday. Many a time had he heard the maid of Professor Chi commenting what a propitious time the young mistress was born in when all kinds of grains and fruit ripened and the weather was neither cold nor warm. And how Ta-hye would live a comfortable life on that account.... And yet, every year, he made a rule of forgetting her birthday until he would get a half notice like today. In-chol thought about how Ta-hye had never forgot his own birthday even once and this remembrance made him feel guilty.

As always, it was a simple repast. Chon Kyong-hun was already there conversing with the professor in the latter's study when In-chol arrived carrying his gift of a birthday cake for Ta-hye.

Ta-hye came out of the Inner-Room wearing traditional-style house clothes which she was in the habit of wearing at this time of a year. Although she did not express her gladness on seeing him by words or other explicit forms of self-manifestation, In-chol was happy to be welcomed just by her wordless smile and the quiet grace of her manner. All at once, the tension that had been building up in his system because of uneasiness about confronting Ta-hye and others at this party dissolved and he found himself congratulating Ta-hye on having her birthday in a carefree joking tone, as usual,

"Congratulations on having your ears out!"

Two women peered out of the Inner-Room. To these also, In-chol offered greetings effortlessly. They were both married and were already mothers. In-chol even knew the fact that Ta-hye had played the wedding march for them at the ceremony.

There were no more guests for the birthday party. In-chol went and sat with Professor Chi and Chon Kyong-hun. In Professor Chi's attitude, there was nothing which appeared changed, but depending on how one looked at it, this constancy in the professor's attitude itself seemed to contain a seed for suspicion in it. An unshakable sense of crisis kept creeping back to In-chol's mind as he sat on in the company of the professor and Chon Kyong-hun.

Suddenly, In-chol noticed that Chon Kyong-hun was listening to the conversation from the Inner-Room with a strained expression on his face. In-chol, too, listened.

— I can now tell whether the baby's crying for milk or because he's not feeling well just by hearing him.

— I don't know why, but my milk becomes so scarce if I should feel depressed or restless. In any case, though, I wish I could wean the baby since he's already close to two years.

— Why can't you, then? You know, your ruination is your soft-heartedness. Just paste your nipples with quinine twice. It will cure him for good. He will never want to come near the breasts. There's nothing heartless about it as I repeatedly assured you. But then, you aren't me. You are the one who said yes to your man just because you'd had him stand in the cold for a couple of hours, waiting.

— Well, I just can't bring myself to put the bitter stuff on the nipples. What if my baby hates me for making him suffer?

Maybe the conversation was not one Ta-hye felt invited to participate in. In-chol could not hear her voice at all. He imagined her just sitting there by the side of her friends with her quiet graceful smile on her face....

Just then, one of the women laughed at a high pitch and said,

— What a fool you are! Aren't we all waiting to coach you

how to raise a kid? What on earth is your worry, you foolish girl?

Then, the other voice said,

— That's right! Why are you hesitating like this? Do you think your father'll live on garbage or something once you're married and gone?

After this, there was a sound of low giggling and mumbled whispering. Then, Ta-hye's voice said,

— Why is it that you girls always end up with that topic after each of your great family-talk sessions? I will leave you now. You two had better discuss your babies some more. I'll go and help bring in the food.

Ta-hye came out of the Inner-Room.

When the table was all laid out in the Inner-Room, In-chol went over along with Professor Chi and Chon Kyong-hun. The birthday dinner was formally started when the maid, who stayed to serve the soup, retreated after saying that since 'the young mistress' hand touched everything on the table, she was sure that the guests would be able to enjoy their dinner.

They all had a glass of wine before starting with the food which was remote from being lavish but elegantly prepared. In-chol noticed that there were croaker and liver *chon* (bite-size patties) which he liked.

After the dinner, they ate the cake In-chol brought, along with the fruit. Then, they all played the cards including even Professor Chi who sang his usual number 'O This Troublesome World' as a penalty when he lost repeatedly. Everybody laughed merrily at the professor's clumsy performance.

In-chol and Chon Kyong-hun stayed on talking with Professor Chi in his study after Ta-hye's two friends left on account of their babies. Then, In-chol, too, left with Chon Kyong-hun.

Walking alongside Chon Kyong-hun, In-chol felt as if he had just finished taking some difficult examination. He felt so exhausted, in fact, that in his dazedness he even forgot

Chon Kyong-hun's presence by his side.

"Do you know what it's like to keep on waiting?" said Chon Kyong-hun suddenly.

In-chol turned to look at Chon Kyong-hun whose thick-lensed glasses were glimmering in the light leaking out of some window.

Without saying anything more on the theme of 'waiting,' Chon Kyong-hun left In-chol when the two walked out of the winding alleyway. To In-chol's eye, Chon Kyong-hun who had left him without even bidding him a farewell properly seemed to be suffering from some inner turbulence. Maybe there's no one in this world who doesn't have a private agony, said In-chol to himself, as he started walking in a direction opposite from Chon Kyong-hun. Then he realized that he could guess the cause of Chon Kyong-hun's distraction. Realizing it, he nodded his head a couple of times in the deepening dusk of the street. So that's why he looked so tense and uncomfortable today, said In-chol inwardly. When they were playing the cards after the dinner, Chon Kyong-hun who had sat next to Ta-hye had made others laugh by making such blunders as picking two or three cards from Ta-hye's hand instead of one. So that was why! In-chol repeated, nodding his head once more.

Next day, he received a call from Ta-hye who wanted him to meet her at a teahouse nearby. In-chol was surprised because it was very rare that Ta-hye called him out to a meeting place in town. They had met only yesterday, moreover, and In-chol knew only too well how particular Ta-hye was about giving one enough time before suggesting a date for a concert or a movie or an invitation to her house. It must be something to do with Chon Kyong-hun, decided In-chol by instinct.

Ta-hye was there before him. In-chol thought that her lightly touched-up face looked somewhat emaciated.

"What's up? Why have I been summoned before Her Majesty?" said In-chol jokingly, knowing already, however, why he had been summoned by Ta-hye.

"Please forgive me for troubling Your Excellency like this," said Ta-hye smiling and pretending to bow deferentially.

In-chol waited for her to speak the word, but until their tea was brought to the table, Ta-hye kept her silence.

"What's the problem, Ta-hye?" said In-chol finally feeling that maybe she found it difficult to broach whatever it was she had meant to discuss with In-chol.

"Why? Do I have to have a problem to see you?" asked back Ta-hye.

"Speak, Ta-hye."

"Really, I have nothing so special to talk about. It's been a long time since I've been to this sort of a place...and...I felt like walking the street a bit...."

Since he had been so certain that Ta-hye would talk about Chon Kyong-hun, In-chol found himself slightly unsettled by the words Ta-hye was saying now. Maybe he had over-stretched his imagination just because of the abrupt question Chon Kyong-hun had put to him that night after Ta-hye's birthday party....

As soon as they finished their tea, Ta-hye got up from the seat saying she found the music in the teahouse too noisy. Outside on the street, Ta-hye said, poking her both hands (she hadn't even taken her handbag) into her coat pockets,

"Let's go see a movie."

"A movie? I don't think there's a good one showing, though."

"Doesn't matter. Let's just go to a place where they have comfortable seats."

This was indeed strange of Ta-hye who made a point of making sure that a movie or a play she was going would be a good one.

"This is a real surprise. Maybe you ate your birthday soup from the wrong side of the bowl?"

"What's surprising about my wanting to go to see a movie? If you want to know the truth, though, I feel like going to a movie 'house' rather than to 'see' a movie."

Ta-hye stopped In-chol as he started calling a taxi. They walked from Chongno to Pil-dong. What they saw was an American comedy which was mostly a lot of noise and bustling about. Even so, Ta-hye commented favorably on it, walking out of the movie house,

"This is better than ones that are overserious about nothing. Your mind lets up, at least, while you are watching this kind of a thing."

In-chol felt that Ta-hye was, to say the least, speaking and acting in a way that was very unlike her today. On their way back from the movie house, also, Ta-hye suggested walking, and they walked up the Ulchiro 3-ga and Chongno 3-ga to come out in front of Tonhwamun where they turned right to stroll along the long stone wall of the Changgyong Palace. Reddish-brown blemishes were noticeable on the drooping leaves of platanus which rustled dryily in the autumn breeze. In-chol was so absorbed in some inner thought that he did not know that Ta-hye had turned her head toward him and was looking into his face.

"What is it you are thinking?" asked Ta-hye.

"What?"

"I asked what are you thinking?"

"Oh, the trees...."

"The trees?"

"I am thinking that these trees would look far better after they've shed all their leaves."

"That's a child's thought!"

Yet, it was not really what was occupying In-chol's mind. He was thinking about the glossy-green leaves of the platanus trees that had been fallen flat on the wet blackness of the asphalt that he had seen some short lifetime ago. And he was thinking about the marks of the ox hooves that he had seen on the platanus leaves covering the steps of the never-ending staircase he had kept on descending in one of his nightmarish dreams.... As he kept moving forward at a slow pace, In-chol saw between the trees his own elongated shadows that deflected toward the stone wall at the upper end, the torso shortened while the lower part comically stretched out. Ta-hye's shadows which were somewhat shorter kept alongside his. Since he was wearing rubber-soled comfortable shoes, he did not make much sound on the pavement while Ta-hye's high heels clicked against the hard surface underneath with a pleasant regularity. For a second, In-chol was overcome by an illusion that ugly footmarks printed by the rubber soles of his shoes were being tugged on forward by his elongated shadows that seemed quite absorbed in the task of pulling the sinister footmarks after them.

"Really, what is it you're thinking of? Your work? Dissertation? By the way, have you finished the plans for Na-mi-*ssi*'s new house?"

"They are in the middle of the construction work now."

"I would like to take a look at it. You think I can do so when it's all done?"

"I guess...."

In-chol was expecting Ta-hye to bring out the topic of Na-mi, but Ta-hye only asked him about her new house and then stopped. There was no question about the fact that Ta-hye was not her usual self today.

As soon as they turned the corner of the stone wall at the Wonnam-dong crossroad, the deep shade thrown by the stone wall of the Changgyong Palace engulfed their two shadows so that now In-chol could not see any trace of them. When they reached the Myongnyun-dong juncture, Ta-hye said glancing at her wristwatch,

"It's time for the piano lessons. I must go."

They got off the bus at Anguk-dong. As they were saying goodbye, Ta-hye said, smiling her saddish quiet smile,

"Meet me again tomorrow, the same teahouse, at ten thirty...."

Coming home, In-chol felt how it had become different with Ta-hye since the revelation of his new identity just as with Professor Chi. True, the professor had treated In-chol

in the same way as he had during all their years of acquaintance on the day of Ta-hye's birthday celebration, and he
somehow knew that Professor Chi would not have told Ta-
hye about his new knowledge. So, what it came down to
was his own sense of the awkwardness of the situation he was
thrown in. He found himself resisting the sweet comfortable
solace of Ta-hye's older-sisterly affection and concern for him
which he had relished in the bygone days. He felt profoundly
fatigued. Maybe I won't meet her tomorrow, he said to
himself.

Yet he met her the next day at the teahouse they had met
the day before, at the hour she gave....

For three days on end, they met, had tea, or even lunch
together. And afterwards, he walked back home.

During these rendezvous, Ta-hye often reminisced about
their common childhood. As if she had all this time lived in
the memory of the things she now reminisced, she talked
about them just as if they had happened yesterday. She went
over the time In-chol had fainted frcm anemia and had to lie
down in the school infirmary. She said that she had envied
him for it and wished she would also have an anemia and lie
in a bed of the infirmary. Yet, she said, seeing In-chol walking home lamely with one of his school friends carrying his
satchel for him, she had changed her mind about getting sick
so she could lie in the white-sheeted infirmary bed. Some of
the things she talked about had nearly faded out of In-chol's
memory. For instance, Ta-hye reminisced about the time
when In-chol had handed in a picture he had drawn but
which the teacher had torn off saying somebody must have
drawn it for him. In-chol, moreover, had to stand at the back
of the classroom as a punishment for cheating. Then, there
was that incident at the school athletic meet when In-chol
kept falling on the ground during a two-persons-three-legs
race because he had been teamed up with one whose pace
he could not keep up with. In the end, the teammate had
dragged him on by force just as he was lying prostrate on the

ground so that for many days afterward he had to limp to and from school. Ta-hye described such details as the season, weather, or some other circumstantial characteristics related with the occurrence of these events. Even while these childhood recollections went on, however, In-chol could not relax or enjoy going over various events of yore with Ta-hye the way he used to.

On the fourth day of their meeting, Ta-hye said she had to return home early because she had lessons to give to her pupils from earlier hours today. From the teahouse, therefore, she started back home. As they walked together in the direction of her neighborhood, she said,

"It's all right now. I don't have to roam about any longer."

After a few paces, she said again,

"I will confess everything. The first time I told you to meet me at that teahouse, you see, I had just met Mr. Chon at the teahouse next-door."

Here she sighed as if in relief that she had told In-chol this much. Then, she continued,

"There was a note inside the package of stockings which he had given me for my birthday. It was a message for me to come out to that teahouse next day. I couldn't not oblige, so I went out. I half knew, though, why it was that he wanted to see me.... He started out in a roundabout way with the story of Queen Sondok and Chi-gwi. You know the story, don't you? How a low-class person fell in love with the queen and so on.... I thought that it was quite childish of him to go about it in that way, but it wasn't as if I couldn't understand why.... When would he have had a chance to talk intimately with a woman? Probably never.... And he...must have thought a good deal about it until he came out with the idea of that fable, I suppose...."

In-chol, too, knew about the queen and the man Chi-gwi, He had heard it from a teacher at the high school. A man of a lowly origin fell so madly in love with Queen Sondok that he came to the brink of insanity, roaming about the town covered with dirt and rags. One day, the queen went to worship the Buddha at a temple and chanced to hear about this wretched roamer. She told her men to find him and bring him to her. In the meantime, however, Chi-gwi who had stationed himself outside the temple wall to meet the queen as she came out of the temple to return to her palace had fallen asleep on the ground next to the wall. When he woke up, the queen had already gone, but he found her bracelet placed on his chest. He was so grieved and maddened by the loss of the cherished opportunity that he caught fire from the flame in his own heart and burnt not only himself but the tower standing nearby.

In-chol thought about Chon Kyong-hun's out-of-the-blue remark on the theme of 'waiting' on the night of the birthday party and laughed out to himself. I had guessed right, after all, he said to himself, and then, still laughing, he said,

"So you see a literature person is different even in proposing to a lady. He knows how to go about the business in a literary, metaphorical way."

"Don't be so flippant. But in any case, I am relieved now. I didn't act like Queen Sondok. Actually, it was quite simple because I have no wish to marry yet. Maybe I have good enough reasons for not wanting to, or maybe I don't. It's all rather unclear to me, I guess.... The reason I was somewhat disconcerted by Mr. Chon's gesture was that he is one my father has so much trust in. It was difficult for me to be rude to him...and besides...I had a feeling that my father wanted me to accept his proposal. I don't know; maybe, I was over-imaginative in that respective. Anyway, it's all ended now. Everything's a matter of the past. Goodbye, then. Come to see us soon, all right?"

Looking at Ta-hye from the back as she disappeared into her alley nearly trotting, In-chol felt a weight lifting from his heart. Ta-hye turned back for a second and with a move of her chin signaled him to go. In-chol answered by nodding his head but kept on watching her disappear, lighting a cigarette.

After having spent a number of days on end in that way, In-chol found himself unable to concentrate on his work after getting back home early on Saturday from meeting Ta-hye. He decided to take an outing to the site of the construction.

The bricklaying was half done on the first floor, and, on the whole, one could now have a general outline of the building to be erected. In-chol inspected the work, taking a round of the construction site and thinking that the house model was being too late in coming compared with the progress of the construction work. I must hurry up, he said to himself.

After receiving that odd letter from Na-mi on the Full Moon Day, he had not had any contact with her, not even by phone. As long as he was not inclined to explain his action of that night in Haeundae, he felt it bootless to try to make an apology or excuse to her. He had, therefore, not answered her letter either by phone or letter. His intention was to get in touch with her when the house model would be finished.

He thought he would drop by a friend's house in Chang-shin-dong as long as he was in its vicinity. This was a man who was now working for the government as an architect at the Urban Development Department of the City Hall. He was one of those with whom In-chol had played the billiard on the eve of the Full Moon Day. In-chol's plan was to maybe have a game or two of billiard and then go on to a tavern with this friend so that he could put a befitting end to his days of roaming and go back to his work starting from tomorrow.

Walking all the way through the Changchungdan area and then the Ulchiro 6-ga, he arrived in front of the Seoul Stadium. A little way past the front gate of the Stadium, he saw a crowd gathered around something. Looking in, he saw that it was a snake merchant in the midst of advertising the medicinal value of his merchandise. Suddenly, In-chol caught sight of his brother In-mun who was trying to push in through the throng of bystanders to get at the inner ring. In-chol, too, pushed between the spectators to get close to In-mun. The merchant was now holding two large snakes entwined one on each arm while his throat bulged at the force of his shouting,

"....Let me, ladies and gentlemen, show you how venomous the snake bites can be. Briefly, their venom can kill five men within two and a half seconds. Why five men in two and half seconds, you rascal, my spectators may ask me. Why not ten men in five seconds, isn't it simpler to put it that way? Yes, except, my dear ladies and gentlemen, that my snakes pour out all the venoms they have in the span of two and half seconds after which they have no more venom left. And this is why, with your permission, my ladies and gentlemen...."

In-chol glanced at the profile of his brother who was still five to six people away from him.

"Our next topic is, what do you do when you are bitten by one of these venomous snakes? Cut your arm off if one bites you on the arm, your leg off if one bites you in the leg, and chop your head off if one should think of giving you a bite on the throat? But that would be unspeakably foolish, would it not?"

Why has In-mun come to this part of the town, wondered In-chol. Has he come all the way here because of this? Does he now concern himself with the snakes, as well, in addition to his birds, toads, and fish? But the snake man, who issued some imitation snake sounds from his twisted lips, interrupted In-chol in his wondering,

"So then, what snakes are the most venomous in the world? That Africa comes out first in this, I can't deny. But which is the country with the next most venomous snakes? It's our country, Korea! What I mean is we rank the second in the worldwide contest of venomous snakes. You may be proud of this all you like, I assure you...." Again, he imitated the snake hissing a couple of times, and then shouted once more,

"I will show you something now. In this here box, I have

all kinds of snakes. Some have wings, some have two heads, some have three tails, some dance to my whistling, and so on. But, before I go on and show them to you, I want to make sure about one thing. I want you now to look at this fellow here...."

And he held up the snake on one arm.

"This is a very curious snake, indeed.... To begin with, he has two cocks. How on earth do you know that, rascal, even if you are snakes' cousin, my reverend spectators may ask me. Whoever asks me this question is a quick-tempered customer! He is one who is in danger of pissing on the back of a matchmaker, as they say. What I just told you is not something I found out by myself but a revelation unearthed at the end of twenty years' investigation by the renowned scholar Dr. Tanaka of Japan. People have eaten this fellow and have found that they gained prowess from eating him but they haven't known why.... Not until our Dr. Tanaka discovered the reason why.... Let me say something more about how Dr. Tanaka's achievement...."

Seeing In-mun pushing his way back out of the crowd, In-chol followed his suit. Even when In-chol caught up with him, however, In-mun did not show surprise. Merely, he muttered in a voice filled with quiet anger,

"What a fraud!"

"Of course, he is a fraud. That's why he is called a *yakchangsu* (peddler of drug, also meaning a talkative liar)."

"You watched, too?"

"Yes, only because I saw you watch."

"It's a total lie that our snakes are the second most venomous in the world. Salmusa which is the most venomous of our snakes is still nothing compared with the Indian cobra or the Taiwanese Hav."

Parting from his brother in front of the Tongdaemun, In-chol walked toward Changshin-dong.

When he got there, however, he discovered that his friend whom In-chol had counted on finding at home it being Sunday had gone out. In his room at the boardinghouse, In-chol found, instead of his friend, a girl who looked out through the open sliding door and told him his friend had gone out at an early hour. The girl looked young enough to have just graduated from a middle school. It was evident, however, that she could not be a sister or a relative. In-chol was aware that his friend played around with women, but now he seemed to be bringing in girls who were barely past their childhood into his room at the boardinghouse. The girl was looking up at the sky with a bored face. It was a clear bright day. Maybe she was discontented that she had to stay put in a hole of a room on a nice day like this. Explaining to her that he had just come by, without any special business, In-chol left.

Next morning, In-chol stood in front of his open window going through warming-up movements as usual. Just as on other mornings lately, he saw In-mun coming in through the gate with the usual carton box against his side. Suddenly, a thought rushed to In-chol's mind and he hurriedly went out of his room to waylay his brother.

"What is in that box, In-mun?" asked In-chol when the latter came up the stairs.

In-mun did not answer.

"It's a snake, isn't it?"

In-mun nodded reluctantly.

"Why do you come in and out of the house with that every morning?"

"I let him loose him in the grass in the mountain at the back so he can suck in the dews."

The memory of the toad squatting in the rain outside his window coming back in a flash, In-chol was alarmed that maybe some morning he would find this creature squeaming about in the house. So he said,

"What's your idea? You can't keep that kind of a thing inside a people's house."

"He won't harm people."

"No matter whether or not he harms anybody, how can one live in the same house with a snake. Throw him away at once."

With a deep discontent on his face, In-mun kept silent. Then, after standing a few seconds in the same spot, he turned and stomped into his room. Ever since this incident, In-chol never saw In-mun again with the carton box against his side.

"Am I in your way?"

It was In-ju who came in with a knock on the door. It was sometime after their common supper. In-chol was touching up his house model which was almost at the last stage of completion now.

"Whose house is it? Is it Na-mi *onni*'s?" In-ju asked.

"How could you guess?"

"From the way it looks...."

This was the first time In-ju ever visited him after that day when she had left her diary on his desk. In-chol had seen her downstairs when he went down to wash himself or to eat meals, but he had the impression that she was feeling gloomy and not up to talking. So he had left her alone.

"Have you been out?" he asked seeing that In-ju was wearing a suit.

"No."

"Oh, then, is the princess contemplating an outing at this hour?" He said in a mock joking tone.

"No, again. I just felt like visiting my brother. With a request."

"Oh, yes? Why, this is an honor. So what's the pleasure of the lady in full dressing?"

"You are teasing me, again. Still, I would truly like you to treat me as a lady in earnest. I need it, at least tonight. All right?" said In-ju going over to the radio. She switched it on and turned the tuner until one heard a sweet dance melody.

"Teach me how to dance, *obba*," said In-ju and then, looking into In-chol's eyes for a second or two, added, "I have learned the basic steps from a friend. But I am told I mustn't dance with a woman leading. So I want you to teach me."

"I am not very good at it, either, you know."

"That's not true. I saw you dance last Christmas time," said In-ju.

On Christmas Eve last year, a group of friends had gathered in In-chol's room with partners and on that occasion the friend at the Urban Planning Department of the City Hall had insisted on teaching In-ju how to dance. But In-ju had been adamant in her refusal. Why, then, does she want so suddenly to learn to dance? In-chol could not help wondering.

"Why this urge for lessons in western dance all of a sudden?"

"Well, if you really want to know, this is not all I have suddenly taken interest in. I am also taking lessons in Korean classical dance. I need it all, for the stage. You understand, *obba*, don't you?"

"Why should I? You hardly give away any secrets to me these days...."

"How can you say that? I haven't kept any secret from you, *obba*. Am I not confiding in you, even now? But, hurry, hurry, before that music ends...." In-ju said a little breathlessly snatching a towel from the peg on the wall for In-chol to wipe his hands with.

"And put on your jacket, won't you? You must dress up when you dance. Not that this suit I am wearing is suitable for the occasion, but it will do in our country as yet...."

The music from the radio continued. To In-chol's surprise, In-ju's steps were already good enough, precise and smooth.

"You are quite good, you know. Perhaps, you might relax your posture a little bit more. And don't look down at your feet. Don't mind making mistakes."

Now the radio was sending out tango music.

"What's the matter with them? They are giving us dance music one after another! Did you make an arrangement with the radio station or something?"

"Don't tease me so, *obba*. They are supposed to be giving this sort of music today. This is something they are doing as a special program. I knew about it beforehand and have been waiting for this hour," said In-ju.

Something seemed to be wrong at the station. The tango music stopped now and then, although each time it was resumed in a second or two.

"What type dancing are you fond of, *obba*?" asked In-ju.

"I don't know.... I don't dislike waltz, though," said In-chol.

"Me, too, although I can't say I know much about waltz yet. I would love to be able to do what they call skating-waltz someday! How lovely it would be.... I picture people dancing to the waltz music of Johann Strauss in a royal ball-room abright with lights from the sparkling chandeliers.... Do you see what I mean, *obba*?"

It was the turn for lesson in blues, now. In-chol taught his sister how to move her feet in quiet graceful steps.

"You know, *obba*. I've found out that everything depends on how much you are determined to do something," said In-ju, and then, as if sensing In-chol's failure to catch what she exactly meant by this, she continued, "You read my notes the other night, didn't you? I complained that Mr. Nam treats me like a baby. But I have decided not to mind it. What's more, I've decided to act like a baby in my relationship with him. This lightened my mind a lot."

"I see our tadpole's got a leg now," said In-chol smiling.

"You're teasing me, again, *obba*. You mustn't underestimate me, though. I am more experienced than I look."

"Aha, I see you're getting back to being a tadpole!" said In-chol teasing again.

Just at this moment, however, In-ju seemed to take a sudden fright at something, her eyes fixed at a point. In-chol looked where her eyes were staring, just to catch the door of his room which somebody had apparently opened ajar closing soundlessly.

"She was peeping in with just one eye!" said In-ju after listening to the inaudible footsteps going down the staircase with a frightened face. "You know she peeps into my room so often these days without any apparent reason? And she looks at my face with strangest expressions on her face. I don't like it at all.... I like it not a bit!" said In-ju in an excited unsteady voice and then shaking her body once as if involuntarily she walked over to an armchair and threw herself down on it covering her face with both hands.

Madam Hong, who had in the meantime reached the bottom of the staircase, muttered bitterly: How unthinkable! How absolutely monstrous! What she had unknowingly feared for many days in the past had, just now, finally materialized before her eyes in a tangible identifiable form. What unthinkable thing are they plotting, what despicable sin are they going to commit? Madam Hong muttered again.

When In-ju was brought into the house after the death of her real mother, Madam Hong had been saddened and disturbed although on the surface she pretended equanimity. Yet, as she grew into a young woman, In-ju never once gave trouble to either Madam Hong or any other member of the family, thus giving Madam Hong's unsettled heart time and motive to calm down. Even so, she had not forgotten her original fear that In-ju carried a seed of evil by having been born out of an unsanctioned and unblessed relationship.

Madam Hong's serious worry over In-ju, however, began this year when the girl who had always been punctual in her hours of leaving the house and returning upset the custom by staying out until any late hour and going out nearly everyday even during the vacation time. Seeing this, Madam Hong had lamented to herself that the girl was beginning to show her origin. Then, tonight, she saw with her own eyes that this mistaken fruit of an unlawful relationship was dancing that whore's dance from the West clinging to In-chol who was her own brother! A *kisaeng*'s daughter she was; who can predict what she will or won't do to In-chol? If it had been some other girl, said Madam Hong to herself, I would not have minded it half so much even if she were up there seducing my son. But she was his sister if from another mother. Madam Hong was deeply, inconsolably worried.

Coming back to her room, Madam Hong knelt down in front of the wall with Jesus Christ's pictures tacked up on it. The pictures showed Christ's life from the time of his birth in the stable through to his crucifixion. She perused them one after another trying to calm herself down. Then, feeling her mind somewhat at rest, she put her both hands on the bible which was lying squarely on one side of her bed and brought her forehead down on the folded hands. Then she began to pray: Lord, what should I do? Please teach this foolish woman slave what she should do about this. Lord, help me save those children from the road of sin. Help me lead them to Your altar, O Lord....

Even after offering this prayer, however, Madam Hong's mind was not as peaceful as she would have wished it to be.

Then, Madam Hong remembered a woman by the name of Ko who was going to the same church as she. The more she thought about this woman friend, the more she became envious of her because this blessed woman had every member of her family attending the church. What was even more enviable than this perhaps was that she was living all by myself without worry or trivial daily problems. She was living alone comfortably on what her son who was at some branch office of a business company was sending her each month. Maybe I will go to her house and forget my worry in a holy conversation with her, said Madam Hong in her mind.

She changed her clothes, and with the bible and the book of psalms tucked under one arm, left home telling the maid that she would spend the night at the house of Madam Ko. Being used to seeing her mistress go off to the mountain prayer-house to stay for several days at a stretch, the maid did not seem to find anything amiss in Madam Hong's action.

When Madam Hong got to her friend's house, Madam Ko was studying the bible with her glasses on. Seeing Madam Hong come in, she got up hurriedly, exclaiming,

"Come in, come in. But what made you visit this widow woman at this late hour?"

Madam Hong sat down on the *ondol* floor and bowing her head half way down, prayed for a couple of minutes. Then she announced to Madam Ko,

"I would like to spend the night here, talking about our Lord with you, Younger Sister." After a half second's pause she continued, "I envy you for all this peace you are enjoying. Even my mind becomes peaceful at your house."

"But in faith, I could never be your equal, Older Sistr," said Madam Ko, to Madam Hong who, however, did not seem in the mood to thank or return the compliment. Instead, she said,

"Won't you, Younger Sister, go for the mountain-prayer with me tomorrow?"

There was a note of entreatment in Madam Hong's voice.

"Well...," said the other woman. "I would love to go, but...I feel I had better be around tomorrow...."

"Why? Are your children coming up from Pusan?"

"No, that's not it. I am just waiting to hear from my son. I thought he would call today but he didn't. So I think he will call tomorrow for certain."

"Is anybody sick in the family?"

"Oh, no! I am waiting to hear the news of my daughter-in-law having a baby."

"Didn't she have her delivery only this spring?" asked Madam Hong in a somewhat perturbed voice. "Is she really with another baby?"

"It's just that I saw my husband night before last. I saw him in my dream when my oldest grandchild was conceived and again he appeared in my dream when my daughter-in-law was having her second. Strangely, he didn't appear when they were getting the girl. I mean their second child.

So, this time, it will be a boy, again, don't you think? I was so sure that I would hear from them today. . . ."

"What a wonderful thing it is that your dreams have such a power. . . . It all comes from all of your family being such good believers. . . ."

"But I, too, have my worry, Big Sister."

"Do you, really? What is it?"

"It says here—and that's why I've had the bible on my lap when you came in—in the Sixteenth to Seventeenth Paragraphs of the Fourth Chapter of the Book Two of the Tessalonians," said Madam Ko putting her glasses back on and picking up the bible from the floor again while Madam Hong, too, opened her own bible which was identical in size, and in that it had the same leather cover, except that hers had more worn look. '. . . There will be the shout of command, the archangel's voice, the sound of God's trumpet, and the Lord himself will come down from heaven. Those who have died believing in Christ will rise to life first; then we who are living at that time will be gathered up along with them in the clouds to meet the Lord in the air.' Taking off her glasses after the recitation, Madam Ko said,

"Here lies my worry. As you know my husband died a believer, so there's no question about his revival. But because he died at thirty seven of age, he will be a young man—and that's how he appears in my dreams, too—while I will be an old woman full of wrinkles when I should be able to meet him in paradise after death. That's my worry. Do you see what I mean, Big Sister?"

"Yes, but there's no need for you to worry at all. I will show you why," said Madam Hong flipping the pages of her Good Book and finding the place. "I will read from Paragraph Fifteen. . ., no, from Paragraph Eighteen of the Twelfth Chapter of Mark: Then some Sadducees, who say that people will not rise from death, came to Jesus and said, 'Teacher, Moses wrote this law for us: If a man dies and leaves a wife but no children, that man's brother must marry the widow so that they can have children who will be considered the dead man's children. Once there were seven brothers; the eldest got married and died without having children. Then the second one married the woman, and he also died without having children. The same thing happened to the third brother, and then to the rest: all seven brothers married the woman and died without having children. Last of all, the woman died. Now, when all the dead rise to life on the day of resurrection, whose wife will she be? All seven of them had married her.' Jesus answered them, 'How wrong you are! And do you know why? It is because you don't know the Scriptures or God's power. For when the dead rise to life, they will be like the angels in heaven and will not marry....'"

When she finished reading from the bible, Madam Hong raised her eyes from the Book and gazed into the eyes of Madam Ko who responded to the other's meaningful look by saying,

"I don't really think that there will be any marriages up there, but wouldn't we at least know each other?"

"I wonder...." said Madam Hong rather uncertainly thinking in her mind how far her own worries were from those of Madam Ko.

Not only her husband, with whom she had been living like with a stranger ever since the birth of In-mun, but also each one of her children was a non-churchgoer. For this reason, she wished that there would only be resurrection for all of them regardless of husband-wife or parent-child reunion in heaven.

Madam Hong's husband had, in the meantime, come home. He changed clothes in his room downstairs and ate the supper brought in by the maid. He did not ask after his wife, and the maid, too, did not offer any information about her mistress' whereabouts. This was how things had gone on for quite some time now between the couple. For the husband, the business came before his wife. His mind was occupied by

the thought that he had to, somehow, pull through the
financial crisis he was in at the moment.

He ate his supper slowly sunken in thought.

According to the report of his Business Manager which he
heard over a drink this evening, all companies in the milling
industry went bankrupt except the Samhwa Milling Company. Samhwa was the only company with a milling factory
that was bigger in scale than the one run by the Taeryuksangsa of which Kim Sang-jin was the head.

Milling industry had been booming for several years on
end and Kim Sang-jin, too, had amassed quite a little fortune
from a milling company he owned. To start with, he had
been able to get an ICA loan for the initial facilitation of the
factory. Since, there was a significant difference between the
official exchange rate of the American dollar and the market
rate, it may be said that Kim Sang-jin's milling business was a
success even from the very beginning. Of course, he had to
donate some of the money to a certain political party and
spend some on a few other public relations activities. Yet, even
after all these expenses were counted out, the business was
definitely a great profit. Kim Sang-jin made some more profit
when he could buy in the relief wheat from America at the
official price which he sold back in part at the much higher
market price instead of turning all the wheat into flour.
Tempted by the prospect of a quick success, others began to
try their hands at the milling business: factories of varying
scales went up. This did not take prosperity out of Kim Sang-
jin's business as a whole, however. Then, last spring, a large
amount of flour came in from America as part of the country's
surplus agricultural products. This flour was sold at a price
lower than that of the Korean product. At first, those in
milling business had thought that this was a temporary
phenomenon which would go away in a couple of months.
Yet, the crisis prolonged for one and half a year and was still
not over. Those in the business were blaming the government
for intentionally ruining them. Yet the government did not

take any actions to alleviate the tension. Factories closed
down one after another. Kim Sang-jin predicted a continuation of the state for another stretch of period.

"They are working just as usual at Samhwa. They haven't
even shortened the hours," the Business Manager had said
while they were drinking together this evening along with
other company staff members. Kim Sang-jin knew that what
the man wanted to say was: What about us?

Tonight, they had asked for a corner room where they could
talk business without hindrance. For this same reason, they
had not even had a waiting woman serve in the room.

"We will make our hours as short as we can. No need to
pay attention to what others do," Kim Sang-jin had said.

Kim Sang-jin had another plan inwardly. He wanted to
turn the present crisis to his advantage. By now, all the
milling factories except that of Samhwa were closed. Kim
Sang-jin wanted to wait out until his last competitor would
topple over.

"Sir,..." said the Accounting Manager hesitantly.

"What is it you want?" said Kim Sang-jin bluntly without
waiting for the other to speak further. "You want to speak to
me about the affairs with the bank?"

"Yes."

"I will go and speak with them in a couple of days."

It was more than two months ago that they were due to
pay back the loan they had taken out at the bank when
building the factory.

"I will go and get an extension on the loan. And I will
take out some more loan," said Kim Sang-jin in a confident
tone.

Leaving the staff members behind in the room, Kim Sang-
jin got up to leave. He put on his shoes and took his hat from
someone who was standing in the doorway with others to see
him off. Then, his eyes spotted the Program Manager among
the group. He was a thin man with a short haircut who was
the youngest of Kim Sang-jin's staff. Answering the boss'

beckoning, the young staff member took a step closer to Kim Sang-jin, looking mildly inquisitive.

"What happened to the matter of the antique that I asked you to see about the other day?" Kim Sang-jin asked.

"I finished the investigation."

"Let's go and take a look right away."

"But, but the store must be closed now."

"Impossible. I just want to take a short look. Come on."

Kim Sang-jin told his chauffeur to drive the car to Myong-dong.

"But the store's in Insa-dong, Mr. President," said the Program Manager, surprised.

"I know. Just make sure that it's a genuine Lee Dynasty white porcelain. And lower the price as much as you can before you purchase it. I have no time for such details."

"I understand, sir," said the Program Officer hurriedly although his face showed obvious puzzlement. "I have had a professional appraiser vouch for it. All that's remaining to be done is settling the price."

"Okay. Get it ready by tomorrow," said Kim Sang-jin stopping the car near Midopa. Then handing his chauffeur some bills, he told the latter to get two bottles of whiskey at the shop across the street.

"And now," said Kim Sang-jin without turning his head when the chauffeur was safely out of hearing distance. "Tell me. How has the other matter gone?"

Only then did the younger man know what it was that the president had taken him out of the group of his colleagues at this hour for.

The 'other matter' his superior referred to concerned the Samhwa Business Corporation that was the sole survivor of the holocaust that befell milling businesses lately. The obsession that this powerful combatant ought to be gotten rid of before the general depression would be over possessed Kim Sang-jin body and soul. With this goal in his heart, Kim Sang-jin had given a secret commission to the Program

Manager to check up on his adversary. That is, he wanted
his young officer to find out whether there were any illegal
dealings between Samhwa and the revenue office such as tax
evasion or bribery.

"As I reported before, the amount of tax money they
evaded runs extremely high. Their records at the Revenue
Office are in a terrible shape. But this doesn't quite solve our
problem."

"How so?" asked Kim Sang-jin almost angrily.

"The trouble is Mr. Lee at the Revenue Office. If we
expose Samhwa's dirty play this time, we will incriminate
Mr. Lee also. That's how things stand."

This was indeed a trouble. Mr. Lee was close with Kim
Sang-jin and had helped the latter on a number of occasions.
Kim Sang-jin could not well betray him. Up to now, however, he had not suspected that Lee had anything to do with
the Samhwa people, as well.

Without any outward comment on the issue of Mr. Lee,
however, Kim Sang-jin took out a check from the inside
pocket and handing it to the younger man said,

"Split this in any way you think right and distribute the
sums around. Imply to them that there will be more."

Their eyes met for a second while the check was handed
over from one man to the other. The younger man thought
he saw a cold glint in his boss' wine-reddened pupils.

The chauffeur returned.

Letting off his young staff member in front of the drinking
house which they had left together earlier, Kim Sang-jin rode
on back home. It was a case of fighting for survival. One could
not afford a friendship at such a time.

After finishing his supper, Kim Sang-jin poked at his teeth
with a toothpick as was his habit and went on to his next
routine of reading the evening paper. Just then, however, he
noticed a letter addressed to him which had been put alongside the paper. He turned over the envelope. Recognizing
who it was from, he broke open the envelope hurriedly and

started to read. The letter which had been registered was long, written in many sheets. It took Kim Sang-jin quite a while to finish the letter. In some places, he read over the same passage once or twice. When he was through with reading the letter, he sat looking vacantly into the air with the letter sheets still held in one hand.

Finally, he got up and going to one wall pushed the bell botton attached to it.

"Is In-chol upstairs?" He asked the maid who answered the bell.

"Yes."

"Tell him to come down here," Kim Sang-jin said, and then changing his mind before the maid finished closing the door after her, he said,

"No, you'd better tell him I want to see him at the *ung-jopshil.*"

CHAPTER FOUR

The Other

When In-chol opened the door to the *ungjopshil,* he found his father standing in front of the picture hanging on one wall. It was a landscape done by Yun Tu-so, a leading artist of the mid-Choson period. In-chol knew that his father had a hobby in antiques such as old porcelain, calligraphy, or painting. Although he was always a busy man, he found time to collect and appreciate these things for which In-chol respected his father. The picture in front of which his father was now standing showing his back to In-chol was an especially expensive piece of art work. Yun Tu-so whose work it was had been grandson to the famous Choson-dynasty poet Yun Son-do whose works In-chol himself had chance to study in his high school days. In-chol liked the picture the more for that reason. Tonight, however, In-chol felt vaguely disconcerted looking at his father stand in front of the painting. For no definite cause, In-chol suddenly felt that maybe his father's hobby in these things was no more than a pose he was adopting to cover up his ignominious origin. All at once, In-chol felt as if a stone wall began crumpling down inside him. His heart began to beat fast.

It was impossible to tell whether or not his father knew that In-chol had come into the room. He turned around after a while, however, and walking over to an armchair sat down. The expression In-chol read on his father's face was rigid and gloomy which made such a sharp contrast with the sense of grace and joy wrought by the delicate interaction between light and dark strokes of brush on the Chinese-ink painting his father had just finished appreciating.

"Where did you go on last Chusok Day?" Kim Sang-jin asked his son in a heavy tone.

Asked abruptly this way, In-chol was somewhat dismayed. Sensing quickly that his father was already in the knowledge of what he had done on that day and knowing it to be the cause of this sudden summon, however, In-chol did not try to cover up his deed. He was, besides, curious how his father had ever found it out.

On the part of Kim Sang-jin, however, his son's silent acknowledgement of his unspoken suspicion was a blow from which he staggered inwardly. Until his son appeared in his presence, he had hoped that In-chol had had nothing to do with the content of the letter.

"I had let you use the car never suspecting that it was for that kind of thing you needed it. I had even told the chauffeur to fill it up on the night before so you wouldn't get stuck on the way. Why did you go there?"

His father's voice was angry although not raised. And he was glaring at In-chol with hate.

In-chol did not say anything. He could not explain the reason why he had to gone to Pundinamutkol to his father.

"You went with somebody, didn't you?"

"Professor Chi was with me."

"What? Professor Chi? What made you drag him into it?"

Now Kim Sang-jin's voice was pitched up high.

"Well, that's not how it happened."

"Then, how did it happen?"

"It was me who tagged along. Professor had been doing some studies about the butchers even before I heard about them from you, father. He had had a plan to go there to watch the cow rite. And I decided to go along."

"Why?"

"I wanted to find out."

"Find out what?"

What should I tell him, In-chol asked himself lowering his eyes.

"And what was it that you could find out, son?"

Hate, only hate, In-chol muttered inwardly. But he said, "I don't know yet."

His father seemed to be struggling with conflicting emotions, but finally he said,

"So, you feel good after offering your big bow to your bigfather?"

"I didn't even meet him."

But what would I have done if he had not had his stroke that day, In-chol asked himself again. Would I have greeted him? If so, what would have been his reaction? Would he have denied me like his son Ki-ryong?

"In any case, your Professor Chi must know about our family now?"

In-chol assented by not saying anything.

"What kind of a boy are you, any way? Why did you jump into fire with gunpowder? All that's left to do is for you to shout the news in all the alleyways."

In-chol saw that his father's high-cheek-boned and strongjawed face was twitching with extreme anger which had turned the complexion into a sinister red.

In the next instant, In-chol felt that he read his father's *paekchong* origin as he sat glaring at In-chol with his red twitching face. It would be irrational to think that a *paekchong* should look in any certain way, but, at least, his own father seemed to have more feel of the *paekchong* on his person than the old man in Pundinamutkol did to In-chol's impression. Again, In-chol heard something crumble in his heart.

"I shouldn't have called you in when your brother came the other night. I should have known that you haven't grown up yet. It was a big mistake. The fruit of my lifetime's struggle has been crushed. Utterly crushed!"

Kim Sang-jin's voice was more pitiable than angered at this point. He continued,

"My plan went wrong with your brother because I had not told him everything, and you, you messed up your life because I told you too much. It's unbelievable! Here, read this, if you like."

Kim Sang-jin thrust the letter sheets toward his son. He kept his eyes fixed on In-chol while the latter read the letter through. Sitting there staring at In-chol while he read the letter, the older man seemed to silently go over the contents of that letter he had finished a while ago in his mind. In-chol stared down at the letter sheets even after he was through with them. His inward eye saw a stretch of tree-lined road on which a foggy dusk was descending. A man was walking along this road without hurrying. The road merged with the fog and a thickening darkness. It was a completely empty road without a vehicle or another human passenger. Then, suddenly, lights came on atop the lamp poles lining both sides of the road and the windows of buildings of various heights threw beams of electric light so that the road loomed up white, reflecting the light. Vehicles and passersby filled the road with movement and noise. The man sped up his pace.

Despite all the lights from the street lamps and the lighted windows of the buildings, however, the road was visible only up to a dozen or so meters ahead; the rest seemed sucked up by the darkness. The man walked faster throwing his glances this way and that as if he were extremely anxious. The lights from the street lamps and the lighted windows merely accentuated the profundity of the engulfing darkness. Spotting an opening to an alleyway, the man hurriedly entered it, as if grateful to find an exit out of the main road. But fog and darkness had taken this by-road as well. Only, to the fleeing man, the alleyway seemed to have enough light to carry him through. Surprisingly, however, there was another man standing not many paces inside the alleyway from its entrance. Although the first man was not aware of his presence, this man had been walking along the same road as the other. Standing immobile in his post, the second man was saying, 'Fare thee well,' 'Fare thee well,' to his unknowing fellow passenger. The fog and the darkness were becoming more impenetrable.

"Do as he wishes if you have finished reading," said his father in a voice sinking with gloom.

In-chol raised his head, awakened from his reverie by his father's voice.

"Burn it!" roared his father.

Without realizing what he was doing, In-chol crumpled up the letter with both hands.

"Over there!" roared the older man again, pointing at the fireplace. He seemed to think that In-chol was about to take the crumpled letter outside to burn it.

Picking up the matchbox that had been placed on the tea table for the guests, In-chol went toward the fireplace. So that the sheets would burn well, he had to smooth out the crumpled letter sheets somewhat. Kindling a sheet with a lighted match stick, In-chol waited until the flame rose up on it before he put in another sheet to burn.

[Dear Father: I hope you are well and everybody in the family is also in good health. As for myself, I do not know where or how to begin my story. Before I have finally brought myself to writing this letter, father, I suffered a truly severe pain that seemed to grind my bones and cut up my flesh. I only feel dejected that there is so much pain and sorrow in our world. Yet, the burden is already fastened on my back; what good would lamenting do for me, then? The only thing I am sure of at this point is that I will not accept this spiteful fate meekly. There is a resolution I have made since I last saw you, father. It is true that when I first had you confirm the unthinkable thing about us, I felt as if the whole world was crumbling down; I felt utterly lost and crushed. As some time passed, however, I began to ponder over a way to survive. Then, something happened to spur my action. It happened last Chusok Day.

On that day, I had not even gone to my mother's grave. And maybe I will never again go there from now on. My intention is not to show my children their grandmother's burial place. You may be angered by this lack of filial feelings on my part, but to tell you the truth, I am ready to commit even a graver sin than this. On the Chusok Day, I was heavy in my heart all day long. In the evening, I invited the Chief of the police station here and Doctor Yu to the house because I could not stand it any longer without letting some of my gloom out of the system by drinking with somebody I was comfortable with. Dr. Yu is our family doctor and the Chief of the police station is my frequent *paduk* (oriental chess) partner. Over the drink, we talked about various things. Then, Dr. Yu told us about a patient whom he had gone to see during the day. From his description, there was no doubt that the patient was no other than our big-father. Instantly, I lost my taste for the drink and became tense. The gist of the matter was that our big-father had had a stroke and became partially paralyzed. The doctor told us also that for whatever talismanic purposes, the old patient had a long knife stuck against his paralyzed side of the body. Listening to this report, I felt a chill run down my back although I was pretty sure that neither of my two guests knew about my relationship with the patient. The police chief on his part identified the old patient as a butcher right way. Upon hearing this, Dr. Yu said, maybe then, the fiftyish man who rode the jeep with him that day and said he was no relative of that old man might be actually a blood relation. The doctor went on to say that the young man who drove the jeep, too, looked worried and solemn which might mean that he was not unrelated with the family either. He added that the young driver did not look as if he were somebody's chauffeur. You may imagine, father, how great would have been

my consternation when hearing these things from the doctor.
I could not guess who this fiftyish gentleman was but I could
not help thinking that this young person who drove that jeep
which the doctor said took him back and forth between his
office and the patient's house is none other than In-chol. It is
my earnest wish that it were not In-chol, but if it had been
him, what business could he have had to show himself
around in that place? I know that you, father, would not
have sent him there. If it had really been our brother, one
thing I can tell is that our secret history will take a shorter
time to be known to the world thanks to him. The police
chief said, when the conversation shifted to the topic of the
paekchong, that a son of an important man in this region (I
will, with your permission, not give you the name of this
man since you would not know him, anyway) caused a
scandal by seducing wife of a *paekchong*. The police chief
who said he had seen the woman with his own eyes said that
she was a great beauty whose husband when he found out
about it threatened to kill the seducer and then kill himself
with a dagger which he carried around on his person for a
time. Finally, the man's father paid a sum of money which,
according to the police chief who mediated the negotiation,
was quite large and this more or less put the end to the
matter for the time being. Soon after the money had been
handed over, however, the family of the butcher disappeared
somewhere so that people began to suspect that maybe the
couple had planned the whole thing from the beginning.
Then, a police officer under this chief had chance to go to
Taegu this spring and he ran into the butcher couple there
who were running a modest-size general store in some back
street. Although there was no doubt about their identity in
the mind of the police officer, the couple pretended not to
recognize the man whom they could not but have known
while living in this small town where people cannot help
knowing all the personnel at the police station or at any
other such places of public importance. The police officer

asked the storekeeper next-door if he knew whether the couple next-door had not come from Kyong-an in Kyonggi-do and whether their name was not so and so, to which the storekeeper answered that as far as he knew they came from Chungchongbuk-do and their family name as he under-stood it was Min (which, of course, was not the name they had in their hometown). The chief of police commented at the end of this story that it was the custom among the butchers to change their names when they leave their home place to live elsewhere hiding their origin. He also said that when the butchers adopt a new name, they prefer to choose one which belongs to an old *yangban* (Korean aristocracy) family. The reason why your humble son has so detailedly reported on this episode is not to tell you how painful it is for me to be listening to this kind of talk but to confess the fact that I for one can understand why this family had to change not only their place of abode but also their name.

You may remember, father, that I had said it would have been better if you had let us grow up as butchers because we would then have had our peace of mind at least. It did not take me long, however, to realize that this was a wrong, immature thought. Rather than living through the life with this terrible tag of a butcher attached to one's person, it would be far better to hide our origin no matter what effort or pains it costs! With this determination, I resolve to accom-plish what you in your lifetime may not be able to accom-plish. If I should fail in this... no, I will make sure that I do not to fail, father. I will see to it that the brand name of *'paekchong'* be dropped forever from our family. I disagree with our aunt who killed herself to save her name. There-fore, I will never seek my answer in measures of that nature. On the contrary, my greatest effort will be expended in preventing others to sense that I have any need to worry about my honor.

Changing the subject a little, it seems to me now that the tragedy of our aunt may have caused my mother to die after she went through the Caesarean delivery of a dead baby which occurred in the winter of the year when our aunt had died. Just to think what would have been the distress of my mother when she learned about our aunt's putting an end to her life with her own hands! I do not much doubt that my mother who was in the same situation as our aunt, as far as the name of *paekchong* was concerned and in so far as they were both women, lost the baby and her own life owing to the great impact of our aunt's fatal action. All this, however, is a thing of the past and what is important now is to prevent this kind of tragedy from ever occurring again in our future.

I have made up my mind to make a clean break with my present life. I want you to know, father, that I am doing this not only to prevent my own ruin but also to avoid whatever damage might be inflicted on my family. I feel that my father would be too thoughtful to ask me where I will be going hence. I do hope you will understand it if I should refrain not only from visiting you but also from writing to you hereafter.

Luckily, nobody at the office or among my acquaintances here seems to guess what I fear to reveal. But who could guarantee that somebody might not discover something about me some time! This thought fills me with unspeakable anxiety. It is customary for the cattle merchants to sell cows and oxen at the local market which opens every fifth day. It seems that most of the cows and oxen that are sold off here go to the slaughterhouse. The sight of these animals which had not stirred my mind in one way or another in the past now makes my heart sink every time I come upon it. It may be that I am of too diffident a nature but I feel that the best thing is for me to leave this place as quickly as possible.

It is near three o'clock in the morning. I am writing this letter while all my family are sound asleep in their bed. In the morning, I will personally take this letter to the post office and mail it. Let me tell you once more, father, how much I suffered before resolving to write this present letter to you. But this is a fate I am born with. I will bear it as best I can. I believe earnestly that my father will not find it difficult to understand his son whose sole concern at the present moment is to find a way to live. Lastly, I would like you, father, to admonish In-chol to carry himself with caution if not for himself then for the rest of the family. No matter where I may be, I will keep on wishing for the best on behalf of my father. Please burn this as soon as you finish reading this.

On the Ninth of the Tenth Month of the
Year of Musul,

Unfilial Son, In-ho

"Gather the ashes and throw them in the garden!" said Kim Sang-jin getting up from his seat abruptly.

In-chol scooped up the fluttering ash flakes with the shovel and the raker, which he started to dispose on a sheet of newspaper, when his father spoke again,

"Didn't you know that it wasn't you alone but the whole family that you were harming by acting the way you did? What is it that you wanted to find out, eh? All there is to know in that place, I, your own father, found out in person long ago! Don't ever act like a fool again! You heard me? Even to people in the house, you must never say anything about your visit to that village or about your brother's letter. Do you understand me? In case you make that kind of a blunder again...."

He did not continue. As if he were straining himself to the limit in order to swallow down the words that came up to his throat, he turned red from the neck upwards.

Even after In-chol went out of the room with the ashes, Kim Sang-jin stood on in the same spot going over the routine of lighting a cigarette and snubbing it out against the ashtray. Finally, he returned to his room where he went

straight to the built-in closet on one wall from which he took
out a glass and the whisky bottle. With these in hand, he
walked over to where the low table was and sat down in one
of the armchairs facing it. Pouring the whisky into the glass,
he sipped it slowly. It was a habit with him to take a drink
of whisky before going to bed at night. Warming his body
with the drink, Kim Sang-jin let his mind calm down. In-ho
did very well for himself, thought Kim Sang-jin to himself.
Yes, very well, indeed. I bet he went through a hell to come
to that decision. I know what it's like, my son. I, too, have
gone through my share of suffering in order not to give my
children that kind of pain, but what was the use! As long as
he has set out to drop out of the family, he had best do a
thorough work, yes, a thorough work. But what about this
other son of mine? What a gutless fool he is! I have to do
something quick to control the situation. But what? Kim
Sang-jin had three glasses of whisky that night.

Next morning, In-chol was summoned again to the *ung-
jopshil* by his father, who was smoking a cigarette in the
same chair as yesterday when In-chol opened the door of the
room. Seeing his son hesitate at the doorway, Kim Sang-jin
told him to take a seat. In-chol saw that his father's face
which had been washed and shaved looked relaxed and
almost benign this morning. He did not speak at once but
kept on puffing at his cigarette for a few seconds longer.
Then, he snubbed off the cigarette and placed both hands on
his knees, fingers interlocking, and, leaning the upper half of
his body toward his son, he said,

"Listen, carefully, son. There is an old saying about how
impossible it is to put back the water into the bowl after it
has been spilled. But that's not what I believe."

In-chol was puzzled. He could not guess what it was his
father wanted to tell him. But his father continued,

"What I mean is, one must, at least, try to put back as
much of the spilled water as one can. If a tool is need for the
operation, one must use it; if haste is the solution, he must

hurry, by all means, but if it would be better to wait, he must be patient. What one must not do is give up. That's right. He must never give up."

Here the older man paused. Leaning back against the back of the armchair, he folded his arms on his chest. Then he asked,

"It's just Professor Chi who knows, isn't that so?"

In-chol kept silence but inwardly he kept searching for the possible motive for this strange manner in which his father was leading the conversation.

"Does he still live in Kyonji-dong?"

"Yes."

"He still teaches at the college?"

"Yes."

"Ta-hye hasn't married, has she?"

"No, she hasn't."

"Since she is the same age as you are, she is somewhat late in getting married. Must be because she doesn't have a mother or any brothers or sisters. But she is a sensible good girl as I remember her."

After saying the above as if to himself, he asked out of blue,

"Is the professor intending to marry her daughter off to one whom he can adopt as son?"

"I don't know."

"She was very fond of you while we lived as neighbors. . . . If it's all right with you, son, I will oblige them in whatever conditions they may propose."

Upon learning what had been behind his father's quizzical talk, In-chol blushed, with shame.

"From my younger days, I have never been afraid to do what I decided to do. And I think what your brother has done this time has been very well done. In a crisis like this, one must not be bound by personal emotions. As I said just now, we have the task of putting back the spilled water. But you must do your share on your own."

"Ta-hye has somebody with whom she is as good as engaged."

In-chol felt his body pressed down with an overwhelming sense of shame which made it impossible for him to say anything more.

For a second, Kim Sang-jin's eyes glared at his son with hate, then he said,

"So what? She hasn't married, has she? Don't you realize that your life depends on your will and action? I am prepared to give you away to the professor if he will have you, do you hear?"

In-chol looked at his father's face for a second. That he had not known his father to be this kind of a man!

"Would I want to give you away especially now that your brother has left me? But I will bear the loss. You are now old enough to act like a mature person. Think about what I've said. One day, you will know that I advised you wisely."

Kim Sang-jin sat in silence for a while, then said in a softer tone,

"If you are not too busy today, I would like you to stay at home and run an errand for me."

In-chol did not say anything, merely waiting for a further cue from his father who now said, again surprising In-chol with his unexpected shift of topic,

"How far is the work done on that banker's house you drew plans for?"

"I don't know," said In-chol although he had an idea that the bricklaying for the first floor must be finished by now and perhaps the concrete work for the second floor must be in progress.

"You'd better go out to the site more; study the practical side of your job, I mean. I heard Mr. Cho, the banker, praise you a great deal when we met somewhere on business. He said you had much talent."

In-chol wanted to leave his father's side as quickly as possible, so he asked, preventing his father from whatever words he might have uttered further,

"What is the errand you want me to run for you today?"

"I want you to go to this banker's house with something I want to send over to him. I can't let another man do the work for me. I will have the thing brought to the house after I go out to the office."

"I don't know where they live."

"The chauffeur would know."

Released from his father, In-chol went up to his room. Although his feet went up the stairs, his body felt as if it were going down the steps lower and lower.

About two in the afternoon, his father's chauffeur brought home a package with an antique porcelain in it. Although he had had time to give the last touch to the house model before the chauffeur came, In-chol had not done it. Instead, he wrapped up the model just as it was and put it in the car along with the package of the porcelain. With a thought of leaving the model at her house in case of her absence, In-chol did not call Na-mi before leaving for her house.

The banker's house which was in Naesu-dong was a fairly old traditional-style house of an impressive size. In-chol waited a while inside the gate which a young maid opened for him, when he saw Na-mi coming out of the house with a light step.

"What a surprise!" said Na-mi, wide-eyed, seeing In-chol standing in the yard. "Why didn't you call before coming? Anyway, I am so glad I came home early today. It must've been a telepathy or something. I only had one class this morning. I am so glad I came home instead of going straight to Montparnasse."

The yard was rather small compared with the house. Seeing In-chol peep into the garden-pond in passing, Na-mi said,

"The goldfish are stupid. They get caught by the mice who eat them. There was one left but last night he, too, got eaten up by the mice. How stupid it is! Do you think it's maybe because their tails are too heavy for them to move faster?"

A few dead leaves were sunken at the bottom of the fishless pond water.

The chauffeur brought in the packages. Na-mi's room was opposite the inner-room. There was a glass case against one wall in which were displayed a variety of dolls including Negro dolls and dolls cut with wood. On the side-surface of the wardrobe standing next to the desk were tacked up some photographs of famous western actors whom In-chol, too, could recognize.

"I can't wait to move into a bigger room. Are these both house models. May I see them, please?"

In-chol conveyed the package from his father to her first, and then proceeded to unwrap the house model.

"Oh, how cute it is!" exclaimed Na-mi, then she examined the model from all angles.

"This is the front door? And this must be the *ungjopshil*. But where's my room?"

"You pass the *ungjopshil*, turn the corner, and you are right in front of your room."

"This is the sunroom? And here's the terrace which is so chic! I'm glad we made the awning come down this low. By far, this is more elegant than what I saw in the picture! This is really wonderful!"

Na-mi chattered happily like a child.

"It looks pretty because it's a miniature. The completed house will make a totally different picture."

"Really? In any case, you are a lucky one because you have the power to make such a beautiful house as this."

"It's too early yet to look for beauty in what I make. I haven't even reached the level of serving utilitarian purposes in architecture."

"No need to be so modest."

"No, it's not that. I just state the fact. Actually, there's an architectural piece which I find truly beautiful. It's a temple named Wasiri which the sixteenth century Russian monarch Emperor Ivan had erected next to Kremlin Palace to commemorate the country's victory at Kazan. The legend has it that the emperor was so pleased with the work that he blinded the three men who were the chief builders of this construction so that they could never build another as beautiful."

"What a story!"

"Of course, it's only a legend, but I feel one can begin to talk about beauty in architecture only when it concerns something of this plane. Architectural beauty is nothing you can come across everyday."

"In any case, you mustn't draw a house plan same as this for anybody again. Ours should be the only one with this shape in the whole country, promise?"

"It's too unfair that I become blinded for a thing like this. I wouldn't mind it so much if I can create a really beautiful architectural work and then lose my sight upon taking a full view of my completed masterpiece!"

They smiled at each other.

Fruit and tea were brought in which they ate and drank together. Na-mi's good mood did not leave her. She did not say anything about the incident at Haeundae and neither her conversation nor attitude denoted any bad feeling she might still harbor over it. And yet, she was acting with spontaneity and genuine friendliness. It was as if she had really forgot the whole unpleasant interlude. Talking and laughing with Na-mi in her room, In-chol could shake off the bad memory of not only what happened in the hotel room at Haeundae but also what took place between his father and himself in the *ungjopshil* this very morning.

They took the microbus near Na-mi's house and went to Montparnasse together. As usual, the inside of the tea-house was dark so that one who first entered it after descending the staircase to this basement teahouse from the street outside could not recognize objects or people very well until after a while. The loud music from the record player filled the hall. Gradually, the plaster masks of Beethoven and Goethe became recognizable on the inside wall of the counter whose gloomy grayness of color, too, now became noticeable.

As soon as they went in, Na-mi exchanged eye-greetings with several people none of whom In-chol knew. As if the atmosphere of the teahouse made her act in a certain way, Na-mi only talked about acting since they arrived at the Montparnasse. The fish in the fishpond, thought In-chol to himself listening to Na-mi's 'theatrical' conversation.

"We are going to have a performance either at the end of this year or in the early part of next year," said Na-mi.

In-chol understood that she meant the acting group centered around Nam Chun-gol.

"We have the funds, and all the trained actors and actresses to fill the parts. Only the script has been lacking but Nam-*sonsaengnim* offered to write it for us. He says he only needs to write it down since he has the general outline drawn up in his head already. It's about a domestic tragedy, he says. From the way he describes it, I am sure it will make a very interesting plot."

Then she told In-chol how this domestic tragedy will evolve. The oldest daughter of a family marries a rich American soldier and goes to his country with him. But the marriage does not work out and she comes back to her parents, house. The cause of the marital failure was her inability to adjust to American ways. After her return to Korea, however, she insists on living in the American style, or in what she believes to be the American style, anyway. Until late in the morning she lies about in the bed where she has her morning coffee and western breakfast brought. She dyes her hair yellow and smokes cigarettes all day long. In time, her family becomes critical of this woman. But it had been her parents themselves who had been instrumental in her marrying an American. She gave financial help to her parents not only while she and her American husband lived in Korea but also after they moved to America. That this family could live in relative wealth, too, is entirely thanks to the support this daughter had given her parents. When her family for whom she had done so much begins to show their disfavor to this woman, she deliberately sets out to destroy them. First, she drives her brother and his wife out of the house to a rented room by persecuting the wife unbearably. Then she seduces her younger sister's fiancé which ends in the younger woman's suicide. She then begins to treat her parents as old servants and goes on to do things calculated to harass and torment her family.

"In the end, the father kills this daughter by poisoning her and goes to the madhouse himself. Intriguing, isn't it?"

"It could make an interesting story if one knows how to write it well."

"That's right. He says it will be a four-act play. Everybody's excited about it. I wish I could play the role of this older daughter. But I don't know. Since Nam-*sonsaengnim* will be the director, maybe he will give the role to your sister."

"You have a talent in shifting to an unexpected topic, don't you? Do I have to take part in your fight over who takes which role?" said In-chol in a somewhat sarcastic tone. But Na-mi was not piqued by this. She merely said,

"I know my weakness is my candor. And I lose by it."

Just then, somebody tapped In-chol on the shoulder saying,

"Oh, hello, Kim *hyong* (a half honorific appellation between males). Long time no see!"

It was Pak Hae-yon who proceeded to take the seat next to Na-mi after shaking In-chol's hand. As usual, his fleshless, ill-shaved face was flushed from drink.

"I haven't seen you around much. Have you been kept busy?" he said.

"No particularly," answered In-chol briefly.

"Do you have a cigarette to spare, Kim *hyong*?" asked Pak

Hae-yon again.

In-chol saw that his hand as it pulled a cigarette out of the pack he held out trembled a little. Somehow, he looked more forlorn and unhappy than when In-chol saw him last. He asked Pak Hae-yon if he could order some drink for him, but Pak Hae-yon shook his head. When the cigarette he took from In-chol was nearly finished, he said,

"Shall we move to the other place?"

Na-mi glanced at her wristwatch and said,

"Already?"

"It's not too early. You must realize it's autumn now. Hours are not long any longer."

"It doesn't matter if it's a bit too early, don't you think?" said In-chol to Na-mi getting up after Pak Hae-yon.

"I have to see someone here," said Na-mi, however, adding, "You two had better go on."

"Then join us there after you see this person."

"Well, rather than that, you may drop by here again if you like after you are through there," Na-mi said.

It was getting dark outside. Indeed, it was not too early for drink contrary to what Na-mi seemed to think.

The tavern was crowded with people and was full of cigarette smoke and human noise. Pak Hae-yon and In-chol went to a table where Nam Chun-gol was sitting opposite a young man with a cap askant on his head. Nam Chun-gol lightly nodded to In-chol but kept on listening to the young man's conversation. His one hand was fidgeting with his pipe. Pak Hae-yon ordered a jug of wine and poured into In-chol's cup and his.

The young man in cap was commentating on the scarcity of dramatic texts in Korea. He was saying that the lack of original work made it necessary for the theater to recourse to translation of foreign texts. He was making the conversation almost by himself with Nam Chun-gol interjecting monosyllabically only now and then.

Pak Hae-yon, too, was taciturn tonight unlike his talkative self that In-chol remembered. Slowly, his body bent forward over the table.

In-chol emptied the cup every time Pak Hae-yon refilled it. He recalled his father's words of this morning. Then, he thought about Na-mi sitting at the Montparnasse. But soon, he became totally unconcerned and concentrated on drinking.

"You see, Kim *hyong*," Pak Hae-yon said suddenly raising just his face without straightening his forward-leaning body. "It was the wife who started the beating first. She did it because the son nagged her to buy him pencils that have an unbreakable lead point. So, she beat him and I, I joined in. My wife just spanked him on the bottom, but I beat him on any place, indiscriminately."

Then, turning to the young man in cap, he said,

"Say, Mr. Son, don't be too ambitious. You can't achieve anything that way. What if it's only one-act play. You'd better put up the original work if you can. Length isn't everything. Besides, a sparrow can break it's leg trying to imitate a crane."

The youngman wearing a cap ignored Pak and went on talking to Nam Chun-gol.

".... The child couldn't even cry out in the end.... What if it's a one-act play! What if it is? Say, Mr. Son pour me a drink, com'on, fill this up for me."

Pak Hae-yon picked up his half-finished wine cup with a trembling hand. He seemed to be holding it out for the young man to fill up but suddenly he lifted the cup as if to throw its content at the young man. In-chol, who tried to stop Pak Hae-yon in the act with one hand ended up by pouring the wine all over the table. As he was about to call the waiting girl to bring a mop to wipe off the top of the table, a young man who had been sitting at the table behind In-chol came and grabbed him by the collar. In-chol merely noticed his short-cut hair style and a bright-colored neckerchief.

"What's the matter, jerk? Are you itching for a kick or something? Why don't you just sit on your ass and drink your drink like you're supposed to, huh?"

Before In-chol could say anything, the other hit him on the chin with a fist. In-chol fell on the floor between two chairs. Something flashed inside his head and then he felt that an absolute silence descended on the scene as if nobody was present within the circumference of perceivable distance. He opened his eyes. The young man of a while ago was standing by looking down at him. He tried to get up, but another blow landed on the underside of his chin and again he fell down on the floor. Lukewarm liquid slowly filled in his mouth. He was aware that something unfair was being done to his person, but he was strangely calm. There was no anger in his heart. Again he felt that it was very quiet all around. It was as if he were lying in a desert land all by himself. Opening his eyes, he saw that the young man was no longer there. But now there were other people. Their faces were all turned toward In-chol. Yet none of them had made a budge to help In-chol. Not even those who were sitting at the same table with him.

Raising himself up in this atmosphere of an uninhabited void, In-chol staggered back to his former seat and sat down. Pouring some wine in the cup, he drank it up along with the liquid that had accumulated inside his mouth. Yes, it was an uninhabited desert land. No, better still, it was a veritable jungle. No matter which way you turned your eyes, there was nobody. Or, there were people but they were jungle people. In-chol poured more wine into the cup and drank it up. Voices and movements were resumed inside the tavern.

The change in In-chol's life occurred quietly.

Ever since the day when In-chol was beaten up by the unknown young man, he became one of the habitués of the drinking house. During the period following this incident, he spent his mornings working on his thesis or reading. In the afternoon, he regularly went to the Montparnasse. He went at first hoping to meet up with Na-mi there, but later he became unconcerned whether or not Na-mi came; he just sat at a table by himself. Pak Hae-yon sat with him on and off during the intervals of his trips to and from the tavern, which provided some diversion for In-chol. The waiting girls came to treat him as one of their more intimate cliental, conveying Na-mi's messages to him or, when they found him sitting alone, bringing him the day's paper to read.

The same pattern applied to his becoming a habitué of the drinking house. He went there at first in the company of Pak Hae-yon. Later, however, he dropped in by himself. Lulled by the cigarette smoke and indistinct noise of conversation and movements, In-chol sat with a wine cup in front of him and a cigarette between his lips. Slowly, he felt himself merge with his surrounding.

While sipping wine at this tavern, In-chol often thought about Ta-hye. How worried will she be if she finds out about my drinking at a tavern every night? he thought. He imagined her reprimanding him in her quiet voice looking at him thoughtfully. He quickly erased this picture, however. She had called him several times lately to find out how he was and to ask him to come to her house for a chat. Every time, he told her he was too busy to take time off his work and did not go to see her or her father. The reason he could not go to see her was that ever since his father insinuated about his marrying Ta-hye he felt such a heavy guilt toward Ta-hye that even imagining a visit to her house unsettled him. Even the memory of feeling light in the heart at the mouth of her alley as he watched Ta-hye half trot into it after having told him everything about her and Chon Kyong-hun gave him now a sense of shame. Should he not have advised Ta-hye to marry Chon Kyong-hun as he himself had told his father? On nights when this doubt came to his mind, he drank more than usual.

In time, In-chol became familiar with the personages

whom Pak Hae-yon had introduced to In-chol on the latter's
first visit to this drinking place. The dentist was one of them
with whom In-chol found himself quite comfortable and
entertained. It seemed that the hunting season had arrived.
He was showing up at the tavern in hunter's attire these
days. His face which had turned back to the ash color from a
russet tan acquired from camping in Soraksan during the
summer was now switched back to the russet color. Maybe
he was not an experienced hunter or maybe the hunting
ground near Seoul where he went after seeing his patients
during the morning hours is poor in game; he was mostly
empty-handed when he arrived at the tavern from his
hunting excursions. As if to excuse himself for the inadequacy
of his hunting skill, he would explain earnestly and repeatedly that the important thing in hunting was not how
many animals you kill but how effectively you can exercise
yourself physically. That's why he didn't even keep a dog for
his hunting, he said. He told In-chol, too, how much he
could reduce in weight through his hunting exercise, adding
that he felt as if he could fly. The strange thing about this man
was that on days when he could catch a couple of hares or
pheasants, he became taciturn merely concentrating on his
drink with his catches and gun pushed aside indifferently.
In-chol said on these occasions, 'It seems you had a good
day.' Then he said shortly, 'Nothing to boast of.' But In-chol
saw that there was pride mixed with indifference in his look.
The literary critic who made a point of lighting his cigarette
from another man's lighted cigarette also was an interesting
man. In-chol did not know at first why it was that this man
never had matches or a lighter. Finally he found out.
Lending him his lighted cigarette one day, In-chol had asked
the literary critic the reason for his lighting his cigarette
always from another man's lighted cigarette. His answer was
that a match light gives one's cigarette the taste of sulfur
while the lighter gives off the smell of gas. This not only
lessens the enjoyment of your cigarette smoking but also is

harmful to your health. It was best, therefore, to light your cigarette from another man's lighted cigarette. In-chol could not help admiring the literary critic's audacity.

The man who had run for the national assembly with a promise to lower the liquor tax in case of his election and, according to Pak Hae-yon, was the strongest in drinking amongst all the formidable contestants in this tavern offered quite an entertainment for In-chol one night.

On this night, the ex-candidate for the national assembly reminisced drunkenly about the time when he had participated in a drinking contest during the Japanese Occupation Period.

"I kept on drinking until the judges stopped me. They said that I had drunken up to the maximum safety limit. Later I found out that I had drunken seven *toe* (about 13 liters) of Japanese wine. I looked around and saw that there were only four contestants left in the race including myself. The contest from this point on was who gets to the entrance gate from inside the building. One of the four contestants who tried to pull himself up to a standing position fell flat on his face on the floor; he could not get up again. Another contestant had the same plight leaving only one rival for me to fight against. My sole competitor who looked about forty was sitting still with eyes closed. Looking at him, I thought to myself I must not let myself be defeated by one so much older than myself. I was then only twenty-three. Yes, twenty-three years old I was and I was not afraid of anything under the sky. It was the fearlessness of my youth that had made me enter the drinking contest just as it had caused me to join the patriotic students' movement as a consequence of which I got locked up in the police detention room for a spell, eating bean-rice. Anyway, I resolved to stand up upright and walk out to the gate with dignity. But it was not easy. I barely managed to pull myself up by the sheer force of my two arms stood against the floor sustaining my weight."

Here, the one-time drinking champion raised himself up

sustaining himself with both arms against the table top.

"People standing by looked as if they were multi-layered images of an identical figure and everything began to spin around me all at once. Even so, I put on the Japanese wooden high-rise sandals, put on the *haori* (traditional Japanese cloak) and silk headdress, and picked up the walking stick just as the rules for the race designated. Somehow or other, I made it to the outer gate and cut the tape. After that, everything was a complete darkness. It was two days afterward that I woke up. I learned then that I got only the second prize because I had put on the wrong *haori*, not the one with my number tag attached on it. Fifty bottles of Japanese wine were lined up above my head on the floor which were the material reward for winning the second prize in the drinking contest. The sight of the wine bottles turned my inside and I felt nausea. But it was by drinking a good cup of Japanese wine nicely heated that I could cure my nausea. This is what they call 'curing the heat with heat,' I guess."

Still standing, he emptied several cups of wine one after another, then said,

"I am finished now. It was only the magic of being twenty-three that made it possible. Yes, the magic of being twenty-three years old."

He mumbled the last of these words and then abruptly walked out of the hall, staggering, although he was not now wearing those tricky Japanese wooden sandals.

After waiting for a few minutes, In-chol went out to see if he were not lying prostrate on the ground outside the tavern building. But he was nowhere in sight.

Returning home that night, In-chol pictured to his mind the sight of the one-time prize-winning drinker staggering onward precariously but without falling.

At twenty-three, In-chol himself was enlisted in the army and was stationed at a front line post. It was an aimless dark period in his life. One wintry day, he was engaged in the chore of pulling logs from up the snow-piled mountain slope.

It was freezing cold and windy. One of the soldiers made a joke about his lower organ being turned to an icicle which he melted back to its original state by covering it up with the envelope of the letter he received from his girl friend. In-chol was too weary to laugh at his joke. Then, this soldier seemed to have let go of the rope in his frozen numbness. The log he was pulling at rolled down hitting In-chol on his shin which sent him flying a couple of feet to fall flat in the snow. When he regained consciousness, the soldier was rubbing In-chol's face with a ball of snow. Every time the wind swept, the snowflakes laden on the tree branches scattered, sparkling iridescently. Over the branches and the flying snowflakes, In-chol could see an indigo sky that was so clear and wide-spread that it looked all the more mindless. In-chol felt a shame. He felt a shame which was so deep that he no longer wished to live. As a whole, the twenty-third year of his life was a period he would much rather forget than treasure in memory.

The one-time heavy-drinking champion showed up at the tavern as usual next day. And In-chol's new life continued at an even pace.

Then, one day, something unexpected happened at In-chol's house.

As was his custom, In-chol had gone home late from the tavern that night. Unlike other nights, the gate opened even before he pushed the bell. It was In-ju who had been standing just inside the gate which she opened as soon as she knew In-chol had arrived. She took him by the arm as he entered the gate saying she wanted to talk to him. By the light from the *hyon-gwan*, he could tell, despite his semi-drunken state, that his sister's expression was unusually serious. Listening to her story, however, he realized that the matter was less grave than he had thought.

According to what In-ju whispered to him, both of them still standing at the gate-side edge of their garden, immediately after In-chol left home this afternoon, the maid had gone upstairs to clean up his room. Before she reached his door, however, she discovered that the door of In-mun's room was open ajar, which surprised the maid because In-mun made a point of keeping his door closed tight while he was home so that nobody would chance to stray into his room and lock it during his absence. He even forbid the maid to clean his room. But on this particular day, he had forgotten to lock it before going out. The maid who had been mildly curious about the inside of this secret room tip-toed inside to take a look. Although she had guessed that In-mun must be cleaning his room once in a while, she had not dreamed that it would be quite so clean and tidy. In this spotless abode of the boy, the maid recognized a fish tank, several bird cages, one cage with squirrels, another with white mice, and another with a toad, all of them arranged neatly in their appropriate places. One by one, the maid inspected these with interest. In the fish tank, she found a large goldfish of motley color and a small one with bulging eyes moving slowly in the water waving their fan-like fins. The birds seemed frightened by the intrusion of a stranger; they fluttered about in their cages excitedly. In one of the cages, the maid found a nest with three tiny white eggs which were very pretty. The two white mice which were the size of a *songpyon* (bite-size rice cake) twitched their mouths as if in discontent, looking wide-eyed at the intruder. Although she did not really feel like looking at the ugly-looking toad from close by, she inspected him also with some thorough-ness before turning to leave the room. Then, suddenly, she caught sight of a wooden case lying on the floor. The top of the wooden case was removed and in its place was fitted an iron net covering the entire surface. Something seemed to move inside the case; the maid looked in closer. Next instant, the maid ran out of the room with a shriek and tumbled down the stairs. The commotion brought Madam Hong and In-ju from their rooms. The maid told them in a trembling voice what she had seen upstairs. Madam Hong went back into her room trembling and in a little while came back out, her clothes changed, and left the house in a fluster.

Although the incident was nothing tremendously grave, In-chol was upset by it all the same. He was angry that his brother was still keeping the snake.

"In-mun's home, isn't he?" In-chol asked In-ju.

"Yes, sleeping, I think. Don't make too much fuss, *obba*. I haven't told father about it. When In-mun learned about what happened after he came home from school, he looked so pitiable and lost. Then, he went up to his room and brought down the wooden case and a shovel. He left the house with these and came back a couple of hours later. But mother has still not come back. I am worried."

"Did she go with her books?"

He asked this question because if his mother had gone out with her Bible and the psalm book, they didn't need to worry because it was clear where she went.

"I was so confused I can't remember. Since she didn't come home by suppertime, I sent the maid to Aunt Ko's house but she said mother hadn't come to her house today."

"Let's go in and see what we can do."

There was no light in their father's room. Since he had been avoiding an encounter with his father within the house after their tête-à-tête of that morning, In-chol was glad that his father had gone to bed. Walking past their father's room quietly, In-chol and his sister went to Madam Hong's room which they entered. They switched on the light and examined the room. The Bible and the psalm book were nowhere to be seen.

"Just as I thought, mother went to the mountain prayer-house," said In-chol.

"But, mother has become so strange lately."

"Don't worry. I am sure she will come back in a couple of days."

"You say that because you didn't see mother this afternoon. I cannot help feeling that something terrible may happen to her."

"Let's go to bed."

Coming upstairs to his room, In-chol went to bed right away switching off the light. Mother would be praying all night in the mountain, he thought. She would be shedding tears and by and by forget the worries this mundane world had inflicted on her soul. If so, now must be the happiest moment for my mother. In any case, I will scold In-mun severely tomorrow morning. Maybe not, though, since he seems to have thrown away the snake already. Because of fatigue, he fell into sleep right away and did not wake up until morning.

It was about seven o'clock in the morning when he opened his eyes. He went through warming-up movements as was his habit and left his room to go downstairs to wash himself. Just as he opened his door to walk out, however, he saw an envelope, which must have been inserted between the door and the doorframe, fall under his feet. Tearing it open, In-chol found inside a letter with In-mun's handwriting. It was a brief note: I leave everything to your kind favor, *hyongnim* (honorific for 'big brother'). After this short message, In-mun wrote directions as to how one should feed and look after each of his animals. There was also the key to his room in the envelope.

Unlocking his brother's door with the key, In-chol went in. In-mun's satchel and school hat were left on top of the desk as he probably had left them down the previous day. In-chol went downstairs and asked the maid if she had seen In-mun this morning. She said that she did see him go out, adding that she thought he was going out for a walk.

Forbidding the maid to tell their father anything about In-mun, In-ju went to his school without even eating breakfast but came home around noon looking dejected. She said that none of his friends knew his whereabouts. Just as In-chol and In-ju had feared, In-mun did not come home that day.

The next day, In-ju went back to In-mun's school. Not

that she had much expectation, but she was too worried and restless to sit waiting. Tending the animals according to his brother's directions, In-chol, too, felt a fear growing in his mind as time passed without his brother returning. The newspapers frequently reported about boys of In-mun's age leaving their houses and meeting various disasters. The second day went without any news of In-mun. In-chol read through the Crime Section of the morning and evening papers thoroughly. Although she did not say anything, In-ju, too, was perusing the newspapers with worrisome eyes. So that their father would not notice anything, they avoided discussing the matter altogether.

Early on the third morning, In-chol was waken up by the maid. Going downstairs, In-chol found In-mun standing outside the *hyon-gwan.* The sky was low and cloudy looking as if it would pour down a spell of rain any second. A glance at the boy told In-chol that his brother probably spent the night in the open. His face was blue from cold and his jacket looked damp.

As if he were a stranger to the house, In-mun kept on standing outside the *hyon-gwan* as if refusing to come in. In-ju who ran out to his side repeated, 'Foolish boy, foolish boy,' with a teary low voice, pulling him in by the hand. In-mun, however, seemed unaffected either by fear of being discovered by his father or by In-ju's emotional welcome. He merely asked apathetically, sounding as if he were addressing the house at large rather than In-ju or In-chol personally,

"Has mother come back?"

CHAPTER FIVE

Autumn Rain

On the night when In-mun stayed on the Paekundae near the Jump Rock, he had watched the lights illuminating the southwestern sector of the city. What he had thought then was that the huge mass of electric lights must have a tiny speck of light from his own house converged in it and that two members of the house from which this speck of light came were now lacking. It was true that his mother had gone to the mountain prayer-house now and then before, but this time she had gone for reasons different from hitherto. Try though he did, In-mun could not understand why people hated snakes so much. He himself was of the opinion that there were few living beings that were cleaner than snakes. Why then would his brother get upset about his keeping a snake in the house and why would his mother take such a drastic action because of it? What is it that makes a snake so different from a bird or a goldfish?

The morning he had left his house, he had gone to the Samchong Park near his house and then went up a mountain slope. He had no aim or scheme; he just kept on climbing up. The leaves had turned to pretty yellow and red, but In-mun's eyes did not notice them. Vaguely, he wished to travel along the ridge in the general direction of the Paekundae where he had gone a couple of times before then. He got lost many times, but he kept on walking unconcerned whether or not he was on the right track. His heart was heavy with the thought that his mother had left home in that abrupt way because of him.

As evening turned to night, he felt cold and hungry. All day long he had eaten only a bag of *konbbang* (dry hard bread originally made for army use) which he had bought from a peddler woman at the foot of the mountain behind Chongnung and some hawthorn fruit he could pick along some path he had mistakenly entered. He knew that there was a free overnight lodging a little way down the slope, but he did not go there. The reason why he chose to spend the night among the rocks in the open without food or cover was that he felt an impulse to somehow make his family pay for their harsh attitude toward his snake and also that in this way he felt he could atone for having made his mother leave the house.

Until he was twelve years old, In-mun had lived under a dictatorship of his mother doing whatever she decided for him to do around the clock. Especially the interval between Saturday night through Sunday was a sheer trial for him. Every Saturday night, Madam Hong would hide In-mun's ball somewhere so that he couldn't play with his friends all day on Sunday. Then, she called In-mun to her side and made him memorize the Sunday school Bible phrase. She insisted that he memorize it so thoroughly that he could recite it by heart even in his bed. Yet, his mind was on something else; he was playing the ball with his friends kicking it this way and that and giving slips to other boys. At times, just as he was about to shoot the ball into the net, something landed on his forehead startling him. It was his mother's hand which she always put there at night offering the night prayer on his behalf. His delicious fantasy of a successful shooting broke into pieces. In-mun closed his eyes tight in despair. During the summer vacation of his fourth year in the elementary school, In-mun went to the suburbs to collect insects for a science homework with a gang of his friends. They chased butterflies, dragonflies, and cicadas all day long until it began to get dark. Ever since this day, he developed the habit of going out to suburban fields with a butterfly net on Sundays. This way, he could have his fun without the worry of being caught by his mother which would surely be the case if he were to play around in the vicinity of his house. In-mun would catch insects, fetch them home, make them appropriate nests, and try to feed them. If any of them should die, he caught another of its kind and made it replace the dead one. Once he put some ants in a bottle with earth and watched them dig tunnels for hours on end. These new hobbies of his became the cause of his staying away from the church. His mother coaxed, scolded, and even shed tears, but all to little avail. He went to the Sunday school only two more times and then never went back. On days when the weather did not permit him to go on his insect-chasing excursions, he read books on insects and animals. It was about this time that the phrase 'seed of sin' began to appear in Madam Hong's morning and evening prayers. She also made In-mun move out of her room to a separate room of his own upstairs. In time, she came to leave him to his own whims and ways and In-mun on his part became more and more unsociable, turning his attention only to his own private little world of insects and animals over which he was a monarch and a devoted caretaker. Yet, this time, just because of a slight neglectfulness in locking up his door, he had frightened his mother into going away from home.

The cold of the late autumn night high in the mountain gnawed into his marrows and although he hugged his knees with both hands and brought his head down against the knees he could not have any sleep. From time to time, some unknown bird shrieked. In-mun was afraid. He listened into the night concentrating all his nerves on his ears. Still, he was not going to climb down to the free lodging.

Almost all through the night, he stayed awake. When the dawn came, he went down to the lodging and obtained some hot water which he drank. Then, he started walking again. Crossing the slope sideways as he was directed by one of the men at the lodging, he looked for the path leading eastward to Tobongsan. Unable to spot it, however, he scrambled about among the trees until almost noon. He was not impatient, however, because in any case he had set out on this journey with the purpose of giving himself a rough time.

Luckily, he met a woodsman who directed him to the path leading to Tobongsan. It was almost evening when he reached Tobongsan and climbed up to the Manjangbong where a few hikers were preparing for their return journey. In-mun, too, started back. From a peddler who was wrapping up his merchandise along the path to go home, In-mun bought some sweet bread which he ate up at once. He went to a spring nearby and drank a great deal of cool water. Suddenly he felt so tired that he wanted to lie down. Climbing on a rock, he lay down stretching all the way. He fell asleep but woke up again soon because of cold. Between sleep and wakefulness, he thought: I must start back home before dawn. Mother must be back by now.

Sensing before anybody could tell him that his mother had still not come home, In-mun went up to his room without another word. In-ju who came after him up the stairs asked him if he should not take a bath and eat something. But he merely shook his head and unlocking his door with the key which his brother had handed to him entered his room locking it up after him from inside. Without changing his clothes, he threw himself on the bed and fell into a deep sleep. Still sleeping, he heard, as if in a dream, a knocking on his door and the maid's voice saying it was past his time to go to school. He slept on.

He woke up around noon feeling a dull aching numbness all over his body. Outside, the rain was pouring. Going down with a somewhat unsteady gait, he ate his first regular meal in several days. Yet he could not eat as much as he had thought he could.

Returning to his room, In-mun paid his homage to each of his animals one after another for the first time since he came back from his wandering voyage. He asked silently, 'Have you been well?' But, of course, none of them responded to his question. Only, they were waiting for him to feed them making wiggly gestures with their bodies as usual. But this made In-mun happy. Ah, my kingdom, he said inwardly, distributing food and water to all his subjects.

The rain kept on pouring. Maybe it was the food inside his stomach after starvation. He felt an overwhelming fatigue again which made him sleepy all over. He resisted the temptation to lie down on his bed, however, and went to his brother's room. In-chol was reading at his desk when In-mun went in. Seeing him come in, In-chol smiled and said,

"You'll have mildew grow on your face if you don't wash up in a hurry, brother."

In-mun, too, smiled. Then he said,

"I wonder if... you could give me some bus money...."

"There's money in the pocket of that jumper. Take as much as you need. Your teacher called a while ago. I said you will come to school from tomorrow."

In-mun had thought his brother would ask him where he had been for the last two days and where he was going now, but he didn't ask. Although he had decided not to answer these questions in case his brother should ask them, In-mun told him voluntarily when he saw that his brother was not likely to interrogate him.

"I'm going to see if I can find mother."

He walked out of In-chol's room and going downstairs washed himself. Then he left the house with an umbrella.

He got off the bus at the Chahamun terminal. Although he had asked Madam Ko the directions to the prayer-house, he felt himself lost in this unknown place. He asked at one of the roadside stores. Luckily, the storekeeper seemed to know about the mountain prayer-house quite well. He told In-mun detailedly. It seemed that the prayer-house was well-known around here.

To the right-hand side from where the road ended was a stream which made clear and rock-hard sound as it flew. About five miles up the gorge along the stream was an orchard on the left marked off by an arch-gate on which was written: The Garden of Truth. Entering this gate, one followed a mildly upslanting pathway between fruit trees to find white-plastered buildings on both sides of the pathway. Thinking that these were the prayer-house buildings, In-mun started to go toward them. Just then, however, a woman came from somewhere among the buildings toward In-mun. In one hand she held up a vinyl umbrella and in the other carried the Bible and the psalm book. In-mun asked her if this was where the prayer-house was. She said it was a little way further up in the gorge.

Passing the orchard, In-mun crossed the stream. From this point, on, it was mostly rock road which was bumpy and slippery from the rain water. Having walked so much since the day before, In-mun felt his legs stiff and unmanageable so that several times he nearly fell on the slippery rocks.

Finally he arrived at the depth of the gorge where rocks the size of houses stood around at random. Standing among these rocks against the mountain slope, In-mun saw a low-lying construction bespread by rain and mist. Going closer, In-mun found a gate with a sign written in two rows:

The First Prayer-house of Samgaksan.
The Prayer-house of All People.

Inside the gate were three houses in a row which In-mun had taken to be just one house looking at it from some distance. The walls of these houses were built with mud and the roofs were faded canvas cloth. On the front side, moreover, the walls did not have even one window or a door. Around the corner on the other side, In-mun found, at regular intervals on the mud house-complex, several doors paneled with artificial glasspanes. In all, the whole setup looked much more like some animal pens than houses for humans. Yet, from inside, voices which were unmistakably human reached In-mun's ears mixed with the sound of rain.

After a few seconds' hesitation, In-mun went up to the first door of the first mud-house and knocked lightly. Although he heard voices inside, nobody answered his knocking. In-mun knocked a little harder and then opened the door without waiting any longer. In the dark interior of the windowless room which was doubly gloomy because of the rain, In-mun saw a figure of a woman in white clothing who was bent forward on the floor and seemed not to notice In-mun's opening the door. She was muttering words breathlessly of which In-mun could not make any sense. Hurriedly, In-mun closed the door. Inside each door he opened, In-mun found women, alone, or by two or three, absorbed in praying, none of them paying any attention to the opening of the door by In-mun. In one of the mud-houses, In-mun saw a woman who was sobbing, beating the floor with her hand. Only when he opened the third door on the second house did In-mun find his mother who was the same with other women in that she was oblivious to In-mun's opening the door and then entering the room, all absorbed in her praying. He decided to sit just inside the door, then it occurred to him that he would be shading off some of the meager light that came in through the artificial glasspanes and so he sat a little to one side from the door. The floor was icy cold.

The mother he saw prostrate upon the floor was not the person he knew in her everyday life. Madam Hong was quiet and short of word at home. Yet the woman In-mun was watching now was pouring out a torrent of words in a fervent entreating manner although he could not tell what she was saying. He felt as if the woman he was seeing were not his mother.

About half an hour had passed when his mother finally sat up. As if her body had become stiff from being bent for too long, she took time in straightening herself from the prostrate position. She turned her head in In-mun's direction once, but as if her eyes could not see anything, she looked away. Then, suddenly, she seemed to realize that there was someone there by the door. Supporting herself with her two arms propped against the floor, Madam Hong leaned forward to peer at the intruder's face. In-mun noted how pale his mother's face looked in the dusk of the room. Then, he saw his mother's forward-leaning upper body shrink back with a start. Next second, she was back on the floor, face down, muttering words of prayer breathlessly. Not knowing what to do, In-mun sat on, until his mother, interrupting her prayer for a second, gasped, without getting up, 'Come here, son, and kneel.' Then without waiting to see how In-mun was responding to her order, she resumed her prayer. In-mun went toward his mother on his knees and bent down by her. Now he could hear the words of his mother's prayer. She was saying: 'Take pity on the lamb that has come back, Lord, and cleanse his sin with Your precious blood. Lead him to God, O Lord.' Gradually, her voice merged into sobbing which made her words indistinct. Listening to his mother's sobbing, however, In-mun forgot the sense of alienation he had felt a while ago toward his mother. He was glad that he had come there. Madam Hong sobbed for a long time. From time to time, In-mun felt as if he were going astray from the stream of sobbing prayer his mother was continuing. He tried to stay with the stream. Through conscious effort, he could for a while longer be with his mother in her prayer, but again he got lost. After repeating this process a few times, he found, at some point, that he was irretrievably cut off from the stream of his mother's sobbing prayer.

Something shook him on the back and he woke up. The room had grown darker than when he had first entered it. But now there was no sound of rain coming from the outside.

"You'd better go home before it gets dark."

"I came to take you home," said In-mun looking his mother

in the eye.

"You go along, son."

"As for the snake...."

But Madam Hong hurriedly interrupted, wincing visibly,

"Don't mention the word! How could you? How could you bring that devil who caused us to be turned out of paradise into our house?"

"I threw him away."

"But the devil still lives in your mind. You proved it even now. You slept when I wanted you to pray with me. You must serve our Lord with three times as much devotion as ordinary believers. You owe it to Him. It is not like any other child that I've raised you."

Madam Hong's voice trembled. The honest fact was that she was discontented with her conception of In-mun itself. It was because her husband Kim Sang-jin was in the middle of his relationship with In-ju's mother then, which made In-mun's birth a sort of an accident or a mistake. After the baby was born, Madam Hong resolved to bring the child before God so that the seed of sin that was her newborn son could be cleansed as much of his sin as possible. She had him baptized before his first birthday and always took him with her when she went to the church for service.

"Maybe you are unredeemable."

"We will spend the night here together since it's late. But you must come home with me in the morning."

"No, that's not possible. So you go on home before it's too late."

Seeing that his mother was not likely to change her mind easily, In-mun decided to leave by himself. As he was putting on his shoes outside the room to go home, he heard the voice of his mother starting to pray again.

It rained for five days almost without a stop. Na-mi was sitting opposite In-chol complaining about the weather. The main objection she had against the weather was that it was delaying the completion of her house.

Ever since In-mun came back from the prayer-house, In-chol stopped worrying about his mother. She will come home when the rain stops, he thought. About In-mun, also, he relaxed his mind and decided to leave him alone for a while, just as he and In-ju had agreed to do. When he thought about how he and In-ju had agonized because of In-mun's disappearance, In-chol felt chagrined but it was not as if he could not understand his brother's motive altogether. Besides, he had gone to the prayer-house in that pouring rain. He must have had some inner conflict to overcome, thought In-chol.

One day when it was still raining, Professor Chi received a phone call from Professor Om who was in the history department. He asked Professor Chi if he could come over to his office. Professor Om was sitting with somebody Professor Chi did not know when he arrived at his office. It was a well-dressed man of about forty or so and on the chair by his side was a large leather bag that seemed to belong to him.

Professor Om introduced the man to Professor Chi.

"It's a great honor to meet you, Professor," said the man handing a name card to Professor Chi.

The name card described him to be a certain Mr. No who was a member of a certain Editing Committee for the Compilation of A History of Korean Cattle-Raisers' Union. Professor Chi could not understand why his colleague had called him to his office to meet this man, who now protruded some staple-bound sheets of paper. Professor Chi saw that an identical sheaf of paper was lying on the table before Professor Om.

"I am so terribly sorry to bother you who must be busy with all sorts of things, but do please help us in our work," said the man.

On the cover of the bound sheets of paper which Professor Chi now recognized to be some mimeographed documentation was written: An Abstract for A History of Korean Cattle-

Raisers' Union. Wondering what help he could give an association of cattle-raisers, Professor Chi lifted the cover page.
Inside, he read a foreword which ran:

'Men were not born unequal originally, but at some historical points and in some geographical areas some human
beings have been subjected to harsh discriminations.... The
case of our society presents a most extreme example. Our ancestors who belonged to the so-called *chonmin* (lowly people)
class received a grossly unjust treatment from the society at
large. It is partly to make up for the wrongs our forefathers
suffered that we, the descendants and inheritors of their
calling, now wish to compile A History of Cattle-Raisers'
Union in a united effort.'

The table of contents showed that the first chapter would
offer a historical survey of the development of the cattle-
raisers' profession from the Three-Kingdom Period through
Koryo and Choson Dynasties. The second chapter was to
treat the themes of anti-Japanese struggle with a separated
section on the Hyongpyongsa in which the evolution and
meaning of such an organization was to be explained along
with the organization's anti-Japanese activities. Also, there
was to be included in this section a listing of the names of
its leaders and a comparative discussion of the Hyongpyongsa and the Taedongsa.

Only when he read this last part of the abstract did Professor Chi realize why it was that Professor Om had called
him to meet the visitor. On a number of occasions lately,
Professor Chi had asked his colleague on the theme of the
butchers, borrowing books and other related materials from
him. What Professor Om had in mind was for Professor Chi
to ask this man about whatever he wanted to know about the
paekchong class. With this new intimation, Professor Chi
read the last page of the abstract which gave the Resolution
of the Hyongpyongsa:

Fairness is the basic principle of a society just as love is the essence of humanity. The purpose of our organization is to eradicate the class differences, erase the insulting name the society has branded us with, encourage education of our children, and seek ways to elevate our life style to that of other rightful members of our society. In what unspeakably low position we *paekchong* class have borne our painful lives! Looking back on what our ancestors had had to go through, we can only weep and lament for pity. For so long, we have been sad, poor, inferior, persecuted, and enslaved. Ah, we the *paekchong* have suffered too grievously for too long!

April 25, 1923
In Chinju, Kyongsangnam-do

After reading through the above Resolution, Professor Chi asked the man,

"The Hyongpyongsa no longer exists, isn't that so?"

"Yes, that is a fact. It dissolved because of the Japanese repression."

"I thought it had disbanded voluntarily," said Professor Chi remembering the farmer in Pundinamutkol telling him that the butchers themselves decided to disband the Hyongpyongsa because they would only be advertising their lowly origin by forming and belonging to such an organization.

"That's not how it was. The Japanese had closed their eyes on the existence of the Hyongpyongsa because they wanted to placate the Korean public in whatever way they could after the March Patriotic Movement. When the power of the Hyongpyongsa grew, however, they forced its dissolution. After the Liberation, the Taedongsa was formed as successor to the Hyongpyongsa."

"Is this Taedongsa still extant, then?"

"Yes, but only in form. It's not doing anything socially active. It's just maintaining its existence under the name of the Cattle-Raisers' Union."

"Why is it then that the Hyongpyongsa was first formed in Chinju instead of Seoul or any one of other bigger towns in the country?"

"I am afraid I can't answer that. All I know is that the organization was first formed in Chinju and then its headquarters transferred to Seoul some time later."

Inwardly Professor Chi thought that perhaps it was not altogether strange that Chinju which, located at a key point on both the land and sea traveling routes, was famous for its luxurious and pleasure-centered culture should have been the site where an organization of butchers first initiated.

"As it is written down in this foreword, no systematic record has been made of how our people have lived and cooperated with one another. That is why we have decided to visit the leading historians who might give us some valuable help," said the man pulling out a notebook from inside his briefcase. In it were written the records of all his visits to different professors of history. Professor Chi read in the list such names as Lee Pyong-do, Yu Pyong-min, Hwang Ui-don, and Yu Yong-dae all of whom were well-known historians.

"I hope you will both be so kind as to 'lead us with a whip,' as the saying goes."

It seemed that the man thought Professor Chi, too, was a historian.

"The business that brought me here is to ask if I could obtain some information about the relationship between our ancestors and the Seventy-two *Hyon* (wise men) that existed in Tumun-dong during the late Koryo Period. If either of you two professors could explain this relationship on the basis of historical evidences, we would be infinitely grateful."

The man spoke these words as if he was thoroughly practiced in the performance.

"This is the first time that I hear of this. Have any of you people heard of any relationship existing between your ancestors and this Seventy-two *Hyon* of Koryo?" asked Professor

Om.

"As you both must know," said the man, "a group of people known by the name of *kwanin* lived in the area next to the Songgyun-gwan, I mean the area next to the present-day Songgyun-gwan University. Among these people were some called *hyonbang* or *tarimbang* who made a trade of selling raw meat. It seems that a few out of the Seventy-two *Hyon* of Tumun-dong came and lived among these people for a period. According to some investigations, only sixty six out of the Seventy-two *Hyon* could be identified by name. As to the remaining six wise men, or *hyon*, four were known only by the surname while neither the surnames nor the given names are known of the last two. We think that these two are the ones that lived among the *tarimbang* people."

While the man talked on in a confident tone as if the essential relationship between the butchers' ancestors and the Seventy-two *Hyon* was a fact beyond doubt, Professor Om listened nodding his head mechanically but without saying anything. Professor Chi, on the other hand, thought that maybe what the man was saying was not too improbable in view of the fact that a man named An Hyang who was one of the *kwanin*, or *panin* which was *kwanin*'s other name, is recorded to have offered up one hundred of his slave-servants to help rehabilitate the Songgyun-gwan which had been devastated during the invasion by a barbarian army from the Chinese border. Part of these may well have made butchering their trade.

Professor Chi had already explored the vicinity of the Songgyun-gwan University in Myongnyun-dong which was known to have been the domicile of the group called the *tarimbang*. What Professor Chi could find out on this occasion was that the *tarimbang* group connived with bureaucrats for the monopoly of their trade. The concrete form by which this connivance worked was that the tradesmen, that is, the *tarimbang*, supported the young Confucian scholars of the Songgyun-gwan during their years of study there with the understanding that these aspiring young men when they should pass the state examination and obtain government posts would protect the interests of their erstwhile benefactors. There was even a shrine by the name of Sungbosa (Shrine of Noble Reward) erected for the men who loyally looked after the *tarimbang*. This shrine is now situated at the back of the Songgyun-gwan University, a little to the east, flanked on both sides by ordinary houses. From the outside, the shrine, too, was little different from other houses in the neighborhood. One entered it through the front gate on which there was no sign. To the left from the gateway were the living quarters where a family was actually living. On the right-hand side was the shrine proper with its faded *tanchong* (red and blue painting) and screen doors from which the rice paper was completely gone. With the permission of the master of the family that lived on the shrine compound, Professor Chi had entered the shrine which was unbelievably ill-kept. Dust was thick on the wooden floor and both the ceiling and the walls were overhung with numerous spider webs. Amongst all this filth and confusion, Professor Chi noticed a shelf-like table stood against the innermost wall. Going closer, he counted twelve dust-covered memorial tablets arranged in a row on the dusty table. Lifting the blackened wooden covers of the tablets, Professor Chi read a number of names who had been highest officials of the government including those of the *yong-uijong* (comparable to prime minister), *chwa-uijong* ('left' minister, next in rank only to the prime minister), and *u-uijong* ('right' minister, next in rank to *chwa-uijong*). Thanks to the wooden covers, the calligraphy on the tablets was distinctly legible despite the passage of time and the slackness in the maintenance of the shrine. The man who was the master of the family living on the premise said that his family had been caretaker of the shrine for two generations. This man who looked to be in his forties also told Professor Chi that the rites were offered until a few years prior to the Liberation but not even once after that. Then he added in a rather complaintive tone that really the Cattle-Raisers' Union ought to see to these things but 'they never did anything to help maintain the shrine, let alone offering the rites.' The caretaker also said that the shrine had been damaged by bombing during the Korean War which he had had to repair on his own. Then, with a sigh, he lamented that before long, the shrine might decay into nonexistence. Professor Chi asked the man if there were some documents left about the *tarimbang* of old time. To this he replied that there was no such thing but the room he was using now was once the office of the *tarimbang* and for this reason there used to be the official signet in his keeping but now it is in the care of the Cattle-Raisers' Union.

On his way back from the shrine, Professor Chi dropped by the Cattle-Raisers' Union office and asked to have a look at the signet. After asking questions such as 'Who are you?', 'Why do you want to look at the signet?' etc., the Union staff who questioned Professor Chi took out from a locker-cabinet a wooden box which was adorned with brass all around its side surfaces. The signet was kept inside this box. It was a square jade signet which was about five centimeters on each side. Professor Chi read four Chinese characters: *hyon-bang-tae-pyo* on its underside surface. Professor Chi made an imprint of the signet to add to his research material. He knew that this was a signet that was used for giving permission for butchering of cows and oxen. It was easy to guess from this how the *tarimbang* had monopolized the butchering right and how great the profit thus made must have been. The *tarimbang* was, thus, affluent enough to sponsor the Confucian scholars during their preparation periods for the state examination, which later brought them back their monetary investment in the form of a continued government protection of their monopoly rights for butchering.

What the visitor to the Professor Om's office was now saying was that a few from the Seventy-two *Hyon* of Tumun-dong had joined this *tarimbang* group for the sake of making their living. Since the butchering had not established itself as a separate trade until the middle period of Choson Dynasty, however, the few that were conjectured to have joined the *tarimbang* could, even if it were a valid conjecture, only be the descendants of the original Seventy-two *Hyon* who existed in the late period of Koryo Dynasty.

As if he, too, were having the same thought, Professor Om said,

"We must not jump into a hasty conclusion, of course, but at least we have the following record on hand. That is, about the time of King Sejo or thereabouts, a certain Choi of a *yangban* house was entrusted to the care of a *paekchong* family as a young child after his own mother died early. Later, as a young man, he continued to associate with this family going hunting with their sons. Then there is another case of a *yangban* merging into the *paekchong* circle. This man took hiding in a butcher's house when he was chased by Yonsan-gun's men. Later, he became the butcher's son-in-law."

The visitor hurriedly made notes of what Professor Om recounted, asking the latter the titles of books in which these records appear. Maybe it was not so much to trace the history of how their ancestors lived and worked together but to prove that some of their ancestors were non-*paekchong* and that some were even *yangban* that the Cattle-Raisers' Union wants to publish what they are now proposing to, thought Professor Chi.

"What you must keep in mind while promoting this project is not to forget the maxim that you must state only the truth of your past and present," said Professor Om in a somewhat strict tone.

"Oh, of course, that is our maxim, too," said the man.

Before he left Professor Om's office, the man said again that he looked to the two professors for their help without specifying, however, exactly what it was that they could help their work in. After the man left, Professor Om said to

Professor Chi,

"I told you to come over because I thought he might have some material that could interest you. But I am sorry it was for nothing that you took the trouble."

That was true. Only, he could gather from the man's account that the Hyongpyongsa may have been formed in Chinju initially and that the motive for its dissolution may be different from what he had thought before meeting this man.

Without losing time, Professor Chi wrote to a former student of his whose home was in Chinju where he had returned after finishing his graduate work. In his letter, Professor Chi asked his former student to find out the origin, activity, and circumstances of the disbandment, of the Hyongpyongsa. A reply came in a few days.

[....I tried to meet Mr. Kang Sang-ho who was one of the chief organizers of the Hyongpyongsa and is fortunately still living. I was, however, prevented from talking to him in person because he is very ill at the moment. Instead, I met the Chairman of the Council of Sponsors for a local middle school who provided me with answers to your questions. Since he took part in the Hyongpyongsa activities as an involved outsider watching every step it took, he seems to deserve our trust in what he relates regarding various aspects of the Hyongpyongsa.]

From this point on, Professor Chi's former student wrote in questionaire form:

⟨— When was the Hyongpyongsa formed?
—It was in the Year of Kyehae, so it's exactly thirty five years ago.
— What was the initial difficulties confronted by the organizers of the Hyongpyongsa?
— An organization named Supyongsa had been formed in

Kyoto, Japan, one year before the inauguration of the Hyongpyongsa. The Japanese phenomenon was a sort of an equal
rights movement on the part of a group of people who considered themselves as socially discriminated. The Hyongpyongsa movement may be said to have been triggered off by
the Japanese example. Mr. Kang Sang-ho, the leader of
the Korean movement came from a family in Chinyang.
His participation in the Hyongpyongsa movement, therefore,
may be said to have been motivated by a purely disinterest
sense of justice and humanity. He was severely criticized by
his family, relatives, and friends, as well as other people of
his community who called him 'a new *paekchong.*'⟩

Professor Chi now understood why the Hyongpyongsa was
formed originally in Chinju. He also knew after reading the
letter up to this point that the so-called Hyongpyongsa movement had not been started by the butchers but by an en-
lightened leader of a non-*paekchong* origin.

The questionaire continued:
⟨— What was the impact of the Hyongpyongsa movement
in terms of public's attitude toward the *paekchong* class?
— After a time, the Hyongpyongsa moved its headquarters
to Seoul, where a national convention of the butchers
was subsequently held which passed a resolution on their
appealing to various governmental posts for an understanding of their position. Thanks to these efforts, 1) a new
law was ratified repealing the old law of marking the names
of the *paekchong* in red in the family register like those with
a criminal record, 2) The old custom of enforcing the male
members of the *paekchong* class to wear *paeraeng-i* on their
head and the females a piece of black cloth on their *chima*
disappeared, 3) They no longer needed to live outside the
limits of a town in a group but were allowed to make their
homes anywhere they liked.
— When was the Hyongpyongsa dissolved?
— Within four to five years of its inauguration.

— Was it in obeisance to the government order?

— Not exactly. You may say that it was a spontaneous happening. At first it was a nonpolitical organization whose purpose was solely in enhancing the social status of the *paekchong* class. In time, however, a segment of communists infiltrated into the organization who ended up by changing the nature of the organization's activities into a communist movement. These communist elements started such tributary organizations as the Meat-Sellers' Union or Carters' Union from their strategic position in the Hyongpyongsa and started to inculcate communist ideas to its members. And others in the community through the Hyongpyong Youth Corps which they installed anew within the Hyongpyongsa for this specific purpose. In this way the original nature of the Hyongpyongsa was in time completely lost leaving only the communists to carry on their inculcation through the medium of the organization. Repression by the Japanese government-general started soon enough with the result that the communist core members fled to Manchuria putting an end to everything. Those who had started the organization as a pure equal rights movement including Mr. Kang dropped out of the Hyongpyongsa when the organization began to be taken over by the communists.⟩

Thanks to this detailed and convincing report of his former student, Professor Chi learned that the disbandment of the organization occurred neither as the farmer in Pundinamutkol recounted it nor as the visitor to Professor Om's office had described it.

⟨This is perhaps irrelevant to our subject, but here the butchers seem to annually commemorate the twenty-fifth of April which is the inauguration date of the Hyongpyongsa with some sort of a ceremony. We may say, therefore, that the Hyongpyongsa still preserves its solidarity at least internally. I have also heard that the butchers have collected

medicine fund for the ailing Mr. Kang. It seems that they are
intending to carry Mr. Kang's coffin on their own shoulders
in case of his demise. ⟩

The above report satisfied Professor's Chi's curiosity suf-
ficiantly for the time being at least.

Madam Ko walked into the *hyon-gwan* breathlessly. It
was the third morning after the rained had stopped.

"In-ju! In-ju!" she called.

Hearing this, In-ju who was combing her hair in her room
ran out.

"Where's your brother?" asked Madam Ko panting. "Bring
him to me quickly!"

Both In-chol and In-mun had come down surprised by the
commotion.

"Has anything happened?" asked In-chol with a worried
restless voice.

"I went to the prayer-house today and...." Madam Ko
seemed too short of breath to continue. Everyone watched
her mouth.

"And I saw your mother lying flat on her back in the
prayer-room," said Madam Ko finally.

"Why?" asked In-mun, stepping out from behind his
brother. "Is she sick?"

"Yes, yes, very sick. She's boiling with fever and altogether
too pitiable to look at. I don't know what ailment it is that
she's having but, if you ask me, I will say that she had a plenty
of reason to get sick. But we will talk about these things later
and right now you must go to her at once. Hurry. She needs
your help. I couldn't bring her home by myself."

"In-ju, go and tell father that we must have the use of the
car," said In-chol, and went back to his room to change his
clothes. If Madam Ko could not single-handedly bring down
his mother, it was clear that her sickness was very serious.

Kim Sang-jin did not seem too surprised to hear the news.

He merely muttered discontentedly, 'She can pray all she likes, but not so she'll get sick on her family!'

Both In-ju and In-mun skipped school and got on the jeep with In-chol. In-ju took a light quilt cover with her. The weather was quite chilly. Especially after the jeep had passed the Chahamun, mountain air that penetrated into the inside of the jeep was cold to the skin.

The uneven road which was barely wide enough for the jeep to pass through ended in front of the arch-gate with the sign: The Garden of Truth. In-chol, In-ju, and In-mun got off and leaving the chauffeur inside the jeep, they walked the rest of the way up to the prayer-house compound.

As soon as the three went near the mud shacks that consisted the prayer-houses, they heard human voices coming out of them in one huge indistinct rumble.

In-mun led his brother and sister to the room where he had last seen their mother. They found Madam Hong lying under a blanket in the room that was in semidarkness despite the fact that it was the morning hour of a fine day. Somebody must have heated the floor somewhat; it was not as cold as the other day.

Their mother's lips were parched and her breathing was rough and uneven. When the children called her, she half opened her eyes but closed them again right away. Her forehead was burning hot to the touch. Then, they heard words coming out of their mother through her parched lips: 'Lord...do not...forsake me...O...Lord....'

An old woman came into the room. It seemed that somebody had told her about the visitors.

"Why didn't someone bring her home or let us know when she first got sick?" said In-ju in a sharp tone, too upset to control herself. "If Aunt Ko had not come by today, I don't know what would have happened to our mother!"

"You're right to get upset. We, too, urged her to go home or to give us your telephone number or address, but she refused to do either. She just kept saying we needn't worry.

It seems that she stayed out in the rain praying and then fainted. She wasn't here in the room when I had brought in the supper tray and I thought maybe she had gone to the out-house. But she still wasn't here when I came back to take away the tray and the food was untouched. Only then I realized that something was wrong and started looking for her. I found her by a big rock up on the slope with her arms around the stump of a pine tree standing next to it. It was such a dismal cold day with all that rainfall. Even a young healthy person would have gotten sick in that situation."

— Madam Hong was praying with her face down on the floor of her prayer-room that day as on other days. Her body and mind were thoroughly fatigued, yet she had to overcome it through her faith and power of prayer. She kept on praying. Then, suddenly, a pillar of fire came down from the sky and stood at a spot within arm's length from her. She raised her head and looked up. On the zenith of the burning pillar, she saw a figure wearing a robe of snow-white brilliance. The halo behind this figure's head was so bright that she could not look straight at the face. After closing her eyes for a few seconds, she tried again to look up at the face. The result was the same as before. Look, can't you see me, a voice that was both stern and gentle said from behind the burning pillar. Then a hand stretched out toward her. She could look at this hand clearly. It was an emaciated hand which was as dry and crooked as a dead twig. And on its palm was a large scar from which blood flew out and merged into the burning pillar of fire. Seeing this, she burst into tears; the sadness and pain she felt was too overwhelming to describe. Come and feel it, the voice said. It is just you that I allow to feel this. She broke into new tears, overcome with gratitude for this grace, but said in a sobbing voice, But Lord, how could I go up that high? Have faith and stand up, then you will be able to feel it, said the voice. She stood up. Suddenly she felt so light that she could fly up through the

pillar of fire as if she had wings and reached as high as His
feet. She knelt down. Although she was within the burning
pillar, she did not feel the hotness. On the contrary, she felt
refreshed as if a breeze were cooling her body. The long skirt
of the robe brushed her on the forehead softly. An indescrib-
able whiff of fragrance embraced her. Diffidently, she
stretched a hand and touched the bottom of the white robe.
Instantly, the burning pillar disappeared along with the
figure that was standing on top of it. Only the rough skin of
a tree stump was left for her to feel—

The children decided to carry their mother on their back
to the jeep. In-chol was the first to carry her. Feeling her
fever on his back, he tried to hasten his pace but found that
he could not move as quickly as he wished, not so much because of the weight of her body but because she hung down
on his back like some unconscious object. In-mun tried what
he could to make his brother's task easier by staying her body
from behind but even this did not quicken In-chol's speed of
movement very much. To make the matter worse, the
pathway to the gate where the jeep was parked was full of
slippery rocks. After a while, In-mun took turn in carrying
her on the back. On the whole, In-mun covered a longer distance then did In-chol in carrying their mother from the
prayer-house to the jeep. In-chol thought it was a good thing
In-mun had come along. They laid their mother down in the
middle of the back seat and covered her with the quilt cover
In-ju had brought with her. Then In-mun and In-ju sat on
either side of her nearly hugging her for support. Eyes closed,
Madam Hong muttered in a feverish whisper the same mono-
syllabic prayer words that she had muttered a while ago back
in the dark room.

Arriving in town, they went straight to the Severance Hospital. The diagnosis was an acute case of pneumonia. Luckily
there was a room available so that they could get her hospitalized.

Her fever dropped on the third day and she recovered a

full consciousness. For whole three days, In-ju stayed with her taking care of her day and night. In-mun, too, dropped in every day after school. As for their father, he only came on the day she was hospitalized and then one week after that. He stayed for a brief while on both occasions. Upon his second visit, he asked his wife,

"When are they dismissing you?"

"The doctor says tomorrow or day after tomorrow," she answered.

"I see. That's maybe better because you will be more comfortable when you are back home," said Kim Sang-jin in an emotionless tone.

"I would like to stay here a few more days," said his wife.

Without saying anything, Kim Sang-jin lit his cigarette.

The nurse who came to take the patient's temperature and count her pulse walked to the window and opened it after glancing at Kim Sang-jin smoking his cigarette. Madam Hong seemed ashamed of her husband in front of the nurse.

Kim Sang-jin who had stepped outside the room looking for somewhere to shake off the ashes from his cigarette left the hospital for good on an impulse.

The nurse who finished her job in the room was about to walk back to the window to close it but Madam Hong told her to leave it open. After the nurse left, she picked up the Bible that had been lying next to her pillow and opened it on a page that she had marked by folding it at a corner. She had been reading this part over many times during the past several days.

〈Do not think that I have come to the world to give it peace because I have come to give it a sword. It is to sever the daughter from the mother, the daughter-in-law from the mother-in-law. I will make a man's enemy out of his family because those who love their family more than they love me do not deserve me, nor those who love their sons and daughters more than they love me. Also, those who do not carry their cross and follow me do not deserve me....⟩

Closing her eyes, Madam Hong prayed, Lord, please please please grant me the strength to carry out what I have resolved to do. Lord, please help me to persevere to the end without succumbing to weakness.

On a Saturday which was the tenth day of her hospitalization, In-chol went through the procedure for his mother's discharge from the hospital and prepared to take her home. His mother surprised him, however, by asking him to take her back to the prayer-house.

"What are you saying, mother? Are you going to commit a suicide or something?" said In-chol shocked to a fury.

"No, it's not that. I feel that I will become healthy once I get there. Please take me back there, son."

Madam Hong's eyes were seeing the pillar of fire that she had seen that day and her ears were hearing the stern but gentle voice she had heard coming from behind the burning pillar. If only she could touch the skirt of that robe and feel the piteous scarred hand once more, she would be the happiest of all souls! For a fleeting second, she wished to tell her son about the burning pillar and the voice that spoke to her but as soon as the thought came she dismissed it for fear that she might anger the Lord by disclosing their secret to her son. Turning to In-mun who had come with In-chol, she said,

"You must not worry about me. Just go to the Sunday service without fail."

In-mun stood speechless.

CHAPTER SIX

The Duet

The next Saturday, In-mun went to see his mother after school without even going home to leave his satchel. When he arrived at the prayer-house, his mother was praying not inside the mud shack but outside by a rock farther up the gorge from the precincts of the prayer-house. A few feet from her was a large stump of a pine tree whose bark was thick and rough. The first words she uttered when she saw In-mun were whether he had gone to the church on Sunday. Unawares, In-mun answered yes. Then, unable to bear standing there before his mother's eyes which were turned toward him but apparently not seeing him, he turned back and went home. The next Sunday, too, he did not go to the church. Unlike in the bygone days, now he did not even look after his animals with attention. Rather, he neglected them for days on end as if on purpose. At school, also, he was apt to fall into a mental vacuum, merely remembering his mother's eyes that were turned toward him unseeingly. They were an indication of his mother's nonexistence. Now, sitting in his seat vacant-mindedly, In-mun sought his mother's eyes of yore when she scolded and coaxed him. He moved about in this state of half-dazedness for several days and then reverted back to caring for his little animals. Then again he would fall back to the mental vacuity. When he was caught in this latter mood, he even felt like throwing away his animals altogether.

When he first heard of his wife's going back to the prayer-house, Kim Sang-jin had blurted out in anger, 'Does she think she hasn't given us enough trouble?' Yet, within his mind, Madam Hong had become so unimportant that it did not matter whether or not she had gone back to the prayer-house.

"How's your father?"

"He died."

"What? When?"

"About a week ago."

Ki-ryong's answers to In-chol's questions were short and mechanical. Their conversation, therefore, halted almost as soon as it started. He had met Ki-ryong by chance on the bus which he had taken at Tongsomun where he had gone to see his academic adviser at his house. It was about five o'clock in the afternoon and his intention had been to go straight to Montparnasse. When Ki-ryong got off at the Chongno 4-ga, however, In-chol got off after him. Before Ki-ryong went into a narrow alleyway around the corner of the Office of Monopoly building, In-chol caught up with him and asked him if he had time to have tea somewhere with him. Without saying yes or no, Ki-ryong made a motion for In-chol to follow and led him to a drinking house within the alleyway. They sat facing each other in a room which was so small that if four men sat around the square low table with its top full of black pock marks made with burning cigarette ends, there would not be room left for anything else. The drinking house seemed to have a couple more rooms of that size.

The news of his big-father's death did not impress In-chol one way or other in any special way. His feeling was as apathetic as the tone of the voice with which Ki-ryong reported it to him. Rather he began to feel as if now something which had remained unsettled had been settled. He thought, moreover, that he would then make this drinking party his last meeting with his cousin who insisted on denying their blood relationship. The lack of communication between cousins, however, was turning the occasion into a mere ordeal of a continuous discomfort and awkwardness. He thought, therefore, that he would put an end to this meeting as soon as they finished the drink that had been brought. He emptied his cup as soon as the woman with a heavy makeup filled it and urged Ki-ryong to drink. Just then somebody called the woman outside the room.

"Why can't you stay put in one place, huh? You can't leave a table so soon," said Ki-ryong curtly to the woman, picking up his cup.

From his way of talking, In-chol could tell that Ki-ryong was one of the familiars of this tavern. He was drinking in the rough manner of an angry man; his eyes were mostly directed at some spot in the air, rarely at In-chol.

"By the way, does that professor of yours still have any use for the knife?" Ki-ryong asked suddenly.

"Ah, the knife. . . ." In-chol said noncommittally.

When he had first heard of his big-father's death, In-chol had spontaneously thought of the butchering knife not so much in behalf of Professor Chi but because he was just curious to know what Ki-ryong was going to do with the knife. When the subject was thrust before him by Ki-ryong abruptly, however, In-chol did not know what to say.

"I believe he would be happy to have it," said In-chol finally.

"Why does he collect things like that? But I will bring it up, anyway, when I go home next time."

There was no hesitation in his tone. Then Ki-ryong added as if to himself,

"It seems people become mad once they give their heart to something although the madness may show in many different ways."

After a pause, Ki-ryong said again,

"My father, when he lost his sight, put the knife over his

eyes and said, 'I can see, I can see.'"

"How did he lose his sight?"

"He had recovered the use of his paralyzed limbs to some extent so he could go to the outhouse with the help of a stick. And he recovered his speech, too, though it never became very clear or smooth-flowing. But then, one morning, he suddenly lost his sight. Ever since then, he made a habit of putting the knife over his eyes and saying, in a stammering blunted speech, that he could see."

The quiet emotionless voice with which Ki-ryong told this story seemed to make it the more pathetic somehow. In-chol thought that maybe there was something of the old man's fanatic belief in his own mother, too. Unable to dissuade his mother from her indomitable determination, In-chol had taken her, along with the bedding and change of clothes, back to the prayer-house where he gave money to the woman who delivered meals to the prayers asking her to heat the floor for his mother and to feed her something nutritious. In-chol still remembered how happy his mother's pale drawn face had looked as soon as she stepped into the prayer-house compound.

"What do you think he had seen?" asked In-chol.

But just then, the woman who had gone out of the room opened the sliding door half and motioned Ki-ryong to come out. Ki-ryong looked at her but did not stir at once. Despite the substantial amount of wine he had drunk, there was no trace of intoxication on his face.

"You are wanted out here," said the woman, this time verbally.

"All right," said Ki-ryong. The woman did not leave. She kept on standing with her hand still holding onto the sliding door.

"Say I will come out in a minute."

"Can't you step out for a second, though?"

"Well, then, bring whoever it is in here. That will settle it, won't it? And bring in more wine, too," Ki-ryong said in a decisive tone. But In-chol read some degree of discomfort on his face. The woman closed the door after throwing a glance in In-chol's direction.

"It looks like you had had a previous engagement with someone. I will go," said In-chol, secretly glad to have the excuse to leave. But Ki-ryong said peremptorily,

"Oh, no. It's quite all right. Let's enjoy our drink."

Ki-ryong looked at In-chol now, for a long second, this time. Although his face and voice still lacked expression, In-chol began to feel something different coming from Ki-ryong; it was close to the soft dampness that your palm feels when it touches the surface of a rock which looks dry and hard to your eyes but is moist and yielding when you actually feel it. Maybe this was something that happens when loneliness of a man piles up so high within his heart that finally it spills out of its confines for lack of room, thought In-chol sitting down again. Ki-ryong filled his cup.

In a little while, the sliding door opened again admitting somebody inside. It was a woman. She was wearing an indigo-blue suit and no makeup. In-chol guessed her age to be about twenty four or five. As if she wanted to take in Ki-ryong wholly with her eyes, she opened them wide once and looked at Ki-ryong when she came into the room. In a second, however, she turned her head toward In-chol letting her eyelids drop back, and looking down. She sat down beside Ki-ryong who proceeded to introduce her to In-chol.

"This is Choi Esther. She works as an instructor at a place called The House of Maria."

The young woman bowed her head lightly in In-chol's direction hardly looking at him. Then she looked at Ki-ryong with something like an accusation in her eyes. In-chol thought then that maybe there was a tone of sarcasm in Ki-ryong's voice as he introduced the woman to In-chol. He, too, remembered reading about this place called The House of Maria. It was an institution for rehabilitating the prostitutes,

sponsored by a wealthy Christian. The photographed pictures of the exhibition showing these women's handicraft had
appeared in the newspaper along with an article about them.
What would be the life of an instructor at such a place like,
wondered In-chol.

"How's your health?" asked Ki-ryong.

"It's got much better," she answered.

"I'm glad," said Ki-ryong.

It was a colorless curt conversation. The woman seemed to
expect Ki-ryong to say something more to her, but the latter
had turned back to In-chol.

"Have you had this kind of an experience?" he said. "A
person gets run over by a car. The bystander thinks he will
bleed himself to death. Yet, he pulls himself up in a few
minutes as if nothing had happened. At these times, the one
who had been watching would say, 'How fortunate it is that
he was not hurt,' but secretly, the bystander feels a bit disappointed. Don't you agree? One feels this kind of disappointment when a fire that looked threatening at first dies down
quickly. Don't you agree with me?"

In-chol could not answer because he was at a loss to know
what Ki-ryong was driving at. The woman spoke before he
could answer,

"Are you angry with me because I tried to call you out?
And you said you were too busy to come out yesterday,
too.... Why do you avoid seeing me?"

In-chol saw a feverish glint in her eyes, noting the unusual
blackness of her eyelashes and eyebrows.

"I don't understand what made you change so much," she
said in a quarrelsome tone.

"It's not going to work between us."

"What is not going to work between us? Say it. I have
lived only for our life together."

Ki-ryong looked at the woman, his own eyes as cool as the
woman's were feverish. But he did not say anything.

"I even looked up a room for rent in Kwanhun-dong

because I judged it to be wise to live in a wealthier area if I am to start a career as a seamstress. But I see all that's no use now. I needn't to have learned to use the sewing machine either. My having earned recognition in that place and been promoted to an instructor's position, too, was a meaningless effort."

"You will be all right at the House of Maria, Esther."

"Don't call me Esther from now on. Call me Hwa-ja. Not just in name but in everything else I will be Hwa-ja again from now on. Give me some drink. I will drink until I become unconscious."

Already, In-chol was nonexistent for her. Snatching Ki-ryong's empty cup with one hand, she held it out for Ki-ryong to fill. Although he had no way of guessing the situation in any way correctly, In-chol felt the urgency of the woman's despair. Yet, Ki-ryong remained unperturbed.

"Nothing can take us back to the past. Our relationship has ended," he said coldly.

"But tell me. What have I done wrong?"

"Neither of us have done anything wrong."

"Then why do you act like this?"

"As I said already, it's not going to work out between us."

"Was it wrong for me to have entered that place? You know I did that with a purpose, don't you? I got my disease cured, too. There are many who have escaped from that place. I, too, wanted to do so in the beginning when I lay in bed suffering with my sickness, thinking I would rather run away and go to you and die by your side. But I stayed and bore the hardship. And now.... I think you are too heartless."

After this long harangue, the woman picked up the wine bottle and pouring for herself she drank up two cups without a pause. Ki-ryong did not try to stop her. Instead, he said, turning to In-chol,

"What I think is that the reason why we feel disappointed upon seeing a person whom we thought was injured in a car accident rise up unscathed or a house on fire rescued without serious damage is that man and the earth and the sky primordially seek blood and fire."

"Tell me frankly. You don't like me any more, do you?"

Ki-ryong did not say anything. Suddenly the woman's body fell forward. Thinking that maybe she had thrown herself onto Ki-ryong's knees, In-chol felt very awkward about being in the room. He regretted that he had not left earlier. But it was not as he had imagined. The woman was only bent forward supporting herself with an arm on the floor. She seemed to weep soundlessly for a few seconds and then suddenly sprang up. Her tear-streaked large black eyes were emitting fire as she said,

"I will curse you! I will curse your eyes, your mouth, your body, your everything! And myself, too! For having tried so hard to become a new person to deserve such a heartless man as you!"

She bolted out of the room. In-chol looked at Ki-ryong who had, to In-chol's surprise, a sort of a smile on his face. Yet, somehow In-chol knew that it was not a real smile that he was seeing on Ki-ryong face now.

"I am sorry if I have been the cause of your trouble," he said genuinely apologetic about having somehow interfered in an intimate meeting between Ki-ryong and his girl friend. But Ki-ryong responded instantly,

"Not at all. I am sorry that I let our party interrupted by unpleasantness. But now we can continue with our drinking in peace."

It was night when the two walked out of the drinking house. The night air was chilly against the skin. Ki-ryong did not go in the direction of the street but went on further into the alley. Walking behind him, In-chol thought he would say goodbye to his cousin as soon as they reach a point where one can make a turn to go out to a bigger street. When they arrived at a junction of crisscrossing alleyways, Ki-ryong turned back to him first and said,

"I acted the way I did this evening because I couldn't act

in any other way."

He lit a cigarette and put it between his lips.

"Come with me. I will take you to a pretty girl," said a boy appearing in front of the two from some dark corner.

"Why not," said Ki-ryong as if he had been waiting for the invitation and started after the boy.

Standing in the same spot, In-chol looked at Ki-ryong walk away into an alley opposite from the street side. The scene of Ki-ryong following the young boy in search of an unknown woman of the street presented such a poignant image of a lonely man of indomitable will that In-chol stood spellbound for a few seconds. Finally, he, too, turned to take the alleyway leading to a street. As he turned, however, he caught a human shadow fleeing into the darkness away from him. Although he could not see clearly, he was almost sure that it was Choi Esther who must have been watching the two men from behind, hiding herself in the deep darkness of the alleyway. Swiftly, In-chol walked through the pathway to the street.

Skipping Montparnasse, In-chol went straight to the usual tavern in its vicinity. It looked as if the majority of the drinkers had been to the tavern, already. Empty seats were found all across the hall. Seeing In-chol come in, Pak Hae-yon called him to his table by waving his hand. When In-chol went and sat opposite him, he said,

"I've waited for you all evening, but maybe it's better that you came late."

In-chol kept his silence waiting for the other man to explain the reason for his waiting and the reason why he thought it was better for In-chol to have come late than early. Pak Hae-yon said,

"It was only a while ago that the scoundrel left."

"What scoundrel?"

"I mean the roughneck who had attacked you for no offense whatsoever."

"Did anything happen again?"

"No, but I was worried that you might walk in before he left."

"Why? What's the harm of our running into each other?" asked In-chol with a smile.

"I was afraid you'd start a fight with him if you see him here."

"Well, I might have been beaten up again, or I might have beaten him up, all depending on the circumstances."

"Well, it's a thing of the past, but if I had not been so drunk that night or if only I had had that national assembly candidate friend of mine with me, I wouldn't have left that jerk alone."

In-chol smiled again thinking how even if that strong arm of an ex-national assembly candidate had been in the hall that time he would not have lifted a finger to rescue another man from danger. He knew it because he knew that this was a human jungle where people are kind to each other while they are drinking convivially, but once anything happens to threaten their sense of safety, instantly they become mortally indifferent to each other. Maybe it was the charm of this jungle character of the tavern that had drawn In-chol here.

On this night, too, Pak Hae-yon drank according to the rules of his usual habit. He went through the routine of finishing a drink, wait, and then finish another full glass, without ever touching the *anju*.

"You want to know why I wanted to see you tonight? It's because of this drama of mine about which I told you months ago, do you remember? I think it was on our first meeting that I told you about it. Now I have the text to go with the plot. Isn't that remarkable? Maybe you remember my telling you that I do not wish to turn this work into a pantomime. Listen, then. Throughout the first, second, and third scenes, the characters appear on the stage one by one, and sit around the electric pole leaning back against it. Every

time any of them appears on the stage, he shouts just one
sentence: 'Ah, this is it!' Just this one sentence. As the action
proceeds to the second and then the third scene, the characters raise their voices higher in shouting this one set sentence. In the desert of red earth where not a tree or a tuft
of grass grow and the size of the sun and its heat augment
as the scenes change, the lighting turns from pinkish red
to scarlet, the cackling of crows grows noisier and the human voices, too, become more manifold and high-pitched.
The third scene ends with many people shouting repeatedly,
'Ah, this is it!' and the curtain falling slowly in the midst
of these exclamations. Tell me, what do you think of
this?"

Normally, Pak Hae-yon gave the impression of talking so
the effect of the drink would spread out in his system the
more vigorously. Tonight, however, the drink itself seemed
to spur his talking.

"My feeling is that it is more suited to a pantomime."

"Then, do you mean that I've worked for nothing all these
months? You mean I ought to make it a pantomime, right?
Changing the subject, though, if you were a character in this
play, Mr. Kim, would you be among those already sitting
around the electric pole or one of the group standing in
line?"

"Well, I don't know. What do you think?"

"I guess you would be sitting with your back against the
pole from any account."

"Do you think so? Well, that's fine with me."

Saying these words, In-chol laughed a little thinking about
Ki-ryong and the young woman and wondering what part
they each would be playing in Pak Hae-yon's drama. At
least, Ki-ryong would be either standing in line or he would
not have anything to do with such a dramatic plot in the first
place. Thinking about them made him remember how
awkward and uncomfortable it had been for him to sit with
them in that pent-up room watching and hearing them in

their amorous quarrel. At the same time, however, he had a
feeling that during that bizarre interlude of human drama,
he had gained something rare and precious.

Just then, Na-mi came to their table and sat across from
In-chol.

"Have you been here long, In-chol-*ssi*?" she asked.

"No, I came only a while ago."

"I waited for you at the teahouse. By the way, have you
seen the movie 'The Miracle of a Rainy Night'?"

"Yes. It's been quite some time, though."

"As for me, I missed it when it showed the first time. I
saw it at the Myong-dong Movie House tonight. Actually,
that's where I come from right now. It was a very good
movie, but do you think that kind of a thing is possible?"

"I don't remember the story very well."

"Well, the leading lady gives a coin to her sweetheart as a
token of her wish for his happiness. He goes to the war and
gets killed. The heroine roams about in rain distraught with
despair at the news of his death; she faints at some point,
then wakes up to find the coin grasped in her hand. Do you
remember now?"

"Oh, yes, yes, I remember."

"Do you think that kind of a miracle can really happen?"

"I should say that we must not try to explain those things
in logical terms."

"That movie came out all right thanks to the excellent
acting of Jane Wyman; otherwise, it would have been just
one of those magic-show type entertainments," put in Pak
Hae-yon sipping his drink.

The door opened noisily and Shin Myong-su walked in.
He was wearing a brown nylon jumper and a blue knitted
hat because of which attire, he looked even younger than
usual, tonight. A quick glance at him showed that he had
been drinking. Swaying his body from left to right, the boy
was searching in the hall for someone. Looking at him one
had the impression that he was a young boy who had drunken

some liquor or wine by mistake or in mischief. Although it was obvious that he had seen the three sitting on this side, he hesitated for a second as if in doubt as to the identity of the three people. He came over eventually, however, staggering, and took a seat at their table. He looked at Na-mi with blood-streaked eyes and said,

"Na-mi-*ssi*... I mean...Miss Cho, I have a request for you. It's nothing but that...I would like you to become my dance partner. Would you go with me to a dance hall just once? I am not as clumsy, myself, as would step onto my partner's foot."

Na-mi shot an angry glance at Shin Myong-su and then said,

"Where did you get yourself that drunk? And why do you bother me? Do you think I am easier to handle than some other ladies?"

"What are you saying? How can I ever find you easy in any way? I just respect you. In fact, I respect all ladies. And it is because I am also a respectable gentleman. But Miss Cho, please go to the dance hall with me just once. I hear that In-ju-*ssi*, too, is carried away by dancing these days."

"Shall we go?" said Na-mi to In-chol, getting up.

In-chol got up and started to follow Na-mi. Seeing them leave, Shin Myong-su said,

"If you need a partner for a dance, just call me, call this Shin Myong-su, all right? And adieu, for now!"

Walking out of the tavern, In-chol wondered in his mind if Shin Myong-su's drunken prank did not have some hidden motive. Could he have tried to make a malicious hint about In-ju, pretending to be drunk?, wondered In-chol. In-chol knew that In-ju was interested in learning to dance. Had Shin Myong-su seen In-ju going into some dance hall with a man? And had he meant to tell In-chol about it by acting that way? If so, who was it that went to the dance hall with In-ju? Nam Chun-gol?

"I don't see Nam Chun-gol around these days," he said to Na-mi.

"Nam-*sonsaengnim*? He's busy writing up that play I told you about. He isn't going to come out of his house until it is finished no matter how long it takes."

"Looks like you won't be able to put it up on stage within the year."

"That's what I fear."

"Does that boy Shin Myong-su play a part, too?"

"I don't know. We won't know until the script is finished. But it will be only a secondary role even if he does play in it."

When they arrived at the Midopa bus stop, Na-mi said, "Let's walk to Ulchiro."

In-chol accepted her suggestion in silence. It was at Ulchiro that Na-mi would be taking the microbus going to Hyoja-dong and for himself it would mean only walking an extra block. They started to walk.

"Will you have some free time tomorrow, In-chol-*ssi*?" Na-mi asked.

"Why?"

"I would like you to come with me to choose the trees to plant in our new garden."

"It's too early for that. You can do that in the spring. And in any case I don't know anything about trees and plants. Why don't you leave it to your father?"

"No, I don't want my father to decide how our new house is going to look. Do you know how often I go out to the site? I go there nearly every day. The work with decorative garden stones has been finished today. I've heard that even if you transplant trees in the autumn, they prosper well enough. I can't leave things I've decided to do undone. You will come with me, won't you? I am going to go to a gardener's in Nokponri. I decided on this place after a careful investigation."

It took two whole days to plant five Chinese-junipers, two crape myrtles, one each of white and purple magnolia, and some roses. Even though a professional gardener supervised the work, Na-mi insisted that In-chol stay at the site during these two days of gardening work to make sure that harmony between the garden and the house be ensured.

"I think that makes the place less dismal," said Na-mi with satisfaction when the planting was over.

"And in the spring I will have some more trees planted. Of course, we will have to choose only good ones."

With the brick outer-wall built up, the garden stones arranged, and the trees planted, the whole place looked quite cozy and pleasant. The house itself, too, was not far from being finished with even the roof work completed. Right now, the work of installing the iron railing along the terrace and the cementing the natural stone slabs on the outer surfaces of the house building were in progress.

"I wish they would work faster but no matter how urgently I push them, they will take their own time. And then that long rain spell! I couldn't believe it! I hate those empty doorframes that makes the place look like a ghost house. So I told the carpenters to hurry up and put up some doors into those holes, but they are so stubborn. They say the wood needs a chance to dry sufficiently."

"That's right. Everything has an order to follow. And the interior work is only beginning. I told you before but I will repeat again, consider yourself lucky if you can move in before the end of spring."

"What are you doing to me, breaking my already broken heart? I realize those working here may think me a heartless girl, nagging and driving them to work all the time. But I will nag and drive them more and make sure that we move in here within this year. You just wait and see," said Na-mi throwing In-chol a resentful sidelong glance. But in a minute she said in a bright tone,

"Are you busy this evening? I want to treat you to dinner."

"Well...."

"Don't be frightened. I only want to treat you to a dinner

which you more than deserve."

In-chol returned home to go out again to meet Na-mi at
four o'clock at a teahouse. She was already there when he
arrived and In-chol saw between the drapes of her scarf
which she had tucked into her coat-front, the white narrow
collar of *chogori*. Surprised, he looked down and found out
that she was wearing a traditional long skirt of crimson
color. He also noticed the *poson* (traditional cotton socks)
and the rubber shoes she had on her feet. Feeling In-chol's
scrutinizing eyes, Na-mi said, pulling off her gloves finger by
finger,

"Tonight, I am the hostess and you are the guest, so I want
you to just follow me in my plan. Senseless questions or pro-
positions are prohibited."

Na-mi tried to look solemn saying these words but she
ended up by breaking into a merry laughter.

They ordered tea and after finishing it left the teahouse.
Na-mi called a taxi and urged In-chol to get in. She said to
the driver, briefly, 'Chongnung.' In-chol glanced sideways at
Na-mi who smiled mischievously as if sensing In-chol's eyes.
The taxi turned left at the Tonam-dong crossroad, and started
climbing the Arirang Slope. There was a road-widening construction work going on from the peak of the slope down to
the stream that flew across the Chongnung plain so that it
made a rough riding.

It was in front of the Chongsujang Hotel located deep inside
the Chongnung valley that Na-mi stopped the taxi. Getting
off the vehicle, she walked ahead of In-chol into the hotel
lobby where she was met by a bellboy standing around near
the counter. It seemed that Na-mi had phoned the hotel
beforehand; the boy led the guests to a western-style room on
the second floor. After inspecting the room, Na-mi said,

"This will do. Can I take a bath right away?"

"Oh, yes. We just heated up the water."

Remembering the time they had gone to the Haeundae
hotel, In-chol started to follow the boy out thinking Na-mi

would have reserved a separate room for himself. But Na-mi stopped him asking,

"Where are you going?"

He turned and saw Na-mi's bright laughing face.

"Didn't I tell you that you should leave everything to me today? I will take care of everything, so you just take off your coat and relax."

Outside the window from which the blind had been pulled up, In-chol saw leafless branches of a tree exposing their bareness in the evening dusk.

"You'd better take a bath first. I will take mine later," Na-mi said, still laughing soundlessly.

Seeping himself in the warm tub water, In-chol thought about how he should interpret Na-mi's bold behaviors of this afternoon. If it had been another woman, I might have got a wrong thought and react in a dishonorable manner, thought In-chol. But it was Na-mi who had the strange power of making these apparently erratic actions innocent and pure, distilling only clarity and bright feeling from words and behaviors that might be interpreted in a different way.

Coming out of the bathroom, In-chol stopped short, struck by the picture of Na-mi taking a pose on a chair clad in a traditional suit of cherry blossom color. She had a heavier makeup than usual today. Her hair had been done up in the style of a young matron or a bride and she even was wearing earrings. The leafless branches outside the window were now buried in the ashen darkness and the electric light which had recovered its vitality during the last half an hour or so exposed the beauty of the picture Na-mi drew at this moment in all its demonstrativeness.

Faced with this new image of Na-mi, In-chol lost his power of speech and stood on as if staked on the spot. What he saw was a beauty clarified with extreme of brightness.

"You disappoint me. I have only one spectator and he doesn't say a word of praise! Can't you say something?" said

Na-mi with a soundless laugh again.

In-chol went toward her and kissed her on her lips which seemed to be telling a great many stories. As if responding to each of these stories, In-chol rubbed his lips against hers.

"That's enough," whispered Na-mi pushing In-chol lightly. "Now it's dinner time." Then looking at In-chol, she said again,

"You'd better wipe off your lips."

Unsatisfied in his desire, In-chol took out his handkerchief and wiped his lips. Stains of Na-mi's lipstick were made on the white of his handkerchief. It was the color of the red seal-ink.

Na-mi took out her lipstick from her coat-pocket and walking over to a mirror hanging on the wall applied it on her lips carefully and straightened her hair.

"People will think we are just married," she said smiling at In-chol in the mirror.

"The bridegroom hasn't shaved."

"That's quite all right. The main thing is that the bride look pretty."

They ordered a Korean dinner at the dining hall which was rather crowded. The guests were mostly pairs of man and woman of which the latter was almost invariably dressed in a fully formal manner. It was only a little while later that In-chol found out that not all of them were hotel guests. When the band music started in some part inside the hotel not far from the dining area, the crowd that had been sitting in the dining room started moving toward the sound by pairs.

"They say it's not right for a woman to invite a man to dance, but...." said Na-mi standing up when they had finished drinking up their coffee after the dinner.

"I hope I won't shame my bride with a clumsy performance," rejoined In-chol getting up after Na-mi who laughed softly at his words.

Na-mi's movements were light. In-chol felt her weight

only at the finger tips of the hand that held her on her back. As if inspired by her pliancy and agility, In-chol, too, moved smoothly. The sweet warmth of the whisky he had drunk at dinner spread out to every tip and corner of his body relaxing him very pleasantly. Every time the music stopped, In-chol took a drink while Na-mi only touched the edge of the drink glass with her lips hardly drinking its content. She joked that western liquor would not go well with the traditional clothes she was wearing and laughed roguishly. The music and the mood of the dancers ripened to deeper mellowness as the night progressed. When dancing the blues, Na-mi brought her cheek close against that of In-chol or sent him signals by pressing her fingertips down against his shoulder, conveying, in this way, her wish that they remain on the spot just swaying their bodies gently instead of moving about. Unawares, In-chol became intoxicated with liquor and desire. After around half past ten, the dancers began to leave two by two.

"Let's make our exit, too," said Na-mi.

While she went to pick up the key which she had left at the front desk, In-chol waited leaning against the rail of the staircase. Just as Na-mi had ordered, he was leaving everything to her tonight. And it made him feel comfortable to do so.

Returning to the room, Na-mi walked to the window to pull down the blind. But suddenly, she exclaimed,

"Oh, what a beautiful moonlight!" Then she added, giving up the idea of pulling the blind down, "Let's turn off the light and watch the moonlight."

In-chol went and switched off the electric light. The room sank in darkness while the window lit up. The moon must have risen high in the sky. The shadow of the window frame was printed in moonlight about one meter on this side from the window. In that square of the moonlight, Na-mi's upper half of body was drawing a dark immobile silhouette.

Walking toward the window, In-chol inserted himself into

the whiteness of the moonlight and looked in the direction Na-mi was watching. A bared tree was standing before their eyes. Because of the white luminosity of the moonlight, and an effect of the intersecting plays of light and shadow made by the moon and the branches, the tree looked bulkier than it probably would be. Shadows of branches that he had seen earlier in the evening were cast on the window sill. The thoroughfare that led out to the inner part of the town loomed up in milky white on the left and the shadows of those who had been dancing in the hall but were now going homeward were moving away hurriedly. At a far end where the thoroughfare merged into the pale-gray darkness of night blinked several scattered lights of human habitats which acquired an unusual yellow hue on this moon-bright night. Sound of the band music was heard remotely as if from some subterranean depth.

"What kind of miracle are you waiting for, In-chol-*ssi*?" asked Na-mi suddenly without turning back. Her voice was low and thoughtful when she asked this which moved In-chol's heart with its ring of sincerity.

"A miracle?" said In-chol.

"Doesn't miracle happen when there is pure and limitless hope? Like in that movie I saw a few days ago...."

"Do you have to talk either about acting or a movie?"

"No, I am not talking about a movie right now. I believe that miracles can occur when people wish for something with the whole of their body and mind. What is it that you keep wishing for in your heart? I mean who is it that you wish for all the time? Isn't it the person who lives in Kyonji-dong? Am I not right? I heard about her from In-ju."

"What does she know?" said In-chol laughing.

"She is a pianist, isn't she?"

"I only know that right at this moment you, Na-mi, are by my side."

Saying these words, he turned toward Na-mi and made her face him by spinning her halfway round. Her eyes went

into the shadow of a lattice of the window. Drawing her into
his arms, In-chol kissed her. Her eyes which were liberated
from the shadow of the lattice by his action were wide open
right in front of his eyes. In-chol looked into her eyes that
were within the moonlight. With a complete fixedness, her
eyes were staring into his, as if they were determined to discover a certain evidence there.

The interphone rang. Disengaging herself from In-chol's
embrace, Na-mi went to the receiver and picked it up. She
said, 'I see. That's fine.' After putting the receiver back, she
turned to In-chol and said exposing only the lower part of
her body to the moonlight,

"It seems my bathwater is ready. I will not be long."

Then she left the room at a light gait. Silence fell on the
room. Not even the band music could be heard now. In-chol
took off his jacket and turning off the light lay back on the
bed. A pleasant fatigue spread through his body. Then the
interphone rang again. In-chol picked up the receiver.

"Is this Room Five?" A voice said.

"Yes."

"The lady said she forgot to take her coat with her when
leaving the room. But she didn't like to take the trouble of
going back up, so she went without her coat. She said she left
her wallet in the coat. And...." Here the voice paused for a
second and then continued, "She said she was going to see
about the affair she told you all about and so she wanted you
not to worry but take a good rest here tonight and come back
home tomorrow morning at a convenient hour."

Only then In-chol remembered hearing something like the
engine sound of an automobile a while ago. Then, too, he
recalled Na-mi's whispering something to the driver who had
taken them here from the town as she was getting off the
taxi. Now that he thought of it, she had been unnecessarily
long at the front desk, too, where she had gone to pick up
the key. Remembering these things, In-chol laughed light-
heartedly, and turning on the light, began to undress.

When the game started, a man started talking in a loud voice behind the spectators' seats where In-chol and his friends were sitting close to the first base. This man seemed to be a so-called baseball fanatic. At the instant when the catcher caught the ball thrown by the pitcher, he shouted a comment using some baseball jargon. And then, even before the judge finished declaring a strike, he shouted his own decree of judgment. He seemed completely well-versed in the names and distinguishing features of the players, and although he made a lot of noise, did not seem to mind for he made them laugh with his histrionic performances.

In-chol turned, at some point, to see what this free-lancing commentator-judge looked like. He was a fattish man in his mid-forties; his face was black from sun tan and his gold tooth glinted in the sun when he opened his mouth to shout a word of comment or judgment or encouragement or advice. As he was about to turn away from looking at this baseball fanatic, In-chol's eyes were caught by something they saw there. On a seat a couple of levels below that of the shouter's seat was sitting Ki-ryong. Thinking that their eyes met for a second, In-chol waited for some sign from his cousin. Yet, he seemed to have got a wrong impression. It was apparent that Ki-ryong had not seen him; he merely continued to watch the game with concentration.

"If there had been women, at least, we could be watching them, couldn't we?" said his friend who was working in the Urban Planning Department in an irritated bored tone.

"Why don't women come watching sports games, do you know?" he said again. "Look, there are practically no women here. I guess there are no more than ten in all."

Since it was Sunday and this was the last game of the season which was moreover a final match between leading teams, there was quite a crowd gathered at the stadium. The seats behind the net and those at the back of the first base were filled up to the full. Except for a few seated behind the net, however, they could not find any women in the whole crowd.

"Women like cruel thrilling recreations, not entertainments of this sort. Haven't you seen on newsreels women throwing bouquets, their hats, and even their purses at the bullfighter who has just slaughtered a bull by sticking his murderous knife into his neck?"

"You are talking about western women. The reason our women don't come to watch games like this is simply that these things have not been advertised and explained enough to the people in general. Why don't you start enlightening women by bringing your own girl out here instead of leaving her cooped up in a room," said In-chol remembering the young girl he had seen in his friend's room at the boarding-house many months ago.

"Don't talk to me about that bitch. Do you know how much trouble I had, getting rid of her? Believe me, it was a task, a real task!"

"Do you really have trouble because of a woman at times?"

"Don't ask me that question. You don't understand. That bitch never let me sleep. For a day or two, that, too, was an added pleasure, but, ugh, let's not talk about it any more."

The man sitting next to them glanced at them accusingly. But the Urban Planning man did not try to lower his voice.

"Why talk about me? Why not you? Bring your girl out here yourself, man!" he said.

In-chol thought inwardly, that's right, both of them like sports. Ta-hye was a swimming and basketball champion at high school and Na-mi said she played tennis. Come to think of it, it would have been better if they had switched their specialties, he thought on. If I should ask them to go to a baseball game with me, which of them would be the first to say yes, though? In-chol mused on....

As if he were telling a great secret, his friend whispered into his ear,

"Don't keep both women to yourself. Choose one and give up the other to me."

"Why don't you shut up and watch the game, huh? Do you think everybody is as corrupt as you are?"

"It's not worth the trouble to treat women with decency, if you ask me."

In-chol was thinking in fact, without the joking reminder from his friend, that he had to put his relationship with Na-mi to some sort of a conclusion.

Just at this moment, however, the runner that had gone as far as the second base was being returned to the home base because of an idiotic failure of the catcher to catch an easy ball. There was a lukewarm clapping of hands.

"Oh, this is too disgusting. They are worse than high school teams. Let's go and play the billiards somewhere," said the Urban Planning man in a really disgusted tone.

"No, let's stay a while longer as long as we came to watch the game," said In-chol although he, too, could not take interest in this game. Yet, there was Ki-ryong sitting close behind him.

The baseball fanatic was no longer talking. Maybe he, too, felt disgusted.

The game ended without giving any moment of excitement to the spectators. Standing in the midst of the retreating crowd, In-chol turned back to look at Ki-ryong. He was coming down toward where In-chol was standing. In-chol made a move to accost Ki-ryong. But he passed by without looking at In-chol once. The friend in the Urban Planning Department asked In-chol if the man was an acquaintance of his. Maybe he noticed the change in In-chol's facial expression and behavior. But Ki-ryong had just passed him by without ever showing a sign of recognition.

CHAPTER SEVEN

Ki-ryong

Ta-hye came to In-chol's house right after In-ju and In-mun left for school. She did not send the maid to announce her coming to In-chol but came right up to his room. Her steps had been so soft that In-chol did not know anybody approaching his room until she knocked at his door. Looking at his surprised face with a smile full on her closed lips, she looked all around the room once and then proceeded to take off her coat. She hung it on the clothes hanger and then taking off her scarf hung it up on top of her coat. It was the suede coat and the brown silk scarf both of which were familiar to In-chol's eyes. And the traditional informal clothes she was wearing underneath, too, were ones In-chol had often seen on her. She was so natural in her movements and in her appearance that a person watching her would have thought that she had just come back to her own house from some outing.

"What are you looking at? Shouldn't you give your attention to your guest?" said Ta-hye.

"Isn't it time you had a new scarf?"

"What a thing to say to a lady!"

"A much more bright color would go better with that coat."

"You mean, from your architectural viewpoint? But to tell you the truth, I've bought a new one but have just left it unused. I feel I would not be as comfortable wearing it as I am wearing this old brown scarf of mine."

In-chol wondered why she had so suddenly come without even announcing her visit by phone. He knew that actually that was what he should have asked her about but did not feel up to it and that was why he talked nonsense about the scarf. Especially since, on his part, he had had that absurd proposition from his father, he felt not a little awkward about finding himself face to face with Ta-hye in his room. Ever since that tête-à-tête with his father, something like poisonous thorns of a cactus pricked him inside his heart injecting their poisonous juice into his blood vein and fattening the cactus with his blood. That was why he had not been able to bring himself to visit her. And now that she was here standing before him, he could not ask her the reason why she came. Maybe his inability to ask her the necessary question was a natural phenomenon.

"I hear you've been very busy. Have you finished your thesis?" asked Ta-hye. "No, not yet," answered In-chol looking at the photograph on the wall partitioning his room from his brother's next-door. The picture showed a forest of trees standing on steep mountain slope laid heavily by the white snow pile. It was a scene in fixity. Yet, In-chol's eyes were seeing the whirlwind and the storm that were devastating the areas outside the narrow region caught peacefully in the arrested picture.

"Look at me," said Ta-hye examining his face with her searching eyes as she was in the habit of doing when they met after a long absence from each other. "You don't look so good. Can I help? I could collect research materials and proofread your manuscripts for you."

"You can offer your exclusive service to your father. But to what do I owe the honor of this visit?" he asked finally.

"Do I have to have a specific reason for coming here?" said Ta-hye with her quiet smile.

These were all familiar things to him—her voice, her smile,

and her way of talking. Yet, In-chol could not react to these
in the same way as he had in the past.

As she professed herself, it was not with any specific purpose that Ta-hye came that day. It was just that In-chol had
absented himself for quite a long time from her house and on
this day she had no piano lessons to give in the morning. Also
it was a day when Professor Chi would be teaching classes in
the afternoon which meant that she had only morning hours
to spend outside the house. These days, she did not feel at
ease about leaving the house entirely to the maid who, ever
since the old woman Chun-hyang became bedridden with
anemia, became entirely too busy to be reliable, partici-
pating in the neighborhood gossip about Chun-hyang's daily
condition and, far more than that, about how the old Lee-
toryong was being tormented by his ailing sweetheart.

The maid brought in the tea on a tray. Putting sugar in
her cup, Ta-hye said with a meaningful smile,

"I saw you once in the street. I had gone out to buy something."

In-chol stirred his tea with a teaspoon without saying
anything.

"You seemed too preoccupied to notice me although I was
only a few yards away."

"When was this?" asked In-chol without raising his eyes
from the teacup.

"The lady stopped the taxi and you both got in. She was
wearing a traditional suit underneath her coat. I watched
until the taxi passed me by. How shall I describe her? Shall I
say she had a dynamic beauty? She seemed to have a great
deal of self-confidence, too. She was looking straight ahead
while her partner kept his head fixed in her direction. That
was Na-mi-*ssi*, wasn't she?"

"Yes."

"What kind of an answer is that? Do you think I asked you
because I didn't know it was she? I knew it right away.
Rather you should tell me where you went with her so

formally dressed. Did you go to a movie house?"

"No."

"Were you invited somewhere together?"

In-chol could not respond to her interrogation promptly. The cactus thorns in the deep of his heart woke up sharpening their needles. As if he himself were the cactus shooting poisonous juice through its thorns, In-chol began telling Ta-hye his tale. From a brief factual report of that night which he had started out telling Ta-hye, his story evolved into a detailed impassioned account of a frustrated desire. All the time he was telling his amorous adventure to Ta-hye, however, he was conscious of his hidden impulse to exaggerate his relationship with Na-mi as a far more serious one than it was. Ta-hye listened with a smile, then, when the story was finished, commented in a light tone,

"What a pity! It should have had a better ending."

Ta-hye could not know about what happened at the Haeun-dae. And it would have been too tiresome to tell her about it now because then he would have to tell her, too, about his abrupt return to Seoul, the incident at Pundinamutkol on the Full Moon Day, his brother's letter, his confrontation with his father, and so on.

"I conclude that she meant to show you her love that way. But it was a method so bold that no other woman could dream of. You must hold onto her, this time. Don't let go of her."

For the first time, Ta-hye realized that she was saying things to In-chol which she didn't mean, and she was not even joking. With both hands, she patted her cheeks that were beginning to blush. In-chol lit a cigarette. Ta-hye felt she had to say something more, but she could not think of anything.

She was walking up a mildly-rising slope. On both sides of the road, she saw all kinds of wild flowers in full bloom. The fresh-green leaves of trees that stood at some intervals among this colorful disarray of wild flowers shone bright in the sun. There was silence all around her. Only the sounds of wings of flying birds and their calls to each other were making inobtrusive music in harmony with the sound of a stream water flowing nearby. She was turned out of her house. She could not remember why. She knew just that she somehow got herself turned out of her father's house. She was wearing the clothes she wore at home; she had not even combed her hair before leaving it. She did not know where she was going. Yet, she was not worried or lonesome. After a while, she discovered a log house and only then did she realize that the log house was bound to be there and it was to this that she had walked so far. In the log house, there was no one, but it was spotless as she looked in through the window. She went into the house. Sunlight that poured in through the windows that were on all three of its walls filled every corner of the interior of the log house. She began to comb her hair here. Although there was not a mirror, she felt that her hair was done in a way that suited her taste better than on any other time. With her hand, she brushed her clothes smooth and gave them a touch-up, retying the jacket-ribbons, pulling down the skirt here and there so the bottom line would be even. In a few minutes, she felt as if she were wearing brand-new clothes. Then, she sat down. There was no boredom or loneliness in her. Suddenly, she heard the bicycle bell ringing outside. The sound was clear and sonorous in the clean air. Knowing that the one she had been waiting for was finally here, she went out to meet him. In-chol was getting off the bicycle. He was wearing worn-down work suit and a wide-brimmed sport hat. Seeing her, he smiled, showing his white shiny teeth. There were wrinkles on each corner of his mouth as if he were no longer young. But she did not mind his wrinkles or the shabbiness of his clothing. Without a word, In-chol took out a bottle of milk from an iron-basket hung over the handle of the bicycle and handed it to Ta-hye. She drank the milk right from the bottle. It was warm and fragrant. After taking a few mouth-fuls, she handed it back to In-chol. They repeated this act a few more times. Then suddenly In-chol started laughing. When she asked why he was laughing, he said, 'Don't you know your whole body has turned to milk?' She looked at In-chol, who, too, had turned to milk all over. She said, 'What about you?' and laughed in her turn. But In-chol was getting back on the bicycle. 'Where are you going?' 'To deliver the milk.' 'Don't go.' 'I won't have to do this much longer.' She clutched the handle of the bicycle and pushed the bell. A clear refreshing sound spread throughout the field.

She would never have chance to tell In-chol, thought Ta-hye, looking at him with eyes that seemed to be staring at something far away. In-chol is in love with Na-mi, she said to herself.

"Does Mr. Chon come to the house often?" In-chol asked exhaling cigarette smoke.

"He took a post at Chonbuk University some time ago," said Ta-hye struggling to become free of her conflicting emo-tions and glad that In-chol brought out a new subject.

"Why there?"

"I don't know. My father advised him to stay in Seoul because it seems the conditions of his appointment, too, were rather unfavorable. He didn't change his mind, though."

Knowing Chon Kyong-hun's personality and his relation-ship with Professor Chi, In-chol could only judge that Chon Kyong-hun's determination to go had to do with his failure to win Ta-hye's heart.

"Queen Sondok ought to have detained Chi-gwi," he said.

"I don't feel like a joke right now. Besides, I don't want to be made Queen Sondok. There's no need for you to feel obli-gated to dispose of me honorably if that is your intention."

Ta-hye was not the usual, tolerant, forgiving and loving woman she had always been for him today. There was turbulence in the words she was speaking now. Both In-chol and Ta-hye became aware of this fact all at the same time. Silence flew between them for a few minutes during which each said innumerable words to the other with a soundless voice. It was Ta-hye who issued her words outwardly first.

"What's the follow-up to your story?"

"I returned her the coat next day."

"And?"

"Maybe I will just quit the whole affair."

"What?"

"It's too much trouble."

I have for too long gone with Na-mi aimlessly, he thought. When he resolved to conclude his relationship with her in some form or other, however, he could not help feeling a third factor which insisted on being considered. That was the dark shadow of his heritage.

"You need not hesitate. You and she love each other; the rest is for you to take the lead."

She knew that she was saying things she didn't mean, but she felt that she could not act in any other way.

"I wish everything was as simple as that."

"What's there to make things not so simple, then? You love each other which should be enough."

"You don't know anything, Ta-hye, you don't know anything."

Suddenly, Ta-hye scrutinized In-chol's face in deep silence. She hesitated a little before saying finally,

"Are you worried because of that thing?"

Wincing, In-chol raised his head. Something struck him hard in the heart.

"I heard about it from father. He praised you, saying that it's not easy for one involved in such a thing to act the way you did. So, what's the big deal about it? You didn't, by any chance, stop coming to my house because of a thing like that, did you?"

In contrast to Ta-hye's voice which was gentle and calm again, a great upheaval rose in In-chol's heart making it impossible for him to utter any words.

"If it really bothers you, go to Na-mi and tell her every-thing. Even today."

"You, too, I wasn't going to see again."

In-chol smiled forlornly. The fine wrinkles that appeared at the corners of his mouth seemed to hide the depth of agony he had gone through. Ta-hye stood up from the chair softly.

In-chol felt that she was coming over to him. The next thing he knew was that a touch of warmth pressed his tem-ples on both sides and then he felt a sweet breath descending on his head and a sensation of moist softness on his forehead. Then he heard Ta-hye's trembling voice say,

"Don't ever let me find you looking so sad. I don't want you to. Go to Na-mi, and tell her. She wouldn't be so stupid as to mind a thing like that."

In-chol felt no need to say anything. In the great emotion that Ta-hye's first touch of intimacy, her sweet breath, and the pathos of her trembling voice stirred up in his whole being, In-chol was conscious only of an urge to give himself totally to Ta-hye for her to dispose of how she will. The poisonous thorns of the cactus broke and fell off one by one in his heart. The cigarette ashes fell from his fingers as if they were pebbles.

"Didn't you hear that all roads lead to Rome? It means that if you are good in one thing, you do well in other things, too. So you just try and catch up with me at least in playing the billiards. Then, automatically, you will become more skillful in handling women."

"Do you think just because I lost to you once or twice, that means you are really all that good?"

Ever since Ta-hye's visit of that morning, In-chol had become restless, unable to focus on any work so that he often called his Urban Planning friend out to play the billiards.

"The billiard balls look like women to you, don't day?" His

friend kept on bantering. "The white ball is charming because it's white and the red one is desirable because it's so red, isn't it? If you are drawn to both, the best thing is to conquer either one of them. Then, believe me, the remaining one will come giving herself up. I will bet anything that she will."

These were words that had nothing to do with him. Silently, In-chol walked over to the cue box and put his cue in it. They walked out to the street. His friend who had started to go in the opposite direction saying he had an appointment with someone came back to In-chol and said,

"Say, let's have tea or something somewhere. I am going to make this one I'm meeting today wait a bit before I show up. It will work better with her, I bet."

Then, straightening his tie with both hands, he went on.

"I will tell you the true story. The girl I'm meeting today who is supposed to have gone to a nursing school is a kind all by herself, you see. She says she can watch the surgeon cut off limbs and split up stomachs without a blink of her eye. Yet she says she once had her finger pricked with something and when she saw blood oozing out, she fainted. And she says, she will never have a baby. She says she would rather die than go through the torment of delivery. But—you must listen to this carefully—somehow she got wind of that girl whom you saw at my boardinghouse, I mean the one who would never let me sleep—and do you know what she did? She started nagging me that she wants to have my baby, never mind her declaration about never giving birth to a baby! Do you understand, fella? This is how women are. You might call that a competitiveness or female vanity or whatever else you like. The point is it's a very handy thing to make use of to your advantage."

This, too, had nothing to do with In-chol, however.

"Get out and wait there," shouted the shopkeeper in the direction of the entrance.

In-chol was just beginning to feel the drink take effect in his body. He had not, tonight, gone to either Montparnasse or the usual tavern, nor had he gone with his friend to spend time so he could give his girl friend a strategic waiting period. Instead, he had come into a drinking house where he had never come. He wanted to be alone. It was raining outside and there was a little wind, too.

—Na-mi would be fretting over the rain. Tonight I am the hostess and you are the guest. So you must follow me in my plan. What kind of a miracle do you wish for, In-chol-*ssi?* It's the person in Kyonji-dong, isn't it? I only know that you are there by my side. Had he spoken those words at the whim of the moment, only?—

"I said, get out!" shouted the shopkeeper again.

"Imagine, following me all the way to this place!" muttered a middle-aged man sitting to the right from In-chol, looking back at the entrance.

In-chol looked, too, and saw a beggar in his early twenties with a bushy hair standing in the doorway drenched in rain and trembling. A closer look, however, showed that it was mainly the rain and the miserable manner in which he hung on at somebody's door that made him look so pitiable. His clothes themselves were not so wretched.

The middle-aged man at In-chol's right whose face was flushed with drink sucked at his cigarette furiously a few times, glaring at the beggar with hate in his eyes; when he could make the end of the cigarette an angry red with fire, he threw the cigarette at the beggar's foot. Frightened, the young man fled outside.

"Why was he so frightened by a cigarette fire?" asked the shopkeeper bewilderedly.

"There's a story to that," said the middle-aged man finishing the drink in his cup.

He asked the shopkeeper for more wine. When the drink was brought to him, he took a sip and said it was not warm enough.

—You must be more aggressive because you are a man. But the reason why I hesitate about concluding my relationship with Na-mi in some way is not only because of the dark shadow in my blood stream but also because of you who is constantly breathing in the core of my body, Ta-hye. Come to think of it, you are the reason, Ta-hye, why I feel compelled to draw my relationship with Na-mi to some conclusion.—

"It was two years ago. A fire broke out in the house next-door in the middle of the night. It was a fire by inflammation of gasoline. Luckily there was no wind and the fire was put out betimes so that no other house except that one was affected by the fire. Only, that one house was burnt entirely out. And four members of the family were burnt to death, the couple, the husband's mother, and their younger son. The beggar you saw a while back is their older son. He was in the yard when the fire started and by running out he saved himself. He is a cowardly good-for-nothing. He didn't try saving his family but just stood there trembling like a branch in whirlwind."

— It was really a surprise, wasn't it. She had said, Don't ever let me find you looking so sad. I don't want you to. Go to Na-mi and tell her everything. She won't be so stupid as to mind a thing like that. She thinks everybody's heart is like hers.—

"Not long after the fire, that rascal went mad. We bought his house. It was through mediation of his uncle on mother's side."

"How could you, when you knew four people were burnt to death in that house? Weren't you afraid?" asked the shop-keeper with an exaggerated surprise.

"Not particularly. Actually we had wanted to buy up that house from before the fire because we needed more room for our garden. But the owners were adamant to our offer. They were so poor they couldn't maintain a house properly so that it became dilapidated rapidly. Yet they wouldn't sell. In the end, the miserable state of that house reached a point where it was likely to make the price of our own house go down. Anyway, they met their misfortune when they could have well avoided it if they had sold it to us when we offered to buy it. Of course, I profited from the result."

— If only you are willing, I will accept any condition. I am ready even to remove you from our family register. So, what's the big deal about that? You didn't, by any chance, stop coming to my house because of a thing like that, did you? Why not, Ta-hye. I did, I did stop coming to your house just because of that.—

"Then, that rascal began roaming outside our wall after he went mad. We had our way, though, to chase him away. We only needed to throw a lighted match or a burning cigarette butt at him and he would fly away as if a tiger were after him."

"Maybe he knows his old house even if he is mad?"

"From some time ago, he shows up where I sit enjoying my drink. Believe me, it ruins the taste of liquor for me. But do you know that the earth becomes very fertile if it has the ashes of burnt cadavers? The trees in our garden seemed to just shoot up. They are so prosperous."

"Unbelievable," said the shopkeeper grimacing.

"But he's right. There's no fertilizer like human cadaver," said a thick voice whose familiarity struck In-chol in the head. He turned to the direction of the voice. On the other side of the middle-aged man was a man in raincoat whose sharp-nosed profile was fixed straight ahead. There was no doubt that it was Ki-ryong. Had he been there when he came in, In-chol wondered. Or, had he come in after him? In any case it seemed to be too much of a coincidence that they were thrown together so often within such a short period of time.

Still fixing his eyes straight ahead, Ki-ryong went on, in a level tone.

"It was during the War(Korean War), I saw a soldier's

dead body lying in a farmland. It stayed there until it decayed. Every year after that, I saw that the grains were richer in that spot. One could even see where the head was and where the body and limbs were by the way grains grew. When you go back, you'd better examine your garden, with a flashlight. Maybe, you will see human figures on your trees there. You may be able to tell which is that young man's grandmother and which are his parents and which the brother. All very clearly, I mean. Be sure to check when you return. I am sure you won't be disappointed."

After this speech, Ki-ryong got up and paying for the drink and raising the collar of his raincoat, he left.

The middle-aged man muttered discontentedly staring after Ki-ryong with bloodshot eyes. Then, he picked up the cup and poured the content which must be quite cold by now into his mouth.

— I will curse you. I will curse your eyes, your mouth, your body, your everything! And Ki-ryong had laughed that laugh which wasn't a laughter at all. The man who has a will that is as invincible as it is lonely. Is he a man who deserves a curse? I wish I could get close to his inner self. Apart from being related by blood, I feel so close to him in some inexplicable way. Why?—

After a while, In-chol, too, got up and left the place.

Father has had his bath and *obba* hasn't come home yet. In-mun says he will skip this time, so then, it's my turn now. In-ju poured a few scoops of warm water over her and then stepped into the tub. This is wrong, all wrong. Women must be the first to use the tub and men must use it after women. It is far more sensible, hygienically and otherwise. But if I were to make the suggestion, our father would fly into a fury although *obba* may not. What a stubborn man our father is! But he is so low in spirits these days, why? Is it because of mother who went back to the mountain before she fully recovered from her illness? I don't think so. I don't think our

father cares that much about our mother. Come to think of
it, what kind of a couple are they? Mere strangers they are.
I think father is gloomy for business reasons. Business is all he
cares about.

Coming out of the tub, In-ju started rubbing herself with a
wet towel which she squeezed into an oblong knot. What
should I buy for tomorrow's table? It's not easy to decide
these things day in and day out. I have never kept the house
without mother for so long. And it's becoming cold. We need
to do our *kimjang* (making *kimchi* in large quantities to last
the winter), too. I wish she would come home now. Why
should she insist on staying in that horrible place? I wonder
why she had peeked into my room that time looking at me in
that strange way. I was so frightened I nearly left home
myself.

In the middle of rubbing her breasts with the squeezed
towel, In-ju looked down. In the vapor-blurred electric light,
the round whiteness of her breasts stood out against the rest
of her body. With her two hands, she lifted her breasts as if
to weigh them. It seemed to her that they had become
rounder and heavier. Although nobody could be watching
her, she felt ashamed and so she went back into the tub
quickly and immersed herself in the water up to the chin.
Maybe I will come back home and take my beads bag with
me when going to meet Nam-*sonsaengnim* tomorrow. Last
week, he said his work did not progress very well. I wonder if
he has worked well this week. I wish his masterpiece would be
finished soon. I wish I could help him with his work but I
know I can't. He said he comes out only once a week to see
me in order to give his brains a rest. So what I can do is to
help him get a good rest while he is with me. Yes, that's
what I can do for him. But what would be the best way to
do it? By not talking unless talked to? But when did I talk
without being talked to? By the way, I think Shin Myong-su
stopped following me around. I didn't know he was such a
shameless bore at first. Did he think that I would thank him

and run to a rendezvous with him if he sends me a ticket to the concert? What a fool! But I wanted to go to that concert. I couldn't go because of him sending me the ticket. But it's not as if I gained nothing form it because ever since then he has left me alone.

"You better hurry up," said the maid knocking at the door. "Your brother has come home."

"Well, tell him to wait a little while."

Coming out of the tub, In-ju rubbed soap onto the wet towel and began to rub herself with it starting from the arms.

The maid went upstairs with a dry towel and handing it to In-chol to wipe the rain water off, gave him the telephone messages as usual.

"There has been a call from somebody who said you would know if I tell you that a call came from your Consultant. His voice sounded familiar to me, he must have called the house now and then. There was another call from somebody strange. He asked for you and when I told him that you weren't home, he said he knew it. I was so surprised. Then after a while he said I should tell you that he brought what he was supposed to bring. But then, again, he told me not to tell you anything. He hung up before I could ask who he was."

The maid looked apologetic as if she felt she had done something wrong.

"When was this?"

"Only a short while ago."

"You can go," said In-chol more brusquely than he intended.

"Wouldn't you like to take a bath?" asked the maid in a small voice frightened by the harshness of In-chol's tone.

In-chol did not answer.

"Wouldn't you like to take a bath?" asked the maid again.

"I don't want to," answered In-chol this time.

Taking the used towel from In-chol, the maid went back down the stairs almost tiptoeing. Going back to the bathroom, she said,

"Your brother doesn't wish to take the bath."

Then, lowering her voice, she said again,

"He is very drunk. He is no drinker although he does drink." Giggling softly, the maid went away.

In-ju understood that the maid had come to let her know about her brother's not wishing to take the bath because she well knew that In-ju liked to take a long bath. But what's the matter with *obba* these days, said In-ju to herself. Why does he drink every night? He must be worrying over something. From what Ta-hye *onni* (older sister, also used for any older female in familiar relationship) told me on the phone this afternoon, it seems he isn't going to her house, either, these days. But why did Ta-hye *onni* want to know Na-mi's telephone number? Anyway, I think *obba* is being foolish. I know Na-mi has her own charms, active and lively, but how can she be even compared with Ta-hye *onni*? If I were *obba*, I wouldn't even think twice. Men are all foolish, and unreliable. I will never marry. In any case, what is it that's bothering my favorite *obba* so much? I tell him everything but he would never tell me anything. It's unfair. Is it because he thinks I am too young to confide in? I told him that he looked like Raskolinikov after his murder of the old woman and he said it must be because he was too tired working on a house plan. Why didn't he frankly tell me that he had a problem planning his life? Why does he lie to me when I am no longer too young to understand these things?

She soaped herself again and again making hundreds of bubbles. And she thought on, and what about In-mun? Why is he getting so funny? He never was talkative, but not as tight-mouthed as he is lately. Besides, he looks as if he were not entirely sane. And why doesn't he wish to take a bath? What kind of a family are we, anyway, nobody seems normal in this house. In-ju rinsed herself many times by throwing warm water over her shoulders.

Lying in his bed, In-chol sank into thought. Ki-ryong must have seen me at the drinking house tonight. But why had he called home knowing that I wasn't there? And what was it he said he had brought?

The rain had stopped but the fog was still there. The damp chilly air of late autumn morning flew slowly but incessantly in a silver-white mistiness.

The slaughterhouse of Miari was at the foot of a mountain which explained the thickness of fog in this part. When In-chol walked into the courtyard of the slaughterhouse, a darkish shadow of a man was walking about noiselessly. Looking more closely, In-chol discerned that he was loading lumps of meat into a vehicle parked within the courtyard. He would carry a lump of meat from inside the house to the truck and unload it in the covered back compartment of the vehicle which somebody inside the compartment would then pick up and pile with other lumps already loaded. Because of the fog, the meat lumps looked as if they were darkish-colored cargo about to be transported somewhere on a mover's truck. In-chol thought of waterfront laborers loading trucks with cargoes just unloaded from a ship.

A man looking like a veterinarian was checking a cow's mouth in front of the house. A man was pulling at the cow by its nose ring while the cow tried to move backward. The veterinarian tugged at the animal's tail to make him come forward. The cow, too, was being treated like an inanimate cargo. Going to a window, In-chol looked in. Through the misty semitransparence of the fog-dampened glass, In-chol saw Ki-ryong who was moving about busily with several other men. The man In-chol saw now, however, was different from the Ki-ryong he had seen outside the slaughterhouse. He looked jovial and simple-hearted.

Deciding to wait until Ki-ryong should be free of his work, In-chol started walking back to the courtyard when Ki-ryong's voice called from behind,

"So you came."

Turning back, In-chol saw his cousin who was walking toward him with the sleeves of his work jacket tucked up and his feet in rubber boots.

"Are you here for the knife?"

No, it was not for the butchering knife that In-chol had come here. He wanted to see Ki-ryong. It occurred to him then that it had been all along Ki-ryong himself that he wanted to get close to and the knife was more or less an excuse for this other purpose. "It's in my boardinghouse right now. What will you do?"

"I will wait."

"We may take longer today. We have to send the supply to the army."

"It's quite all right. I have time."

"I am not sure if I will be through in the morning or in the afternoon. A man has to come out from the barracks. Couldn't I meet you in the evening?"

"Any time is all right with me."

"Then meet me at five o'clock at the same house in Chong-no 4-ga."

Ki-ryong hurried back into the house.

Walking back through the fog, In-chol thought to himself: If he isn't sure whether he'll be through in the morning or in the afternoon, it means that he wouldn't be busy throughout the day. He might have been able to take a little time off and fetch the thing from his boardinghouse unless it is very far away. Maybe he, too, wants to spend time with me under the pretext of the knife. . . .

"It's been several days since I brought this up. But somehow I couldn't bring myself to call you to come out for this which is only a butchering knife after all. I couldn't decide what to do, and then. . . ."

He didn't go on although it was the sequel to the above explanation that In-chol most wished to hear. Without many more words, they repeated the gesture of pouring and drinking wine. Yet, unlike on the preceding occasion, they did not feel uncomfortable or awkward with each other. They felt something like a subterranean water stream connecting their hearts together.

"You don't get drunk easily. You must be very strong with drink."

"Not at all. I only learned to drink after I came up to Seoul. It's only my face that doesn't show it."

"Have you been in town long?"

"Since right after the War. I've been here four years."

In-chol threw a glance at the thing underneath the low table. It was wrapped in sheets of newspaper. He had not opened it when Ki-ryong handed it to him. At most, it would be a sharp-edged iron slab of a certain length, he thought. He no longer felt for his big-father the intense hate he had felt, the hate that had been so inextricably interlocked with this knife. He did not think that his reconciliation with the dead old man was the kind that people often arrived at after the person whom they had hated had passed away. Only, he had since come to understand that everybody had an object of preoccupation or attachment which could but appear irrational in the eye of other people the way his big-father's belief in the butchering knife had seemed so unbearably irrational to his eyes. As he thought more about it, he came to sympathize and comprehend his big-father more and more. Now he rather wished to learn about the dead man's life and beliefs. He asked the same question that he had asked Ki-ryong the other night,

"You told me your father said he could see with the knife laid over his eyes. What do you think he saw?"

Ki-ryong put down the wine cup which he had lifted to his lips and said,

"How could I know that? Maybe he saw the heavenly world."

Ki-ryong was smiling, looking at In-chol and lifting the cup to his lips again. Yet, his expression had changed by the time he was finished with his cup which he put down on the low table. He was staring at In-chol without a trace of smile.

Then, he said,

"I thought of blood when my father had that over his eyes."

His sensitive-looking narrow-cheeked face and prominent nose looked tense.

"I don't mean the animal blood but the human blood with which that had been stained."

Almost instinctively, In-chol looked about to see if anybody had heard although he knew that there was nobody except Ki-ryong and himself, not even a waiting woman.

"You mean what happened during the War, don't you?" said In-chol remembering what Professor Chi had told him when showing him the picture of an old man with his eyes closed. He had said that the old man had stabbed to death the father of a man who had caused both his son and grandson to die during the Korean War.

"You know the story, then," said Ki-ryong still looking into In-chol's eyes.

Professor Chi had said after telling him the story, 'He doesn't look cruel enough to kill a man with his own hand even if it be an enemy, does he?' And he had thought in his mind that it would not be right for one to think of the old man's action in terms of whether or not it's cruel. This was before he found out that the old man and he were related. He still thought the same about the matter.

"I think what your father did was rather natural, under the circumstances, I mean."

"You don't need to console me. Do you want to hear the real story, though? It was not my father that did it but me. I killed the man."

Only the eyes that looked into In-chol's eyes with piercing intensity showed inner turbulence but his voice was as calm and expressionless as ever. In-chol persevered under the icy coldness of Ki-ryong's stares with determination.

"Tell your professor that he ought to sharpen that on the polishing stone now and then. Otherwise, it will lose its value."

After a pause, he said again,

"I shouldn't have said it. There's no reason why the professor should polish that thing. We butchers polish our knives for fear that they may rust, but after the event I got to think of it this way. There was another reason why my father polished and sharpened this so meticulously. It was not only to keep it from rusting but to remove the human blood that had been smeared on this as best he could. Especially since it was me, his own son, that had put the blood on it."

Ki-ryong's monologue went on,

"My father worshiped this. After I committed murder with that, he worshiped it with a fanatic fervor. All kinds of things came to take place in our village in those days. A dumb boy began to talk after having his mouth touched with that, another person had his or her ailment cured with that. It was a farce. Suppose, a child is touched with that butchering knife on the mouth suddenly, wouldn't he be frightened out of his wits? No wonder he made some sort of a sound which was his way of screaming. Some children learn to speak late and maybe there occurred some happy coincidence that way. People in our home village had belief in that knife, all right. But then, human beings have a habit of changing and exaggerating facts in order to boast of their having seen something special and wondrous. That's how all kinds of incredible stories circulated making many people develop such a reverence toward that knife. My father, in any case, used to say that the man who was killed with that knife was sure to have gone to the heaven. I know that my father came to worship the knife more and more as years went by because he wanted to lift the sense of guilt from my mind. The trouble was as my father tried harder and harder to obliterate my guilt, I became more and more aware of the blood smeared into my skin. The strange thing is that about the actual murder I committed, I wasn't feeling half so guilty."

In-chol poured wine into Ki-ryong's and his own cups in turn while his cousin paused before he went on,

"It was two days after the National Army had recaptured the capital. That night I escaped from the People's Voluntary Army into which I had been forcibly enlisted. I came home only to find that my brother and nephew had been killed. Without losing a minute, I ran to the enemy's house with that thing. I broke into their rooms and their kitchen, everywhere. There was nobody there. Then my eyes caught sight of the enemy's old father crouching in a corner of the storage shack. He was holding something in his hand, although because of the darkness of the interior of the shack, I could not at first tell what it was. Then I knew. It was the same kind of an object that I myself was gripping in my hand. It was a butchering knife. Yet he was not holding onto it to fight me. As soon as he saw me, he begged to be left alone so he could take his own life. I detested him for being so miserable and humble. I leapt to him and killed him in one stroke. In any case, I was so grieved and mad at the time that I could not have allowed him his last wish. I saw my father standing outside the storage shack. He snatched the knife from my hand and pushed me hard in the direction of our house. He didn't say a thing. A little while later I heard my father's voice shouting behind me: 'I killed a maaaan!' I turned back. In the darkness of the night, my father was shouting the same words again and again with that thing raised high above his head. I understood, then. After the incident, my father polished the knife more faithfully than before and developed a fanatic belief in it. After the War was over, I came to Seoul and have been working at the same place ever since. What I wanted to do was something else. Ever since I was old enough to think for myself, I had resolved not to follow my father's footsteps. My father had wanted to have my brother succeed him in his trade. The reason I chose the career my father wanted me to was that the more my father tried to take the guilt consciousness off my mind, the heavier I felt my responsibility for something which I can't quite put to words. You might say that I chose this profession so that I might see more blood of other kind. I was not very sad when my father died. You may think me a heartless son, but I dare say that I might have wished my father dead. Yet, when I did wake up to the fact that the one person under the sky who knew that I had killed a man was no longer living, I felt desolate and lost. You probably cannot know what this feeling is. One thing clear, perhaps, is that I am one who cannot stand a stable life. Maybe the reason I am telling you my story tonight is that I want you to be the one person on earth who knows my guilt, replacing my father. Returning to my boardinghouse from the tavern last night, I thought about you, remembering how you had had a look of agony and some inner perturbation as you sat drinking by yourself. That was why I called your house although I knew you wouldn't be there. It was an act of impulse, you might say. But I also felt the need to commit myself to an action before I should change my mind. Maybe I need an action and event to keep my life going although such words as these may not be quite adequate to describe my case with. Anyway, stability and security for me mean a life that is dead. The same rule goes with women. I am that kind of a man. But let's drink. I've talked too much tonight. I guess I couldn't help it, though."

For the first time, In-chol felt an undercurrent of emotion in Ki-ryong's tone of voice.

He could not remember how he came to drink at a tavern in Miari. He remembered as far as insisting, when they left the drinking house in Chongno together, that he would see *'hyongnim* (honorific for older brother, cousin, or other males of varying degrees of intimacy)' to his home. Yet he could not remember how they had arrived at Miari. He remembered going to the outhouse to vomit several times at the Miari drinking house and, during the moments of respite between vomiting, making long speeches the way Ki-ryong had in that other tavern. He remembered also explaining to Ki-ryong why he had looked as if he were in agony at that other drinking house where Ki-ryong had walked out without once accosting him. He had told Ki-ryong that he did not know himself why he could not acquiesce to reality and live according to the dictates of the circumstances to which he was accustomed to. He did not understand why he was roaming about aimlessly day after day. Or, should he, like his brother In-ho, seek an escape? In-chol seemed to remember Ki-ryong laughing when he said this last and he seemed to have advised his cousin not to laugh because laughter destroys the perfect harmony of his facial expression.

When Ki-ryong tried calling a taxi for his drunken cousin, In-chol said, 'I'll sleep in your room tonight. Do you mind?' He put his arm on Ki-ryong's shoulder for support and limped along on a bumpy dark road. On the way he met Shin Myong-su and he asked, 'Where you going?' in his drunken voice.

At some point, he had dropped the thing that was wrapped in the newspaper and when Ki-ryong tried to pick it up for him he had stopped him by waving his arm ostentatiously and picked it up himself.

He remembered going into a small room and lying in a pallet bed. Ki-ryong had taken a few books off a pile that was standing at random in one corner of the room to put his head on in place of a pillow.

In-chol woke up past eight o'clock next morning. Ki-ryong was not in the room. In-chol guessed that he had gone to his work. There was a bowl of water by his pillow. The room was not as small as he had thought the night before. The papering of the ceiling and the walls, too, were quite clean and nice. In one corner of the room, there was a fairly large amount of books stacked against the wall. Most of them were social science materials written in Japanese. He got up and put on the clothes, then he opened the newspaper wrap-

pings. It was an approximately ten-inch long knife that looked
as sharp and spotless as if it had been ground and polished
quite recently. From the way the blade was worn in, however, one could tell that it had been heavily used. On its
wooden handle was engraved the winding dragon design of
which it was impossible to tell the beginning and end. The
grooves made by the engraved winding line were black with
age-old grease stains. After looking down at the knife for a
few minutes, In-chol wrapped it up again with the newspaper and left the room with it.

His head throbbed with a dull pain and his insides turned
over. Yet his heart was light. What had been Ki-ryong's reaction when I said I would sleep the night in his room?, he
asked himself. He was almost sure that Ki-ryong did not dislike the idea. It seemed to In-chol, moreover, that Ki-ryong
had smiled many times last night, which was unimaginable
from his previous remembrance of his cousin. In-chol pictured to his mind the Ki-ryong that would be working busily
in his work clothes within the slaughterhouse full of blood
and grease smell.

He paused catching sight of a burning charcoal fire by the
roadside. The angry red of the burning charcoal dazzled his
eyes. When he reached the bigger street, again his eyes were
drawn to a red fire just before the smaller road ended. The
fire was at a welder's shop where a man was blowing the
bellows on the fire in which a few iron bars were stuck askance.
In-chol stopped to watch. Then he walked up close, saying,

"Could you make me an iron fixer with this?"

He unwrapped the knife and showed it to the man at the
bellows who, letting go of the implement, looked up with a
darkish-red rustic face looking bewildered.

"I don't know.... For an iron fixer, though, people usually
use a different material," he finally said.

"It doesn't matter. I would like you to make one using
this," insisted In-chol.

"You can get one much cheaper at a hardware store," said

the man.

"I don't care about the cost. Here, I will give you an advance payment of two hundred *hwan*. Have it ready until tomorrow."

But In-chol was not going to come to pick it up.

PART THREE

CHAPTER ONE

Another Beginning

Ta-hye was looking into a mirror. She took off the scarf that was around her neck. She was not comfortable with this one which was new. She touched her neck with a hand. In-chol had said a more colorful scarf would go better with my coat. And I had answered that I had one which I had bought but left unused. This one was a bright silk fabric in which red was the dominant color. As if with determination, Ta-hye passed the scarf around her neck again. She felt she could guess why Na-mi wanted to meet her. Probably, In-chol told Na-mi about his family and now she wants to see me who has known him from childhood and is, like herself, a woman.

Her voice that Ta-hye heard on the phone sounded quite unique, clear-spoken with distinct intonation. She told Ta-hye what color clothes she would wear so that Ta-hye could recognize her without difficulty. She said she would wear a beige coat. She didn't know, of course, that I have already seen her, said Ta-hye to herself. She was wearing traditional clothes that time.... Ta-hye remembered the crimson color of her long skirt that showed beneath her coat. The contrast between the snow-white *poson* and the bright red of her *chima* was striking. Ta-hye thought she would recognize Na-mi at once no matter what she would be wearing for their rendezvous today. She drew Na-mi's oblong face with a faint smile on her red lips and her large eyes touched up with the eyeshadow.

The image that Ta-hye drew in her mind of Na-mi presented a personality so different from Ta-hye's own, yet Ta-hye thought that the two of them might get along quite well once they meet. She smiled at herself in the mirror. Stretching her neck a little, she passed her hand around the scarf on her neck. She felt a little more comfortable with the new scarf than when she had tried it on the first time.

Her mind was calm as she left home to meet Na-mi. For an early winter, the weather was mild this afternoon.

With her mouth shut tight, Na-mi made a smile twisting the corners of her mouth delicately. It was a face of a woman who had confidence in herself. Na-mi made up her mind to keep this smile all through her conference with Ta-hye who was the cause of In-chol's incomprehensible indecisiveness. He would come toward her with aggression and then suddenly retreat. And Na-mi decided that this was because of the existence of the other woman Ta-hye. She had suddenly felt an urge to find out how they were all interrelated by contriving a meeting with Ta-hye. She had been light-hearted enough about this venture to draw a script to be played by her so that Ta-hye could never suspect her real motive.

A woman pushed open the entrance door of the teahouse gently and, stepping inside, looked around the hall calmly. She walked toward Na-mi who had in the meantime fixed the prepared smile on her face and made a slight gesture of getting up to meet the other woman. When Ta-hye stood by her table, Na-mi said,

"Please sit down."

They examined each other unhurriedly. Then Na-mi said, still with the smile,

"I knew it was you the minute you came in!"

Yet she had not even asked Ta-hye what color clothes she

would be wearing on her part when telling her about her beige coat.

"Me, too," said Ta-hye glancing at the notebook and the purse in front of Na-mi on the table. Maybe she had been to school, thought Ta-hye. Although she had said, 'Me, too,' however, the woman she met here was not the woman she had drawn in her mind. She had the same large eyes but her lips were not as decisive as those of the other Na-mi and her face, too, was narrower and longer than the other face. Could it be the change in her makeup?, wondered Ta-hye. Or, had she used too much imagination in depicting Na-mi's face to her mind's eye lately?

"The telephone line was mixed up with some other party this afternoon, wasn't it?" asked Na-mi interrupting Ta-hye's thought.

"Oh, did it? I didn't notice although there was a moment when I couldn't hear your voice."

"Maybe, you didn't hear, but it was interesting. The voice said what fun is there in a woman meeting a woman. And he said he would be wearing a red coat so I should recognize him and let him join our table. What a buffoon!"

Just as she had thought, Na-mi was a lively and innocent girl. Although they had just met, Ta-hye felt tension melting away between them, already.

"I, too, wanted to meet you. Thank you for calling me first," she said.

It was true that she had wanted to meet Na-mi. That was why she had asked In-ju for Na-mi's telephone number sometime ago. Yet she had been putting it off.

"I got your number from In-ju-*ssi*. She wouldn't give it to me so I had to force it out of her, in a manner of speaking."

"You must be joking. Since it was quite some time ago that she last talked with me on the phone, I believe she couldn't recall it instantly herself. In fact, In-ju almost never calls me on her own."

"Do you think so? My impression was that she didn't like

me to get to know you. To tell the truth, I wasn't sure that I
would call you even while asking In-ju for your number, but
when In-ju hesitated to give it to me, I definitely had to see
you."

"That sounds like an impure motive, doesn't it?" said Ta-
hye in a joking tone.

"There's nothing in this world that's hundred percent
pure. Certain things merely have the appearance of purity."

Ta-hye thought Na-mi was an interesting woman. Maybe
In-chol was drawn to this characteristic of Na-mi especially,
she thought.

"I hear In-ju is training to be an actress, is that right? I
never thought of her as a person temperamentally suited for
stage."

"That's not true. She is sensitive, so she understands dramatic texts very well. And she is good at acting, too. She isn't
an exhibitionist; she just does her job well. I think she will
play a big part in the play our theatrical group is going to
put up on stage at the end of this year, or early next year, at
the latest. I hope you will come to our performance. I will
send you the ticket. It's possible that In-chol-*ssi* will do the
scene designing. But I don't see him much these days. In
fact, I have never seen him for... let me see how long it has
been...."

Na-mi calculated the days since the day on which In-chol
had returned her coat after spending the night by himself at
the Chongsujang Hotel.

"I haven't seen him for three weeks."

Ta-hye counted the days in her turn. It was about two
weeks ago that she had visited In-chol at his house. Hadn't
he told Na-mi, then?

"Maybe he is busy writing up his thesis. It seems he has to
have it printed and handed in by the middle of December."

Not likely, said Na-mi inwardly and for a split of a second
her face lost the equanimity it had so far succeeded in
maintaining.

"I am not sure about that. You see I called him at his house today and he wasn't there. And to my knowledge, he is drinking a lot these days. A person saw him in the street only the other night, drunken from head to foot."

It was Shin Myong-su who gave this report to Na-mi. He had told her that In-chol was walking in the street with someone right before the curfew hour, completely drunk.

"I think he is avoiding me. I don't understand because there's no reason why he should. I played some mischief on him last time we went out together but he isn't so petty as to have that against me. Why doesn't he tell me he no longer wants to see me if that's the case. He needn't try to avoid me."

Ta-hye decided that this was the moment.

"Why don't you try and find it out?"

Na-mi took a sip from her teacup taking care that she does not leave the lipstick mark on the cup. Then she asked, her prepared smile once again securely fixed in its place,

"You mean I should ask him first?"

"Yes. Don't think about your pride. He needs you now. He...yes, he loves you. I think there's no other way of putting it."

Na-mi leaned back against the back of the chair laying her head on its ridge. She wasn't smiling any longer. When she read or heard the word 'love', she had always felt unconvinced and awkward. Yet, when the word was spoken with the voice of this woman Ta-hye, it sounded natural and convincing.

It was clear to Na-mi that Ta-hye knew her relationship with In-chol, thought Na-mi. Had In-ju told her? She did not think so. In-chol must have told her of his own accord. But what about me? Had In-chol ever told her anything about Ta-hye? Never.

"I know too little about In-chol-*ssi*."

She wanted to add, 'to feel loved by him,' but didn't.

"Is it possible for us to know anyone entirely? What is

more important than knowing may be a readiness to understand, and I think you, Na-mi-*ssi*, have the capacity for such understanding."

"I don't think I comprehend what you mean. What is it that I need to understand? Is there anything that I misunderstood?"

Is she thinking that I have misunderstood her relationship with In-chol?, thought Na-mi for a second while putting the last question to Ta-hye.

"Maybe I did not make myself clear enough in my haste to come to the essential question. But in any case, please take an initiative and see him. You will then know that he has had no intention of avoiding you. Something is troubling him. It is because he cares for you that he is not seeing you."

This put Na-mi in a greater confusion than ever. What Ta-hye was talking about did not seem to have anything to do with her relationship with In-chol. Then what was it that was making it so difficult for In-chol to see Na-mi? She wanted to ask this question to Ta-hye but refrained from it. What was it that this woman knew all about but she did not. Her self-respect, however, forbid her to ask the necessary question. One thing clear was that she was being excluded from the knowledge of the thing which represented In-chol's present agony but Ta-hye was sharing the knowledge with him. The world of mystery in which In-chol and Ta-hye coexisted was encircled with a wall so tight-knit that she could not hope to penetrate it. At the same time she realized this, Na-mi became aware of the fact that her feeling for In-chol was not strong enough to make her risk breaking through this thick wall. The half-cynical, half-mischievous smile came back to Na-mi's face.

"I just realized that I don't care for In-chol-*ssi* as much as you seem to think. I don't have much urge to find out why In-chol-*ssi* is agonizing."

"I don't think that's true. What is true is that In-chol-*ssi* loves Na-mi-*ssi* and Na-mi-*ssi* loves In-chol-*ssi*."

"What I feel is you might exchange your name for mine in the sentence you've just uttered."

"What a thing to say!"

Ta-hye was embarrassed. She felt as if Na-mi had thrown an arrow at something which was buried deep inside her heart. Yet it was not just a pain that she felt from the other woman's penetration into her secret wound.

While Ta-hye was appraising the mixed effect of Na-mi's poignant remark, Na-mi herself was thinking how their rendezvous was taking an opposite direction from what might normally have been expected. Was it not Na-mi herself that had asked to see Ta-hye? Yet, she was being made to feel as if Ta-hye had summoned her to give her some specific message she had to convey to her.

"Let's change the subject, shall we?" said Na-mi smiling effusively. "I hear that you are always busy because of piano lessons you give the kids, is that right?"

"Yes, I am afraid that is rather the situation."

"I've asked to see you today because I had a request to make."

Ta-hye watched Na-mi's mouth without saying anything.

"I wanted you to help me buy a piano."

This was a pretense Na-mi had prepared in advance.

"Help you buy a piano?"

"I saw two Schimmel pianos at an instrument store near here and I would like you to see which of the two is a better choice."

"I wonder if I could be a good judge in such things. You had better ask somebody who has a more professional knowledge about the make of a piano. You might ask a tuner to help you."

"No, I want you to play both pianos and decide which has better sound. I decided to make my choice that way."

"This is to buy a piano for your new house, right?"

"Yes. To tell you the truth, though, it's more for ornament purposes than for use that we want it. I don't even know how to play a piano properly. I wonder being a pianist you find this an insult to your profession. I hope you will forgive me, though. After all, I am a woman. I like to indulge in a little luxury."

As Na-mi herself said, having a good quality piano for ornament purposes did not seem out of proportion with her general configuration of personality. Seeing Na-mi put on the gloves which she had taken off and placed on the tea table, Ta-hye, too, got up.

After choosing the piano with Ta-hye's help, Na-mi said goodbye to the latter outside the instrument store to go to her father's bank that was in Sogong-dong.

Ta-hye was a woman of tranquility, gentleness, sensitivity, and class. What more does In-chol want? It really seems, though, that he is in some sort of a trouble, but why doesn't he tell me? He suffers more if he sees me because he cares for me? Nonsense. I will say that he lacks candor. Well, it's just as well. I will not see him, either. Yes, it would suit him to be left in the protection of that matronly woman I just met, yes, that would suit him very well!

While immersing herself in this reverie, Na-mi reflected that maybe it was because she really didn't care for In-chol, just as she had confessed to Ta-hye a while ago, that she now thought these thoughts. She started crossing the street when the signal for 'stop' came on. Waiting for the 'walk' signal, Na-mi said to herself: It's about time I lower the curtain on the interlude of my relationship with In-chol.

As usual she used the side entrance to enter the bank office. The guard that was sitting at a desk by the door stood up and greeted her. Na-mi took out a chewing gum from her coat pocket and giving it to the guard went to the staircase leading to the second floor. As she was halfway up the stairs, she grimaced, conscious of the smell of the paper money.

There was a guest in her father's room. Going to a chair

placed close to the window, she sat down. Her father who was sitting in an armchair by his desk and the guest who was sitting opposite him were talking business, using such words as 'terminating operation', or 'description of assets.'

Picking up the pile of official monthly publications of the bank from the small table in front of the chair she was sitting on, Na-mi leafed through them, perusing only the comic strips. She knew that it was one of the workers at this bank who drew these comics which featured a bank clerk as hero, portraying different scenes from his home and office life. As a whole, there was no wit or humor in the entire work.

A girl who did various chores of the office brought Na-mi a cup of coffee saying that she had not put either cream or sugar in it. Na-mi nodded her head once in acknowledgement of the girl's punctiliousness of memory. It was Na-mi's custom to drink the coffee black when she visited her father's office. She once explained to her father that it was to kill the smell of the paper money with the unmixed aroma of the coffee and was scolded by her father for being flippant. Yet, she continued to drink her coffee black whenever she came here.

She took a big swallow from the cup. Just then she felt a movement at her back and turned her head. A strong reflection of sun against a window on an opposite building hit her in the eye and she felt dazzled. It was a burning fire rather than sunlight that she saw on the opposite window. She had an illusion of the melted glass after the sunlight would have receded. On the outer window sill one floor below the one with the burning fire was a pot of plant in full bloom which looked like cineraria. What would happen if the burning fire of sunlight would pour down on that plant? No doubt, the flower, leaves, and the stalk would all together burn down in a minute, thought Na-mi, smiling a cold smile. Yet, she did not wish the plant to be the victim of the burning fire. She wanted herself to be at once the burning fire and the plant that gets burnt down.

"Thank you for everything," said the visitor getting up.

"I will do what I can," said her father getting up also to walk the man to the door.

"What brought you here," asked Mr. Cho coming back toward his seat after the guest was gone. "There's a staff meeting today, so I am a bit busy. What is your business with me?"

Yet there was no impatience in his manner. Maybe he just wanted to hear without delay the matter that had been the cause of his daughter's visit. It was very rare that Na-mi went to see her father at his work place without business.

"I thought my reason for coming here was self-evident."

"But it's been only days since I gave you your monthly allowance."

"It's not allowance money I want."

"What, then?"

Just at this moment somebody knocked at the door and the man who had just left came back in.

"Excuse me. I forgot to take my hat," he said and taking his hat off the clothes hanger by the door walked out again nodding and smiling to the two in the room. Na-mi noticed his gold-rimmed glasses and longish powerful-looking front teeth.

"That man came to take out a loan, didn't he?" asked Na-mi.

"That's right."

"Does he need money very badly?"

"Why do you ask?"

"I just thought he might, seeing how he forgot his hat and so on. It's a sign that his mind is somewhere else."

"By the way, you know him, in a way. He is the father of your friend Kim who drew our house plan."

"Oh, is that so? You should've told me. I'd have liked to look at him more carefully. Anyway, I could see that he looks entirely different from his son. He is more thick-boned, for one thing. So that was his father...hmmm....This is a strange day for me."

"Why is that?"

"It's nothing. You don't need to know, papa. But I want you to give me a loan. I picked the piano."

"Already? Aren't you doing things in a rather lopsided fashion? It will be months before the house will be completed, won't it?"

Then, Mr. Cho seemed to remember something. He said, "I almost forgot. Look at this."

He handed Na-mi a letter sheet which he took out of a drawer of his desk.

"It came this morning. I can't make either head or tail of this thing."

Na-mi unfolded the sheet, then exclaimed,

"What is this?"

Rather than a letter, it was an ugly caricature of ill taste. There was a drawing of the frontal view of a building on the sheet which actually was a page torn out of a notebook. What had shocked Na-mi was that four cow-hooves were drawn at the bottom of the house and on its top were two ox-horns with some span between them and a long knife was laid across on these horns. Even a quick glance could tell Na-mi that the picture of the house drawn on the sheet resembled their new house. She looked at her father and the latter looked at Na-mi.

"I wonder who could have played such a vulgar joke as this," said Mr. Cho.

Na-mi asked her father to hand her the envelope in which the drawing came. The address of the sender was given shortly as Myong-dong and his name was given out as Kang something. Yet, of course, they would be false. The letter was merely addressed to: Bank President. Also, it looked as if the sender wrote the envelope with his left hand in order to avoid detection.

"Let's report to the police," said Na-mi.

"I don't think so. It's just somebody's prank."

"You have anybody who might have something against you, papa?"

"I wouldn't know, daughter."

"I wonder it's one of our would-be neighbors. I mean somebody who thinks he is injured by our building the new house there."

"I don't think anybody would suffer any injury because of our house. We aren't building a factory or anything like that there."

Na-mi was looking intently down at the drawing and then she suddenly exclaimed,

"Ah, that's it. Look, papa. Now I understand why whoever it is put ox-hooves and ox-horns to our house. It's because our new house has a Spanish-style roof. And Spain is a country of bullfighting. Maybe you are right, papa, maybe it's somebody's practical joke."

Inwardly, Na-mi thought: I will see In-chol. Not because I have any other thought but because, if I showed this to In-chol, he might know who could have played this kind of a joke on us. So the purpose of my seeing him is entirely business.

"I will see to this matter, papa," she said folding up the sheet of drawing and putting it in her purse. "But you must see to it that I get my fund for the piano soon. In all Seoul, there are, at the moment, only two pianos that are worth having. We must get one of them before they are both taken by other people. I settled the price at one million and three hundred thousand *hwan*. It's the minimum price, I think, it will carry at all times. I mean it's a good investment for you, papa."

"We must find out if it's well-made, though, I mean inside and all. There's no call for a hasty action."

"You always so underestimate my capability, papa. I don't like it. I already had a professional try out the instrument for us. Don't you worry about such matters but just give me three hundred thousand for a deposit. I arranged to pay the rest upon delivery. You said you had a staff meeting to attend. So hurry up, papa, and give me the money."

As usual Mr. Cho was no match for his daughter in this kind of a conference. He wrote a check for the amount Na-mi asked and handed it to his daughter.

"Thank you very much, papa," said Na-mi happily, then she raised the check to her nose pretending to sniff at it.

"Why are you sniffing at it?" asked her father.

"To see if it has a smell."

"Smell? Oh, you mean the smell of paper money."

"Yes. I don't care for the smell but at the same time I can't feel that I have money unless I have a whiff of that smell. But, I smell it, papa. Just a tiny bit of it."

"What a girl!" said Mr. Cho but without irritation. "Have you dropped in at the construction site, though?"

"Not yet today. I'll go there after I hand in the money at the instrument shop."

"It has been quite warm these several days, but they say a cold spell will come next week. It's not good to do construction work at a freezing temperature. I think we'd better stop the work until next spring."

"No, no, papa. I don't want to. Let's keep on as long as it is possible," said Na-mi with petulance in her voice, then changing the tone, she said, "Well, my business is over. I'll go now. See you, papa."

Coming back home, Ta-hye felt as if she had been betrayed by someone, or something. Hadn't there been no hesitation in Na-mi's attitude? She said that she didn't want to know what it was that was annoying In-chol. If so, what would be the good of In-chol's telling Na-mi about his family's past? When her thought arrived at this point, Ta-hye felt a pity and sadness for In-chol.

She had come to believe that In-chol was more attached to Na-mi than any other woman he had had anything to do with in the past and that Na-mi on her part was going along with his inclination. She had thought, therefore, that it was on account of his relationship with Na-mi that In-chol was agonizing so deeply over the newly-disclosed origin of his family. Now that she has found out that In-chol's great agony had no way of being alleviated by Na-mi, Ta-hye felt as if In-chol were being betrayed and this feeling of betrayal she felt in sympathy with In-chol somehow made her feel as if the betrayal were committed at her own expense. But why was it that this betrayal was not giving her a real pain in the heart? Then, she remembered Na-mi's words which she had spoken with an edge. She had said, '...you might exchange your name for mine in the sentence you just uttered.' Ta-hye had been somewhat taken aback by those words; yet, to be quite frank, she did not wholly deplore them. All of a sudden she felt the curtain that had been screening her from In-chol ever since their common childhood days lifting, exposing In-chol as a male to her face.

Upon returning home, Ta-hye called In-chol at his house at once. He wasn't home and it was In-ju who talked to her.

"Do you know where your *obba* has gone?"

"He went to Samgaksan in the morning."

"Samgaksan? What for? Did he go mountain-climbing?"

"No, it's because our mother's there at the prayer-house. She told *obba* to come and that's why he went. If you have a message, why don't you give it to me? I will convey it to him when he returns."

"No, it's all right. I just felt like calling him up, that's all."

Hanging up, Ta-hye felt that it was just as well, perhaps better, that In-chol wasn't home. She was not even sure what she wanted to say to him at this point. Had she wished to tell him that Na-mi did not love him?

The door bell rang. The maid who went out to the gait came back to the window and said,

"It's the kid from Kye-dong."

She meant one of Ta-hye's pupils who came to take the piano lesson. Before going away, the maid reported,

"I saw Lee-*toryong* going home with a big pollack he bought at the market."

The maid looked up at Ta-hye with a snicker as if she expected the latter to share the enjoyment of the common passtime of the neighborhood.

It had been about ten days since the old woman Chunhyang had passed away after suffering from a severe anemia. It was said that until her last breath, the old woman had not let go of the whip with which she slashed at the old man on his shin for discipline and punishment. At the funeral, the middle-aged daughter who had never been seen to visit the old couple was present. On the night of the funeral, the old man spent all night at their back-porch although the air was very sharp during the night. The old man was worried that the burial site of his wife was wet from some water leakage in the ground. Since the daughter supervised the whole procedure of the funeral, the old man had refrained from saying anything, but he could not help feeling as if he had let his wife sleep in a wet bed and for that reason he would not sleep comfortably in the room.

The next day, he started an investigation on how he should go about moving the old woman's body to a new burial site. After a hundred tedious and difficult procedural steps, he could finally accomplish the work. There was a rumor that he had mortgaged the house, which was his sole property on earth, in order to carry out this project.

The old man was also very particular in his ritual observances for the deceased. He put up the memorial table in the warm, lower section of the *ondol*-floored room the two had shared and made an offering of warm rice-water in place of the usual cold water. Even the pollack which he was reported to have bought at the market today probably was to prepare the evening ritual table for his dead wife with. with.

These days, when Ta-hye ran into the old man in the alley, she could not help noticing that his cheeks were more sunken, his shoulder-bones more prominent, and his hair whiter than when his wife had been alive. She could not, therefore, share the mirth the maid wanted her to partake of.

The sound of the pupil going through the finger exercise in preparation for the lesson came to Ta-hye's attention and she realized that she had not even changed her clothes. Going into the Inner-Room, therefore, she took off her street clothes and put on the comfortable clothes she wore around the house. Then, suddenly, she was overwhelmed with a sense of consternation. It was because she found herself wishing, out of blue, to either beat up someone or else be beaten up by someone. She had never been driven to such loneliness before.

CHAPTER TWO

Two Women

His mother who was prostrate on her face upon the ground looked as if she had fainted face downward from exhaustion. In contrast with the gigantic black rock and the huge stump of a pine tree, her body clad in a white traditional suite looked unbelievably scanty. From this meager body escaped words which were too indistinct for In-chol to decipher. She seemed to be moaning, entreating, and sobbing, all at once. In-chol noticed the faint tremor on her bony back. He stood on, waiting for his mother to come to the end of her prayer. Slowly the thought that he had been for too long neglectful of his mother dawned on him and he resolved once more, as he had made up his mind coming here, to take his mother home with him today.

Finally Madam Hong raised her upper body. When she saw In-chol, she at once folded her two hands on her knees and, dropping her head, closed her eyes. Then In-chol saw her parched lips moving, but he could not hear any sounds coming out of them.

Madam Hong raised her head again, opening her eyes.

"So you are here, finally," she said.

"I couldn't come sooner because I was busy," said In-chol though he knew that it was not exactly true.

Looking more carefully at his mother from the front, In-chol found out that his mother was not more emaciated than when he had seen her at the hospital. Rather, because of the sun tan, she looked somewhat healthier. Her eyes, too, shone more brightly than ever. Yet, they were not looking at him; they seemed to be staring at something that was behind him.

"Is everyone all right back home?" she asked in a voice devoid of expression that seemed to be addressed to the void. In-chol felt that what his mother should have asked, instead of 'Is everyone all right back home?' was, 'Is father well?' He recalled the scene that had taken place at home that morning.

After sending off the woman who had come to the house with his mother's message with the promise that he would come to his mother very soon, In-chol had looked in the direction of the garage to see if his father was out. The jeep was there which meant that he was still home. Ever since his father had spoken to him about Ta-hye on the morning after the memorable night when there was that stressful confrontation between him and his father upon In-chol's reading his brother In-ho's long letter, he had been avoiding any opportunity to be found in his father's presence or speak to him. Luckily, his father ate his breakfast and dinner in his room separately so that In-chol did not have to see him at mealtimes. On rare occasions, when they met in the house, In-chol made himself as inconspicuous as possible and disappeared from his father's sight quickly. But today, he had to see his father.

He knocked at his father's door and went in. What he saw upon entering the room, however, dismayed him. In front of his father who was sitting in his pajamas in an armchair facing the tea table were the whiskey bottle and a glass. He knew that his father drank a glass of two of whiskey at night before going to bed, but he had never imagined him drinking whiskey at this early hour, still in his pajamas. Then he remembered that lately he had seen light in his father's room as he returned home late from his outing or went to the toilet in the middle of the night. He recalled, too, that his father had taken to wearing glasses which he had not seen on him before.

"A message came from mother," he said without proceeding into the room.

His father's eyes when they were raised from the documents he seemed to have been perusing were mildly bloodshot. He thought that his father looked very tired.

"Is she still in that place?" he said, not really needing an answer.

His father's tone of voice was so apathetic that In-chol had laughed to himself in disbelief. Now that he was seeing and hearing his mother who, too, was so incredibly indifferent to the well-being of her husband, however, he realized that his father's apathy was not a one-sided phenomenon.

"Let me take you home, mother," he said.

Hearing his voice, his mother closed her eyes again as if to hide from In-chol her glance which had looked beyond him at some invisible object. Then she said,

"I like it here."

"You can come back another day. Come home with me today."

"No. I want to live here for good."

Her obstinate decisive tone reminded In-chol of another voice he had heard only several hours ago. It was with an intention to consult his father about his mother that he had gone to see his father that morning. But his father seemed to think that In-chol's business with him was borrowing the jeep to go to his mother.

"I will need the car right away. Don't take it," his father had said in the voice he used when he was angry, once again perusing his documents.

"I think you are being too obstinate. It's going to be very cold soon."

"What, you're calling *me* obstinate?" his mother said raising her voice a little. "In any case, I find it comfortable

to live here. If all of you will go to church and your father, too, will become a believer, I will come home without question, but not before then. You all may be my family in body, but not spiritually. You are strangers in spirit to me."
spirit to me."

"Even so, you can't stay on here like this. And you are not even well. Let's go home for now, anyhow."

"I am not afraid of the bodily sickness. What I am afraid of is the sickness in soul. If a person's soul gets sick, he will fall into hell. Compared with this, nothing one can suffer in this world is frightening. Think of it, you too! When we are fallen into the fearful flames of burning sulfur, not even parents and children can wet each other's tongues with a drop of water. I am comfortable here. You had better know it. The reason why I called you here today is...look at that thing there," said Madam Hong pointing at something up the mountain slope. It was a rock of a great size and deep gray. Wondering what his mother could mean, In-chol returned his eyes back to his mother, who said,

"I want you to build me a house which is just like that."

In-chol noticed that it was with an entreating tone that his mother said the last words, quite different from her angry, accusing tone of a while ago. Looking back at the rock, In-chol found out that on the side of the large rock was some construction which was separate from the rock but looked as if it were part of the rock. It was a hut.

"I can't do it on my own. I've gathered these rocks here but that's all."

In-chol had noticed that there were rocks near where his mother had been praying but he had thought nothing of them until his mother said these words. So then, it was his mother who had brought those rocks here! The rocks that were quite numerous in number were of variable sizes some of which looked too big to have been carried by his mother.

"If you will build me a house like that here, I will be able to fare the winter without any trouble."

Even as he was climbing the slope up to where the hut was standing against the large rock, he knew that he could no longer hope to take his mother home with him today. The hut was built with rocks piled up to form three of its four walls, the remaining one wall being afforded by the face of the rock against which it was standing. A patch of tent cloth was pitched over it to make a roof. In all, it was about half a *pyong* (about 3 square feet) and was barely high enough for a person to sit in. It seemed, however, that it had an *ondol*-floor; there was a furnace at the bottom of one wall and a chimney.

Looking around, In-chol saw that there were other huts like this one in the area, at least three of them standing quite close by. Invariably, the huts were built against a large rock which formed one of their four walls. The sizes and the styles of the huts were more or less alike except that a couple of them had, in addition to the front door, a window fitted in with artificial glass. It seemed that at the moment some of the huts were vacant; there was a complete silence in them. Others, however, were emitting low but feverish sounds of human voices as their occupants prayed on.

In-chol looked back down at his mother who looked tinier than ever from this distance. She was praying again prostrate on the ground. In-chol felt that whatever may be the state in which their separate souls may be at present, the first thing he could do for his mother was to build something which would protect his mother's body against the harshness of the winter weather.

It was on this day that In-chol realized for the first time how high was the wall that was separating his parents one from the other. But it was not in any near past that this separation originated.

For Kim Sang-jin, marriage was a dumping-ground where he could bury all the refuse of his dishonorable past. He wanted to discard the part of him that was shameful there and let a new self come to life. This was the same with his first wife who was In-ho's mother and the present wife alike. Even this purpose-oriented matrimonial relationship with Madam Hong, however, was marred when she became a Christian. If Kim Sang-jin ever experienced an affective relationship between man and woman, it was only through his relationship with the woman who had given birth to In-ju. Yet, even this relationship had not been touched by the passion that he devoted to his business. He gave himself to the affective life with the woman conditionally, only when he was with her, but to his business, he maintained a continuous and unflagging devotion. And even to this day, his love of business had suffered no blunting or abatement.

Madam Hong's story was different. Although Kim Sang-jin had never been a very affectionate and expressive man, she had relied on him as a trustworthy husband if short of words and slow in showing affection. She used to think that a woman's life fulfills itself in raising children and looking after her husband. In those days, however, she was totally ignorant of the fact that her husband was having an extramarital affair. Only when In-ju was brought home under her care after the woman died did Madam Hong wake up to the fact. And she was with In-mun at the time. After giving birth to In-mun whom she considered 'a seed of sin,' Madam Hong did not allow her husband to come near her. She had felt that keeping her husband off was the way to go near God. From this time on, the wall between her and Kim Sang-jin grew up higher and higher with passage of time.

In-chol went to the building materials store in Chahamun and came back with a laborer whom he hired to help him build the hut. Coming back to the prayer-house, he went over the thought many times that building this stone hut for his mother was the same as building a higher wall not only between his mother and father but also between her and the rest of the family. Every time he went over this thought, he was oppressed by the realization that as a son he did not have a filial affection strong enough to move his mother's heart.

Even if it was just a hut that was being built, one had to lay some sort of a foundation since it was meant to fend off the wind and snow storm. Like other huts in the vicinity, one wall would be offered by the face of the rock against which the hut would be standing which meant that he only needed to finish three walls.

First, In-chol told the laborer to remove the stump of the pine tree which interfered with the construction of the hut. Hearing this, however, Madam Hong who was standing by jumped up, exclaiming,

"No! You must leave the tree alone!"

"Why, mother?" asked In-chol bewildered. "We must clear the site."

"You must not touch it! I want you to build the hut so the stump will be inside it," Madam Hong declared.

In answer to In-chol's puzzled look, she explained reluctantly,

"I have a good reason to wish it. Please do as I tell you to."

In-chol kept on staring at his mother, more puzzled than before.

"I need it for my prayers," said Madam Hong in a more placating tone, but instead of telling her son about her encounter with the white-robed incarnation which she knew she should not give utterance of, Madam Hong merely repeated, "Just do as I tell you to, son."

In-chol, too, was no longer anxious to hear a more detailed explanation. Although he had no way of guessing why his mother needed the tree stump for her prayers, he had his own association of memory which was not unrelated with what was happening here with his mother. What he was recalling now was his big-father taking his round of the slaughterhouse with the knife wrapped in the red cloth. In-chol felt pity for his mother. He felt an impulse to grab his mother by the hand and tell her that what she was doing was erroneous.

Yet it was merely his wishful thinking. Suddenly he broke into a laughter. He was laughing at himself because for good or for bad, he had never been so passionately devoted to anything until now.

Since all the rocks were roundish and smooth, it was a taxing job to pile them up. In-chol could not leave the job to the laborer who seemed unused to that kind of work; he worked along with him. Before they could finish the walls up to one foot after laying the foundation, already it was evening. Promising his mother that he would come back early in the morning, In-chol went home.

Next day was Saturday when In-mun had only a half day of school. He went to the mountain prayer-house without bothering to go home to leave his satchel. In-chol was mixing the cement when In-mun arrived. Laying down his hat and satchel on the ground, In-mun helped his brother, fetching water or carrying rocks. One could see that he was enjoying the work.

"You are a very good worker, In-mun," said In-chol, proud of his younger brother. He wiped the sweat off his neck with his handkerchief which became wet immediately. The weather was fine and quite warm like the day before. The roof was pitched and the stones were laid for the floor. While the laborer spread the mud over the stones, In-mun went for the fuel wood.

The area near the prayer-house did not offer much in the way of fuel wood, too many people having gone through there gathering whatever they could burn. Going deeper into the mountain, therefore, In-mun climbed the trees to break off dead twigs. He also gathered dry leaves and grass. Once he climbed a tree with an intent to break off a dead twig which he had spotted from below. Just as he reached his hand for the dead twig, however, something fell from above, brushing against his shoulder before it dropped on the ground. When In-mun looked down in surprise, he found out that what he thought fell from above was only a squirrel who was scurrying to a rock nearby which the little animal climbed up rapidly. Only when he reached it's top did the squirrel pause with his bushy tail folded upward against his back and his wary eyes peering up at In-mun. Next second, the squirrel fled away out of sight. It was a plump well-groomed squirrel.

Turning his eyes away from the squirrel, In-mun caught sight of a dragonfly perched on a wild flower. Its wings were fluttering faintly iñ the quiet wind of early winter. How could an insect like that still be living in this kind of season! Wondering, In-mun crept down from the tree and tip-toed up to the dragonfly, which did not fly away even when In-mun went up close. Maybe he is too weak to fly, thought In-mun and blew at the insect gently. Although its body and wings shook at the whiff of In-mun's breath, the dragon-fly did not fly up. Stretching out a hand, In-mun caught it between his fingers. It was dead. As if only its husk had been hanging onto the plant, it made a dry hollow sound when In-mun's fingers touched it. Yet, it did not let go of the flower it was holding onto. In-mun picked it up forcibly. When he looked closely, he saw that the dragonfly had bits of the wild flower between its tiny claws. In-mun regretted having pulled the insect off the plant and tried to put it back onto it spreading its folded claws gently so that they could support its body on the flower. It was impossible, however. Just as if it were a dry blade of grass, the dragonfly fell off on the ground. In-mun felt there was no time to lose over this kind of thing and started collecting fuel woods again.

Although In-mun brought several armfuls of fuel in the form of twigs, dry leaves, and grass, they were not enough to dry the mud floor of the hut. Finally, it was decided that they go down to Chahamun to buy regular fuel wood. It was arranged that In-mun would go along with In-chol and bring the wood back to the mountain while In-chol went on back home.

Before leaving the prayer-house, In-chol went to the room where his mother was praying but could not say goodbye to her because she would not rise up from her prostrate position. Remembering that his mother had not come out to the site of her new hut ever since the previous afternoon, In-chol asked the woman who was cooking for the prayers if she knew whether or not his mother was sick. The woman answered that she did not think so. The fact that he had to ask another person about his mother who was right in front of him made In-chol feel once more how high the wall separating him from his mother was.

Sending In-mun back to the prayer-house from Chahamun where he bought a load of fuel wood which he paid a carrier to take to the prayer-house following In-mun, In-chol said to his brother,

"You come back home before it's too late."

"I am not going home tonight," said In-mun who made it clear by his tone of voice that his mind had been made up on this matter since earlier that day.

"All right, then. Go on back to the mountain before it's dark."

"Yes, but I want to ask you something," said In-mun in a tone by which In-chol could tell that this, too, had been premeditated like the decision to stay overnight in the mountain.

"You haven't ordered the door yet, have you, *hyong* (older brother)?"

"I am going to order it, maybe tomorrow morning. I have the measurements here. But why do you ask?"

"It doesn't have to be a smooth work, does it?"

"Of course, not. Why would a hut like that need a handsome-looking door? Any simple board-door would do well enough, I think."

"I want to try making it myself."

"You?"

"If it's a simple board-door that's needed, I think I can

make it. I will buy some planks and...."

In-chol knew that his brother had been collecting tools such as a plane or a saw to play with. And then, thought In-chol, why not? Maybe, by letting him make the door for this place where their mother was going to reside for long or short, he might help the relationship between his brother and their mother to develop into something more communicative and natural than what he and his mother had between them. He sincerely wished it to happen. In-chol gave his brother the money to buy the planks with.

Arriving at the prayer-house at dusk, In-mun borrowed the matches from the woman who cooked for the prayers and right away went about making the fire in the furnace of the new hut. The wood they bought at Chahamun was not sufficiently dry so that it was difficult to build up the fire. He burnt a lot of the fuel he had gathered during the day before he could make the new fuel wood flame up.

"I will tend the fire while you go in and eat. You must be very hungry," said the woman who cooked for the prayers, coming up to In-mun.

When he went into the room, there was a candlelight and a tray of food which he could see by the candlelight. The sight of food suddenly made him feel an acute appetite and he picked up the spoon to eat. But his mother intervened,

"Just a minute, son."

It was with a reprimanding tone that she said this. Only then did In-mun remember that in his hurry he had forgotten to pray before eating. Closing his eyes, therefore, he said silently, 'I thank You for this food, Amen,' and opening his eyes went for the spoon again.

"What kind of a prayer is that? You should pray more lengthily and wholeheartedly," said Madam Hong with disgust. She knew that her son had been going to the church from some time ago and she had been thinking that it was the power of her prayers that had made it possible for the 'seed of sin' to become a believer on his own initiative. Yet, it seemed that the devil was still living in some corner of this child.

"You mustn't act that way. You must always remember that it is only God's grace and the price of the suffering of our Jesus who was crucified for our sin that are keeping us alive. If you do not serve our Lord truthfully you are not my son and I am not your mother. But...."

In-mun saw that his mother's face which he saw in the candlelight looked hard.

"Why does your brother live in such an abominable way? Why does he not fear God? I heard him laugh in a loud voice yesterday beginning his work on my new house. He doesn't seem to realize what kind of a place this is. And what kind of a house he is building, either! I detest looking at him. As soon as this work is done, I want him never to come back here."

His mother's voice was harsh and resolute. It was not the voice of his mother who used to sermonize to her children in a surreptitious, almost apologetic manner. Since she came here, moreover, his mother's heart seemed to close tighter and tighter against In-mun every time he visited her.

The draft came in through the cleft on the door shaking the candlelight. His mother's shadow elongated ominously coming up close to him. Despite his hunger, In-mun could not finish his bowl of rice. He walked out of the room. Returning to the hut, he asked for a burning stick of wood from the woman who cooked for the prayers and was now tending the fire for him. With this as a torch, In-mun looked inside the hut.

"I think we don't need to put in too much wood now. Just keep the fire alive," said the woman.

In-mun saw that the center of the mud floor which was giving off a gust of vapor had been dried into a lighter color but the space all around it was still wet.

"You'd better come in and sleep after a while," said the woman going back to the prayer-house compound.

Although he answered that he would do so, In-mun decided to spend the night here at the hut. He did not think that he would be more comfortable by his mother than here.

Although it had been a fine warm day for the season, the night air was icy. On account of the warm vapor in which was mixed the smell of mud and the heat from the furnace, however, In-mun did not feel much cold. Apart from the crackling sound the wood was making as it burnt, the whole mountain was silent. But it did not frighten In-mun. He felt that it was probably because of the fire near him that he could afford to be unafraid. It seemed mysterious that a trivial thing such as a little fire had that kind of a power.

When the fire in the furnace waned, the darkness poured in from everywhere. It was a darkness that was closely knit with thick and thin threads of black which shifted incessantly from thick to thin shades and backwards. As if to chase away this darkness, In-mun threw in several more sticks of wood. After some time of repeating this, he could tell by the way the darkness rushed in that it was time to throw in more wood and each time he confirmed that the fire in the furnace was flickering from lack of new wood.

The way the wood burnt, too, was variable. When he first put in a piece of wood, he would think that this or that part would catch the fire first but as often as not his expectation was betrayed and he had to witness a totally different part of the wood flaming up first. Only then would the part which he had expected to catch fire first would flame up as if it had been waiting for its turn. After this, flame rose up from everywhere which never stopped in one shape but went through a series of metamorphoses. They seemed restless for something. Whatever it was that these flames wanted, they were very beautiful to In-mun's watchful eyes.

Unawares, In-mun dozed off. But instantly he woke up remembering that he must not fall asleep. Opening his eyes, he saw something flit through the fire in front of him. He thought that he saw this moving thing somewhere although he could not offhand remember where he had seen it or what it was. Looking in close, he found out that it was the squirrel that he had seen in the afternoon. The squirrel was fluttering through the fire this way and that as if in complete abandon. What if he burns himself to death doing that?, said In-mun to himself. But already the body of the squirrel was one red burning coal that kept on moving the more swiftly than a minute ago across the fire of the furnace. Is he running like that because it cannot stand the pain of heat?, asked In-mun to himself. Then a voice whispered into In-mun's ear, 'It's because the squirrel is in hell, burning in the flames of sulfur. He will never be freed from them!' In-mun closed his eyes tight. Still, he could not avoid the sight of the burning squirrel which was moving at a higher and higher speed. But what was this? The squirrel that was burning in fire was not the squirrel he had seen earlier that day but the squirrel he used to look after at home. It was one of his animals whom he had at one time felt urged to throw away all at once but soon went back to tending arduously. Finally, however, he had left all of them, including this squirrel, to starve to death. The movements of the squirrel were no longer those made by a living thing in pain but were joyously rhythmic. In-mun wanted to smile at seeing this, but he was crying.

Na-mi was not at Montparnasse. Deciding to wait for her a while, In-chol took a seat. He knew that he had been avoiding Na-mi for the past couple of months. But was it necessary? I will see her, said In-chol to himself. He knew that Na-mi had called him at home many times while he was out. I will keep on seeing her like before, he said to himself again. And despite Ta-hye's advice, I would not tell her about our past. Not until I can be surer about my inclination toward her.... I will tell her when I am so passionately in love with her that I cannot stand it....

The waiting girl brought him the day's paper and told him

that Miss Cho had gone out with a woman friend. If so, I
would not see her tonight, thought In-chol.

C'est une chanson qui nous resemble,
Toi qui m'aimais....

Although there was no Pak Hae-yon in sight, this song
which was his favorite came out of the gramophone. Had
he gone to the tavern, wondered In-chol. Before the song
ended, In-chol walked out of the teahouse.

Just as he had guessed, Pak Hae-yon was sitting at a table
in the crowded hall of the tavern. He was not alone but
with the man who was supposed to be teaching philosophy
at some college in town. It was the same atmosphere all the
time.

"Hello, hello, Mr. Kim. Long time no see! I nearly forgot
your face," said Pak Hae-yon boisterously when he recognized
In-chol, making him sit down beside him. "I hear you've
been kept very busy lately."

"Not really, I don't think."

"I heard that you are the one who drew plans for Miss
Cho's new house, is that right? I knew that you studied
architecture but never knew that you were actually practicing. It was only very recently that I found out about it
from a conversation Miss Cho was having with somebody.
She seemed entirely content. Said it was a truly stylish
house."

In-chol smiled without saying anything.

"You see, architecture and drama have a lot in common.
Let's, therefore, drink to it, shall we?"

He poured into the cup fetched by the waitress.

"Architecture?" murmured the philosophy professor who
had been leaning forward with his chin poised on his palm
and his elbow pivoting against the tea table. "It's the most
useful and solid field among all the pursuits that can be
called art. Don't you agree?"

Saying this, the professor turned his drink-blurred eyes at In-chol, freeing his palm from the weight of his chin which he lifted from it.

"Have you ever thought of comparing our traditional style in architecture with those of other countries?" said the professor again as if delighted that a new topic came up.

Not particularly wishful to make a conversation with this learned man, In-chol merely nodded without saying anything.

"It is an interesting subject for scholarly investigation," said the philosophy professor, he, too, nodding his head once. "One can compare the Japanese style with ours, for instance, with an interesting result. You see that everything about a Japanese house, whether its roof or anything else, is rectilineal. Compared with that, our traditional houses are made practically in curves. Think of the curved line of our roofs and our eaves that look like a large bird with its wings spread out. Everything about our traditional house delineates the curve. From this we can draw the conclusion that our ancestors had a superior aesthetic sense than those of the Japanese."

In-chol lent only one ear to the philosophy professor while watching the entrance for sight of Na-mi.

The soliloquy of the philosophy professor continued,

"It's the same with clothes. The Japanese *kimono* is rectilineal, all straight lines. Now, let's consider our *hanbok*. First of all, the underside curve of the sleeve of women's jacket and the uptilting curves of its frontal hemline are outstanding examples of how Korean attire is designed in curves. And what about our *poson?* Isn't the contrast with the Japanese *tabi* striking, indeed? And this applies to the shoes of the two countries as well. Consider the rectilineality of Japanese *tabi* or *chori* compared with our *chipshin* (straw sandals) or *namakshin* (wooden high-sandals worn in wet weather), or the *katshin* (leather shoes)."

"You have a point there, but what about the food, the re-

maining requisite of the three basic conditions of human sub-
sistence? Or, what about the drinks?" interjected Pak Hae-
yon who had finished two cups of wine with measured intervals in the course of the philosophy professor's soliloquization.

"The same rule applies there, too, to be sure. Let's compare the Japanese clear wine with our thick wine, for instance. You can't deny that one gets inebriated in a roundabout, that is, curved fashion with our *takchu* compared with
the *chongjong* which makes you drunk in a more blunt and
direct manner. Yet, I must confess that there's one aspect of
life that does not fit into this classification."

Just as the philosophy professor was about to continue,
after giving a couple of nods to his own perspicacity, however, Pak Hae-yon put in,

"You mean the natural environment? Like mountains and
rivers?"

"No, I am referring to something more quotidian and
practical."

"Language?"

"No, something more concrete. I feel that your sense of
perception falls below the mark here, Pak-*sonsaeng*. It's
women that I mean, women."

"Women?"

"Yes, women, women, women."

After uttering these words as if he were spitting them out
of his mouth, the philosophy professor abruptly got up and,
picking up the paper bag from the tea table, staggered
toward the counter. Suddenly In-chol felt nauseated by all
these repetitions—the same atmosphere, the same house, the
same drink, and the same people and same topics. . . .

"What are you thinking, Mr. Kim? You are missing a good
scene, look!" said Pak Hae-yon in a low tone.

Looking in the direction of the counter where Pak Hae-yon
was pointing with his chin, In-chol saw that the philosophy
professor was pulling money out of the *Chindallae* cigarette
pack.

"He got caught in hiding the money between the pages of his notebook. So, he now carries his money in his cigarette case like that. But you don't know when his wife will find that out, too!"

"Other members aren't coming tonight, it seems," said In-chol thinking that he should have left the table before the professor did. But he still could not shake off the wishful thinking that Na-mi might drop by.

"The attendance level is pretty low these days. The national assembly candidate went down to the provinces to sell the last of his land and the dentist is kept busy with his seasonal hunting, and...Mr. Nam is locked up in the house writing up that play of his and it's been several days since I saw Miss Cho here."

"It's been quite some time since Mr. Nam stopped coming out here. It must be a true masterpiece he is composing," said In-chol remembering his unsuccessful attempt to waylay Nam Chun-gol after reading In-ju's diary a short time before the Full Moon season. And he had never run into him at this tavern since.

"It's not the length of the period of work that makes a masterpiece although I don't know how great a play Mr. Nam is capable of creating. By the way, Mr. Kim, I am conceiving another play these days," said Pak Hae-yon.

Hearing this, In-chol who had been languishing more than usual from the atmosphere of frustration this place never failed to evoke for him decided to leave; there was no telling when Pak Hae-yon's talk would end once he started on the theme of a new play. But his decision was vetoed by Pak Hae-yon who exclaimed,

"No, you can't desert me like this when nobody else is coming to keep me company. You must realize that you, too, are now one of the leading actors of our theater."

In-chol could not help smiling at these words. What he said was true, however. Unawares, he had become a leading actor of this theater of drunkards. But he left the tavern all the same.

Am I really a leading actor of this house of drunkards? I must be, since I even played the role of being beaten up by a gangster very convincingly, and truthfully, to boot. The siren of a fire engine came from a street nearby. The sound receded through the Ulchiro crossroad and turning toward the Namdaemun from the Central Post Office intersection. When the first siren sound died out, another of the same nerve-stirring sound came, going through the same route before it, too, died out.

In-chol turned into Myong-dong. We feel disappointed when a house on fire is rescued without a serious damage. It's because man and the earth and the sky primordially seek fire, Ki-ryong had said. In-chol thought how long it had been since he saw his cousin Ki-ryong last. I wonder how he would fit in in the atmosphere of our tavern, In-chol thought on.

A drunkard came staggering from the opposite direction. He was about the same age as In-chol. He was mumbling some words of a song as he passed by In-chol which sounded like, 'I can't sleep because I don't have my bottle....' In-chol turned his head to look at the young man as he walked on in the direction from which In-chol came. He was staggering on, with his head bent down and his mouth mumbling the song words. In-chol repeated the words in his mouth, 'I can't sleep because I don't have my bottle....'

"What a pleasant surprise!" said a voice when In-chol nearly reached the center of Myong-dong with its night places ablaze with neon signs. He looked up and saw Na-mi.

"This is such a coincidence," Na-mi spoke again.

In-chol felt the same.

"I was just thinking of you, In-chol-*ssi*, walking through here. We ran into each other hereabouts once before, didn't we? I mean right after we returned from the seashore. I was thinking about that time when suddenly I saw you coming toward me."

"Do you also have the habit of recollection? I didn't know that of you."

"Why did you think I wouldn't? Do I look like such a bleak person to you?"

"Are you alone?"

"Can't you see that I am?"

"Shall we walk a little, then?"

In-chol's intention was to walk to the Ulchiro crossroad with Na-mi where she would probably catch the microbus to go home.

"Let's go to a teahouse first."

"I feel like walking after the stuffy air of the tavern," insisted In-chol relishing the refreshing night air of early winter after a mild intoxication at the tavern.

"Let's sit in a teahouse just for a while," said Na-mi alreading walking toward a teahouse by the road.

"You have had a lot to drink, haven't you?" said Na-mi when the two were seated across a tea table.

"Do I look drunken to you?"

In-chol had not intended to drink that day. If only he had met Na-mi at the Montparnasse, he wouldn't have had any drink for the night. He had wished to spend some time with Na-mi with a clear head. Yet, he did not think he was really drunk right now.

"Your eyes are red."

"It's not because of the drink."

He could have said, 'That's how all *paekchong*'s eyes look,' but buried these additional words in his mind. He felt a heavy fatigue.

"By the way, In-chol-*ssi*, do you have anything against me?"

"Why? What could I have against you?"

"Why, then, haven't you ever answered my call? You know I've called you many times."

"I couldn't. I would have if I could."

"Why do you quibble with words like that? I want a straight talk. And you aren't looking at me. Are you bored with me? Then, I will make my business short."

"Why do you find fault with me? If I am bored, it's because of something that only has to do with me, not you."

"Don't try to make excuses. I told you, when we met a while ago, that I had been thinking about the time when we two had met that other time, didn't I? I will tell you the truth. I was thinking about that occurrence as a thing of the past that has no relation to the present. But I am sure I will forget it even as a thing of the past because remembrance of things past does not suit my temperament. Just as you pointed out a while ago."

Na-mi was saying these words in a clear, unhesitant voice without even playing with her fingers as most girls would. She continued,

"Even if I bore you, I want you to hear me out. I have just seen a movie at the Central Theater with that friend of mine from Inchon. She went straight to the railway station to catch her train and I walked by myself thinking. First I thought about my friend from whom I had just parted. She got herself engaged lately after a series of relationships. Many times, she went near the point of engagement with a man and then called it off. What is interesting is—I want you to hear this carefully—that the one she recently got engaged to is the one with whom she had fallen in love first. According to her, her numerous peregrinations with other men has been only to verify to herself that the first man was the one whom she most desired. You know what I am talking about, don't you? I mean that I am now one of those objects of preparatory experimentation."

Immediately, In-chol understood the meaning of Na-mi's metaphor.

"That's a misunderstanding. My relationship with Ta-hye is not what you think."

"Then, what kind of a relationship is it?"

In-chol had no immediate answer to this question.

"Frankly speaking, I have no wish to try to penetrate the thick curtain with which this woman Ta-hye is enveloping you."

In-chol sat in silence. Whatever he might have said would have sounded like an excuse. Yet, his heart was bereaved by the decision of this girl to leave him. At the same time, however, he had a feeling that things were settling down to the right order.

"From now on, our relationship is strictly that of business. First of all, I want you to come by the construction site more often."

In-chol remembered he had not gone there even once lately.

"Secondly.... It was because of this matter actually that I called you so many times."

Na-mi took out of her handbag the folded letter sheet which she unfolded and put down in front of In-chol's eyes. Upon glancing at the drawing once, In-chol was utterly taken aback. Yet, he immediately raised his eyes and looked across at Na-mi.

"This was mailed to my father. Would you be able to guess whose practical joke it is?"

"How could I know it?"

"Look closely. Since this obviously is a caricature of our new house, I thought maybe you might have some idea and so...."

Na-mi stopped, sensing a strange change of expression in In-chol's eyes. He said,

"I wouldn't know who it is but I think I can guess why anybody would have sent this sort of thing."

Na-mi felt that In-chol's eyes looked as if they caught a sudden fire.

"The message of this drawing is that one who is *paekchong* drew plans of this house."

Na-mi was staggered. Not because of the fact that the one

who drew plans of her house, that is, In-chol, was *paek-chong* in origin but because of the strange, ominous laughter In-chol emitted finishing the statement. It sounded as if it had started from some faraway darkness at the back of In-chol which, as it came closer, turned into a cry of inexpressible ecstasy.

In-chol was thinking, 'Things have strange turns of settling themselves. I had thought that I would tell Na-mi about it when and if I should ever become so in love with her that I could not stand it without doing something radical like confessing my secret to her....' It then occurred to him that something he could not foresee but that had its own logic of happening had come to induce him to make his darkest confessions to the two persons who were closest to him unpremeditatedly. In any case, however, his mind was more in peace now that the secret was all out.

"You'd better go home now."

Only when he was parted from Na-mi did In-chol begin to wonder who could have played such a vulgar and nasty practical joke on Na-mi's family. Neither was he able to guess who it was nor was he sufficiently interested in finding it out, however. He merely thought that he would have a haircut before going home in case the barbershop near his house was still open.

Na-mi reported to her father what In-chol said just as she had heard it from him. Mr. Cho did not say anything. For three days on end after this, Na-mi entreated her father as he was about to leave the house to go to the bank in the morning to give the loan to In-chol's father. Every time, Mr. Cho merely listened without promising anything.

On the third night, Mr. Cho called Na-mi to his room and told her that she should not see In-chol except on business relating to the construction of the house. The face and tone of voice with which Mr. Cho said this had the hardness that Na-mi had never felt on her father.

This surprised Na-mi. Yet she smiled inwardly because there was something in her heart which was still too new for her to know distinctly but challenged her in a delightful way. She remembered the fire that was in In-chol's eyes just before he made his confession. She wanted to burn herself in this fire which seemed strong enough to burn itself and anything or anybody else near it. And his voice as he said, 'You'd better go home now' had a poignant tinge she had never heard from him before; it seemed to penetrate into her heart although the voice itself was rather expressionless. What he meant was for me to go home because there was nothing more between us now. But she had wanted to be by his side for as long as he would let her. And this was a feeling she had never experienced before that night. I must have him for myself, she said to herself. I don't care what kind of origin he comes from or who is standing there between him and me. And I don't care how much my father is against it, or with what thick curtain of shadow Ta-hye tries to protect In-chol from me.

CHAPTER THREE

The Weight of a Cat

"Would you care for coffee or tea, *toryonnim* (high honorific appellative for boys or unmarried young men, used by servants or brothers' wives)?"

"I don't care."

"I will make tea for you then. But now I want to tell you something. It's about a fortuneteller I consulted some time ago because I'd heard that he is really good. And he was, too! He said I should have been in great luck if I had met one with the surname of water-origin. I thought about it and he was right! Because the name of this house where I am now is Chi that has the water-origin. Someone told me the name *chi* means 'pond', so it has the water-origin. I am right, am I not?"

The maid talked on garrulously. Professor Chi was still not back from school and Ta-hye was giving lessons to her pupils. In-chol had gone into the professor's study to wait for her until she should be through with the lessons. There was a coal stove in the study and it was on this stove that the maid was boiling the water for the tea.

"I wanted to ask the fortuneteller to read your and my young mistress' Four Pillars and Eight Letters but she would not give me her birth hour though I knew her birth month and day. What about you, *toryonnim*? What are your birth year, month, day and hour?"

"I don't have those things."

"You are teasing me!"

Going to the shelf to pick up a book to read by way of avoiding conversation with this talkative woman, In-chol caught sight of a notebook lying on the professor's desk. On the cover were written the words: Notes on the Theme of the *Paekchong*. In a reflex movement, In-chol snatched up the notebook and returned to his seat with it.

The contents of the notebook were mostly memoranda, scribbled down rather randomly without order. He read:

〈Wrote down the story I heard in Pundinamutkol, Kwangju-gun in my separate notebook.〉

〈The Chinese character meaning ox or cow is a hieroglyphication of the ox-horns. The character symbolizing ox or cow was used as the peripheral character for all words signifying male and female animals. Ex. 牡牝〉

〈The word signifying all things of the world, 物, also has the character 牛 as its peripheral character.〉

〈The mythical Emperor Shinnong of ancient China had the ox-head upon human body. The origin of this myth is conjectured to be in sanctification of oxen and cows.〉

〈The title names of our Shilla Period such as *kakkan*(角干) or *kakchan*(角粲) both of which have the character signifying ox-horns in them may be indicative of sanctification of oxen and cows in ancient Korea.〉

〈In the Exodus of Old Testament, there is a passage describing worship of golden calf.〉

〈In the West, water, moon and the ox are considered the symbols of fertility. While interpreting water as the male essence, the moon which influences the flow of this water and also has the tendency to wax, wane, appear, and disappear is also deemed to be a powerful symbol of fertility. From the fact that the crescent and the ox-horn resemble each other in shape and the fact that two ox-horn shapes are needed to make the character meaning the moon, the ox was made a symbol of fertility also.〉

The writings were small with frequent spots where the words were crossed out so that it was not easy for In-chol to read them. In-chol took a long breath to relax himself, and then realizing that he was sitting at the edge of the chair with his upper half of body bent forward, he shifted his posture sitting back in the chair more comfortably and loosening the tension that had been building in his body. He turned the pages of the notebook on another place.

⟨ The appellations of endearment people used for oxen or cows: *Osanari* (secret royal envoy), Prince, Holy One, Mountain Old Man, Royal Jade Carriage, etc. General appellations for the *paekchong*: White Rake, The Skull, The Butcher, etc. The words the *paekchong* use to vilify other classes who look down on them: Marinated Shrimps (meaning the people jump up and down busily but once they are marinated with salt become as limp as jelly), Hooks on the A-Frames (meaning they are as insignificant as hooks on the A-frames), Hiccups (meaning the words which the people speak in derogation of the *paekchong* class are no more sense-making than hiccups).⟩

⟨Wrote down the story I heard from the *paekchong* in Suam-dong, Pyollae-myon, Yangju-gun in a separate notebook.⟩

"Here, it's ready," said the maid bringing the teacup to him.

Then, throwing a glance in the direction of the 'piano room,' she muttered,

"That child always takes longer than other kids!"

Finally she left the room. In-chol sipped the tea a few times, then he went back to the notebook.

⟨The Chinese do not seem to look down on the butchers. Many characters in Suhoji run butchering and lodging businesses in combination and yet enjoy prestige in their respective localities.⟩

⟨One graduate who studied in France and came back said that he saw at some café that a man drank coffee in complete equanimity wearing blood-drenched work clothes. 〉

〈One seventy-three-year-old man from the Pyong-anbuk-do said that the people of the northern parts of Korea do not look down on the butchers as in the south. Nor do they ostracize them, forcing them to live in segregation, he said. There is no generational succession of the trade, either. Those who peddle such things as the fine combs or baskets going from a house to another are all from the southern parts of Korea. These too, the local people treat without prejudice. There is, however, hesitation, on the part of the people, where marriage is involved. 〉

〈The *paekchong* nickname those who are their likely candidates for marriage as the 'Sticky Leech,' meaning that all they want is to extricate money from them the way leeches suck up the blood of their victim. They call this kind of a mixed marriage, 'Egg-Rolling,' meaning that it is as tricky and difficult as rolling the eggs. 〉

〈Have been to Pundinamutkol with In-chol on the Full Moon Day. Wrote down the scene of the Full Moon Rite of the butchers in a separate notebook. 〉

〈If the butchers are descendants of the Khitanese or the Jerchenese émigrés in Korea, or, if they are prisoners of war, why is there no trace of their collective living in the northern parts and only in the south we see remnants of these villages? According to a diagram presented in a book issued in 1933 by the Japanese Government-General under the title of: Korean Villages, in the Chollabuk-do, there were five *paekchong* villages with fifty-five houses and the total population of three hundred and forty-nine; in the Kyongsangbuk-do, two villages with fifty-eight houses and a population of two hundred and sixty-one; in the Kyongsangnam-do, two villages with forty-five houses and a population of two hundred and thirty; in Kang-won-do, where a large number of *paekchong* had gathered from all parts of the country three hundred years ago, there is now only one village with thirteen houses; in Hwang-hae-do, there are supposedly three *paekchong* villages according to documentary evidences but no number of the houses or inhabitants are given. As to the provinces to the north of Hwang-hae-do, we have no record. ⟩

⟨ Like Koguryo, Paekche was originally formed by the Puyo tribes who were known to have followed the flow of the water in deciding the foundation site of their country. That Yangsuchok followed the water flow as they hunted and made baskets with willow branches is perhaps to be considered in connection with this. ⟩

⟨ Is Choi Chung-hon's record on the Yangsuchok a far-fetched theorization? The founding king of Koryo had forbidden to appoint to government positions the people from the southern reaches of Kumgang, that is, the site of Late Paekche for the reason that both the nature and human spirit were impoverished in those regions. The descendants of Late Paekche who resented this (especially the upper-classes) organized a group called the Yangsuchok which they induced a segment of the Khitanese invasion army to join. They then instigated the Yangsuchok to run across the country disturbing the peace, disguising themselves as Japanese invaders. ⟩

⟨ Heard from a man who came to see Prof. Om of the History Department about the Hyongpyongsa. The inaugural speech and descriptions of the organization are as given in separate sheets. ⟩

In-chol could find inserted between the pages of the notebook a folded sheet of paper and an envelope on which the sender was given as somebody in Chinju. In-chol unfolded the paper. Among the mimeographed writing on the paper he read such phrases as 'abolishing injurious appellations,' 'living like true citizens,' or, 'looking back on our past will only make us weep all day long.'

In-chol closed his eyes feeling an urge to shout at the top of his voice. He heard the door open. Opening his eyes, In-chol folded up the notebook.

"Have you waited long?" said Ta-hye coming in with her quiet smile on face.

In-chol had been oblivious of the fact that the piano sound had ceased and the child who had been taking the lesson was gone.

"Why are you looking like that?" said Ta-hye examining In-chol's face, no longer smiling.

Only then, In-chol remembered that he still had the note-book in his hand and put it back on the desk.

"Oh, that? That's nothing to be gloomy about. You must utterly ignore all these trivialities. They belong to the past only. Even my father is, I think, giving up his research on the topic."

For no specific reason, In-chol felt that it was probably Ta-hye who was asking her father to give it up.

"It seems he was carried away by his study of the subject at first; he wanted to prove that those people have not been lowly from a very early period. But what would be the good of turning these forgotten facts over now? I think my father, too, came to feel in this way."

In-chol felt that he could well follow the evolution of the professor's intellectual passion for this subject. He probably wanted to come out with an incontestable proof that the *paekchong* class was not originally a lowly people but found out that the task was too big for him to accomplish. But what difference does it make whether the *paekchong's* an-cestors were the Khitanese émigrés or a tribe of Late Paekche? Isn't the crucial question in the present? The solution is in going the way one wants to go without regard for anything else. But is this possible?

"What's this? You still insist on brooding over it? I say, for-get it. It's such nothing!"

"I don't want to hear you say any more of those things, Ta-hye. I would rather that you shout to me, 'Get out, you son of a *paekchong*!'"

"Let's go out for a walk, shall we?"

Ta-hye seemed at a loss how she should hold up In-chol's inner strength that was threatening to crumble. Although there was another child coming soon for the piano lesson and her father, too, was likely to come home any minute, she felt she had to take In-chol somewhere out of this house.

"Let's go to some music hall. I feel like drinking a glass of whiskey tea with you listening to good music, what do you say?"

In-chol felt as if he would choke to death if he stayed on any longer. So he said,

"I must go now."

Ta-hye was distraught which was a thing unheard of in her.

"Nonsense!" she said.

"I must see someone."

In-chol said this at random, but now that the words were out, he thought that it would not be a bad idea for him to go to see his cousin Ki-ryong. "I have a cousin at a slaughter-house in Miari whom I want to see. He makes me feel restful when we are together. I came here because I had something to report to you. I have said goodbye to Na-mi."

Ta-hye was silent.

"I told her everything. Now you don't need to worry."

"What did she say?"

"Nothing."

"Are you sorry?"

In-chol looked straight at Ta-hye. Ta-hye looked back at him with caressing eyes which had recovered their usual calm. In-chol turned his eyes away.

"Maybe it was just as well because if she doesn't understand that kind of a thing, she doesn't deserve you. Forget about everything. Please."

Her voice was quiet but there was a tone of resolution in it.

The alley was flanked with rows of faded old-style houses.

Although it was a crooked and narrow passage, In-chol felt as if he could walk through it with his eyes closed. Nothing had changed here. Whenever he walked into or out of this alley to visit or return from a visit of Ta-hye, In-chol had felt as if he were coming back to an old home from which he had been away for some time or as if he were going away from his old home on some business. But that was not how he felt now except that Ta-hye was the same old Ta-hye. The atmosphere of her house which she created was also unchanged. Yet on this particular day, In-chol had come away from these changeless familiar things as if in flight. At the same time, he realized painfully that it was none but himself that had changed.

Only when he got aboard the bus headed for Miari did In-chol remember why he was going to Ki-ryong. It was because seeing Ki-ryong was the one thing In-chol could do without the consciousness of self-escape.

Ki-ryong had moved to another boardinghouse. A man whom In-chol did not remember seeing at the time he had come to spend the night in Ki-ryong's room came out and directed In-chol to Ki-ryong's new lodgings which was right at the back of the slaughterhouse and was not difficult to find. In-chol walked along the field where the harvest had been finished. He passed by the front gate of the slaughterhouse which looked entirely vacant at the moment. Turning around the corner of the slaughterhouse, In-chol saw a low mountain with a fairly dense growth of pine trees only a short distance ahead and a hut which could have been the abode of the mountain-keeper. The mud wall had fallen off in places and the tin roof was red from rusting. About fifty meters from this hut to the left was a quarry from where the sounds of hammering and chiseling came mixed with the sound of the stones cracking.

Arriving at the hut, In-chol called, '*Hyongnim!*' instead of announcing himself in any other more ceremonial manner.

No answer came out of the hut. Thinking that maybe the noise from the quarry distracted one from hearing his voice, In-chol called once more, a little more loudly. Again, there was no answer. Upon a more careful examination, In-chol thought that the hut did not look as if anybody were living in it. Maybe I came to the wrong house, thought In-chol, and looked about to see if there was another likely human abode that fitted the description of the man who gave him directions at Ki-ryong's former boardinghouse.

He decided to leave and turned back when he heard the sound of a door opening at his back. He looked around. Ki-ryong was standing there holding the one-panel door with his hand.

"Oh, you were there," said In-chol, gladdened.

Ki-ryong, however, said nothing, nor did he show any other sign of welcome. Maybe I shouldn't have come, thought In-chol.

Ki-ryong was still standing, watching him in silence. Then he gestured with his head for In-chol to come in. He did this as if he didn't really wish to but felt obligated to do so since In-chol had come out a long way to see him. In-chol was about to say, 'let's go somewhere if you are not busy,' but stopped just before the words came out and went into the hut.

The inside of the hut was dark since the lighting was bad. The wallpaper was faded to a dirty yellow and the floor was covered with cut-out soiled cement sacks, all of which combined to make the inside of the hut look very dingy and depressing. A thick-volumed book which, it seemed, Ki-ryong had been reading was lying spread out on the floor. In-chol felt sorry again that he had come to disturb Ki-ryong's peaceful moment.

"Maybe I should have turned back without coming in today."

"Not at all. It's just that I didn't, at first, recognize your voice," said Ki-ryong.

In-chol guessed that what his cousin meant was that he would not have opened the door if he had thought that the visitor was anybody else but In-chol although he did not say it in so many words.

"When did you move to this place?"

"Several days ago. Circumstances compelled it."

Just then, something moved out of the pile of books next to a wall and came up close to In-chol. It was a cat. Surreptitiously, he started climbing up to In-chol's knees. It was a red-bean color cat with white on its neck and belly. In-chol remembered he had not seen the cat in Ki-ryong's former lodgings.

In-chol did not like cats, so he pushed the cat off his knee with one hand. The cat, however, pounced back onto his knee and settled down comfortably. Seeing this, Ki-ryong remarked,

"I have never seen anyone as honest as that animal. He chose your knees because he judged that it would be warmest there." Then he added an explanation about the cat, "It belonged to a lodger who lived in this room before me. The old woman who owns this hut told me that the cat disappeared the day before the man who was the cat's owner died, and came back after his funeral was over. He was a laborer at the quarry. He had a tuberculosis of the lung and came to the slaughterhouse now and then to get the cow blood. It seems he loved that cat a great deal. The old woman says the dying man asked for the cat many times before he died. Yet, that animal took to me from the very first day I moved in here, begging food and coming inside my bed cover at night. This doesn't mean that he has much affection for me, either. He is always solitary. I liked him for that. I, too, took to him right away."

After saying these words, Ki-ryong gave the cat with a meaningful stare, then, he said,

"Shall we go?"

Standing up, Ki-ryong changed into the street clothes that

had been hanging on a nail in one wall. While he changed, In-chol sat on as if he could not lift the scanty weight of the cat that was purring on his knees.

In-chol urged Ki-ryong to drink more, thinking that his cousin was far stronger in drinking than he was. He could not tell whether the tavern where the two were sitting opposite each other was the same one to which they had come the other night after their carousing downtown. He had been so drunk that night. I must not drink too much, tonight, thought In-chol. Ki-ryong took the cup from In-chol and drank slowly without hastening to return the cup to In-chol. In-chol was glad that he didn't.

Ki-ryong was like a man drinking alone. In-chol asked again,

"When did you move to your new place?"

"Didn't the man say anything when you went to my former lodgings?" said Ki-ryong instead of answering In-chol's question.

Hearing this and seeing Ki-ryong's pensive eyes turned on his face, In-chol recalled that the man had indeed looked at him in a rather strange way.

"I mean he may have thought that you came from the police. There have been visits and summons from the police lately and the owner of the boardinghouse did not like it. So I moved to a new place. And I don't blame him."

"Why police?"

"Nothing serious. Some time ago, there was a murder robbery back here. Somebody hit a passer-by on the head with an ax and robbed him thoroughly. The problem is the wound made by the ax. Although it was a pitch dark night, the wound was made precisely in the middle of the man's forehead. So the police deduced that the one who killed him must be exceptionally skillful in using an ax. In such a close proximity of the murder scene was the slaughterhouse, too. The natural thing for the police to think was that one of the

men working at the slaughterhouse did it. And the scene of
the crime is closest to my former boardinghouse. I was inter-
rogated many times, as a result. Most bothersome it was. In
the end, I asked them how deep was the wound."

Pausing, Ki-ryong laughed once. Then he continued,

"They said, as low down as the chin. Then, it hasn't been
done by one of the butchers, I said. If the murderer had been
a butcher, he would have hit just deep enough so the ax-
blade would be barely buried inside the skull but not any
deeper. I told them I would show them how it is done if they
wished."

Ki-ryong's tone of voice was as calm as ever. In-chol believed that he would really have proposed an experimentation to his interrogators.

"Did they catch the murderer?" he asked.

"If they did, the man in the other boardinghouse would
not have given you a strange look. In any case, they can't
catch a criminal with such stupid thinking."

Ki-ryong laughed a short laugh, once more. Then, devoid
of laughter, he looked across at In-chol and said,

"You look thinner than I last saw you. If you don't like
drinking, don't. Forgetting loneliness by drinking is an un-
worthy thing to do. The drink does not humor you in such
weakness."

In-chol felt that Ki-ryong understood his recent state of
mind.

"Man is destined to be lonely. That is why history is made
and men kill each other or die of their own accord. Man and
earth, and sky seem to have cried for blood from time imme-
morial. And it was to be exorcised from loneliness that they
have done so. This blood does not have to be the actual red
thing. It can be the blood that is invisible and flows only
within our heart."

In-chol remembered Ki-ryong saying something like this in
that other tavern in Chongno 4-ga some months ago. He had
said those words in relation with some problem he had be-

cause of a woman. I wonder what happened to her, thought In-chol.

"Is the lady I met at the drinking house the other night still living in that Maria something house?"

"Yes. I think so. I met her some time ago. She looked as if she were having a good life. She told me that now she is completely a member of The House of Maria. And she thanked me for that. If I had not turned her away that time, her life would not have had the stability it now has, she said. In short, she disposed of her loneliness very quickly and efficiently."

Ki-ryong's eyes which seemed to get clearer as he drank more liquor were fixed on In-chol as he told him this.

"Hadn't you known beforehand that she would go through that kind of metamorphosis?" asked In-chol.

Ki-ryong did not answer this question but, instead, went on with his verbal meditation on the theme of loneliness,

"There is no question that if a person wants to recover from a sense of alienation, he or she must begin by overcoming loneliness in whatever form it was thrown on him or her. Too many people, however, seek to forget this loneliness through such things as the blood of Jesus. They then decide that they are no longer lonely."

Although Ki-ryong was talking about the woman with the name Choi Esther who made her home in The House of Maria, listening to him In-chol could not help thinking of his own mother. Isn't she committing the very fallacy which Ki-ryong is condemning? Isn't she mistaken in her conception of what is religion?

Unawares, In-chol was pouring wine into his own cup repeatedly. Drinking cup after cup, he was thinking about his own words about his mind becoming peaceful when he was with Ki-ryong. Today, Ki-ryong was not speaking to him in honorific form and this pleased In-chol. Yet, he was conscious of the fact that it was not an easy peace or comfort that he was getting from Ki-ryong. In Ki-ryong's utterances, there were countless number of knife blades that flashed in many different directions at once and it was when some random strokes of these flashing knife blades cut him through in many places that he could have the comfort of the peaceful feeling he relished. In-chol poured the wine again into his own cup.

In the reverse order from the other night when they had started in a drinking house downtown and moved up to one in the outskirt of Miari, on this day, they started from a tavern in Miari and then moved on downtown. In-chol took Ki-ryong to the tavern near the Montparnasse where he had wished to bring his cousin once.

Inside the tavern which was not very crowded, In-chol saw Pak Hae-yon who waved a hand in In-chol's direction to call him to his table. Nodding to him in acknowledgement of his invitation, In-chol went to another table which was un-occupied and sat down across from Ki-ryong.

"You seem to come here often," said Ki-ryong without even looking around the hall.

"Does it look like that to you?"

"Your whole person began to assimilate with the atmos-phere in this place as soon as we entered the alley."

In-chol laughed. That Ki-ryong had, under his guise of utter indifference, had this kind of perceptive power even after so much drink surprised him in an exquisite way.

When the drink was brought to their table and they started drinking, Pak Hae-yon came over carrying his own cup in one hand.

"You are somewhat late today," he said sitting next to In-chol. Then, putting down his cup on the table, he said to Ki-ryong,

"Please, excuse me."

Ki-ryong merely looked at Pak Hae-yon saying nothing.

In-chol had foreseen that in so far as Pak Hae-yon was present in the tavern, his time with Ki-ryong at this place would turn out in this way. Come to think of it, however, he might have wanted to bring Ki-ryong here so that the latter could take a look at all these leading characters of this theater of the drunkards.

Pushing his face close to In-chol's, Pak Hae-yon said,

"I see you've brought a new member."

What he meant was 'a new actor for the theater.' In-chol wavered whether or not to introduce these two to each other but decided not to. Or, maybe, it would be more correct to say, he decided that it was perhaps not possible. Ki-ryong's taciturnity combined with his habitual expression of apathy gave him the impression that the latter forbade him to.

"Our national assembly candidate seems to have come back from the provinces with the money he was paid for his last property which means that he will show up here re-gularly every night from now on like before and Miss Cho was here, too, only a while ago. She said she came to see if you were here. I told her that your attendance rate is pretty low these days. You'd better buckle up and improve your grade, if you don't want to become a dropout, that is. And... according to Shin Myong-su, Nam Chun-gol, too, seems almost through with his new play. He's moved to a hotel to give the work a last touch-up, Shin Myong-su says. The problem is...."

Here Pak Hae-yon brought his head closer up to In-chol and said, "the hotel expenses. Do you know where they come from? They are coming from Miss Cho! Can you guess her motive? Simple. Since it's Mr. Nam whose hotel bill Miss Cho is paying so that he could write up the play in which Miss Cho wants to play a role, one does not have to be very smart to know what is making Miss Cho to spend money on Mr. Nam at this point. She is doing that to have the leading role herself. I don't know how this kind of thing appears to you, Mr. Kim, but if you ask me, I think it is plain sordid, yes, sordid is the word! Everything and everybody is sordid. Of course, it's none of my business. What I should concern myself about rather is the new play I myself am conceiving as I hinted to you the other night, remember? It is related with architecture, so I will tell you what it's like."

There was a tone of entreatment almost in Pak Hae-yon's voice. To avoid smelling his alcohol-rank breath, In-chol turned his head aside a little. Ki-ryong was continuously drinking, oblivious to Pak Hae-yon's talk whether genuinely or in pretense.

"To the right of the stage flows a river and the left side is a construction site. In the river, there flows no water; only sand and pebbles are covering the space where there should be water. Grasses and all kinds of trees are growing everywhere along and beyond the riverbanks and the construction site, too, is encircled with these growths. Time can be set freely. Doesn't matter whether it is morning, midday, or evening. When the curtain rises, the laborers are mixing cement, pebbles, and sand which would be used for laying the foundation. At some distance on the riverside, a row of laborers with a stone-carrier on their back are entering the riverbed to fetch the sand and pebbles to mix with the cement. It is easy enough to enter the river. Although the area between the riverbank and the riverbed is a marsh land so that the laborers' legs sink into the mud now and then, all of them reach the riverbed without fail. The trouble is in getting out of there loaded with sand and pebbles. Because of the weight of their loads, the laborers keep falling into the soft mud holes underneath. They sink up to the knees, to the waist, to the armpits, then their shoulders and finally their heads go under. Yet, none of them thinks of freeing himself from the burden on his back. Thus, they continue to sink into the mud. Even so, one or two of the crew succeeds in climbing up the bank while more labor hands with empty stone-carriers keep arriving at the riverbank. There is no need for elaborate stage effects. Only the voice of the superintendent shouting, 'Hurry up. Hurry up. More sand and pebbles!' can be heard coming from the wing at...."

"At regular intervals?" interjected In-chol.

Pak Hae-yon smiled somewhat shamefacedly and said,

"You find a similarity between this and the one I told you about before?"

"They are not just similar but identical."

"But it's not so, Mr. Kim. There are many dissimilarities. I mean variations increase as the play proceeds. In the second act, for instance, more laborers with loaded carriers succeed in climbing up the riverbank. This has become possible because the marsh land has been filled in with the corpses of the men who had been buried in it. The work at the construction site, as a result, proceeds smoothly and now the voice of the superintendent shouting, 'Hurry up. . . .' and so on is not heard as conspicuously as before. In the third act, no laborer with the loaded carrier sinks into the mud. The corpses have filled up the entire marsh land between the riverbank and the riverbed where the laborers have been traveling back and forth. The construction has progressed excellently and now we see a building through the trees and plants which is finished up to the fifth floor. Now the superintendent is not shouting at all. Everything is being done quietly and peacefully. The curtain comes down. How is this, Mr. Kim? Don't you feel that this is more optimistic and constructive than the other one? That's why I name it. . . ."

Just then, Ki-ryong suddenly interjected,

"An idea game."

Stopping short in his revelation of the title he was going to give his new play, Pak Hae-yon turned his head to Ki-ryong looking at him with eyes that were intoxicated with drink and the excitement of the story he had just come to reveal to the audience of this table.

"Who is this man?" asked Pak Hae-yon finally, turning his eyes away from Ki-ryong to In-chol.

In-chol did not reply. He thought he would leave the tavern with Ki-ryong in a minute.

"Who are you to insult a person's creative work. . . ."

But again, Ki-ryong stopped him short by uttering,
"It was a small village by the harbor...."
He lowered the wine cup from his mouth taking time to do
so. From the way he uttered the sentence, one could tell that
he had not so much interrupted Pak Hae-yon in his talk as
was too absorbed with his own preoccupation to pay attention to others. He continued staring at a spot in the void in
front of him:
"About a dozen hovels stood by the seashore facing sea-
ward. A soldier was ambushing in a hill overlooking this
harbor village. He was waiting for the night to come because
then he can go down to the village and loot some food from
the villagers. He had a rifle with him."
Ki-ryong picked up the wine cup and took a sip as if to
wet his lips. He continued,
"Three men came out of the hovels and started to dig holes
in the sand. After they dug up about half a dozen holes, they
went back inside the hovels. After a while they came back
out, this time dragging about half a dozen people who were
bound up with ropes around the arms. Among the half a dozen
or so captives was at least one woman who was carrying a
child on her back. The three men dragged the captives to
where they had dug the holes and making them kneel inside
the holes, one in each hole, they buried them with sand, just
their heads poking out."
"This is what happened during the War, isn't it? It's a
scene of villagers killing fellow villagers, isn't it?" asked Pak
Hae-yon with interest, forgetting his resentment of a while
ago.
"It was an hour of the evening tide. Every time new tide
of waves came in, the distance between the sea and the buried
captives grew shorter while their three captors watched at
some distance standing on the sandbank. When the tide
finally swallowed the buried captives, the three men walked
back toward the village. It was at this moment that the
soldier started fire. He fired countless shots at the three men

as if he were in a frenzy."

"Who's this soldier? Is it you?" asked Pak Hae-yon pointing at Ki-ryong with a finger excitedly.

Ki-ryong did not even turn his head toward Pak Hae-yon
but picking up his wine cup lifted it to his lips.

"I don't understand his action. Why didn't he shoot down
the three men before the captives were buried by the water?
Why did he wait to kill the men until their victims drowned?
Which side do you...." Pak Hae-yon went on.

"The soldier did it because he was lonely."

"Because he was lonely?"

Without another reply, Ki-ryong got up from the table as
if he did not feel up to offering any more explanations to Pak
Hae-yon.

"Shall we go?" he said to In-chol. "I don't think they
have good wine here."

"Wait just a moment," said Pak Hae-yon hurriedly, he,
too, getting up.

Ki-ryong walked to the counter to pay. Pak Hae-yon
turned to In-chol saying,

"I don't know where you two are going, but can't I come
with you? I find that man very interesting."

Hearing no answer from In-chol, Pak Hae-yon went after
Ki-ryong who was walking toward the entrance after paying
the bill.

"*Hyong-ssi* (semipolite way of accosting another male of
similar age group)," Pak Hae-yon called. "I am sorry to
impose myself on you like this on our first meeting, but
couldn't you let me borrow the story you've just told us? I
want to revise it as a play and see what happens...."

In a flash, Ki-ryong turned back and pushed Pak Hae-yon
on the chest. With his two arms spread out, Pak Hae-yon fell
back on the floor. He fluttered his arms a couple of times in
the air as if calling somebody to help him up. In-chol pretended not to see and walked out the door after Ki-ryong. He
felt as if it had not been Pak Hae-yon but he himself that had

been thrown onto the floor by Ki-ryong. No, rather, it was
the entire staff of actors that appeared in this theater of the
drunkards that Ki-ryong had knocked down on the floor.

Ki-ryong was lighting a cigarette a few yards away. When
they were out of the alley, In-chol asked,

"Shall we go somewhere else and have a drink?"

"Better not have any more tonight," he said.

They walked in silence toward the bigger street. Suddenly
Ki-ryong muttered,

"Man is incapable of attaining the wisdom of a cat."

Luckily, the cold spell came later than expected. Because
of a change in the plan for the interior decoration, however,
the completion of Na-mi's house was further postponed.
Every time In-chol went out to the site, which was not
seldom these days, he ran into Na-mi there. He wondered
if Na-mi stayed longer there in order to meet up with him.
It was, more than anything, her attitude toward him that
gave him this suspicion. Yet, hadn't she proposed to him
that they maintain strictly business relationship and nothing
more? What made her change her mind? But hadn't he
changed himself? Nowadays, In-chol was much more carefree in relating to Na-mi. It was because now he could keep
himself separate from the world where Na-mi belonged. He
could not deny that it was partly through a conscious effort
that he could maintain this separateness from Na-mi, but he
was content. As he grew more noncommittal in regards to
Na-mi, however, she grew more personal and insistent toward
him.

On the day when it was finally decided to call a halt to the
construction work on account of the fall in temperature, too,
In-chol ran into Na-mi at the site. Na-mi said she was glad
that at least the upstairs hall could be put to use at Christmas
time. She told In-chol that she would like to invite him to
celebrate the temporary completion of the work with her,
and without asking In-chol's opinion, took him to the Chong-

sujang Hotel again. Recalling what had happened at this
hotel months ago, In-chol wondered what kind of a drama
Na-mi had in store for tonight. Whatever plot she had, now
he was an outsider, a spectator.

Na-mi's eyes were open in the darkness. Whitish blur
above made her wonder if the color of the ceiling had been
white. Or, was it gray? Or, a cream-yellow? Try though she
did, she could not remember. Her one obsession throughout
the dance at the hall or conversation at the table was con-
summating her relationship with In-chol tonight. As soon as
they returned to the room, therefore, she had pulled down
all the blinds and turned off the light with her own hands.
At the same time, she was aware that she was acting in a
way she had never acted in her life.

There was complete silence in the room. Only the hissing
sound of the steam heater at the head of the bed broke the
silence now and then. In-chol was immobile by her; maybe
he was asleep. He had not had much drink tonight.

The pain on her lower abdomen was almost all gone now.
Yet there still was some sensation which reminded her of the
time when, as a child, she had tried on her grandfather's
thick-lensed spectacles. Even after she took off the glasses,
she had felt as if something were still hanging there across
her nose. What sensation would In-chol be feeling now, she
wondered. She wanted to ask him. And she wanted to tell
him about how she felt. It seemed to her that she could tell
In-chol anything just as she felt it. This was not the same as
what she had experienced with Nam Chun-gol. With him,
the mental and intellectual part of her would not follow the
lead of the action. With In-chol, she was still lingering in the
intoxication the action brought. But what about In-chol? As
if in deep sleep, he was lying completely still. Shall I wake
him up?, she wondered. She recalled the words he had muttered separating himself from her a while ago. Shall I leave
some more room between me and him while I sleep, then?

Na-mi asked herself.

Na-mi felt alone in the darkness. Now there was not even the hissing of the steam heater. For a long while Na-mi was the sole keeper of this complete silence. Then, she fell asleep.

With an indifferent expression, In-chol was standing off a few paces off. Na-mi waved her hand to him signaling him to come to her side. In-chol pretended not to see it; he kept on standing in the same spot with a vacant face. Na-mi caught up with him. Every time she came up to him, however, In-chol removed himself to the same distance that there was between them before. She could not remember how many times this had been repeated. Suddenly, she saw a pond right in front of her; she was standing on its bank. The pond water was boiling over so that it came up to the bank where she was standing. A large goldfish was swimming in this boiling water wagging its tail in a leisurely style. She cried, 'That is In-chol! I must catch him quick!' She ran after the fish this way and that along the bank. The pond water boiled up more fiercely, flooding the bank. The more furiously the pond water boiled over, however, the more relaxedly the fish swam about. But suddenly, the fish was thrust out by the force of the boiling water so that it fell on the surface of the bank. Instantly, blood poured out of its body; its skin peeled off and the flesh fell off. In the end, there remained nothing but the white bones. Na-mi lay down beside the carcass of the goldfish. The blood that had flown out of the fish wetted her. She wanted it to make her skin peel off and make her flesh fall off so that she, too, would become mere white bones. But the blood only made part of her skin wet and flew on away somewhere.

CHAPTER FOUR

The Mask

Kim Sang-jin was sitting at his supper table but kept on drinking whiskey without touching food. He drank the whiskey straight tonight. Soon, he felt his chest burn, then the back of his neck and next his head caught the fire. The fire burnt up everything except one thing which it only urged on to blossoming. It was the thought: how should he get through the financial crisis.

It was about ten days ago that his milling factory which had finally gone into short hours stopped running altogether. The depression on the milling business as a whole was still continuing except that from general indications at the market, one could foresee a change for the better in a near future. A temporary closing down of the factory, therefore, was no serious question. The more important problem was how to procure the fund with which to resume the operation after this spell of depression.

Kim Sang-jin still had not made this year's installment for the loan he took out at the time of building the factory. And his plan to take out another loan ended in failure, too. Kim Sang-jin could not understand why Mr. Cho, the bank president, had become so cold toward him all of a sudden. Far from granting him another loan, he even started threatening Kim Sang-jin that he would appeal to the law if the latter should fail to make the necessary annual installment within a

short period. Was he being pressured by someone to perse-
cute me? Maybe somebody who has connection with the
Samhwa Milling Company?

Kim Sang-jin's position in relation with the Samhwa, too,
was problematic, to say the least. According to the Business
Manager of Kim Sang-jin's company, the other company's
act of tax evasion and bribery had been proved incontestable
on an informal basis; legally, however, there was no way of
proving it. The latest report was that the Samhwa was in
league with an official source far more powerful than what
Kim Sang-jin had on his side. It was likely that their illegal
behaviors would be covered up. That was not all, however.
By some means Kim Sang-jin could not guess, the other
company was still operating although it was as clear as day
that they were not making any profit. What bank could have
given them the loan, wondered Kim Sang-jin. It was a war,
veritably. War of survival. If it was so, one had to fight for
victory no matter what desperate means one had to use.

Taking off his glasses, Kim Sang-jin pressed his both eyes
with his fingertips. He put the glasses back on. The factory
building and facilities were already mortgaged at Mr. Cho's
bank for the loan he had taken out which meant that he
could not utilize them again at this point. He had, therefore,
mortgaged the company building and the house he and his
family lived in at another bank for a loan. If only he could
get this loan, he would use that money to bribe someone in
higher quarters who would have the power to help him get
the necessary loan.

As if to keep the fire going in his system so that the blossom of his determination would not wither, Kim Sang-jin
poured some more whiskey into the glass and drank it.

The door opened quietly and the maid came in with the
rice tea which she put down softly on the table. She left the
room as if fleeing. He is not eating his dinner. Is it because
he doesn't like the way the foods are cooked that he skips
dinner every evening lately, she asked herself. But it's not

me who cook the foods. It's the Food-Mother (general term for female help who cooks and tends other household chores), she said to herself again.

"What's the matter with you these days, *obba*? You are home every evening. Have you stopped drinking? Or, is this the short peaceful moment before a fearful storm?" said In-ju sitting in a chair opposite In-chol. She was still in her street clothes. Her cheeks were flushed as if from being exposed to the cold air outdoors.

"Why don't you knock at a person's door?"

"Oh, pardon me, I was in a hurry to show my older brother something."

In-chol put down the book on the side table. These couple of days, he had been leafing through various foreign magazines and journals which he was subscribing to but had left in a pile unopened during the period he had been kept busy with Na-mi's house and his thesis.

What In-ju was in such a hurry to show In-chol were some printed sheets which apparently somebody had torn out of some book.

"Look," she said.

On the top sheet was attached a white slip of paper which had these words scribbled with a ball-point pen.

⟨If you do not understand what is written here, ask In-ju-*ssi*; if she doesn't understand it, either, ask In-chol-*ssi*.⟩

"What's this?" said In-chol with a misgiving.

"This was mailed to Nam-*sonsaengnim*. I couldn't understand it, that's why I've brought it to you, *obba*."

In-chol lifted the white slip of paper to read what was underneath. He read a title: Hahoe Pyolshin Mask Dance.

"This is a drama, isn't it? If neither Mr. Nam nor you understand this thing, how could I who has nothing to do with that kind of thing understand it?"

"Well, I, too, can see that it's a text for an old mask play; I don't understand why whoever it is sent this to Nam-*son-*

saengnim and why he or she directed him to ask me or *obba*. There was no name or address of the sender on the envelope."

In-chol started perusing the text.

"There are such filthy expressions in it!" said In-ju.

From the first to the third scene, there were only directions and it was only from the fourth scene that characters were supposed to appear on the stage exchanging dialogues. But what In-ju called 'filthy' came up only in the fifth scene where the Aristocrat and the Scholar compete over who is the better of the two. The Scholar—One must have learning. I've read all of Four-so and Three-kyong (Seven Chinese Classics). The Aristocrat—What's that? Four-so and Three-kyong? As for me, I have read Eight-so and Six-kyong. The Scholar—Where are these Eight-so and Six-kyong? Choraeng-i (Aristocrat's servant)—Don't you know the Six-kyong which even I know? They are: *Palmantaejangkyong* (complete Buddhist sutras), Monk's *Parakyong* (gong-like instrument), blind man's *ankyong* (spectacles), medicine man's *kilkyong* (root of Chinese balloon flower), maiden's *wolkyong* (menstruation), and slave boy's *saekyong* (farmland slaves were given as annual fee).... The Aristocrat and the Scholar at this point make up with each other, saying their claims to superiority are equal. They call a woman named Pu-ne and together they dance joyously. The scene which answered In-chol's apprehensive premonition came after this. The *Paekchong* enters carrying an ax and ox-balls. The *Paekchong*—Buy some *al* (ball, egg, etc.). The Aristocrat—Get lost, rascal. Don't you see we are having fun? And what's this *al* you're babbling about? Who needs such a thing? The *Paekchong*—Don't you know *al*? Choraeng-i—*takal* (eggs of hen), *nunal* (eyeballs), *sae-al* (birds' eggs), *taegamtongbulal* (great lords' testicles). The *Paekchong*—That's right, that's right. I mean *pulal*. The Scholar—What? The *Paekchong*—Don't you know *soebulal*, the ox-balls? The Aristocrat—Rascal, how dare you speak such a filthy word to us? Nobody's going to buy, so get lost! The *Paekchong*—These are good for *yanggi* (virility). The

Scholar—What? Good for *yanggi*? Then, I will buy it.
The Aristocrat—No, it's mine. (The Aristocrat and the
Scholar both snatch at the ox-balls.) The *Paekchong*—Oh,
my balls! You're bursting my balls!

In-chol could not go on reading.

"It's a satire on the aristocrats and the scholar class of old
time. Nothing very interesting."

In-chol did not add that there was in it a satire on the
paekchong class with its vulgar use of language and base
behavior.

"I know that much."

"Then, what don't you know?"

"I want to know the motive of the person who sent this
anonymously."

"Maybe the unknown person wanted to tease you a little
because you are so carried away by acting."

In-chol knew that his answer did not make much sense but
it was the best he could try.

"No, I don't think so. There must be some better reason
for it. But I see that you are as much at a loss as I am. What
should I do, now? I can't just let it go; I feel terrible."

"Why? It's just some fool's idea of a practical joke."

But the truth was that In-chol himself was feeling quite
bad. What despicable character was it that was doing this to
them? There seemed no doubt that it was the same one that
had sent that drawing to Na-mi's father. Who was this evil
and cowardly person that was using this sort of underhanded
method to harm us, wondered In-chol feeling a belated anger
welling up from his heart. To In-ju, however, he said casually,

"I hear Nam Chun-gol's new play is almost finished, is
that right? Did he give you a good part?"

"I don't know. We are all waiting. But I don't think getting a good part is all that important."

"Well, but it won't harm you to get one, I don't think,"
said In-chol, still trying to divert his sister's mind from the
thought that was oppressing them both.

"That's not how it is in acting. It is wrong to think that leading characters have so much control over the performance," said In-ju in a tone that conveyed to In-chol that his strategy was working.

"From what I hear, though, people seem to be competing to get a leading role. I've heard an outline of what Nam Chun-gol is writing from Na-mi. I mean the plot with a woman who married a G.I., broke up, and then coming home destroyed her own family. It won't be an easy part to play but could be a profitable challenge for Miss In-ju, I think."

"You mean you don't have confidence in my ability to act? You mustn't underestimate me too much, *obba*. I could act that part if I would."

"What does the playwright-director think?"

"He doesn't say anything about parts as yet although he might have decided in his mind."

There was a knock on the door and the maid's voice said, "You'd better take the bath, *toryonnim*."

"All right, I'll come down in a minute."

In-chol was glad to have the excuse to cut his interview with his sister short. A thought came to him, however, and he asked,

"Would you like to take it first?"

"Isn't it the rule that you take the bath first when you are home?"

"Well, I will yield my right to you today as a special treat."

"That's not how it should be put, though. What I think is that from the way our bath system goes, it's more hygienic for women to be the first to use the bathwater."

Before going out, In-ju added,

"You know I take long, don't you? And since I feel quite unclean today, I think I will take even longer to cleanse me, all right?"

In-chol laughed in acquiescence. But how could one

cleanse the inside of one's heart by taking a long bath? All the same, he liked the way his sister went about things in a thoroughgoing manner and he was glad that he managed not to tell her anything about what could be the motive of the person who sent Nam Chun-gol the text of the mask play.

In a minute or two, however, In-chol's mind became gloomy again. It may be possible to protect In-ju for the time being, he thought, but as long as this person is alive somewhere, it would be only a matter of time for In-ju to learn everything. It was only a period of reprieve for In-ju now.

Just then, In-chol seemed to hear a characteristic low voice speaking to him. It was the voice of Ki-ryong. Tell her everything, the voice said. Let her take care of the rest of the business. But In-chol could not bring himself to tell In-ju even after she finished her long bath.

Na-mi was rushing in on In-chol rapidly. After the work was stopped at the site, she met In-chol in town. Since In-chol no longer liked to go either to the Montparnasse or the tavern in its vicinity, the two spent time together at places like music halls where they could listen to the music while drinking tea or coffee. At parting she gave In-chol the time and place of their next meeting. Even if In-chol was late or didn't show up altogether, Na-mi did not blame him. When they walked in the street, too, Na-mi did not complain even if he should walk ahead of her or lagged behind. She would hasten her steps and catch up with him or slow her pace down and, passing one arm through In-chol's when he was by her side, walk on, trying to keep pace with him.

One day, Na-mi said that it would be a memorable Christmas party this year. Then she said that she planned to announce their engagement on the occasion. The music hall gramophone was playing a violin concerto by Bruch. Still intent on the music, In-chol merely looked at her. She was saying, 'Are you listening to me, or aren't you? Papa is against it, but you wait and see, I will defeat him. Papa will come around. You, too, In-chol-*ssi*, you must get a consent from your parents if only for form's sake.'

In-chol gave it a thought. My father needn't be consulted. Didn't he once suggest a diplomatic marriage with Ta-hye, even? Besides, he is right now too deep in agony over the financial trouble of his company to care about anything else. Anyone can see it. It seems he isn't having any luck in getting the loan from the bank. He will welcome a marriage with the daughter of the bank president Mr. Cho. He will welcome it hands raised. But...but.... In-chol repeated this same word again and again, listening to the sweet and beautiful music from the gramophone.

His thesis came out of printing and he decided to give it one more reading although he had proofread it before it went into print. He found not a few misprints. More disturbing than these were the shortcomings he found in its contents.

The defects in his thesis were the reminders of the events that had been happening to him for the past number of months. He was sorry that he had not given more time, thought, and energy to this work, but there was nothing he could do about it at this late hour.

With a finely sharpened pencil, he began to correct the diagrams he had inserted within the thesis. It was about nine o'clock in the night. Suddenly, the bell on the wall rang the signal for the telephone. He picked up the receiver from the phone at the head of the bed.

"You are Mr. Kim In-chol?" asked a male voice which In-chol could not identify.

"Who is this?"

"I am Shin Myong-su. You know me, don't you?"

"Ah, yes, yes, I do. But what made you...."

"Something urgent happened. Please come to the front of the Capital Theater."

"What happened?"

"In-ju-*ssi*'s not home yet, is she?"

"So, what then?"

"You will find out when you come. The questions had better be postponed. Hurry up and come to the front of the Capital Theater."

"Tell me, what happened?"

"Just come out and see for yourself."

He hung up. In bewilderment, In-chol put on the heavy coat on top of his house clothes and left home hurriedly. He had to go near Tonhwamun until he could catch a taxi. What on earth could have happened? Why did he ask if In-ju was home? Has anything happened to In-ju? In-chol could not sit still even in the running car. When they had to wait at the signal, the interval seemed to last forever.

He got off the taxi in front of the Capital Theater. Except for a few passers-by, there was no one there. Only one ticket collector was sitting inside the entrance door of the theater. It being quite past the beginning hour of the last feature, the whole place looked deserted.

In-chol took one more careful look around and then he saw a man coming toward him. It was Shin Myong-su who was wearing a beret.

"Has anything happened to In-ju?"

"Come with me," said Shin Myong-su starting to walk in the direction of Ulchiro.

"Has anything happened to In-ju?" In-chol asked again.

"You will soon find out."

It seemed that Shin Myong-su was drunk. He was staggering a little. Then, after a while, Shin Myong-su turned the corner to enter the street leading to the Chungbu Police Station. A roasted chestnut seller was shouting: two piles for one hundred *hwan*! I'll give you two hundred *hwan*'s worth of chestnuts for one hundred *hwan*! A little way away from there were two beggar boys scuffling with each other. Maybe they were fighting over who would have the roasted chestnut that had fallen off the peddler's sales tray.

Shin Myong-su halted when they had walked about fifty meters along this street. Pointing at a building across the street with one hand, Shin Myong-su said,

"She's in there, now."

It was a two-story building with a sign on the front that said that it was a hotel of some name. It did not look like an expensive place.

"She's in that room at the left end on the second floor," Shin Myong-su said again.

As soon as he recognized the place to be some sort of a hotel building, In-chol felt his heart pound.

"Of course, she is not alone. You know what I mean, don't you? This has been happening every night these several days."

In-chol seemed to see everything all at once. So, he finally....But In-chol's anger was fired at Shin Myong-su.

"You, scoundrel, why do you watch other people from their behind like this, eh?"

His adversary fell back one step.

"What scum of a man are you, to follow people around like a spy!" In-chol shouted again.

"You don't understand, at all," said Shin Myong-su recovering voice. "One might have expected a praise. But to be shouted at like this is something I never even imagined."

"Are you still proud of what you did, you scum?"

"I did it only, only for In-ju-*ssi*. Really, I did it for In-ju-*ssi*'s future. And for your honor."

"What? Who told you to be our protector, huh?"

"I...I...love In-ju-*ssi*. Really. It's been several days since I first knew In-ju-*ssi* was coming to that hotel. I put up with it at first. I made up my mind that I would bear everything and wait until In-ju-*ssi* will change her mind. But something happened today. She came out of the hotel and buying a bag of roasted chestnuts went back inside the hotel. And from the way she moved and acted, I could tell that she was happy and contented. Suddenly, I could not stand it. That's why I called you up."

"It's up to you to love her or not, but from now on you must never behave in such a filthy way as this, you hear me? It won't do you any good to disobey me!"

A blind masseur passed by them blowing at his pipe and crossed the street to the hotel side. In-chol did not wish to be standing with Shin Myong-su any longer. He was conscious of the fact that he had been taking his anger out on the wrong person. He turned away from Shin Myong-su. A thought suddenly came to him, however, and he returned to Shin Myong-su whom he grabbed by the throat.

"You did that, too, didn't you?"

Taken completely by surprise, Shin Myong-su became helpless in In-chol's angry grip.

"Why are you doing this to me?" he protested staggering backward.

"You sent that drawing to Na-mi's father and you sent that mask play text to Nam Chun-gol, didn't you?"

Shin Myong-su did not answer.

"Answer me, you scum! There's no one except you who could have done such a dirty thing!"

Still with his throat in In-chol's grip, Shin Myong-su nodded, moving his head with difficulty.

"You filth! Can't you do anything except in such an under-handed fashion?" said In-chol tightening his grip on Shin Myong-su's throat. "Don't you know it's filthy to act in that way?"

Shin Myong-su gagged. Maybe In-chol's grip was choking him. In any case, there was no point in holding a man by his throat when he wasn't resisting in any way. In-chol let go of him.

"You do that kind of thing and still have the nerve to say you love In-ju?"

"But I do," said Shin Myong-su rubbing himself on the throat where In-chol had held him. "I did all that because I love In-ju-*ssi*. In whatever way possible, I wanted to make others move away from her so that I could have her. Frankly, I wanted In-ju-*ssi* to become unhappy. After she would have become unhappy and people stopped caring for her, I would have loved her, keeping her all to myself. I am not reciting from a dramatic text now. I would never have minded it no matter in what social situation she would be placed. You must believe this of me."

"How did you find out about our family?"

"I didn't know anything for sure. It was mostly my guess work. All I knew was that you seem to be associating with that kind of people. This was pretty long time ago. One morning I stood at the bus stop in Miari to go to school when I saw you coming from the opposite direction. I wanted to greet you but you didn't see me. You looked very tired and I wondered where you could have gone in that area that early. Then, I met you again in Miari as you, too, must recall. You were very drunk that night. I don't know if you remember this, too, but you asked me that night where I lived. My house is close to the house where your drinking companion of that night had room and board until very lately, although I know that he is now living at another place."

Inspite of himself, In-chol laughed voicelessly. It seemed comical that he had confirmed Shin Myong-su's arbitrary conjectures voluntarily.

Back at home, In-chol tried to calm himself down. At least, now he knew that it was Shin Myong-su who had sent the drawing and the text of the mask play. Even if he had taken that incriminating action on mere conjectures on his part, it was borne out by the truth and there was no helping it, now.

In-chol tried to resign himself to the matter concerning In-ju and Nam Chun-gol, as well. The man was married and had children, but what could he do at this point since the water was already spilled. He picked up his thesis which he had put down to answer Shin Myong-su's summons, but he could not concentrate on it.

Footsteps were heard climbing up the stairs. Then there was a knock at his door. It was In-ju.

"Did you want to see me, *obba*?"

He had told the maid to send In-ju up to his room as soon as she should come in. Although he had decided to accept what had already happened, he could not sit back and do nothing.

"Where have you been?"

"Same place as other nights," said In-ju without hesitation.

"Where is this same place?"

"It's a hotel at the back of the Capital Theater."

"Who's been with you?"

"You know who, don't you?"

Standing up abruptly, In-chol slapped her on the face. Rather than her admission of the fact, her absolutely blasé attitude had angered him intolerably.

"I order you to stop this acting nonsense at once! I thought you would be different. That you could sell your body to get a part in a lousy play!"

In-ju stood absolutely motionless, merely looking up at him with penetrating eyes. One of her cheeks which had been flushed by the cold outside air was redder because of his slapping.

"Are you so proud of what you did that you can look at me in the eyes like that? Are you, eh?"

Once more, In-chol slapped In-ju.

"You are misunderstanding things."

"I am misunderstanding?"

"I am going there to help Nam-*sonsaengnim* with copy work."

"You can speak, can't you? You've already forgotten about your mother?"

In-ju stood on, erect. Her face, however, turned pale at the mention of her mother and tears rose in her eyes shaded by her long eyelashes that reminded one of the fine ribs of an elegant fan. Then, the tears rolled down her cheeks and fell onto her scarf and the collar of her coat. "I have believed that at least you would have trust in me," she said, her face distorted with anger and grief. "No matter what other say, I thought you would trust me. But, but all you think of is dirty things. Now I don't have anyone. You have stopped believing in me for long, now. I can see. And you've been deceiving me, too, I know. I met Shin Myong-su coming out of the hotel."

Turning violently, In-ju ran out of the room not bothering to close the door after her. In-mun who had come out of his room hearing In-ju run out of In-chol's room and down the stairs, looked from the staircase to In-chol's room once, and then went back into his room.

In-chol heard the sounds of the front door banging, rapid and confused footsteps, and finally the gate creaking open.

Without knowing in which direction she was going, In-ju kept on running. Her sole thought was that she had to go to Nam Chun-gol.

Many times, she nearly bumped against other passers-by or was thrust back by someone, but she did not cease to run. He had said that if she can come and help him tomorrow, they could put the manuscript in some sort of an order until day after tomorrow. He had asked her if she wasn't wearied by all the work and had apologized to her. He is so silly, he doesn't know that I am so happy to work for him! I don't care if he gives me only a very minor part. I will do whatever he tells me to, not only in acting but also in other things, too. Yes, I will do that, now.

The scarf came off from around her neck and fluttered wildly in the wind. She let it flutter and fly away if it will as she kept on running. You will accept and trust me, won't you *sonsaengnim*, she cried out to Nam Chun-gol with her inner voice.

Finally, she came to a spot where she could see the hotel

where Nam Chun-gol was. She saw light on his window. He isn't in his bed, yet, thought In-ju. Ah, that's he, looking through the window! Can he see me? I can even see his pipe! I can almost smell it. I must go quickly to that room where I can smell the tobacco he uses in that pipe. Ah, he saw me, that's why he's opening the window! Just then, a bright light rushed to In-ju's side with a screeching sound; In-ju was thrown unconscious on the ground.

In-ju opened her eyes with great difficulty, but she could not see anything. Her consciousness, too, was blurred. She closed her eyes again. She did not know how much time had passed; she reopened her eyes. This time, she saw something milky in front of her. She opened her eyes wider. But it was no use. Her consciousness became blurry again.

Many times, In-ju regained consciousness for a brief while and then fell back into a coma. She heard a sound after some time and looked in the direction of the sound. Something came into sight but what it was she could not tell. After another long or short while, she heard another sound; she opened her eyes and looked in the direction of the sound. Somebody was standing there but she could not tell who. Again she heard a sound and opening her eyes she looked in that direction. Although indistinctly, she saw a face. Ah, that's right, I have Nam-*sonsaengnim* who cares for me and I was alive until a short time ago. But why isn't Nam-*sonsaengnim* smoking his pipe, now? Then, her vision faded. Some time later, she opened her eyes again. Another person was standing beside Nam-*sonsaengnim*. That person was putting a handkerchief to the face. Why is that person crying? She closed her eyes. Ah, that's right, I had a brother, yes, a brother whom I liked best in the world. But why is he crying?

A long time passed before In-ju became aware that aside from Nam Chun-gol and In-chol, there were a doctor and a nurse by her side and that she was lying on a bed in a hospital room with a white ceiling and white walls. Still, she did not know why she was lying here. Then, she remembered: Ah, I bumped into something. She began to feel herself here and there with her hands. Nothing seemed wrong. She moved her legs. She could move her left leg but her right leg would not obey her. Moving herself from waist up, she brought a hand to the right leg. There was nothing from the knee downward. Then, she lost consciousness again. When she came to again, she tried to spring up to a sitting position but fell sideways. She repeated the same movement a couple more times with the same result. The doctor and the nurse held her down. She cursed them with all the foul words she knew. But no voice came out of her throat. She cursed them anyway, until she fainted again.

The dawn was still far off. It was dark outside when In-chol walked out of the University Hospital with Nam Chun-gol. The cold air he inhaled through his nostrils filled up the inside of his head and he felt a light dizziness. Nam Chun-gol took the pipe out of a pocket and filling it with tobacco, started smoking it.

Some unknown animal was howling on the other side of the wall of the zoo nearby. It was a long pitiable sound. A horse passed by making resounding sounds of hooves against the pavement. Although one could not be sure because of darkness, the horse seemed to be pulling a vegetable cart. Whitish vapor fumed at the animal's nostrils.

In-chol and Nam Chun-gol walked around the wall of the Changgyong Palace which had the zoo on its grounds in the direction of Tonhwamun. In-chol was thinking about what the doctor had said about the probability of saving In-ju's life. It seemed that In-ju would live. But she'd lost one leg. When she ran out of the house, why had he not stopped her? Why had he not been softer toward his sister? No regrets could do any good now. What future would there be for In-ju? His heart choked for her. But what could anybody do to save her future for her? It was a task she herself would have to cope with.

"I was standing by the window to rest my head. Or, maybe, I was thinking of In-ju, standing there like that. At times, I wish to have In-ju by my side. Of course, I restrain these wishes as well as I can. I wouldn't have been that considerate with other women. But In-ju was an exception. I wanted to protect her. Strangely enough, however, I saw In-ju just as I was thinking of her by the window. She was running toward me. She looked driven. Suddenly, I felt an urge to hold her in my arms tonight. Do forgive me for speaking these words. But this is my truthful feeling. I wanted to cry out something to In-ju, so I opened the window. I thought our eyes met when that automobile...."

Nam Chun-gol spoke slowly as if he were listening to his own narration.

In-chol was thinking how he had wanted to have a talk with Nam Chun-gol once. It was bizarre that it was under these tragic circumstances that their intended conversation took place.

"In-ju had wanted to recite passages from my work at the group's Christmas party," said Nam Chun-gol as if to the void, pulling the pipe out of his mouth.

CHAPTER FIVE

Christmas Eve

Wearing a red Chinese dress, Na-mi stood at the door bestowing a motley-colored paper hat on the head of every guest. Although this was something the guests were not used to, it seemed to become the atmosphere of the party hall.

Chandelier lights were ablaze in the second floor hall of Na-mi's new house. Oil stove was lit and music flew out of the gramophone. Since the house was built on an elevated terrain and, in all the house, only this upstairs hall was lit brightly, looking from outside, one would have thought that the party was being held in a floating space of light among prevailing darkness.

The lack of snow gave a sense of imperfection to the outside of the house but everything within the party hall denoted the Christmas mood. The myriad electric bulbs on the big Christmas tree standing in the middle of the room effectively enhanced the festive feeling of the evening; Christmas carols continued from the gramophone.

There were about fifteen guests. Ta-hye and Chon Kyonghun who had come up to spend the winter vacation in Seoul, too, were among them. Aside from these, Nam Chun-gol and one other person whom In-chol remembered to have sat with Pak Hae-yon on the night when he was beaten up by some unknown gangster were about all that In-chol could identify among the invited. In the meantime, Na-mi was going around introducing the guests to one another. Among other invitees were that friend of Na-mi's who was supposed to live in Inchon and her fiancé. The rest were all theater-related people.

Na-mi went toward the Christmas tree threading between the guests. Upon arriving there, she pulled the cork off the champagne bottle she had carried all the way there. With a sound of explosion, the cork came off. It popped up into the air and then fell on the floor. Somebody shouted: Bravo! And everybody laughed merrily.

Champagne bottle in hand, Na-mi announced,

"It's an all night party tonight. I hope you will all enjoy it! To start off our night, I suggest that we sing *White Christmas* all together!"

The guests clapped their hands and everybody sang. At first, the tunes were desultory, but in time the singing became a well-tuned unison. When the singing was done, the guests were invited to the food table prepared in one corner of the hall in the western style. Na-mi filled two glasses with champagne and handing one of them to In-chol, said,

"A toast to my talented architect!"

They clinked their glasses which produced a clear pleasant sound. In-chol poured the liquid into his mouth and filled the empty glass with whiskey. People were talking in groups, their champagne glasses in hand. Some were drinking beer by the food table. In-chol walked toward Ta-hye. With a glass of coca-cola in hand, she was sitting on a chair that had been scattered in twos or threes side by side around the hall. Chon Kyong-hun was with her. Ta-hye who was wearing a wool suit and a long pearl necklace did not harmonize with the atmosphere of the hall very well. Only the paper hat on her head reconciled her to this room to some extent. Had she come because she wanted to?

"I hear that a terrible thing happened to your sister," said Chon Kyong-hun seeing In-chol. "I just heard it from Ta-hye-*ssi*. What a tragedy!"

"When I first went to the hospital, she covered her head

with the sheet and would not look at me," said Ta-hye whose eyes filled with tears instantly.

"How's life down there?" asked In-chol to Chon Kyong-hun as if in a hurry to change the subject.

"It was quiet and nice at first but in a little while I began to miss life here," said Chon Kyong-hun. "I think maybe I'll come back to Seoul in the spring. One who's used to living in Seoul seems best off here."

"Maybe that's not the only reason in your case," said In-chol smiling.

"By the way, though, this is a fine work you did here. You are an accomplished architect, now," said Chon Kyong-hun avoiding the subject In-chol hinted.

He couldn't even have taken a good look at the house in this darkness, thought In-chol. He is just being courteous.

"Won't you go to the hospital with me later?" said Ta-hye. "She must be feeling terribly lonesome left by herself on a night like this."

From Ta-hye's tone of voice, In-chol could see that she had been thinking about In-ju continuously in the midst of this gaiety. The music changed from Christmas carols to a fox trot and somebody shouted,

"Let's dance!"

A man with his hair combed back from the forehead walked out from the corner where the gramophone was playing and spread the talcum powder all over the floor.

Sitting up in the bed, In-ju began to spread the cold cream on her face. This was the first time since her hospitalization that she was doing anything of this sort to herself. Slowly, taking as much time as she could, she began to massage her face with tips of her fingers.

Suddenly, she stopped her massage. Her eyes were fixed on the black spot at one corner of her upper lip reflected in the small mirror of her compact powder case. People made various comments on this tiny black spot. Some said it made

In-ju's face more attractive; others said she had better have it removed because her fair clear complexion would become the fairer, then. She wondered, looking at the black spot now, if it really made her look prettier. I would ask Nam-*sonsaengnim* about it and decide whether or not to have it removed, she said to herself. Then, she thought, maybe he will come to see me tonight! Since *obba* was here during the day, he won't come again. He would be at Na-mi's party with Nam-*sonsaengnim*. It must be a wonderful party that they are having. Who is Nam-*sonsaengnim* dancing with most? I think he will come by because there's no curfew tonight. Then, it occurred to In-ju that maybe it was because she was expecting Nam Chun-gol that she was making up her face. At this thought, her face which had almost recovered its former healthy complexion flushed uncontrollably.

The transistor radio on the side table by the bed was sending Christmas carols all evening. She dialed it to another channel which was no different. She looked all around the room. All the walls were white and so was the ceiling. Even the door was painted white. The window opposite from the door, too, except the glass panes which were dyed black with darkness outside at the moment, was white. In this uniform whiteness of the room, In-ju had been getting used to her misfortune.

In-ju stared at the window and at the darkness that filled the window, spreading out endlessly beyond. Just outside the window which was the sole source of sunlight during the day stood a ginkgo tree and beyond it stretched another hospital complex lying sideways from this side with rows of other rooms. Through the bare branches of the ginkgo tree, one could look out at these rooms.

One day, soon after she could move about a little, In-ju chanced to look out of the window when her eyes caught the figure of a young man at the opposite window from hers. He, too, was looking out of the window. She could not tell what he was looking at. All one could tell was that he was sitting completely still with his eyes fixed at a point beyond the window of his room. In-ju looked away from him. She could not stand the atmosphere of extreme loneliness that the sitting man created around him.

She acquired, ever since this day, a habit of looking out at his window. Depending on the position of the sun, sometimes she did not have a very good vision of the opposite window but mostly she could confirm the figure of the young man sitting by the window with his eyes fixed at some point outside. According to the nurse that came to In-ju's room, the young man had a heart disease and was ordered a complete rest in bed by the doctor. He disobeyed this order, however, and sat out at the window whenever he could. At times, In-ju saw the immobile figure move to wipe the windowpane with a handkerchief. In time, In-ju did not pay so much attention to the figure within the other window. Maybe she got more used to her own loneliness.

In-ju looked at the crutches that were standing against the headboard of the bed. She did not abhor them as much as when she had first started learning to use them.

In-ju hummed the melody that was coming out of the transistor radio. She was wishing for somebody to come to see her before night would be over.

Dancing with In-chol, Na-mi glanced at Nam Chun-gol now and then.

"You see that woman who's dancing with Nam-*sonsaeng-nim*? I introduced her as an actress incognito, but it was a lie. I never saw her before tonight. Since she came with Nam-*sonsaengnim*, I decided to let her be known as such."

In-chol looked in the direction. The woman had a long hair that came down on her back. Na-mi's friend from Inchon was scolding her fiancé from time to time for lowering his hand to her waist instead of keeping it on her back. Her fiancé seemed to be making excuses such as that the floor was too slippery for him not to lose balance. She would then say,

'Nonsense! You're just a country bumpkin!'

The man whose hair was combed backward was dancing with a girl whose eyelashes were unusually long. She was so much shorter than he was that it looked as if she were being carried by him with her feet off the floor. When they made turns, her feet actually swung in the air. Yet, they danced well together, their steps in perfect harmony.

Giving pressure to the hand which she was putting on In-chol's shoulder, Na-mi whispered rapidly,

"Papa is still being obstinate. But I am going to announce our relationship when the party reaches its peak. I left one bottle of champagne unused for that purpose. I am sorry about papa but what can I do?"

In-chol did not say anything, benumbed by the willfulness of the girl who was making one decision after another completely on her own. Yet, inside him, there was a persisting thought that he had to say something.

Tango music shifted to waltz. Passing the hand that had been on In-chol's shoulder through his arm, Na-mi walked over to Ta-hye who was watching the dancers sitting by Chon Kyong-hun. Na-mi gently pulled Ta-hye up by the arm and handed her to In-chol. Ta-hye protested that she did not know how to dance, but Na-mi pushed her off to the middle of the hall with In-chol and disappeared in the direction of the food table, picking her way dexterously through the dancers. She seemed content with what she had just managed to achieve.

Ta-hye told In-chol that she only learned a few dance steps in her high school days and she did indeed make some blunders at first. But soon, led by In-chol, she was dancing smoothly.

"Are you having fun?" asked Ta-hye.

"Well...."

"My expectation went completely astray."

"What expectation?"

"I had thought that you wouldn't appear here tonight."

"Why?"

"What else could I expect after hearing the report you made to me on your last visit to the house?"

"I've decided not to report to you about anything any longer."

"Why? Why are you changing like that? Can't we go back to our old relationship?"

Like with Na-mi a while ago, In-chol could not find any word to utter. Only he felt that he had to say something. Chon Kyong-hun was sitting by himself fidgeting his thick-lensed glasses for lack of anything else to do. Maybe he really didn't know how to dance at all.

Na-mi pulled Nam Chun-gol to a corner where there were not people within hearing distance. She began her interrogation,

"Who's the woman that came with you?"

Nam Chun-gol did not answer.

"What does she do?"

Again, Nam Chun-gol remained silent. There was a short pause, then, Na-mi spoke again,

"I thought I might recite some parts from your new play. Which parts would you recommend?"

"I don't want any part to be recited tonight!" said Nam Chun-gol all but bluntly.

"Why not? Isn't this a good occasion for that? I mean in commemoration of the completion of the play?"

"I don't want it, I say!" said Nam Chun-gol in a tone that sounded almost harsh.

Na-mi didn't speak again. She seemed to be able to guess why Nam Chun-gol was so cross. She did not mind his having spoken to her in such an ungenial manner.

To Kim Sang-jin, the gaiety of the night meant nothing. Closing his eyes, he leant back against the seat of his car. He was returning from a meeting with his company staffs. Although they pretended that they were having the *mang-*

nyonhoe (end-of-the-year celebration) in advance, actually the gathering virtually was the ceremony for the disbandment of the company. Nobody spoke much tonight, everybody looking solemn and glum. Somebody said they would retreat to make a better new leap and a couple of men agreed, but everybody knew that these were mere words. In order to allow his staff members to drink to their fill on this occasion which was likely to be their last chance to drink together, Kim Sang-jin had got up early to go home. Upon leaving, he told the Business Manager to let them drink and eat as much as they wanted no matter how much it would cost.

Retreat to make a better leap? But how? The only word he could think of with certainty was: a total annihilation.

The more he thought about it, the less he could understand it. A sudden change of attitude on the part of a bank president had knocked him down so completely. What really bewildered him was why the bank president had so suddenly changed his attitude. If only he had been firm and unyielding from the first, Kim Sang-jin would have stopped the operation of the milling factory much earlier. It would, of course, not have solved his problem, but at least he could have minimized the loss or investigated other sources for help. Although he had tried to make some money by mortgaging the company building and their house, nothing was likely to come out of it within the end of the year because of various bureaucratic red tapes. He tried to invite Bank President Cho to a dinner outside so that he might have another chance to broach the matter to him, but the bank president declined his invitation on the plea of end-of-the-year engagements. That afternoon, he had gone to see Mr. Cho unannounced. Although Mr. Cho received him warmly as before, his essential answer was as unchangeable and negative as all his previous answers of late. It was as if all the answers were made out of one basic mold. 'There's nothing I can do, I am sorry,' he said. 'It's the new policy of our government and the ICA not to allow postponing of installment for any loan from now on. It's not as if I didn't know your difficulty but it's all out of my personal reach. I must repeat that you must make the overdue payment before the end of the year.' There was nothing Kim Sang-jin could do against this in-flexibility.

Everything was crumbling down all at once, and Kim Sang-jin could not help feeling that he had been a victim of some intrigue. He had been able to equip his factory with facilities thanks to the loan he could get from the ICA. Yet, such a great amount of low-priced flour had been imported from the very country where the ICA had its headquarters that the milling businesses toppled over one after another. The Korean government surprisingly did not take any action against this but merely looked on. To make the matter worse, the ICA pressed for the immediate repayment of its loans, threatening with confiscation of property through law in case of fail.

"We are there, *Sajangnim*(president of company)," said the chauffeur's voice. Opening his eyes, Kim Sang-jin saw him holding the open door of the car with one hand. They were in front of the entrance of the University Hospital. Kim Sang-jin had told his chauffeur, when he was leaving his staff members, to drive the car to the hospital. He did not understand why he had wanted to come to see his daughter at this hour of the night. It was not because this was a Christmas Eve. What is it, then?

The surgery patients were hospitalized on the second floor of the inner complex. Passing through a dark corridor full of draft and smell of antiseptics, Kim Sang-jin went up the stairs with heavy feet. In-ju's room was in the middle of a row of rooms upstairs. Kim Sang-jin opened the door without knocking and went in.

"Oh, father!" exclaimed In-ju in a surprised voice from the bed where she was sitting up.

Pulling a folding chair to him, Kim Sang-jin sat down.

Maybe one bolt was missing on one of the legs, the chair tilted a little to one side under Kim Sang-jin's weight.

"Sit on this chair, father," said In-ju turning off the radio and pointing at another chair closer to the bed.

Kim Sang-jin did not move to a new chair, however. He merely took off his glasses and wiping off the vapor on the glass put them back on.

"You look all right," said Kim Sang-jin after giving her face a prolonged look.

In-ju thought that it was probably because she had made up her face, but said,

"I feel very well, now. After the Christmas holiday, I think I will get a dismissal."

Kim Sang-jin was still looking at In-ju. He was, at the same time, sinking deeper and deeper into a pensive mood searching for another face in his daughter's. Then, he knew. He now understood why he had wanted to come to see his daughter tonight. Her mother had looked exactly like her, he said to himself. Her eyes, mouth, nose, everything about In-ju except the healthy complexion (for her mother had turned quite pale in her last days) was a replica of what her mother had. It was to cover her paleness that her mother put on heavy makeup, thought Kim Sang-jin. Even if he broke his promise to come to her because of some business at the company, she never complained or looked sullen on his next visit. She was, in fact, the only woman he had ever loved with the love of man for woman. Even when he was run down with various duties of running a business, she had the knack of making him forget all his fatigue as soon as he was with her. Why had I not been more considerate and loving toward her while she was alive? Kim Sang-jin thought on, still looking at In-ju.

In-ju found her father acting strange tonight.

"Shall I peel some fruit for you, father?" she asked eyeing the plate of fruit lying on the side table. "Would you care for some persimmons?"

"I don't want any," said Kim Sang-jin in a heavy tone. Then he got up.

"I will go home, now."

In her father's eyes as he looked at her saying these words, In-ju thought she saw something she had never seen there before. At the same time that she realized this, she felt a shiver run down her spine. Only when her father closed the door behind him did it occur to In-ju that she had not even offered a farewell greeting to her father. What she had seen in her father's eyes still lingered in her consciousness, frightening her. Should I call him back even now, she wondered. Should I ask him what his trouble was? But she did neither of these things. Whatever it was her father was resolving in his mind, she felt that she would have no power to stop him.

A coughing sound came from some room on the same floor. As if to escape from some fearful thought, In-ju snatched up the mimeographed text of: *Those Who Must Go* from beside the radio and read at random.

⟨Mother—(throwing a surreptitious glance at her daughter) Look, daughter, why do you contradict your father in everything? Do you have no pity for him? Ae-ra—Is asking one's father to buy American cigarettes for her daughter contradicting one's father? He used to do things for me the minute I said what I wanted. I mean while I brought in American goodies laden in a jeep. Mother—Those were different times. Ae-ra—You put your mind at rest, anyhow, mother. They say what started on earth will be resolved on earth. Mother—Now, what is that supposed to mean, daughter? Why do you always talk in riddles? Ae-ra—I will end up by being killed off. (as if in a soliloquy) I can just feel the stares of sorrowful ghosts that are watching me from all corners of this room.... ⟩

In-ju turned the page. She was looking for the passage which she had chosen to recite at the Christmas party held at Na-mi's house tonight.

The door opened suddenly. Looking up, In-ju screamed, unawares. A patient with his entire head bandaged was stumbling into her room. It seemed that he came to the wrong room after going to the rest room or something. Footsteps came running to In-ju's room. It was a nurse, who took the patient by the hand and led him out.

In-ju sat in stupor for some while. Her mind's eye was seeing the strange shining thing in her father's eyes just before he left her room. I must call home, she said to herself. I must tell him that he must not carry out the thing he has made up his mind to. At the same time, however, she wondered if it was not her paranoiac sensitivity that was imagining things about her father. She pushed the bell at the head of the bed. A nurse came.

"Could you give me some sleeping pills. I need to sleep."

Kim Sang-jin told the maid not to bring in his supper. Then he asked the maid from the back,

"Is nobody home?"

The maid hesitated for half a second, not being used to such a question from the master.

"The big *toryonnim* left home in the afternoon and the little *toryonnim* seems to have gone to the mountain directly from school."

"I see."

Kim Sang-jin was glad that there was nobody home. He went into his room and locked the door.

At this moment, In-mun was climbing up the mountain after leaving the room where his mother was praying. Although it was windless, the mountain air was biting. Choosing a rock at the top of the mountain, In-mun sat up on it. Then, staring into the darkness, he thought about the sermon he had heard at the church last Sunday.

Peter saw that Jesus was speaking with Moses and Prophet Elijah on the top of a mountain which he climbed. Peter suggested that he build three huts there, one for Jesus, one for Moses, and one for Elijah. Jesus, however, climbed down the mountain. The point of the sermon was that escaping to the mountain was not the answer worthy of a true Christian spirit. The ultimate answer was in going among the people, mixing with them. If so, didn't his mother, too, need to leave this mountain and go back to the world?

In-mun who was not even wearing a coat felt very cold. All of a sudden, he thought of the snake which he had buried in the earth at the Samchong Park. I wonder what happened to him, thought In-mun. Would he be coming back out after the hibernation. He had made a hole in the earth so he could breathe. It had been a long time since he had last thought of him. Was it because there really was a devil inside him that he thought of the snake, now? Mother would be upset if she finds out that I am not by her side, said In-mun to himself. Yet he kept on sitting there despite the cold that was making him shake all over.

The atmosphere of the party grew more merry and mellow as time passed. Dance was interrupted for the opening of the presents which were going to be allotted to each guest by a lot. As soon as they received packages wrapped in colorful papers, the guests opened them emitting shouts of joy and surprise. A necktie came out of a package given a woman and a man pretended to cry for disappointment holding up a woman's chemise in one hand. From Ta-hye's package, a large toy puppy came out which she hugged happily. Clapping her hands for attention, Na-mi told whoever received the packages wrapped in striped paper to raise their hands. Five hands went up. Na-mi announced that those will receive another present each. There was a loud cheer. She said, then, that the additional present was presentation of a song by the group. Singing ensued accompanied by clapping of hands to beat time, and then, loud applause.

"I thought you would surely be invited. How come you're

not?" said Pak Hae-yon looking at Shin Myong-su with drunken eyes. Then, he added, "Of course, I wouldn't have gone even if I'd been invited. That's for certain. Let them dance and make noise as much as they like. As for me, I prefer to sit here and drink."

There was a sort of a party at this tavern, also, tonight. The dentist had brought two pheasants which he had shot and with these cooked up for *anju*, the habitués were sitting in a group separate from ordinary clients, drinking and eating. The dentist was still in his hunting attire; one could see that he had come here directly from his hunting. His shotgun was standing against a wall and there was even a pointer lying on its belly by the gun, dozing despite the commotions in the hall. Now and then, the dog opened its eyes to peer up at its master who used to say that he did not need a dog for hunting but must apparently have changed his mind about it. The national assembly candidate who did not touch the *anju* but merely kept on drinking wine suddenly said,

"Say, how can we know that you didn't buy these pheasants at the market?"

Everybody laughed heartily at this joke. Only Shin Myong-su sat on without a laugh. Just then, the literary critic who had already got himself drunk somewhere else came toward the group mumbling something that sounded like part of a poem: This is the Water of Indang / Jump in! Jump in! / The boatsmen shout and / The drums resound....

"Oh, I see that there's a banquet here. I must partake of some of this before I jump in," said the literary critic squeezing himself in and sitting down next to Shin Myong-su.

Shin Myong-su got up and left the tavern. Myong-dong was milling with people although it was so late in the night. Going to a flower shop, Shin Myong-su bought a stalk of camellia. With this in hand, he walked to the bus stop in front of Midopa and got on the microbus headed for Tonam-dong. He got off the microbus in Wonnam-dong and walked up to the University Hospital. Remembering Na-mi's direction, he climbed the stairs to the floor where In-ju's room was. Somewhere a child was crying. The sound came from far off but the quietude of the surrounding seemed to magnify the sound. A nurse passed by him hurriedly.

Arriving at In-ju's door, Shin Myong-su stood for a few seconds, hesitating. Then, he turned the doorknob without knocking. His intention was to put the flower on the floor just inside the door and then leave. With a sudden courage, however, he pushed the door halfway in and peeped inside. It seemed that In-ju was asleep. Trying not to make a sound, Shin Myong-su tiptoed to the bed. In-ju was lying face up-ward with both her hands tucked inside the cover. Every time she breathed, the bedcover went slightly up and down below her chin. Shin Myong-su put the flower on that part of the cover and looked down at In-ju. Then he went around the bed to the other side, always on tiptoe, and again took a long look down at her. At least for that moment, In-ju was wholly his.

Unlike the foggy atmosphere of the party hall, In-chol's head became clearer with the deepening of the night. People were dancing again. Nam Chun-gol was sitting on a chair alongside the woman with long hair. She was talking and Nam Chun-gol was smoking the pipe, listening. Maybe he was not actually listening to her but was sunken in his own inner thought. Maybe he is thinking about In-ju, said In-chol to himself. A woman who had been dancing suddenly broke into laughter. Her dance partner was saying in the manner of a theatrical recitation, 'Go to the nunnery, Ophelia, go to the nunnery.' In-chol poured whiskey into his glass.

"Give me some of that in this," said Ta-hye who had come to his side without his knowing.

In-chol poured a little whiskey into her coca-cola glass from his own.

"More," said Ta-hye.

In-chol poured some more. Na-mi had come from somewhere and together she and Ta-hye clinked their glasses.

"You'd better make merry a little. I wish we had had the piano delivered. We could have asked you to play something for us, then," Na-mi said lifting her drink to the lips and watching Ta-hye take a sip from hers.

"Come on, let's dance," said In-chol putting down his glass.

"I wanted to sit drinking with Ta-hye-*ssi* for a bit," said Na-mi coming into In-chol's arms.

"What if you get drunk?"

"You mean what if she does, right?"

In-chol looked down at Na-mi's face which was flushed from the drink and also the excitement of playing the hostess for tonight's party.

"You are mine. I asked you once if there's a true love between man and woman. Do you remember? I said that time that everything was acting—living, loving, grieving, or rejoicing. I will take that back, now, if you will let me," whispered Na-mi.

But hadn't it been for some time that she had proved in her action that those words didn't mean anything to her any more? Wasn't he feeling rather overpowered by the sincerity of this girl who was coming toward him negating everything that separated them from each other?

Putting the pills in his mouth, Kim Sang-jin washed them down with the remainder of his drink. Somebody was tripping him by the leg. He fell on his face weighed down by an unbearably heavy load. He grabbed a stone thinking he would throw the stone at the one who had tripped him. Nobody stopped him this time. His brother was nowhere to be seen, nor his older son or his other sons. He threw the stone with all his might. The one who fell down before his eyes was no other than Kim Sang-jin himself.

Ta-hye's hand was warm. They were dancing blues. In-chol halted in one place and merely moved his body to the rhythm of the music.

"I've lost my dream," said Ta-hye, her eyes looking somewhere beyond In-chol's shoulder.

"What do you mean?"

"I used to dream up long stories with you as the hero. But I find that I am no longer able to do that."

"I guess that means you must grow up like everybody else."

Ta-hye closed her fingers on In-chol's hand and bringing her face away from In-chol's shoulder looked into his eyes, pulling her head away a little as if to see better. In-chol's eyes were looking at her, too. A smile formed on her lips and her eyes glistened with tears. In-chol wanted to tell her to close her eyes. But before he could say this, his lips were pressed against her forehead. She received them in complete acquiescence. In-chol felt the moistness of her forehead on his lips.

When the blues was over, In-chol led Ta-hye to the chairs and sat her in one of them. Then he left the hall right away. Nobody was watching him.

Outside, it was dark and cold. His body that was used to the warmth of the well-heated room trembled involuntarily. In-chol thought of the coat he had left inside, but did not want to go back to get it.

Is it my fate to relate to both Ta-hye and Na-mi as a spectator to the performer? Is there a true relationship that leaves the people involved as separate individuals? One must overcome one's alienation; he must learn to bear loneliness. This was what Ki-ryong said, or, he said something to that effect. And he was right. But does one need to be alone, cut off from everyone, to know the meaning of loneliness? He, for one, didn't think so. If that is the case, might it not be better for one to commit himself to others with courage and try to live with his loneliness without denying others? I must see

Ki-ryong. I must see him and talk this over. Taking off the paper hat from his head, he hung it on a branch of a tree in the yard.